I0664991

FRIENDS 2 LOVERS

VOLUME I

THE UNTHINKABLE

BY

JONATHAN ANTHONY BURKETT

Jonathan Anthony Burkett
Publications

Faith doesn't get you around problems in life
and relationships, it gets you through it.

ISBN: 098529700X

ISBN 13:   9780985297008

TRUE LOVE

Existing in life together, knowing the best for one another
Altogether, as well as having confidence and dedication
Into living a sophisticated existence as one
Lovingly and contentedly

True love comes from the heart
Declaring companionship along with precision
To having a constant understanding
For one another

Enclosing disbelief
So as to believing
Real love is all that it takes
While in the midst of discomfort and catastrophe

True love carries conflicts
Challenges and then happiness
But more importantly
Living life
Lovingly and contentedly

People I give thanks to for being in my life and giving words of encouragement unto me:
Lynn Burkett (Grandmother)
Arnold Burkett (Grandfather)
Marise Christophe (Godmother) and many more.

ACKNOWLEDGMENTS

I first give thanks to my Lord and Savior Jesus Christ, and my Father God, whom I will glorify always and forever for being right here by my side day and night, and for taking me through all my troubled times throughout my life.

With gratitude, I wish to also thank all the people who have come into my life and touched, inspired, and illuminated me through their presence.

PART I

CHAPTER I

"Claude! Troy! Ya'll get up! It's time to get ready for the first day of your senior year!" Charles Daniels called out as he turned on the lights in Claude and Troy's room with a bright smile. Charles was feeling proud of himself because his youngest son, Claude, had worked so hard in school, especially during the last three years, to earn and maintain a strong grade point average.

Claude was seventeen years old and an Aquarius—friendly with females, honest, rough, independent, unpredictable, and intellectual. A handsome young man that kept his hair cut, his body in shape, and his clothing style up-to-date with the help of his big brother Troy.

Claude had a nice smile that all the girls he'd met loved. It didn't hurt that he was sweet, and liked making the girls happy. He loved going out to party, dance, and drink, but he never got into smoking like Troy.

Claude wasn't perfect, though. Just like anyone, he had two sides. Often, Claude came home dirty, scratched or ripped up from a fight with a schoolmate or with people who just hung around the high school looking for girls to talk to at the end of the school day. He hated to be messed with, yet he loved to fight because that's all he grew up doing to prove he wasn't someone to mess with.

Charles was proud that Claude was keeping up in school, even though he'd grown up keeping bad company like Troy and a few other friends. He believed that Claude would stay self-motivated no matter what obstacles appeared.

Claude told his father that he dreamed of becoming a businessman with his own multi-million-dollar hotel company. That the rich and famous would love. First he wanted to work with other companies to learn from them how to help a company grow and become strong and well-known. Claude eventually wanted to own his own National Football League and National Basketball League teams and allow only the best of the best athletes to play for him. Claude was ambitious, unlike his brother.

Troy, by contrast, was bad like his father, Charles, used to be on the streets. He was twenty years old, muscular, wore dreadlocks, and liked jewelry that showed he had money, even though he was held back two years in high school. Troy was always getting into trouble, always stealing and then selling it on the streets. But he was all about hustling to make money for himself and for Claude. They spent it on school stuff mostly; clothes, shoes, hats, and other fly gear.

Susan, Claude and Troy's mother, knew what Troy was doing but never told him to stop because, to her, at least he was doing something positive with the money. Until then, Claude and Troy had had to share clothing because their parents said they only made enough income to pay the mortgage and utility bills. However, whenever Troy made money on the streets, he would put half toward making more money and use the rest for himself, Claude, and their parents 'bills. He usually paid the water bill because he and Claude liked to take thirty-minute showers twice a day, like they were stars about to walk the red carpet.

In school, Troy struggled with numbers and needed four more math credits to graduate. He felt that the math teachers with whom he'd studied throughout his high school years were too demanding of him, which — he assumed — meant they didn't like him. However, this year, he'd requested an older female teacher who had a reputation for being supportive and tutoring all of her students so well that they passed. Troy felt that with her help, he would be able to graduate in the same year as his younger brother.

Charles and Susan wanted the best for both their sons, but they had much higher hopes for Claude than for Troy.

For Troy, a high school diploma was as far as they assumed his formal education could go. He didn't seem to want any more than that; he wouldn't stop his hustle. Charles and Susan knew this led to trouble, though they had no idea how much. Still, they feared for Troy in a way that they never had to with Claude, all the while loving him and trying to be understanding parents.

"I already know Claude will graduate, just as much as I'm guaranteed to graduate this year," Troy said to his father with his head still on his pillow and his eyes closed. He wanted some more time to sleep before school.

"I want you two to make me proud," Charles said loudly enough for both boys to hear. His words were focused mainly on Claude, though.

Downstairs, Susan was happy about the first day of school. She had risen early to start cooking a special breakfast for her boys.

"Claude and Troy, come on and get up!" she called out to them. "Breakfast is gonna be ready soon!"

Claude and Troy finally had motivation to get moving. They washed up and headed to the closet they shared. They liked to pick a side of the closet at the start of the school year and then switch every week or two. This expanded each of their wardrobes, which was more closely studied and valued among their peers than any book or equation.

After dressing, they gathered their school supplies. They knew supplies didn't matter much on the first day. But they wanted to make their parents, especially their mother, feel good and proud of them by seeing them walk out of the house with folders and pens in their hands, like they were both on their way to orientation at a good college.

Looking at Claude while folding his folder and putting it inside of his back right pocket, Troy stepped to Claude and looked him in the eye. "Time for your big brother to give you a few words of wisdom, if you know what I mean."

"Let me have it then," Claude replied, trying not to sound startled.

"This is your year for the girls and all the parties. I already know that you have plans for you and Kelly. But, until your time with each other comes, enjoy the single life, bro. Be free. I couldn't see myself being put on lockdown straight after high school like how I see you've planned it out for yourself."

"Yeah, I know that already, fool. That's why when you get that one girl pregnant by accident again, like what happened to Monique, she's going to put your ass on child support, and that'll have you begging her to be your girl again after you start seeing the amount of cash you'll be paying," Claude replied while giving Troy a good nudge.

"Ha-ha, very funny. But let me tell you that won't ever happen to a man like me because I play all my games right. And of course, I'm going to be there for my child, whenever that time comes. The mother, she won't ever have to worry about money and food because they'll already be getting it every night and day." Troy's tone was serious.

"Well, I didn't see you saying that when you begged Monique to have that abortion," Claude said. He was pushing for a better explanation.

"I wanted to finish school first, that's why. Plus, I couldn't see her being my first baby's mama, with her mother on drugs and father on steroids trying to be Detroit's all-time backyard fighting champion and drug dealer always running from the cops."

"Oh, so that's why you dropped her off at the stop sign instead of in front of her house?" Claude asked, laughing harder now.

"No, I was alright. He hardly was ever there anyways because if he was, the police would've been locked his fat, dumbass up. But that's not what I wanted to say to you."

"Then get to it, man."

"Alright, alright, bro. I just want to encourage you to try and do your best at every challenge that comes to you in life. And from now on, I'll handle all brawls that come. You just worry about getting into college and doing the right things."

"Come on, you guys!" Susan called out again. "It's time for breakfast. Right now! Don't think I'm going to allow you to be late!"

"They won't be, darling," Charles chimed in. "I'm taking them both to school for a little bit of good luck this year."

Charles was really taking the boys to school because he knew they never went straight to school after leaving home every morning.

Coming out of their bedroom, Troy was not happy. "I'm a grown man. I'll take myself to school."

"Well then, go and get your own place because while you're still in my house, you're still my responsibility."

"I'm not a little kid anymore," Troy said, seething.

Claude came out of the bedroom laughing at how seriously Troy took their father's comments.

"Of course you're not, son," Susan interrupted. She wanted everyone in a good mood. The boys needed to be focused 100 percent on school only, and not on family problems.

The dining room table was set: Susan across from Charles and Claude across from Troy; King across from Queen and Prince across from Prince.

"Okay, everyone. Enough arguing. It's time for a word of prayer, giving our Lord and Savior Jesus Christ thanks for all that he has brought to the table this morning," Susan said.

All of them except Troy sat down with a smile on their faces and with their eyes on their plate. However, after seeing his plate, Troy's facial expression changed fast. They all began to wonder to themselves how long it had been since Susan had cooked a breakfast like this.

"Hold hands and close your eyes, everyone, as I pray for us today," Susan said after she sat at the table. "Father God, as we come to you today, we thank you for bringing us this far in life as a strong and loving family. Father, I pray that a blessing may come up on us this year as our children are now young men and are about to graduate from high school. Keep them strong and help them to stay out of all the trouble that I know may come their way. Protect us and bless us, Father, on this special and wonderful day that what we are all feeling will brighten this family's goals of achievement and future hopes and dreams. Everyone around the table now say 'Amen.'"

"Amen," Claude, Troy and Charles said together.

Opening her eyes, Susan put her hands over her mouth in shock at seeing her family, whom she was just praying for one second before, already eating their breakfast.

"Sorry, Ma. But having the smell of this food in my nose without being able to touch it was too much for me. But I still, and always will, love and respect you, and God, of course," Claude said with his mouth full.

"Just as long as you've given your Father God thanks for this day and all of the food that he has been providing for us, I guess it's all right this time, son," Susan replied with a grin.

"Susan, how come you don't cook for me like this?" Charles asked with mock offense. "Usually it's your mother cooking a wonderful breakfast and dinner like this for us."

"Sweetheart, what's to celebrate? Your paychecks still aren't enough for all of the bills for this house, which I'm mostly paying for by myself. Or are you making more than you told me you're making? You did come out of nowhere with that new car that I see out there in our driveway," Susan replied coolly as she took her first bite.

"Well, that's true, Ma," said Troy laughing too much for Charles's taste.

"Stay out of this and let the adults talk this out with each other!" Charles said to Troy. Then his eyes shifted back to Susan. He tried to compose himself.

"Susan," he began slowly. "I'm curious to know. In all the years we've been together, what *haven't* I done for you?"

"You've never taken me out on our anniversary, but you have the money to go out and buy a new car that you see other people driving. Where did that money come from?"

Charles realized she had a good point. "We'll talk about that later."

Everyone ate in silence then.

Afterwards, they put their dishes in the sink and immediately began walking towards their rooms. Susan stopped them.

"Who is going to clean up and wash up all of the dishes? I was the one that cooked and served our breakfast."

"We don't want to be late," Charles, Troy, and Claude replied in unison.

"What are you going to be late for, Charles? You don't go to work until 9:00 a.m.," Susan said, with a serious face.

"I planned to drop them off to give them some good luck this year, remember?" Charles said. "They need to know that I'm going to be there for them and with them through every important time in their lives until they are on their own." Charles spoke slowly so that Susan would know he was serious.

"I'm guessing then that when you come back home, you will wash up the dishes and clean off the table before you go off to work today?" Susan asked.

"Well I got some runs to make afterward, and I'm going into work early today to make some extra money so that I can keep you living and looking luxuriously," Charles replied, grinning.

Claude and Troy began laughing out loud.

"But you don't even have on your work clothes or shoes," Susan said.

"Shit! Thanks for reminding me, sweetheart," said Charles. As he looked down to see what he was wearing, he felt guilty now about the lie he was telling.

Charles ran to put on his work clothes and then ran out of the house. "Hurry up, Troy and Claude! Let's go before your friggin' mother asks me to do something else."

"Run, that's all men do whenever they hear the word clean," Susan said to herself as she turned to go do the dishes. She wanted to have the kitchen looking and smelling clean just like her mother's was.

Susan and her mother, Mrs. Anne, had such a strong and well-connected relationship. They'd always been able to talk to each other—about God, nature, other cultures, finding and keeping that right man, the difference between right and wrong, sex, and just about any other topic that caught their attention. Susan and her mother talked about it all with each other. That's how Susan learned to be such an understanding wife and mother.

* * *

On Claude and Troy's way to school, the music was blaring loudly, and Charles's rims were spinning. He drove a fully loaded BMW 7 Series. He paid for it with money he made from investing in a tractor-trailer that moved retail store electronic supplies and illegal drugs like Cocaine, Cannabis, Heroin, Ecstasy, and Opium all over the United States. No one in his household knew about this. All they knew was that the car was in Charles' name, and the police were not looking for it or him, though, though they ticketed him a lot for speeding.

As they pulled up to the front of the school, Claude and Troy saw everyone greeting one another happily.

"All right, boys. Go up there and get those good grades, and I may even let you take a girl out in my car for a date or two this year," Charles told them.

Claude and Troy only laughed because they knew that no one would ever be allowed to drive their father's car. Whenever they went out as a family, they drove their mother's Suburban, not their father's BMW.

Claude stepped out of the car, still laughing. "Don't go back home, or else Mom might have you sweeping and mopping the floor since you didn't want to wash the dishes like she told you to."

Claude closed his father's car door, and he and Troy walked up to the crowd. "What's up?! How was everyone's summer break with the girls?" Claude asked.

Charles drove away slowly, taking another look at the boys through his rear-view mirror.

Beep, beep, beep, beep.

A man with a 2008 Tundra truck behind Charles began blowing his horn. Charles kept creeping up slowly and ignoring him until . . .

Bam!

The man's truck slammed into the back of Charles's BMW.

Charles got out of his car with his mind set on going to the man's truck window to break it and then to punch him in the face for hitting his baby. Without even looking to see who the man was, Charles picked up a rock and threw it at the car, busting the windshield. The man jumped out of his truck, looked back at it and spat out, "Son of a bitch!"

With his fist balled, he began walking up to Charles and threw a hard punch, but Charles dodged it and then threw his own fist at the man's face, knocking him down on his back. Charles then started kicking the man in the face for hitting his car in the first place.

The man's son got out of the truck and started to run for Charles. The boy punched Charles in the back of his head as hard as he could.

By now, the fight was drawing attention and Claude and Troy looked back to see their father getting punched.

"Oh shit!" Troy yelled, pulling Claude to follow him.

Together, they ran to their father who was on the ground getting stomped in the face, back, and neck.

Then the man got on his knees and started punching Charles in the face. It was an all-out brawl, and Charles looked to be on the wrong end of it.

Claude pushed the boy's father off Charles, and Troy punched the son in the face. Claude gave the man a hard shot to the head, and after that, started beating him down to the ground.

Claude and Troy picked their father up, took him back to his car, pushed him into the backseat, and then Troy drove off as fast as he could before the police arrived.

The other father and son had been helped up by another man that was dropping off his daughter and warned them to go before the police or the school security arrived to arrest them.

* * *

As they got farther away from the school, Troy began to slow down to avoid attracting attention on the road. He knew that his mother had left already for work, so he drove back to the house. Then Troy called Charle's manager to explain his absence, knowing Lorenzo was cool enough to understand.

Claude and Troy made sure that they cleaned up every drop of blood in their father's car. Luckily, Charles had leather seats so it was easy to clean it all up. After that, they cleaned all the blood off their father and threw away the clothing.

They really didn't want their Mom to know what happened. She would be too upset and worry unnecessarily.

"Mom is going to see all of the bruises and cuts that you have all over your body eventually," Claude said to his dad.

"I don't care. Don't tell your mother anything about what happened today. Either of you."

"We already know that," Troy said evenly.

"Claude, come over here and sit down. I want to talk to you, son," Charles said.

Claude stepped closer as Troy walked to the bathroom mirror to make sure he didn't have any visible scratches or bruises himself.

"It doesn't make no sense if I tell your brother what I'm about to say to you," Charles began in a slight whisper "It'll just go in one ear and out the other."

Claude nodded uncertainly and turned to see if Troy was listening.

"Son, what went on today, I'm sorry for it all. I never meant for it all to happen and end up the way that it did. I should've been a mature man and just kept on driving. I'm asking you to forget how you saw me behave. That's why I'm going to find out whoever that man and his son was, and I am going to apologize to them because, son, your dream of becoming successful is all that matters to me right now. And you need a good example in me. That's the part I want you to remember. Okay? This ends with me. I don't want this to affect you."

"I understand, Dad. And I'm not going to want to start anything up with that boy again. He wanted to help and defend his pops the same way that I wanted to help and defend you. It's cool."

* * *

Later that afternoon the house phone rang. Troy answered, "Hello."

"Troy, how was your first day back to school, son?"

"It was great, Ma."

"How was Claude's day?"

"I'm sure his day was wonderful too because he's still telling Dad all about it. He's telling him about all his new classes."

"Really? Claude? He never tells us that kind of stuff."

"Oh, yeah," Troy said, keeping calm. "He came home real excited. He can't stop talking about his schedule. He might be tired of talking about it by the time you get home, though."

"Okay, if you say so," Susan said with a laugh. "Hey baby, tell your father I'm working late tonight. A couple of people are paying me extra money to get their hair done for some party. They'll be taking a lot of pictures, so they want to be looking glamorous."

"All right, I'll tell them. Don't work too hard."

"I won't, baby. You just make sure any dishes that get used, you wash them all up and keep my kitchen looking clean."

"Okay, Ma, I'll tell them that too. Bye."

"All right, baby. Bye."

Troy hung up the phone. "That was Ma, and she said any dishes that you'll use, clean them. And she's working late. By the time she gets here, we'll be sleeping. So we're good. No way to get questioned."

"Perfect," Claude said, breathing a sigh of relief. He hated lying to his mother.

"Perfect is right. I'ma make sure I go to bed early for the first time in twenty years to avoid any kind of confrontation. I don't want to be a part of any argument. I'm not trying to do anything that might make Ma kick me out of the house. I'm twenty. Shoot, she can do that!"

"I'm glad that you finally figured that out," Charles said with a laugh.

When Susan got home a few hours later and saw her husband's face bruised as he slept, she shoved him awake.

"Wake up, Charles! What happened to your face? And don't tell me nothing happened today because I know something had to have happened. I didn't see you run out of the front door today looking like this!"

Charles pretended to be asleep.

Susan got up and Charles would hear her rumbling in the medicine cabinet in the bathroom. But he kept his eyes closed.

Susan came back and rubbed a cotton ball drenched in alcohol across the scratches on her husband's arm.

"Aww, why the hell did you do that for?!" Charles screamed out.

"What happened to you today?" Susan asked him again.

"Damn it! I got into a fight at work, and why are you waking me up like that? Don't get me mad up in here, Susan! Do you hear me?!" said Charles.

Susan just turned around, got up to get ready for bed, and prayed that Troy and Claude weren't involved.

CHAPTER 2

The next morning, Claude and Troy got up early for school to avoid seeing their mother. They weren't taking any chances that she might ask them questions about the fight.

"You know, maybe Dad's already talked to her about it. Last night I heard him screaming about something," Claude said.

"About what?" Troy asked.

"I don't know. I couldn't make out the words. But I heard yelling, and then it got quiet."

"Well I'm ready to go now. I'm not about to sit here with nothing to do. And I got business to take care of anyway. Are you ready?"

"Yeah, almost. I've just got to find my wallet."

"I'll be in my car. Hurry up."

"Alright, alright," Claude said, looking through the pockets of the pants he'd recently worn. "Oh, here it is!" he announced raising his wallet in the air like a medal.

"Good. Now bring your ass on."

On the drive to school, Claude hoped that the fight from the day before wouldn't grow into something big, as fights tended to in high school. If that happened, the problem for him and his brother would likely last until the end of the school year. Claude didn't want anything messing either of them up in their senior year.

"Get out of the car."

"Huh," Claude said, snapping out of his daydream.

"Get out. We're here," Troy said with the car still running.

"But…where are you—"

"I'll be back before school starts."

Claude looked dubious.

"C'mon, man. Seriously. I promise I'm coming back I had some plans for making money yesterday and never got the chance to. I gotta handle that today."

Troy was being nice about it, but Claude could tell he was getting annoyed. Still, he couldn't bring himself to get out of the car.

"And I never knew that I had report to you about my plans for the day," Troy said, reaching over Claude to open the passenger door. "But since it seems like it now, is it alright if I go out and make some money, captain?"

"Yeah, if you say so." Claude then got out of the car and started walking toward the school. He noticed his best friend Kelly sitting on an outside bench and his heart skipped a beat. He headed her way, trying to surprise her with a goofy grin the whole while.

* * *

At home, Susan wouldn't leave the fight alone with Charles.

"I got into a damn fight with a customer because he kept on screaming at us and saying that we didn't fix his car right," Charles explained for the umpteenth time to his wife. "He threatened us saying that he was going to take us all to court if we didn't give him his money back."

"So why did you have to fight him then?" she asked.

"That man started throwing our stuff around. I wasn't going to just sit down and let him do that to our workplace."

"Well, you should've just called the police and let them handle it instead of getting yourself in more trouble. What if he really decides to take it all to court now? What do you think is going to happen to your job?"

"If he does, all that we have to say is that he started it because he was throwing our supplies around and even threw them at us. So I decided to defend myself and my workplace because that's just the kind of man I am," he replied.

Susan wasn't sure what to believe, but she knew what she wanted to believe.

"Are you sure this is over, Charles? I mean, what if he comes back?" she said as she fidgeted with her hands. She always got fidgety when she was worried.

"Baby, I'm sure," Charles said, reaching for his wife. He kissed her hands softly. "It's just a few bumps and bruises. I ain't broken. And that man's not coming back."

* * *

Troy drove to his friend Keith's house to pick up his work for the day. Keith and his girlfriend Amanda, a classmate of Troy's, hopped in the car. Troy dropped Keith off at work on the way to driving himself and Amanda to school.

Amanda was, a beautiful gold-digger, but Troy didn't have a problem with that. He didn't like that she gave unsolicited advice. As soon as Keith got out of the car, she jumped into the front seat and started in on Troy.

"So I heard about what happened yesterday, Troy," Amanda said, sitting sideways in her seat to face Troy head-on.

"Heard about what?" Troy was used to this with her.

"I'm so disappointed in you. When are you going to develop a mature mind, Troy? Think about it, all that's going to happen is trouble for you and your brother. Be smart this year. Think before you react," said Amanda.

"Are you serious right now, Amanda?"

"What?" Amanda asked incredulously.

"Um, how about whenever you have problems with another girl up in school, don't you give that girl pain while you're giving her a piece of your mind?" said Troy.

"But you're older and have a younger brother who looks up to you. My situation's different."

"You cannot be serious."

"I'm dead serious. You're a role model, aren't you?"

Troy didn't want to agree, but he knew she had a point. He had intended to go hunting for the boy who'd punched his dad, but with Amanda in the car and Claude on his mind, he decided to let it be.

"All right, I'm going to listen to you this time."

Amanda smirked victoriously and shifted her position in the car to the front.

"*This time.* Don't get a big head."

"Whatever," she said grinning.

"But for real, if that boy ever starts anything up again with me or my brother, I'm going to finish it."

* * *

Back at school, Claude and Kelly caught up what they'd been doing all summer long. Class was about to begin, but he was milking every moment with her.

Suddenly, he saw the Toyota Tundra truck from the previous day pull up. The windshield was fixed, but the boy who got out had a black eye and the driver kept his head down. The young man walked straight into the school door without making contact with anyone. And he looked angry.

I better not have no classes with that boy, Claude thought to himself.

"What's up, Claude?!"

Claude nearly jumped out of his skin.

"Man, you alright. I didn't see you all summer, bro. What's up with that?" It was Thomas, Claude's friend.

Then he turned to Kelly. "Hey, Miss Kelly! How're you doing?" Thomas bent down to give her a big hug.

Kelly giggled. "I'm good, T. I'm good."

Thomas was like another brother for Claude because he had Claude's back 100 percent, and Claude had his back 100 percent in any situation, no matter what. Plus, they had gotten to know each other through their church. They even used to go to the same daycare.

Thomas was cool, loved to joke around, and was mostly laid back. He was a church boy whenever he was around his family and a bad boy when he was on the streets. But deep down, he wanted to be neither. He believed in God, but he didn't see himself being in church for the rest of his life. It would be to boring for him. He wanted to live a fun and exciting life, not a life with people telling him what to do and what not to do.

"So man," Thomas said, nudging Claude. "What have you been up to?"

"I was chilling all summer with Troy and his friends. Going to party after party and having girl after girl every week and doing grown man things. Do you understand what I mean, or maybe you haven't seen that life yet, church boy." Claude said with his hands folded high on his chest.

"Oh Lord," Kelly said, laughing. "I think that's my cue. Bye, fellas."

"Nah, Kelly, you gotta stick around to hear my come back," Thomas said.

"No, no, I think I've heard enough."

They all laughed.

"I've been in that life way before you were even born," Thomas said, turning back to Claude.

"How are you going to experience all of that way before I was born, when we were born the same year? Don't say anything else, bro. All you're doing is making yourself sound uneducated right in front of the high school that you've been attending for three years now," Claude replied laughing and shaking his head.

The school bell rang.

"Where did Kelly go?" Claude asked.

"Over there, with her other friends," Thomas replied, turning his head in her direction.

"What other friends?" Claude asked, grabbing his shoulders to turn him back around toward him.

"The other friends that don't forget about her every summer," Thomas said with his eyebrows raised.

"Whatever you say, Mr. Uneducated, who seems to know more about friendships and relationships more than his education and future career."

"Yeah, whatever. But I know how to call a woman."

"Man, that's low," Claude said with a laugh as they walked together to their first class.

Claude's first class was French II, a language that he had no clue about and did not want to learn since French I ended. But his French teacher was a beautiful woman with a sexy body and long hair who seemed very nice.

"Class," Mrs. Green said loudly. "Today, before I resume where you left off in French I, my objective is to teach and for you to learn and experience something new. Some of you may not be interested, but I want you to be able to say, 'Yes, I've learned a different culture's language to help me in a career here in the United States of America, which is a country of many kinds of cultures and people.' And we all are one with one another, no matter the ethnicity or race," Mrs. Green said.

"I would love to experience something new with you in detention, no matter the time or place. And don't worry, I have money," a student named Willis replied. He had been a class clown since fourth grade.

Mrs. Green laughed with the class and then said, "This is going to be your second strike, Willis. Yesterday you made similar remarks. Don't be immature. You don't want a problem with me, do you?"

"Mrs. Green, the size of your booty is the problem. Can I spank it?"

"Third strike, Willis. I'm calling the principal. You're interrupting your classmates' education and my time," Mrs. Green said.

"Or *you* can spank *me?!*" Willis tried.

"Security!" Mrs. Green called into the intercom.

"You know you're going to miss me, boo. Especially my bright handsome smile."

"Security, I need you to come remove a student right away. He's been disruptive and offensive."

A moment later, two campus security guards arrived to escort Willis out.

"Bye, sweetheart," Willis said with a smirk as he was dragged out of class.

And that was just Claude's first period.

After French class, Claude took the long route to his next class, hoping he'd run into Kelly. No luck.

Second period was World Geography. Then Journalism, and then Calculus with Ms. Gusby.

Ms. Gusby was known as one of the meanest teachers, but she was also one of the most valuable because she was the principal's girlfriend. So Claude did his best to participate in class and make a good effort. He knew that even if he wasn't a perfect student academically, showing a good effort impressed most teachers. It was a good thing, too, because Calculus was going to be Claude's hardest class. He was happy that he'd already passed Algebra II, which would allow him to graduate. But he wanted to challenge himself and impress Ms. Gusby.

Next was lunch.

Claude never ate the school's lunch. He and Troy always drove off campus for pizza or fast food, and he'd bring back something healthy for Kelly.

As he brought her lunch that day, he spotted some guy flirting with her. It shouldn't have bothered him as much as it did. Claude knew that any guy who dated Kelly would have to get his approval first. That's just how he and Kelly were: best friends. But his feelings for Kelly had grown stronger and he didn't know what to do with them. That was why he'd avoided her all summer.

But he didn't want to lose her to someone else. He never wanted to see another guy looking at Kelly the way he himself had started to look at her. She was beautiful, smart, sweet, funny, and sexy in a girl-next-door way. She was everything he wanted in a partner and he wanted her for himself. But first, Claude felt he had to step away from the kind of shadowy life he was living. Kelly deserved better.

Over the years, Kelly had developed feelings for Claude, too. She introduced him to her parents and her sisters, Evette and Shellion. They liked to tease her that she and Claude were a couple, and she'd just blush and tell them to shut up. Claude was everything to her. She liked that he spoiled her with small things to keep her happy, but just his undivided attention was enough for her.

"Kelly!" Claude called out from across the cafeteria.

Kelly looked back smiling to see Claude walking up to her. Just to annoy him, she sucked her teeth and turned back around to the flirting guy.

"I know you're not saying forget me," Claude said with mock offense. "I guess you don't want this salad." Claude was holding the bag in the air.

Before Kelly could respond, the guy turned around and eyed Claude. "You that despicable motherfucker from yesterday, right? That was trying to beat up my fucking father?"

"Yeah, and you're that dumbass boy that got his ass kicked. I can't believe it," Claude said with a dark chuckle. "You better go and try to find some other damn girl to talk to this school year. I can tell you right now, you're not good enough for her." Claude stood still and unmoving, only looking deeply into the guy's eyes.

"Bitch! Payback is coming real soon I promise you. And don't worry, my father remembered who your fucking father is. He been waiting for him," the boy said.

"Get the fuck away from her. Keep it moving, that's all I'm saying." Claude's voice was low but intense.

"Yeah, motherfucker. Ask your daddy. Charles Daniels, right?"

Claude's jaw clenched.

The guy continued. "Ask him who used to make fun of him about wanting to be a Purple Gang member."

"Get the fuck out of here before I stomp your ass again."

"Whatever," the guy said walking away. Then he turned back around and looked at Kelly with a smile. "See you again soon, Kelly, and I am sorry for all of this that's happening right now in front of you. I'll talk to you later since we've been rudely interrupted. As a matter of fact, hopefully, I'll be able to take you out to the movies this Friday night. What do you say?"

"I'll think about it, Robert," Kelly replied and looked at Claude to gage his response.

"Oh, so Robert's your name, slick mouth? And hell no, Kelly! You're not going out with that fool." Claude was furious now.

"Why not?" Kelly wasn't really interested in Robert, but at least he asked. And she liked that it made him angry.

"Because I said so!" Claude replied.

Kelly looked at Robert and smirked. "Sorry, Robert. I guess that means I can't go out with you. You heard 'em."

Robert stared Claude down. "I'm going to make you fucking hate me more than you've ever hated another man in your life!"

"It's too late," Claude replied.

Robert stepped up into Claude's face. "You need to make sure you and the rest of your family remember who my father is. Obviously you need to get to know who you're starting things up with. We don't play childish games."

From the other side of the cafeteria, one of Troy's friends spotted what was going on between Claude and Robert and texted Troy.

Bro, someone wants to fight your brother right now for his girl. I think it's that guy you were telling us about.

As soon as Troy read the text message, he ran out of class and toward the cafeteria, ready to knock someone's lights out. When he rushed in, he saw Claude and Robert standing face to face, with their fists balled.

"You two need to stop before you start fighting," Kelly said. "There's no reason for this at all."

Out of nowhere, Troy jumped over a table and punched Robert in the face and began beating him up. Kelly was going to try to break it up, but Claude held her back so that she wouldn't get hurt. All the other students began to crowd over Troy and Robert as they continued fighting. They looked as if they wanted to kill each other. A security guard came running in and immediately called for backup. A couple of students in the back of the line heard him calling for help, and they began screaming out, "Security! Security!"

Claude looked back and saw the guard standing there and turned around pull Troy and Robert apart. Then he kicked Robert in the face and dragged his brother in the opposite direction of the security guard.

When all of the guards finally arrived, they only saw Robert on the floor with blood all over his face and clothing. Claude and some of his friends had taken Troy into the boy's bathroom to clean him up. Troy's shirt had too much of Robert's blood on it, so they threw it in the garbage. Troy's friend, who was willing to walk around school the rest of the day in an undershirt, took of his Polo shirt and gave it to Troy to put on.

The guards carried Robert to the school nurse.

"What happened to you, honey?" she asked.

"I got jumped from behind," Robert replied softly.

"Were you involved in the fight that happened yesterday before school? You already had a black eye," one security guard said.

"No, I wasn't able to make it to school yesterday," Robert said.

"We hope you're not lying to us because we already have the police reviewing our cameras," security replied.

"How about you just shut up, clean me up, and call my father to come get me?"

The nurse exchanged curious looks with the guards, but she reached for the telephone. "What's his number?"

* * *

The school called Robert's father, Stanley, to tell him about the fight. Fifteen minutes later, Stanley rushed through the school's office doors.

"What happened to my son?" Stanley asked the administrators and security guards. He could see blood all over the shirt Robert had worn. The nurse had peeled it from his body and draped it across a chair.

When Stanley focused his attention on Robert, the scratches on his face, chest, and arms just about flew him into a rage.

Robert tried to downplay the fight. "Dad, they just wanted to settle the score. I guess they thought would be the best to get me while I was by myself."

"So they want to start something up?!" Stanley said through his teeth. He was trying to keep his composure. "Fine then. We're going to give Charles and his sons something to remember us by."

Then he turned to the principal. "You want to just stand back and see my damn son get abused and beaten up like that and not have any information or do anything about it? I want Robert out of your school. Right now!"

The principal hustled to a computer to locate all the proper transfer documents. Then he handed them silently to Stanley.

"Don't think this is over. Not by a long shot," Stanley said, stepping into the principal's face. "I'll be back later to do something about what has happened!"

After school, Claude and Troy had planned to go straight home with no hesitations or distractions, but while walking out of the school, Claude saw Kelly walking by herself.

"Hold on, Troy. I have to go and say something to Kelly real quick. I know she's upset about today."

"Alright, man. Hurry up. I got things to do."

"Just be cool. I'll be just a sec," Claude said, already heading in Kelly's direction.

When he finally got to her, he wasn't sure where to begin. "Sorry about today, Kelly."

"Please, no more arguments and no explanations because my head is already hurting. Claude, it's time to grow up and stop acting like some thug on the street. I thought you were more mature than that."

"I am. But that whole thing was bigger than just you. It has something to do with my father, and I had to stand up for that. I'm not even all sure what's behind the whole thing. I'm going to go home and find out. But I am sorry that you had to see all of that."

"I understand I guess. Just make sure that you don't mess yourself up in the process. Okay, Claude? You've got me worried now."

"Don't worry, Kelly. I promise you I won't mess up."

He nudged her playfully. He couldn't walk away without seeing her smile.

"Stop, Claude. You play too much!" Kelly said, trying, with little success, to stay angry.

Claude nudged her again, this time harder. "I said I promise I won't mess up, Kelly. You believe me, right?"

"Yeah yeah yeah, I believe you," she said with a full smile.

* * *

After school, the principal called all administrators and teachers to come inside the cafeteria for a meeting. He wanted to find out what had happened at the fight.

"Does anyone know what happened?" he began.

"Yes, I think I do," one teacher stood up and said. "Troy Daniels was in my class when the fight happened. Then he suddenly ran out without even asking me or telling me where he was going. He never came back."

"What's his full name?" the principal asked.

"Troy Daniels."

"All right, does anyone else have any other kind of information for me?" the principal asked.

No one replied.

"Thank you all," the principal said and immediately jumped off the stage. He went straight to his office to start making plans about dealing with this problem that the school was now facing.

* * *

"Dad!" Claude screamed out as soon as he walked through their house's front door with Troy.

"Wait, Claude, make sure you throw out the garbage today because we forgot to do that last night. Ma must have seen it, and do me a favor and put my homeboy's shirt back in my car so that I won't forget to give it to him tomorrow when we go back to school," Troy said.

"Alright," he replied.

When Claude went outside, Troy hurried into his father's room to wake him up and tell him everything that happened.

"Knowing the kind of guy Robert seems like, I've got to start going to school strapped," Troy said to his dad after he finished describing the fight.

"No, get that damn shit out of my ears," Charles answered.

"I just beat that man up today for messing with Claude. He's going to want payback," Troy explained.

"Well, then let him bring a gun or some kind of weapon on school campus and then end up getting locked up for it because I know they're watching him more now," Charles replied.

Coming back inside of the house, Claude realized that Troy had gone to talk to their dad without him. He rushed in to see what he'd missed, trying to hide his annoyance at being left with garbage duty.

The fight had mostly been a blur for Claude. But he remembered the one thing Robert insisted he ask Charles.

"Dad, a wannabe Purple Gang member. Who used to call you that?"

Charles looked at Claude surprised because he hadn't heard anyone call him that in years.

"That's what that boy Robert said his father used to call you," Claude continued.

"Oh man. So it *was* Stanley," Charles said with his hand over his face.

"Who is that?" Troy asked.

"Stanley. That's the man who killed Alan's father because of me and then disappeared," Charles replied.

"Alan?!" Troy and Claude said together.

Alan, Kevin Wall's son, had been Claude's friend since they were teenagers, and was the same age as Claude, but more ruthless than Claude and Troy put together.

"Well, does Alan know that Stanley is the person behind his father's murder?" Claude asked.

"No, because he doesn't need to know. His mother changed him into a better man ever since his father died," Charles said.

"Revenge. I know that's all on Alan's head. That's why he hardly talks to anyone anymore except for us. But it's been a long time since I've heard from them," Troy said.

"Well, I can't tell him anything. His mother would be angry if I did. She's planning on telling him herself one day. Maybe on his eighteenth birthday she'll finally do it. Plus I haven't heard from them either—don't even know when was the last time I talked or even saw her. It's been years," Charles said.

"So what are we going to do about Robert and his father?" Claude asked.

"Take him down before he takes us down or move to another state, which we don't have the money to do right now. And I'm sure your mother is going to want to know the true reason why I would want to move to another state in a time like this," Charles replied.

The house phone rang, and Claude answered. "Hi, Ma."

"Hi, baby. Is everything alright? You left for school so early this morning. I was going to cook breakfast for you again."

"Oh, I'm sorry, Ma. I wanted to compare my notes from class with one of my classmates before school started. Troy and I grabbed something to eat on the way."

"Oh, okay. Well, tell your father I'm working late again tonight. Please make sure you eat and clean up after yourselves."

"Okay."

"You're going to be so proud of me by the end of this week because I've been making a lot of money since your first day of school and that prayer that I said for us all."

"That's good, I'm happy to hear that. Now that means you could save up and have money for my homecoming and end-of-the-school-year prom."

"Maybe, anyways, your father is the one who deals with those kinds of events for you because he's the one that seems to have a lot of hidden money around."

"Alright, I'll talk to him about it then."

"Make sure your father gets something to eat for me with his bad self getting into fights still."

"We all fight in this house."

"Well, he shouldn't be one of them that's fighting. He's supposed to be a mature role model for you two now that you're almost grown."

"I understand, but no one's perfect."

"Alright, I have to go now, Claude. I see my next customer has just arrived and she's paying me good money to do her hair."

"Alright then. Bye, Ma."

"Bye, baby. And behave yourselves," Susan called out before hanging up.

Claude turned to Charles. "Dad, does Ma know anything about what had happened yesterday?"

"No, I told her I got into a fight at work with one of my customers, like how I told you before," Charles replied.

"Did she call your boss to find out if everything that you had told her was true? Because you should know how she is by now. Plus, your boss will lie to her, but he won't lie to his wife, and I just remembered Ma does her hair from time to time still," said Claude.

"No. But you just reminded me about his wife and your mother talking," Charles replied.

"Tell us about Stanley," Troy said, changing the subject. He didn't want them to get distracted from the main issue.

"Alright, but keep it all between you two and me."

"We will," Claude and Troy replied together.

"Well first of all, just to let you know, it all started from high school when I was as bad as you, Troy, and always getting into trouble for stupid reasons just like you do. Stanley and I were part of two rival groups that hated each another, for no real reason except popularity. We were always fighting one another for props and to be the most feared guys in the streets.

"To make a long story short, it all started to get real serious after one of our homeboys got hurt and had to be brought to the emergency room because his head got busted open badly by one of the other guys. So we went for payback and ended up shooting one of Stanley's homeboys in the back while they were running from us. They came back that same night after Alan's eighth birthday while we were celebrating. As I was congratulating Alan's father, Kevin, on his son, somebody in Stanley's crew pulled the trigger. The bullet was meant for me, but Kevin pushed me out of the way and wasn't able to move fast enough. It hit him in the head. After that, everybody went running. I tried to help Kevin. Call 911 and all that. But there was nothing anybody could do to save him at that point." Charles sounded tired.

"Well, tomorrow his son better not come at me with nothing else, or I'm going to put him in the hospital," Troy replied.

"Keep everything calm you two, and don't start anything up. Only *defend* yourselves," Charles replied.

"Alright," Claude replied.

Charles looked at Troy with a serious expression. "You too, Troy. I mean it."

"I hear ya," Troy said after a beat.

"Well, I got homework to go do, and I need time to sleep because me and Kelly are going to be hanging out together tomorrow. She loves to walk around her neighborhood and talk. I need rest," Claude said.

"Well, make sure you wrap it up tight, son. I want the first grandchild to be named after me, but that should be a long way off." Charles replied and started laughing.

"Now Pops, you already know me and Kelly won't be taking anything between us that far right now," Claude said.

"Alright then. Goodnight, son, and stop with the talk, trying to make yourself sound innocent 'cause I already know that you've thought about it," Charles said.

"Goodnight," Claude replied and walked off, shaking his head.

Charles then turned to Troy. "Alright, take my gun with you to school tomorrow, and don't show it to your brother or even let him know that you have it on you because, I already know they're coming back for us. I'll also try to make it out there after school."

"Alright," Troy said.

"And don't worry. Nothing is going to happen. I'm not going to let anything happen to you or to Claude," Charles said. He thought that, if anyone should get killed, it should be him. He already owed someone his life.

CHAPTER 3

Charles got up early to go to the school to search for a hiding spot so that when Robert's father dropped him off, he could deal with the problem. Claude and Troy also got up early for school. Troy didn't want his mother to see all the scratches and swelling on his face from the previous day's fight with Robert.

When Susan got up, she realized the house was empty. She knew she was being left out of something important and possibly dangerous, so she got down on her knees and went to the Lord in prayer, asking for protection, knowledge, wisdom, and understanding on her household.

Instead of dropping Claude off to school first, Troy took Claude with him to his friend Keith's house because he didn't want him out of his sight. However, he told him to stay inside the car until he came back out; he was just making a quick stop so he could quickly speak with one of his friends about money issues.

Troy went inside of his friend's house to tell him to come out to his school at 2:30, fifteen minutes before school ended. He wanted back up that didn't include Claude. Claude needed to be kept away from everything.

"No matter what, I want my brother kept out of it all," Troy repeated again to his friends.

"We heard you the first time, man," one of them replied.

"So you'll have my back?" Troy then asked his friends.

"Yes, of course, bro," they all answered.

Troy walked out and looked inside of his car. "I'm doing this for you," he said to himself.

"What the hell took you so long up in there?" Claude asked him as he was getting back into his car.

"Oh, uh, I forgot a book for class." Troy replied.

Claude looked down at Troy's hands. "I don't see a book."

"Yeah, I just realized I left it in my locker."

"Man, you the most forgetful brotha I know!" Claude said with a laugh.

When they finally reached school, Claude's friends walked up to him and started telling him that his father was in a corner, watching out for him and his brother. They guessed that he wanted to see if Robert was going to start up another fight.

"That's what it seems like," they all said to Claude.

"My father is just probably trying to make sure we're at school and not out here doing something that we're not supposed to be doing. We should be cool, though. I mean, Robert ain't gonna come back after us again after he just got his ass whooped yesterday," Claude replied.

The school bell rang, and everyone started walking through the school doors and into class. Administrators and security guards were everywhere keeping an eye out for any problems. Everyone was a little tense.

Charles kept looking for Stanley and Robert to show up. He didn't see anything, but he was leaving nothing to chance. *Maybe he decided to drop him off at the side entrance and not in the front of the school because he knows I'm watching*, Charles thought. *I'll just come back here after school to see if I can spot him picking up his son.*

* * *

"Hello?"

"Hi, how are you doing? Is this Susan, Mrs. Anne's daughter?"

"Yes it is."

"This is Nurse Vanessa from Memorial, and we are calling you to let you know that your mother has had a heart attack, and she is asking if you could come to the hospital immediately and be here at her side."

"What! Is she alright? How, what made her have a heart attack?! All right, I'm on my way right now, and, please, tell my mother please don't worry herself because everything is going to be all right, I promise," Susan replied.

Susan ran inside her room to put on her clothes and shoes, ran to her car, started it up, and backed out fast onto the road. She drove as fast as she could to get to her mother, crying loudly the whole time. "No, Father, please not now! I'm going to need her here for me after I tell Charles about all the secrets and mistakes I've made during our relationship. I don't think I can survive without you, Mom. I need you! I need you in my life! I need your love and encouragement! I need your smile, because other than my children's smile and happiness, it has been the one thing that has kept me strong and moving in life."

* * *

Back in school, the announcements came on in first period. They talked about how strict they were going to make the school year.

"If anyone causes any more trouble on this school's campus, we will not hesitate to expel you. There is one person from yesterday's B-lunch incident who will be expelled today. Let this be a clear example of how serious we are, people."

In Claude's first period, Mrs. Green explained class that they shouldn't get into any trouble because it might hurt their chances for admittance and scholarships.

Troy could barely pay attention to what was happening in his class. He hoped that no one had snitched on him because if someone did, he would make that person his second enemy of the year. Just then, a security guard came to Troy's classroom door. His teacher got and opened up the classroom door for him.

"Troy Daniels, the principal would like a word with you inside of his office," the guard said. "So whoever you are, please stand up and come with us."

Troy got up without saying a word and walked out of his class with an angry expression on his face. The guard walked Troy straight to the principal's office and told him to have a seat right outside of his office door.

"Sit down there, and don't get up or move without someone's permission. He will be here to talk to you about what happened yesterday in B lunch with you and that other boy."

"Yeah, whatever," Troy replied.

* * *

Driving her car as fast as she could, without watching out for the police, Susan finally reached the hospital where her mother was. She ran through the emergency room entrance.

"Hello, I'm looking for my mother, Mrs. Anne?" Susan said as soon as she saw a nurse.

"Yes, I believe she's in Room Four," the nurse replied.

"Thank you," Susan replied.

Peeking inside of room four, Susan couldn't believe her eyes. It was her mother in a hospital bed for the first time since she had given birth to her.

"Hi, Mommy," Susan said nicely with a smile, though she was still crying. She bent over to kiss her. "What happened to you?"

"She had a heart attack," said a nurse who came up behind Susan. "She passed out in a store while she was shopping. Luckily, a store employee was there to catch her before she hit the ground."

"Is she going to be alright?" Susan asked.

"The doctor doesn't know yet. Her age and fragility make a difference. I'm going to go and call him now to tell him that you're here. You're her daughter, right?" the nurse asked.

"Yes, I am and her only child too," Susan replied.

"Susan," Mrs. Anne said softly as she woke up out of her sleep.

"Yes, Mother, I'm here for you. I'm here, and I won't ever leave you alone again. I promise you," Susan said, smiling after hearing her mother's voice as well as wiping the tears from her eyes because Mrs. Anne never liked to see her cry.

"Don't worry, I'll be alright because I'm a strong believer in Christ, and when my Father calls, I answer. I just wanted to see you one last time. I know the boys are in school right now. But I wanted to see you. I love you so much," Mrs. Anne said breathing hard and coughing after every couple of words.

"I love you too," Susan replied.

"I thought I was going to be here to see our first-ever black president Barack Obama, but it seems my time has come before his time has arrived. I'll still vote for him in heaven," Mrs. Anne said coughing and laughing softly.

"I don't want you to leave me yet. Please don't go, please don't let go, fight back, Momma, fight back!" Susan cried.

Mrs. Anne closed her eyes and smiled. "I've always dreamed of you being the best in the family. Especially when I was told that I wouldn't ever be able to have a child in my whole entire life, and somehow still I did. I had you. You are a blessing and now I want you to teach, bless, and lead your children the same way your father and I did before he died much too soon. But now, I'm going to be happy to join my husband, in heaven . . . I—"

Mrs. Anne's eyes closed slowly, and her monitor flat lined.

Susan cried and cried as she slumped to the hospital's floor, wishing for her mother to come back to her. The nurses gave her tissue to wipe her eyes and told her that they would stay by her side until a family member came to pick her up. A nurse named Jodi was a member of Susan's church and called their pastor to tell him about what had just happened. She knew that bringing their pastor to help her was one of the best things for her, other than calling her husband and children to come, but she didn't have their numbers. Nurse Jodi wanted their pastor to come and hold her while praying for her as she cried in pain because she had just lost her mother and best friend.

* * *

At school, the principal walked back into his office and found Troy sitting there. "Follow me," he said evenly. Then he closed the door behind him.

"Troy," he continued, "It's obvious that you were the other person involved in the fight yesterday. You somehow got away but I know you were involved. We gave you a chance to graduate at your extended age because of some reported health problems that you had, but that's over now. You've messed up that opportunity. Mr. Daniels, you are expelled from this high school."

Troy screwed up his face and slammed his hand on the principal's desk and looked at him.

"Anything that you would want to say to me or explain, before I call your parents?" the principal asked Troy.

"No!" Troy said with a mean look. Then he walked out of his office and to his car in the students' parking lot. *Payback is all he's going to get from me now.* Troy drove straight to his friend's house and made sure all guns were loaded up and everyone was ready.

* * *

After school, Charles was at the side entrance, and Troy and his friends were at the school's front entrance. Claude and Kelly planned to go by her house to talk and connect with each other again. The school bell rang, and Troy and Thomas hadn't seen that Claude and Kelly had already left to go to her house because they were walking in the middle of the crowd together. They stayed out in the front, waiting for Claude to get out of school. Kelly's friend Sasha and her mother Brooke saw them walking and offered them a ride to Kelly's house. Sasha's mother already knew about Claude and Kelly's close friendship with each other, and she always teased them about it.

"Thank you for the ride home," Claude and Kelly said as they got out of the car.

"Bye, and don't go in there doing anything that you wouldn't do with each other in front of your mother, Kelly," Brooke said, looking out of the car window and grinning.

"Bye Kelly, bye Claude," Sasha said as her mother began to drive off.

Sasha was a shy, nice, and intelligent friend of Kelly's. Her father and older brother were in the Marines, so it was just she and her mother Brooke taking good care of one another. Motivated day and night by her mother, Sasha was taught from home what to expect from a young man just wanting sex from her—which of course she knew didn't always go like how her mother explained it. With all of what her mother was trying to make her become, Sasha was lost when it came to choosing a career. She wanted to get out and live life on her own. However, after telling her mother Brooke slowed down on all of the speeches that she was giving Sasha and began trying to be more of a listener, not a commander in her house.

* * *

While Charles waited, there was a lot going on. Everyone was holding conversations with one another, football and band practice had just begun, and a lot of people were waiting at a city bus stop for the bus.

"There he goes, right over there. I don't see his brother though, but I'm still going in now," Robert said to his Dad on the phone while he sat in the car with his friends.

Stanley never replied because he was on his other cell phone with Tim Escobar, a drug lord who's brother had recently been shot in the back. Tim was in the mood to kill.

Robert didn't wait for his father's order. He threw down his phone and hit his foot on the gas pedal. "Let's kill these motherfuckers!" Robert hollered to his friends.

Shots were fired at Troy and his crew, who were all standing by their cars across the street from the school. Everyone around the schoolhouse began screaming and running for cover. Troy pulled out his father's gun and started firing back at the car where the shots erupted from, busting the windows and hitting one man inside. Thomas began running from the car but fell down as two bullets ripped open his back.

Charles heard all the gunshots and the screams of the students and parents, so he turned his car around and went toward the sound. The school's security guards called the police, and some of the students ran for cover back inside the school. When Charles turned the corner, he saw a car turning the next corner and his son's body on top of his car with that same gun he had given him sliding down his hands. His eyes were wide-open as if he were still alive and looking at him, asking for help.

Troy's friends saw that Troy and Thomas were dead. They jumped back into their cars and started going after Robert and his friends. Charles knew that he had to leave the scene because he had a loaded shotgun on the passenger seat, and that would implicate him if the police searched him and saw it in his car. Tears began streaming down his eyes, and he immediately decided that he was going to kill the man who killed his best friend and now his son.

Another car slowly crept up behind Charles, but he wasn't looking back to see it coming. He began speeding up to try and catch up to Troy's friends who were following the shooters' car. They caught up to the car with intentions of slamming into the back of it while the second car sped up to slam it on the side and began shooting at the passenger-seat windows with guns and shotguns. The car made a quick left turn, and both cars ended up crashing into each other. Troy's friends helped one another out of the car and started running. It was only Charles left to get payback.

Charles took his shotgun and shot the back tires so that the car would slow down, and then he shot the car's back window. That made the car crash into another car that was parked on the side of the road. Charles got out of his car with his shotgun in his hand and his mind set to kill whoever was left in that car. It was Stanley's son, Robert, and two of his other friends, but they were all dead already. The other car that had been following Charles came up behind him. The driver pulled a gun out the window and then pulled the trigger several times and shot Charles four times in the chest as soon as he turned around. It was Stanley. Charles saw him before he fell down, and then said his last word: "Claude."

Stanley got out of his car and ran over to him. "I killed your best friend, and then my son killed your son, so you decided to put your life on the line and killed one of my sons. But look at this now, you ended up getting laid-down in the process by me, your number one enemy. Now rest in peace," Stanley said to Charles as he lay in silence.

Then Stanley shot Charles in the head.

Stanley ran from the scene, looking around to see if anyone saw him. He went back to his car and rolled up the windows, barely having time to kiss and say goodbye to his son's body.

Across the street, a man screamed to the police on the phone, "He just drove off in a black car heading east on Clover Street!"

* * *

Claude and Kelly were at the house, talking about all that was going on.

"Please, Claude, don't get into any of this. You'll make it worse. I'll be so mad at you. And then I'll tell my mother who you *know* is gonna tell your mother. Then you won't be able to see me because of all the trouble you'll be in," Kelly said.

Claude tried not to blush. "Okay, I won't get involved."

"Make sure you're not just doing it for me, but also for yourself Claude. I mean it."

"I'm not, I'm not," he said smoothly. He was happy they were talking. "Let's talk about me and you now, and why you are so mad at me still."

"You left me alone all summer, Claude, knowing that I wanted to hang out with you before your last year in high school. You're gonna be leaving me for college in a few months. Plus, you already know my mother wouldn't let anyone in the house except you. I was lonely. I missed all of the fun things that we always do with each other, like playing video games, and stuff. And I didn't go out and get any exercise this summer because you, my stretching and exercising partner, were nowhere around."

"Well, I'm sorry that I didn't come and see you all summer, but my brother just had me going everywhere with him, and I was enjoying it so much that my mind was just set on all that we were doing. I would've loved spending each and every day with you much more, of course," Claude said.

"Then why didn't you?"

Claude knew she had him there. He did want to see Kelly, but he got caught up with Troy's crew. And one day lead to another day and before he knew it, the summer was over.

"You're right," he said finally.

"Whatever, Claude."

"No, I mean it. You're right. Kelly, don't you believe that making you happy makes me happy the most?" Claude said with all the sincerity he could muster.

"Not until now."

"All right, to help prove it to you today, before I leave, I'll cook a special dinner for you to show you I'm sorry, and we'll call it our first special date."

"Okay," Kelly said nodding her head. "I'd love that."

Latoya Brown, Kelly's mother, walked through the front door, tired and hungry. "How are you doing, Claude, my favorite son in the whole entire world?" Latoya asked.

Latoya was a great mother to all three of her girls. She'd had Evette at only 16 and the father, her ex-husband Colin, was a deadbeat. But she had managed to raise three fine young women. She was proud.

"I'm doing great. How are you doing, my second greatest mother in the whole entire world?" Claude replied with a smile.

"I'm doing greater now that I get to see my son after so many months of my daughter being unhappy because he forgot all about her," Latoya said.

"Oh, not you too!" Claude said clutching his heart. "Ms. Brown, I apologize to you to for that."

"Words can't show me that you really mean it," she replied.

"That's why, as an apology, I'm going to cook a special dinner for Kelly because I've been practicing after watching my grandmother cook," Claude said.

"And me," said Latoya.

"Yes, and my second mother, but you'll have to ask Kelly," he said.

"Can I join, Kelly?"

"Yes, you may join me, Mother, and you already know that you didn't have to ask me."

"I know, I just asked because Claude asked me nicely to ask."

Claude took Latoya's car and went to a grocery store to buy fish, cabbage, carrots, broccoli, onions, cucumbers, spinach, mushrooms, and tomatoes to make a special healthy dinner because that's the way Kelly liked it and wanted it. On the way back, Claude saw a lot of cops driving around, looking for somebody as if something big had just happened, but he didn't get stopped and questioned.

"Did you see that out there?" Claude asked Latoya.

"Yea, I heard people got shot at a high school and in the middle of the road today. They need to stop all of that violence," Latoya replied, shaking her head.

"It wasn't at our school because before we left there was nothing going around about a fight or anything else," Kelly said.

Claude began cooking. First, he cleaned and seasoned the fish and then steamed it along with a lot of the vegetables. Claude made a nice salad for them as their first course and served it to them like a waiter at a fancy restaurant. After Kelly and Latoya finished their salad, it was time for their wonderful and healthy-looking dinner to be served on the dining room table. Claude had Kelly feeling special when she saw and smelled the food.

"You're lucky that Evette and Shellion aren't here, or else it would've been more work for you," Latoya said.

Claude laughed. "No, because I'm sure they have men already for all of this special dinner cooking and treatment."

Claude poured wine for them both because he knew Latoya allowed Kelly to drink it. Then he gave them each a dish of fish and vegetables. He was happy to watch them eat, smile, and laugh with one another while giving him orders to get different things for them at the table.

After they had finished eating, Latoya started to bring up some funny jokes about Claude but then said to him, "I think you should start coming back over my house more often again because whenever I come from work at night, I feel tired and hungry, and I don't like fast food, and my daughter can't cook yet. But my only son can. I need you here to feed Mommy."

"Um, I have homework?" Claude replied, knowing it was a good excuse.

"See how much he loves you, Kelly. You better keep a friend like him forever because he's willing to cook for his best friend, but not his second-mother," Latoya said.

"You don't have to tell me anything, Mom. Claude isn't going anywhere."

There was an awkward silence then. Latoya looked at Claude smiling brightly and then back at Kelly, who was smiling even brighter. She hoped her Kelly and Claude were headed in the direction she thought they were.

After they finished eating, Claude cleaned up and walked Kelly up to her room. "I hope you've forgiven me."

"Of course." Then she kissed him softly on the cheek. "Goodnight, Claude."

"Goodnight, Kelly."

When Claude got back downstairs, Latoya was cleaning up. "Claude, let me give you a ride home. I don't want you walking so far by yourself with all those police officers already out there looking for someone."

"Yeah, that'll be great, Ms. Brown. Thanks."

Minutes later, they pulled up in front of Claude's house.

"Look, there's police at your house," Latoya said, totally confused. "I hope they're not looking for you, Claude."

"Um, I'm not sure I should go in," Claude said nervously

"No! I'm going to take you in there so that if they ask any questions about where you were all day, I'm going to tell them that you were at my house after school," Latoya said confidently. "It's going to be fine. Trust me."

Claude saw the police searching through the house with his mother in her pastor's arms, crying and screaming dramatically. Claude and Latoya got out of the car.

"Officer, what's going on inside?" Claude said across the lawn.

"Sir, do you live here?" the police officer asked sternly.

"Yes, yes, my parents own this house. I live here with them. What's happened to them?"

"My apologies, sir. I have firm instructions not to let anyone besides family through."

"Yeah, I got it. So what happened?" Claude was growing impatient.

"There was a shooting today. Five people were fatally shot, two from this home. I'm not at liberty to say anything more about the case except to say that we're looking for evidence and asking questions about what was going on in this home and in this neighborhood."

Latoya started to cry. "Please tell me that you're not talking about his brother and his father. Troy Daniels and Charles Daniels?"

"Yes, I am, ma'am. Also a Robert Wright and a Thomas Green," the police officer replied.

"Oh my Lord!" Latoya wailed. Claude held her up.

"Ma'am can I get your name, number, and address just in case we need further information, please?" the police officer asked.

"Yes, of course," Latoya answered. "And you should know that Claude was with me and my daughter all day at my house, talking and eating with us. I'm sure he had nothing to do with any of this."

"Thanks for that, ma'am. Right now, I just need your information."

Latoya gave the police officer all her information and was then asked to leave.

Before she could get to her car, she turned around and saw Susan running over. They hugged each other tightly.

"I'm here for you," Latoya whispered.

"I don't know what to do, Latoya. My mother died and now my husband and son have been murdered. On the same day?! This is too much for me to handle! I can't do this! I want out! I want my family back!" Susan held Latoya as she cried.

Claude looked on, unsure what to do. He looked to one of the detectives. "I can't believe this is happening right now." *Thomas was shot too?*

"It looks like it started from inside the school," the detective said, stepping closer. "You know any reason why that would happen?"

Claude knew the detective was fishing, and he wasn't in the cooperating mood.

"Man, don't even talk to me right now," he said, growing irate.

The church pastor walked over and put a shoulder on Claude's shoulder. "Claude, I know it's going to be tough. First your grandmother, and now this."

"My grandmother?" Claude asked.

"Oh, I thought you knew. Wow," the pastor said, trying to find the right words. "Claude, your grandmother had a heart attack this morning. She died in the hospital a few hours ago. I'm so sorry."

Claude dropped himself in a chair. "I don't believe this, I don't fucking believe this! No!" Tears began to fall down his eyes. He then bounced up and punched through the glass in the front door. He looked down at the broken glass and then went on a spree in the house of breaking things.

Police officers ran inside to try to calm him down. The pastor stood back both to let Claude get his feelings out and to avoid getting hit.

"Don't touch me!" Claude yelled to the officers.

"We just want to help you, that's all," one officer replied.

"I never needed no officers help and damn sure don't need it now. So get the fuck out of my face and go protect and serve someone else!"

One officer reached his hand out to Claude. "We're here for you."

Claude immediately punched the officer in the face. "Get out of my house!"

"Claude, you have to calm down," the pastor tried.

"Claude, Claude," an officer said. "Calm down or else we'll be forced to arrest you."

"Arrest me?" Claude said and then began throwing more punches.

It took the officers a little time to hold down Claude but they had got him down and held him down. "We understand how you're feeling right now, but you need to calm down."

From outside the house, Susan and Latoya could hear all the ruckus. Susan saw police officers wrestling with Claude as he was trying to break free.

"Get off of my son!" Susan screamed as she ran back into the house.

"They're trying to calm him down right now, Susan. I'll make sure they don't arrest him," the pastor replied.

"Why would they arrest *him*? This is crazy!"

The pastor then helped Susan up to her room to lie down and told her not to worry because he wasn't going to leave her and her son while they're going through these hard times. So he offered to sleep on the sofa in the living room for the remainder of the week, to be there for them.

"Who killed my father and brother?!" Claude screamed while the officers held him down.

The police told Claude that his father and brother were killed along with five other people, and that guns were found inside the cars. "Do you know anything about all of what happened today? And don't lie to us," the police officers asked Claude.

"I don't know anything. I was with the lady you saw me pull up with just a while ago," Claude replied.

"Did they have any enemies?" the police asked.

"No," Claude answered, breathing heavily through his nose.

"All right, tomorrow we would like for you to come down to the police station with your mother so that we can talk to you about all of this. Don't worry, we'll contact your school for you about your absence," the officers told Claude and then began letting him up slowly.

"Fine," said Claude.

After all of the police officers cleared away from his home, the pastor asked Claude if he could join him in prayer for him and his mother.

Susan was inside of her bedroom feeling trouble and sadness like she has never felt before in her life. She couldn't handle the pressure and the way she was feeling. It was as if something had just ripped her heart out of her, chewed on it and then spit it out and walked away. Not looking to see the expression, or caring about the kind of expression it left on her face. Not being able to handle lying down in her bed without her husband to hold, she began to shake and have chills. "I don't want to live like this," she told herself.

Susan called her hair salon and asked one of her workers to take over things for a couple of days, without even giving an explanation.

After a prayer, Claude went to lie down on his bed and fell asleep with tears dropping from his eyes. He asked himself why he wasn't there when they needed him the most.

The pastor heard his words as he stood by the door to make sure that he was all right. "Because it wasn't meant to be that way. Your Father God had someone to guide you in another direction instead of the direction of trouble and death and the rest that went on today. You should be thankful that you're still here for your mother, and not only for your mother, but for yourself. Now I want to encourage you to learn from your father's and brother's mistakes and know that they're watching down on you now, hoping that you won't do the same as them. Don't go looking for revenge, Claude.

"Remember, for everything good that you do and learn in life, there comes a reward, and remember, my brother, the more you strive in life and succeed, the more you will be hated. But the more you fail, the more they laugh. Your father strove and succeeded in life. He had a good job and a great family. The enemy got jealous and continued testing him until he couldn't take it anymore. Learn from your father and be like your father. Don't let the enemy turn you around when you're so close to getting out of here and doing better for yourself. Let your Heavenly Father handle this. Remember, sacrifice is what earns blessings in this life."

"Thank you," Claude softly said. He appreciated the pastor's wise words. But he couldn't help but to fall asleep with the revenge still in his mind. In the middle of the night, he woke up and screamed out, "Robert!"

The pastor heard him and ran to Claude's bedside. "Are you alright?"

"Yes, I'm alright," Claude replied.

"Who told you that Robert was one of the other guys killed?" the pastor asked.

Claude looked at him for a long moment and then ran out of the house with only one person on his mind: Stanley.

He ran to Alan's house and knocked on his bedroom window. When Alan roused from his own sleep, Claude motioned for him to come outside.

"I heard about what happened today, and I guess now you know how it feels to lose a father," Alan said to Claude as he came out of his house.

"That's what I came to talk to you about. If you want to be in this with me, you can be," Claude said.

"What?" Alan asked.

"That same man that killed your father just killed my father," Claude said. "His name is Stanley."

"Stanley?" Alan asked.

"Yeah, Robert's father. Robert's the boy that my brother fought with because of me," Claude said.

"Your father and my father were best friends, so tell me why didn't your father tell me?" Alan asked.

"He didn't want to mess up your life anymore. After your father's death, we heard it took a while for you to recover. And once you did—you know, staying out of trouble, out of gangs, and into school—my father didn't want to rock the boat."

"I can understand that. Truthfully, I was doing really bad. Many nights I wanted to commit suicide, but I didn't because I still had a mother to look over me. But then when my mother died from stressing herself too much, I dropped into an I-don't-know hole," Alan replied.

"No one ever told me that your mother died too," Claude said.

"Well, yes, she did. But I never told anyone, and now I feel like I have nothing to live for. No one but myself, and I feel like I'm not going nowhere in life because of it all. My uncle that lives here now with me, he doesn't do nothing for me."

"I feel you. So you in it with me?" Claude asked him again.

"Tell me when, and I'll make sure I find out where he's hiding until then," Alan replied.

"All right, just be ready when I call," Claude said.

On his walk home, Claude asked himself if his decision to seek vengeance would be worth it in the end.

The pastor must've sensed what was on his mind. "I hope you remembered my words to you, and that you've decided not to crash into another problem that might have you farther away from that finish line than you already were."

Claude glanced at the pastor and kept on walking, not looking back. He didn't want the pastor to see all the tears.

"Before you go back in your room, Claude, remember that you have your father, your brother, your grandmother, and your friend Thomas looking down on you, hoping and praying for you to use your head and learn, and for you to be the best man that you could be, for them and yourself."

CHAPTER 4

Claude got up early the next morning and woke up with red eyes because he'd cried throughout his sleep. So much had happened in just one day.

He took a shower to compose himself and got ready for the meeting at the police station. He walked to his mother's room to check on her. He needed to know if she was doing all right; whether she was feeling better than the day before. But when he had reached his bedroom door and peered in, she wasn't anywhere to be found.

"Pastor!" Claude screamed. Looking around the house for him, Claude couldn't find the pastor either.

Claude called Latoya and asked her if she could be the one to take him down to the police station. Without any hesitation, Latoya said yes. She got ready quickly, dropped Kelly off to school, and then went to pick up Claude.

"How are you feeling about yesterday? I cried like crazy the moment I got home and locked myself in my room," Latoya said when Claude got into her car.

Claude just looked at Latoya with his red eyes and put on his seat belt.

"It hurts so deeply, Ms. Brown. I know I shouldn't, but I want revenge from the person responsible for this. It may not be the right to do, but I think revenge is the only thing that would make me feel better."

Latoya was quiet for a few blocks. Then she said quietly, "Claude, tell me what really meant the most to your father?"

"Me having a good future."

"All right then. Even though he's not here in your face and this world anymore, he still wants all of those dreams to come true for you. As he's looking down smiling, he's thanking our Father God that you're still here today. I'm here for you, don't worry, and I always and forever will be no matter what. Okay, Claude? You're like my son, that's how much I love you, and I would like for you to talk to me like a friend because I also want to be an lifetime encourager for you too," Latoya said.

"Thank you and I love you too," Claude replied.

"I want you to remember what your father wanted for you. And what about your mother? You do know it's better for family to be there for each other in these kinds of situations?"

"Well, when I woke up today, Ma and the pastor were gone. They had never told me they were leaving. I have no clue where they are or when they're coming back."

"They're probably at the police station right now, and if they're not there, they are probably at the church praying for you and for her. She's hurting as much as anyone."

"I don't know what to think because I already have so much going through my head right now," Claude said, trying to fight back more tears.

"Whatever you do, don't stress yourself too much. I already know that I can't stop what you're feeling right now. However, I do know that I could encourage and help you through it all," Latoya said.

Claude and Latoya finally reached the police station, and all Claude hoped for was that they didn't catch Stanley yet because he wanted to see Stanley lie in as much blood as the tears he himself was shedding.

When Claude walked into the police station, a detective walked up to him right away. "How are you doing today, Claude Daniels?" he said.

"How do you know my name already when we just arrived?" Claude asked the detective.

"I saw you last night, but you didn't notice me," the detective answered.

Claude sat down quietly, looking at the detective.

The detective turned to Latoya. "Well, hello, ma'am, my name is Detective Arnold, and I will be one of the officers that will be investigating and helping out in this case."

"He's shocked and hurt about it all," Latoya said. "That's why I'm going to be here today to help answer and explain all that I can for you."

"You're not his mother?" Detective Arnold asked.

"No, but I'm here for him. My name is Latoya Brown."

"Well, I thank you for that, Ms. Latoya Brown," Detective Arnold replied. "So tell me, has there been anything going on before all of this had taken place yesterday?" he asked Claude.

"No," Claude replied.

"So, no fights? No troubles in school, before school, or even after school?"

"My brother got into a fight with someone during my lunch because someone was messing with me, but they never got caught," Claude said.

"What about after school or even before school?" Detective Arnold asked.

Looking into the detective's eyes, it seemed as if he knew about it all already, so Claude figured he might as well stop lying.

"On our first day back to school, my brother and I had gotten into a fight with some man and his son in the student drop-off spot because the man was beating up on my father. I don't know why," Claude said.

"So your father never knew that guy?" Detective Arnold asked.

"No," Claude answered.

"Are you sure?" Detective Arnold asked.

Looking into his eyes, Claude screamed, "I'm sure!"

"Well, according to the videotape that we watched from a camera across from the school, it seemed as if they didn't recognize one another at first, but I'm sure when they realized who one another was, it escalated. Tell me, did you know that your best friend, Thomas, died too?" Detective Arnold asked.

"Yes, I was told that last night. But how the hell could he have gotten involved?" Claude asked.

"Looks like your brother and his friends were waiting for you to come out of the gate, so Thomas decided to wait with them," Detective Arnold replied.

Claude started breathing hard and balling up his fist. *Stanley, you're dead.*

"Also, we have the whole shoot-out in front of the school on tape. It looked like you and a girl came out of the school in a large crowd on the left side of the school instead of coming out of the front entrance of the school where your brother and best friend were waiting for you. Your brother had started shooting at a car when those inside shot at him first. Your brother was shot from someone inside of the car, a black Lincoln, and then your father came from the other side of the school in his BMW and followed your brother's friends toward the shooters.

"Then another car with dark tints came behind him out of nowhere. From there, we have nothing on camera. However, after investigating the scene, a witness described that first, a guy came out of his BMW with a shotgun and went toward the Lincoln, and then another car came up behind your father and shot him. That person then came out of the car and shot him in the head and then ran, looking inside of the Lincoln, saying goodbye to one of the victims. Out of all the witnesses from the school, only one could describe the man in the car. However, he disappeared and couldn't be found by anyone as we searched through the streets last night," Detective Arnold explained.

"Well, I don't know where he could be or who he is."

"Well, all I've studied from this investigation so far was that Robert, one of the shooters that was killed, was Stanley's son, the murderer of Kevin Walls, who was your father's best friend. We have been looking for him for years now but haven't found him even though it seems now like he's been right under our nose all this time, and we're thinking that he was the one in that car we saw, and the man that murdered your father," Detective Arnold continued.

"You keep a lot in your computer system, don't you?" Claude replied.

"We're going to try to find Kevin Walls's son, or do you already know where he and the other two boys that were involved in yesterday's incident are?" Detective Arnold asked.

"No, I don't," Claude lied.

"Well, we're going to try to find him, so if any clues or questions come up, give me a call. Here's my card with my cell phone number on it," Detective Arnold said as he gave a card first to Claude and then to Latoya.

"So what are you going to do now?" Latoya asked when they got outside the police station.

"Go home and talk to my mother about it all."

"Well, I don't think she needs to hear about all of it now. Just go home and be there for her, okay?"

"Okay."

When Claude got home, his mother still wasn't home, but the pastor was.

"Where is my mother?" Claude asked him.

"I've been looking for her all morning. I don't know, so I'm about to go and check by her mother's house," the pastor answered.

"Alright, I'm coming with you," Claude said. Then he turned. "Ms. Brown, thank you for the ride. I guess I will be seeing you later?"

"Yes, Claude. You'll be seeing me later. I'm gonna come check on you and your mom this evening."

"Okay. And I want to thank you for wanting to be here for us."

"I'll always be here for you two, son."

Latoya's phone began ringing as she drove off.

"Hello," she answered.

"Yes, this is the detective you and Claude Daniels had met up with today, ma'am."

"Oh, hi."

"Is Claude with you right now, Latoya?"

"No, may I take a message for him?"

"Are you familiar with the name Anthony Richards?"

"No."

"Well, that's Claude's birth father in our system, not Charles Daniels."

"What about Charles Daniels?"

"That's Troy Daniels's father, Latoya."

"I didn't know that, and I truly don't think that's true and if it is, then Claude knows about that."

"Well, there was another case on Charles Daniels at one time because he wanted to get back at Anthony Richards for getting his wife pregnant. However, Anthony Richards didn't know that Susan was married and already had a child. It's all on paper that she did it because he had money, but when she had the baby, Charles didn't want to put him on child support because he said he didn't need someone to do a real man's job for him. Plus they were already married."

"Why are you telling me this?"

"I'm just trying to get information. That's how we begin an investigation, ma'am."

"Well, you'll have to ask Claude's mother about all of that. It sounds more personal than I know anything about. But I hope you'll wait until she gets over all that has happened to her. You drudging up old gossip isn't going to help." Latoya felt defensive of Susan.

"I'm going to ask whatever questions need to be asked to get to the bottom of this murder. Besides, I'm going to get in contact with him for Claude," Detective Arnold said.

"I don't think that would be a great idea," Latoya shot back.

"Well, he's going to need someone to help him and help provide a roof over his head because nobody knows when his mother is going to get over this. Plus, Mr. Richards might have some answers for me."

"Well you do what you need to do," Latoya said before hanging up.

When she got home, she sat on her bed, telling herself that this was all too much for Claude in just three days. She didn't know what more she could do for Claude. She'd never been in a situation like this before, but she was determined to stand by his side through it all.

Suddenly her phone began ringing again. This time it was Claude's mother.

"Are you okay? Is everything all right?" Latoya asked.

"No," Susan replied.

"I've heard about all of what has happened, and I'm sorry to hear about it all."

"I'm sorry myself, that's why I called you, Latoya."

"Do you want to come over and talk about it? The detective said some wild stuff to me earlier. I have some questions to ask you if you don't mind, though I understand if right now isn't a good time."

"Ask me now before I tell you what I have to tell you."

"No, you go ahead and ask me what you have to ask me, Susan, because your information might be more important right now."

"Go ahead, Latoya. I'm hearing and listening to you right now because it might be your last question for me."

Latoya didn't really think about what Susan had just said, but if she would've really listened to her, she might have figured things out and could have helped.

"A detective called me and told me that the name of Claude's real father is Anthony Richards. Is that true?"

Susan took a long, deep breath. "Yes, it is. I cheated on Charles and had a baby by another man. It all started after we had Troy. Charles wasn't making enough money to feed the both of us, or so I thought because he's always was hiding money from me. On our anniversary, I dropped Troy off at my mother's house because I thought he'd want to take me out. But he ended up being to busy for me on our day. He apologized later and gave me three hundred dollars and told me to go shopping. But I wanted to go somewhere nice. So I took my own self to a nice restaurant. That was when I met Anthony. He was sitting at a table by himself just like me. We both looked so lonely since everyone else around us had another person at the table with them.

"We kept looking at one another and then he finally got up from around his table and asked me if he could join me. I had nothing better to do, plus I was feeling low so I said why not, I wouldn't mind making a new friend. After telling me about all that he does—a bunch of finance stuff—I began telling him about my goals and about what has been holding me back for so long. 'Let me help you,' he said to me. 'I would love to. I enjoy helping others.'"

"I can see how he got your attention," Latoya said with a small laugh.

"Right," Susan continued. "So we talked more that night and got to know one another. I was so happy and excited about him wanting to help me, that I ended up kissing him that night out of nowhere. He seemed like the man of my dreams, Latoya. He was handsome and sexy. Plus I wanted someone to make me feel better that night. I began meeting up with him once a month whenever he would come back to Detroit from New York or Miami. We became close after he helped me to open and advertise my beauty shop all over Detroit. I needed a way to thank him even more, plus I began having feelings for him. So I began sleeping with Anthony and I stopped having sex with Charles. I thought Charles was cheating on me anyway, so I didn't feel that badly about it.

"Much later on, I found out that Anthony was a single millionaire who mostly paid women for sex. But I didn't know that then."

"So how'd you get pregnant? Weren't you, um, *careful?*" Latoya asked, choosing her words.

"We were usually. But one night he forgot the condom."

"Uh huh," Latoya said, listening hard now.

"But I told him to keep going because I don't like a man that starts something that he can't finish."

"Oh Susan—"

"I know, I know!" Susan said, lowering her head. "Really though what was going through my head was money. The one way I saw of a way getting it was to get pregnant by a rich man. And Anthony was it. So that night I stayed on top while we had sex. The minute he told me that he was about to cum I began riding it harder. He didn't tell me to stop. We both knew what could happen."

"True, true..."

"Afterwards, we talked about the possibility of me getting pregnant that night."

"What he say?"

"He said they he was tired of just looking at his money as his family. He said he'd been abandoned as a child and didn't have anyone in his life; nobody that he was responsible for. He said he was ready for a child."

"Woooooooow, Susan. I can't believe you'd been able to keep this quiet all these years."

"I know. It wasn't easy. When my stomach started getting bigger, honestly I wanted to break up with Charles and move in with Anthony. But I knew that I really loved Charles. Like, with my heart I loved Charles. And I was only dealing with Anthony because of his money. So I ended up telling Charles about me and Anthony. There was no way around it. He noticed my stomach getting bigger and he couldn't even remember the last time we had had sex."

"Oh my God, what did Charles say when you told him?" Latoya asked.

"He was very upset at first, threatening to kill whoever my baby's father is. I told him why I did it, though, and out of nowhere he came up to me and began apologizing for not being the kind of man that he knew I wanted in my life. He said he realized that it was Anthony who helped me to open up my beauty shop, and not a bank loan with my bad credit. Well Latoya, he forgave me, and that's why I never wanted to leave him because my love grew stronger for him after he had it in him to look past what I did. On the day that I was going have Claude, he threatened Anthony and told him to leave the hospital after giving the nurse his information. Charles proclaimed himself as the birth father and told Anthony he'd kill him if he ever came around again. Anthony never called me again."

Latoya couldn't believe it. "Susan, I can't believe it."

"I know, it's a lot to take in. But you're like Claude's second mother, and you love him."

"Yes, I do, as if he was my own child."

"Well so did Charles, bless his soul."

Latoya was nodding into the phone. "Yes, I totally understand that. Claude's a hard kid not to love."

Latoya and Susan were quiet for a moment.

"Where is Anthony now?" Latoya asked.

"I don't know. I haven't talked or ever tried contacting him since Claude was born."

"Your mother knew about this?"

"My mother is one of the only people who knew. You know I could never hide anything from her."

"Right."

"And she understood."

"Wow, well why don't you come on over and bring a change of clothes. I think you should sleep over. We'll talk all night long. I'll cook something good. What do you say?"

"You know what? Right now, I think I need to spend some time with Claude. I think I'm gonna stick around here."

"That's probably the right thing. I'll call you later, okay?"

"Okay, Latoya. Thanks for listening."

"Anytime, Susan."

Hours later, someone knocked on The Brown's door.

"Answer the door, Kelly!" Latoya yelled from her room. She was crying in her bedroom and didn't want anyone to see.

It was Claude.

Kelly answered the door wearing boxer shorts and a white shirt that, if Claude looked hard enough, showed her nipples.

"How are you doing?" Claude asked, trying to keep his eyes up.

"I'm okay. How are you doing?"

"You could just say, awful. I've never cried so much before in my life."

"Why? Come upstairs in my room so that we can talk," Kelly said.

They both began walking upstairs as Kelly held on to Claude's hand. "Lock the door so that we can talk privately," she said. "What's wrong? I want you to talk to me."

"Didn't you hear? My grandmother died, and so did my father, brother, and Thomas. And then to add to it all, my mother is missing," Claude replied as tears began to fall.

Kelly wasn't sure what to do, It was her first time she ever saw Claude cry. She wasn't sure what to say to make him feel better.

"I want to be here for you," she said finally. "I don't really know what to say to you though. I could only show you and give you my love in this kind of situation, and I'm talking to you from the heart because I know words won't make you feel any better right now."

Kelly hugged Claude, and they held each other tightly as more tears ran down Claude's eyes. Tears began to run down Kelly's eyes as if when she held him tightly and closely to her, they became one, and she could feel everything that he was feeling deep down inside of him.

Memories of Claude's family and Thomas began running through both of their minds and every time they pictured someone in their minds, more tears fell and they grasped onto one another even tighter.

"I love you," Kelly said, holding onto him. Then she tilted his head up to her and kissed his lips softly. It was such an affectionate feeling for the both of them that their hearts pounded in their chests, and their chests pounded on each other. With both eyes red, faces wet, and hearts locked onto another, they thought about how this moment was meant to be. Gently grasping Claude, Kelly laid him down.

"Claude, everything is going to be alright," she said, running her hand across his chest.

Every touch Kelly gave Claude amazed him. He never thought that heartbreaks in a person's life could create such a strong romantic and needing feeling from another.

Kelly kissed Claude one more time softly and told him that she didn't know why, but she wanted to follow her heart by showing how much she loved and cared for him. Sticking her tongue into his mouth now, she slowly positioned herself on top of him and put her hips on his.

Claude moved his hands to her waist and slowly slid them down further.

Kelly started a circular grind and began to feel her hormones rising out of control for him.

Claude began rubbing on Kelly's body, then slowly lifted up the shirt to reveal that, indeed, she had on no bra. He began licking and kissing on her neck. He made his way down to her shoulders, and finally to her breasts. He sucked them gently.

Kelly moaned and started to grind harder. Then she lifted her body up, took off her boxer shorts, and kept her tears-filled eyes on Claude. "I love you," she said again.

"I love you too, Kelly," Claude said, wiping his face.

Kelly began taking off Claude's clothing for him slowly while rubbing on his sexy body softly. Claude had then stood up in front of Kelly as she pulled down his pants and then his boxers to see what she's always called mini-me. A bright smile appeared on her face and she couldn't resist rubbing on it for the first time. Again they then began kissing as Claude began slowly laying her back down gently on the bed and then slowly moving her head up to her pillows.

They made each other feel good again with the joy and feeling of true love from each other, which they both had sometimes dreamed of giving to each other.

All Claude and Kelly could think of was the tender, loving moment that they both were sharing with each other in that moment.

Kissing, with legs wrapped around the other, hands rubbing all over each other's bodies, Claude and Kelly began making love. Feeling pain at first and, immediately after, a sensational, exotic feeling filled with pleasure and love which made her tremble, Kelly was delighted because unforgettable moments like this she could cherish and never regret.

* * *

Susan had to pull over on the side of the highway bridge. She had just finished talking to Thomas's mother. She wanted to give her condolences in person. Susan apologized to Thomas's mother over and over, though she knew there was nothing she could have done.

On her drive home, she listened to gospel music, and she cried. "I can't wait to make it to heaven," she said aloud. She repeated this over and over. "I can't wait no longer! My life isn't how I want it to be, nothing is. I can't see myself living day-by-day feeling this much pain inside of me. My mother and my husband...," she said, trailing off.

Susan slammed her head against the steering wheel. "I can't live like this! I don't know how. I feel so weak. I don't want to live this kind of life, Father. I don't."

Then she got out of the car.

Beep! Beep!

A car zoomed by at eighty miles an hour as Susan stood on the edge of the road. She began walking towards the other side of her car where she saw how high up she was. She then climbed her way up on the wall of the highway, her heart began beating, the wind blew her up as well as the nightgown that she still had on and then without any hesitation or even thinking about her son, she jumped.

* * *

Falling asleep in each other's arms, Claude woke up looking at Kelly and thanking her for holding him and for being there when he needed her love the most.

Before walking out of the room, he reached over for an air freshener and sprayed the room before leaving to help to leave a fresh scent.

When he got downstairs, Claude looked back at Latoya's room door and whispered, "Sorry, I was just following my heart, and the feelings that she gave me made me not think of anything but her love for me during our moment."

Then he lay down on the couch and fell asleep with nothing on his mind except kelly's words and love.

CHAPTER 5

"Kelly! Get up, you're going to be late for school," Latoya said loudly.
Kelly was still knocked out from last night's moment of a dream come true. Latoya went over to Kelly and pulled her nose, telling her to wake up so that she could be on time for school.

"Ouch, Mom," Kelly said. Kelly's eyes widened and she screamed out "Claude" because she thought he was still in the room with her, lying down naked.

"You were dreaming about your best friend again, Kelly? I hope it was a positive dream and not a wet dream. And why does the air in here smell so clean, but you still have a lot of stuff on the floor and food right here by your bedside from last night's dinner? And since when did you start sleeping naked, little girl? Get up and start getting ready for school," Latoya told her again.

"Okay, Mom, now please leave my room so that I can start getting ready for school."

Latoya walked out while looking back at her to make sure she wasn't going to put her head back down on her pillow again.

Oh my goodness, I thought Claude was still here in the bed with me. My mother would've probably gotten so mad if she was to ever see us naked in bed together. Still, I don't know what got into me last night to actually show Claude how I truly feel about him because I'm usually shy about it. I loved it though, Kelly thought to herself. *It was as if we, well, I was truly releasing and showing all of the love that I have for him, and it felt like he was too, but not in a brotherly and sisterly way. I just wanted to show him and make him feel loved again, and plus, I've always dreamed about him being my first. I hope he doesn't tell Mom about it.*

Claude was downstairs, sleeping on the couch and looking totally knocked out with his mouth wide-open, snoring. When Latoya had gone downstairs to make some coffee, she saw Claude and realized it must have been him knocking on the house door last night. She hoped he was feeling better and figured she should tell him what the detective had told her yesterday.

Claude started to wake up while Latoya was in the kitchen singing one of Yolanda Adams' big hits. Claude got up off the couch and walked into the kitchen with a smile on his face and said, "Good morning, what's for breakfast?"

"Good morning, Claude. Sorry, son, but if you want breakfast, you can make it yourself," Latoya replied.

"That's cool, Ms. Brown, I know how to fend for myself," Claude said smiling. He felt good to wake up in Kelly's house. Cooking for himself wouldn't spoil that.

"Claude, after you're finished eating, I want to talk to you about some things that were said to me last night, not only from Detective Arnold, but also from your mother."

"Okay," Claude said cheerily.

"And how come you're waking up this morning with such a bright smile on your face?" Latoya said. "What you'd do? Have a great dream or something?"

"Nah," Claude laughed. "I'm just happy because I'm in a place where I feel loved and comfortable."

From the kitchen, Claude looked up goofily at Latoya. But he could see that she looked really anxious. "Hey, Ms. Brown. You know, you can tell me right now whatever it is that you want to tell me. That look on your face isn't gonna let me eat my breakfast in peace."

"Okay."

"I hope this doesn't have to do with the police thinking I had something to do with the shooting," Claude said, looking up from bowl of cereal he'd just poured.

"No, Claude, it's about your father."

"What else did he do now?"

"Nothing, he was just never able to be there for you."

"Yeah, he was," Claude said. "He's one of the main people in my life that inspired, encouraged, and grew me up into being a better young man in life today. He could be overbearing sometimes, but Dad was always there for me. Sometimes he was a little *too* there." Claude laughed and took a mouthful of food.

"No, I'm not talking about Charles."

"Then who are you talking about? He's my only father."

"Well, um, how should I——? Maybe I should let your mother handle this."

"Handle what? Tell me."

"No, I think it isn't my place."

"Ms. Brown, if my mom was gonna tell me, she'd of told me," Claude said taking another bite. "Is this something you think I need to know right now?"

"Yes…"

"Then tell me."

"Okay," Latoya said, moving closer to Claude. "First, the detective called me asking for you, but I told him that you weren't with me at the moment. So I told him to give me the message, and I'll give it to you, and then your mother called me, and I asked her if it was true. She told me the same thing, and that is, a man named Anthony Richards is your true, biological father." Latoya hadn't realized she'd been holding her breath until she let out a big one after she said all of this.

"What?" Claude asked, not believing his ears.

"Charles wasn't your biological father, Claude."

"So I have another father out there?" Claude asked.

"Yes, and his name is Anthony Richards."

"How do you now. Is there DNA proof? My parents never broke up once Troy was born."

"True, but your mother had an affair after Troy. She told me this herself yesterday. She was going to tell you eventually, I'm sure. But the police are asking about the whole thing now, thinking maybe it relates to the murders. That's the only reason I'm telling you this now. And the more I think about it, I wish I'd have at least told your mother I was going to tell you this first. She's got enough surprises to deal with."

Claude sat their in silence with cold, soggy cereal in his mouth.

"Charles found out about the affair right after Susan got pregnant with you. He didn't care that you weren't biologically his. He claimed you anyway. And your parents' love for each other grew more strongly because of you."

Claude couldn't see the love part. He was too shocked by the news. "So a guy named Anthony Richards is my biological father?"

"Yes."

"And my dad knew I wasn't his flesh and blood, but he didn't care?"

"Yes. To Charles, you were as much his son as Troy was."

Claude sat there and missed his dad even more.

"So did the detective say anything at all about Stanley's whereabouts yet?" Claude asked wanting to change the topic. He didn't want to hear anything else about his dad not being his dad.

"I haven't heard anything about all of that," Latoya replied.

"Where did my mother say she was when you talked to her?" Claude asked.

"She said she was going to wait for you. I think she wanted to tell you this. She'd just finished telling me. She was on her cell phone, though. It sounded like she was on the highway going somewhere, so I don't know where she is exactly. She'll turn up."

"You're right. I think she just wants to be alone. She didn't even leave the pastor a note," Claude said.

"Well call her again. She's probably home. It's still pretty early."

"Okay, I will."

"Oh, and before you do, um, Detective Arnold said that he was going to find Anthony Richards. Again, it's about the shooting. So just work with them please, Claude. I know it's going to be tough. But just work with them please."

Before Claude could respond, Kelly walked downstairs. She smiled at Claude, but he was too caught up in his thoughts to smile back.

Kelly pretended not to notice. "I'm ready now for school, Mother."

"Okay, Claude, you're on your own for a few hours. Stay here in my house, and I'll see if I can get off work early today so that we can go and talk to Detective Arnold face to face about everything, " Latoya said.

"I will."

Kelly and Latoya walked out of the front door together and got in the car and drove off. "What's going on now?" Kelly asked as they began heading toward her high school.

"Susan's still M.I.A. and Charles wasn't Claude's biological father," Latoya answered.

"So they don't know who his biological father is?"

"Yes, and the detectives are looking for him. That's what Claude and I are going to go to the police station to find out about later, baby."

"Can I come, please, Mother?"

"You would also have to ask Claude about that. It's all his personal business, sweetie."

"Claude doesn't hide anything from me. You already know that."

* * *

Claude began looking for his cell phone to try calling his mother again. He couldn't find it anywhere downstairs where he had slept the night before. So he went upstairs into Kelly's bedroom where he knew might have dropped it. Looking around the room, he saw a photograph hanging halfway out of Kelly's pillow.

Walking over towards the bed, Claude ended up stepping on his cell phone. He picked it up and then reached for photograph.

It was a picture that Claude and Kelly had taken two years before. They were posed together, after Claude had just finished playing football with Troy and some of their friends. Claude didn't have on a t-shirt and Kelly's head was on his chest along with her arms wrapped around his waist. He was smiling as he held up a football in the air with one hand while the other hand was wrapped around Kelly.

I guess Kelly sleeps on this moment for us every night, Claude thought to himself. Then he put the photograph back inside of the pillow and walked out of Kelly's room smiling.

Claude continued, trying numerous times, to call his mother, but it seemed as if she had turned it off. Claude called the pastor to see if he had heard anything.

"Hello, Pastor, did anyone hear from my mother?"

"No, I've been hoping that she had called you."

Claude let out a big sigh. "I'll call you if I hear anything."

"Okay. And I'll do the same."

"Okay, one more thing: did you know Charles wasn't my biological father? I just found out today."

"Yes, I did, Claude."

"I can't believe everyone knew except for me."

The pastor couldn't think of anything to say.

* * *

Over at the police station, Detective Arnold had been able to locate Anthony Richards, a busy businessman who traveled a lot.

Anthony was in New York for work, though his main residence was in Miami. He told the detective that he'd be on a 2:00 PM flight to Detroit. He promised to come straight to the police station.

Anthony still didn't have any family to speak of. But he'd grown up to do pretty well for himself. He liked the finer things in life and was willing to pay for them. Luckily his income as a financial investor paid well and he could afford the life he wanted.

It had always bothered him that had a son that he couldn't see. He would, in fact, have been willing to give up all his professional accomplishments to be a real father. But when Charles threatened him, he knew Charles meant it. And if Susan didn't want him either, he figured there was no reason to complicate matters further.

So he was happy to know that he would finally have a second chance at getting to know Claude, though it was under horrible circumstances.

* * *

Latoya was able get off work early because she told her boss that she had some business to handle with her adopted son. She picked up Kelly from school, and as they walked through the front door, they saw Claude on his knees, praying. They joined him and prayed for him and for Susan to make it through everything that had happened. Claude had been crying the whole time he had been on his knees, praying to his Father God. Getting up, he was surprised to see Kelly and Latoya down on their knees too. When they all stood up, he thanked them and gave them a hug and a kiss for their love and support, and put on his jacket to go see Detective Arnold.

On their way to the police station, Claude, Latoya and Kelly hoped that the police had found Claude's mother. When they reached the police station, they looked to see if her car was there.

"No, she's not here," Claude said, looking around.

They saw a man walking toward the police station's entrance. He was a rich-looking businessman and had just hopped out of a Mustang. "Mr. Richards," Latoya had seen on his nametag. She also noticed a resemblance to Claude.

The man opened the door and waited for them all to enter before he did. He headed down one hallway while Claude, Latoya and Kelly headed toward Detective Arnold's office. When the detective saw them, he got up from his chair and began walking toward them.

"Hello, Claude, how are you doing today?"

"You should already know that answer," Claude replied.

"Well, I'm sorry for it all, and I know it's hard on you right now to be going through it all by yourself."

"Well, I have two people there for me, and they are still right here for me. They've been giving me back a lot of love and attention," Claude replied and then looked back at Latoya and Kelly and smiled.

"Well, that's great to hear, Claude. I have a nurse over there waiting on you, so please go to her, and she'll tell you what to do," said Detective Arnold.

"Okay," Claude replied.

"Latoya, please come into my office and let me talk to you privately please," Detective Arnold said.

As they walked to his office, another officer had been asked to direct someone toward Detective Arnold's office.

"Hello, sir. He told me that you're Detective Arnold," Anthony said.

"Mr. Anthony Richards?" Detective Arnold asked.

"Yes, that's me," Anthony replied.

"It's nice to finally meet up with you. However, wait over there, and the nurse will be back shortly for you. I'm going to talk to this lady, and then I'd like to have a couple of words with you," said Detective Arnold.

"Is this the guy that I've been hearing is Claude's real father?" Latoya asked.

"Yes, ma'am," Detective Arnold answered.

"I assumed. They look just alike," Latoya replied and then turned toward Anthony. "Well, hello, sir, I'm Ms. Latoya Brown. I'm your son's second mother."

"Well, it's a pleasure to meet you, Ms. Brown," Anthony replied.

"Please, call me Latoya."

"Okay, Latoya. I'm Anthony."

They smiled at each other cordially.

Detective Arnold stepped forward. "Come in here first please, Latoya. We don't want you two to start a discussion with each other about this whole entire situation yet," Detective Arnold said. "We need to talk to you separately first."

Anthony and Latoya exchanged looks.

"Okay, who's first?" Latoya asked Detective Arnold.

"You are. Please come this way. And Mr. Richards, if you'd please wait here—"

"Sure, no problem," Anthony said.

While Detective Arnold began talking to Latoya about Claude and his mother inside of his office, Kelly decided to walk over to Anthony and have a private discussion with him to find out for herself if it was all true about him and Susan and what they had going on with one another secretly. Also, she wanted to know if he really cared and wanted to be there for Claude.

"Do you have love for your son?" Kelly asked.

"Yes, of course, even though I don't know him and have never seen him before. He's my blood, and just by that, there's love inside of me for him," Anthony replied.

While in Detective Arnold's office, Latoya was being told that the police had sent out more search crews to help find Susan. They couldn't find Stanley either, and they were hoping that he hadn't kidnapped her.

"So please keep watching out for Claude for us, and I'll make sure to keep calling to check up on him," Detective Arnold then said.

"Have you been given any tips or phone calls from any one of his locations?" Latoya asked.

"No, but we know that he's here," Detective Arnold began. "We have reliable sources that say Robert had been sleeping at his friend's houses from time to time. They said his father slept at a nearby house not too far away, but they didn't know which one. We believe that he's trying to hide from us before leaving Detroit. How he was able to enroll his son into a high school without us knowing, I do not know."

"All right, just make sure you keep searching and are alert so that he won't be able to get away."

"Of course." Detective Arnold paused for a moment. Latoya could tell he was searching for his words. "And, um, yeah. That is Claude's father over there. As you already know. He's the one that we have in our system as his real father. He is quite successful. If you think it's okay, I was going to ask if he would help Susan with the funeral arrangements. I know it's a delicate situation."

"I think it wouldn't hurt to ask. Maybe he'd like to be helpful that way." Latoya felt optimistic that Anthony would help. Susan had described him as someone who liked to help.

"All right then. We'll talk later, Latoya," said Detective Arnold, opening the door. "Come on in now, Mr. Anthony."

Latoya slipped out of the room, then Anthony slipped in.

"Mr. Richards, thanks for coming in today," Detective Arnold said.

"Anthony. Please. And you're welcome."

"Okay, Anthony,"

"Is everything alright with Claude?" Anthony asked, getting right to the point.

"Yes, but we're still trying to find his mother."

"Susan."

"Yes. She's been missing since yesterday. Claude has been staying with Latoya, but doing a lot of thinking about his living situation. We expect Susan to come back. She's distraught right now and probably went some place to get her head together. But we have to think of all the scenarios."

"Sure," Anthony said uneasily.

"Claude Daniels is on file as your biological son. The man who raised him has died, and his mother is now missing. Your son is going to need a legal guardian."

"I'm happy to take him into my home. I have property here in Detroit."

"Perfect! I'm glad to know you're willing." Detective Arnold said.

"Of course. He's my son. I don't know him, but I'd like to."

"Okay, well until we get this sorted out, just sit tight. The nurse will be here for you shortly. You can wait back out there and she'll call you when she's ready for you. Oh, as a matter of fact, there she goes right now with Claude. Come on," Detective Arnold said, waving an arm.

Detective Arnold and Anthony walked out of his office toward Claude and the nurse.

"Hello, Claude, how are you doing today?" Anthony asked, extending his hand for a shake.

"Alright," Claude answered and then continued walking without looking back.

"He's a very nice guy," Kelly said to Claude.

Claude couldn't have cared less. The only thing on his mind was his family and his missing mother.

"Are you two ready to go?" Latoya asked Claude and Kelly.

"Yes!" they replied together.

"Let's go out for dinner," Latoya suggested.

"That's fine with me," Kelly replied.

"What about you?" Latoya asked Claude.

"Whatever you want to do," Claude said.

They went out to a nice seafood restaurant with many choices to put on their plates. However, they all chose the same thing because they didn't know the restaurant was so expensive.

Latoya couldn't take her eyes off of Claude from across the table. "Claude, you do know we're going to be here for you every step of the way no matter what, right?"

"Yes, I already know that. I know you won't just leave me stranded out in the wild, Ms. Brown," Claude replied as Kelly laughed.

"I was just making sure you know that I'm here for you, so if you want to talk about something, let me know. Don't hold it in and let it block up your mind and stress you because I'm sure you don't want to start making me sad and depressed because of what you're doing to yourself."

"I won't ever do that to you, Ms. Brown. I love you to much," Claude replied.

"What about Kelly?" Latoya asked.

"Of course, my best friend too. I think I love her more than you," Clause said and looked at Kelly, smiling.

Latoya made a face after Claude had said those words. "I don't think I like that," Latoya replied.

"She's my best friend," Claude replied.

"I'm your second mother, and I don't see how you're going to love a friend more than your second mother," Latoya said.

"I love you too, Claude, more than the whole world and my mother," Kelly said.

"Well, since you love him so much, you pay for his dinner," Latoya told Kelly.

"But I don't have any money, Mom," Kelly replied.

"I give you fifty dollars every two weeks for allowance, and this is just the first week of school. Where did all that money go?" Latoya asked Kelly.

"I have to save the rest for next week's lunch."

"But I give you more than enough."

"I bought some things, and I'm saving up for some other things that I need for school."

"See, Claude, she doesn't love you. If she did, she would have been willing enough to feed you."

"Mom, stop please because you're the one always telling me that I need to learn how to save up money."

Claude was laughing because a mother and daughter right in front of him were arguing with each other for his love and about money.

"Immature! I tell you, Claude, that's why she needs to start following and being more like her mother," Latoya said. The restaurant's waiter walked up and asked if they wanted any dessert.

"No, they're not gonna have any," Latoya replied quickly.

"Why?" Claude asked.

"Because I'm not loved and appreciated the most, so no, unless you two are going to pay for it yourselves, no dessert."

"Well, do you wish to make a separate order for yourselves?" the waiter asked Claude and Kelly.

"No, put it all together, and yes, I would love a cheesecake," Kelly replied.

"Me too," Claude replied.

"Okay," the waiter said and walked off.

"I hope you have money for all of that," Latoya told them.

As soon as the waiter got back with their desserts, they ate them and then Kelly and Claude left the table together and went out to the parking lot and sat on Latoya's car. Watching as they were walking out together, Latoya thought to herself, *I hope my dream for those two come true. I honestly and truly do.*

They started talking about how wonderful it all had felt for the both of them last night to be in each other's arms, to give and to get love romantically from each other.

"I wonder if we're in love with one another," Kelly asked.

Claude then leaned over and gave Kelly a kiss. "I love you, and you should've already figured out that answer, even though I'm still asking myself the same thing."

Latoya was left with a bill of sixty-seven dollars and fifty-six cents, plus a tip for the waiter of course. She only laughed and paid the bill because she had felt that they deserved a nice night out. Walking out of the restaurant, Latoya's phone began to ring. As she looked at the number, she saw that it was Detective Arnold, so she ran and gave Claude her phone.

"Hello."

"Is this Claude Daniels?"

"Yes, it's me, Detective Arnold. I just needed to tell you Anthony Richards has been confirmed as your father."

"So what now?" Claude asked.

"We're going to have to make some arrangements for a meeting for you two to talk with each other about things because right now, you need a guardian to be there for you."

"Why can't I stay with Ms. Brown?"

"Because she's not a blood relative. And because your father wants to take you in."

"My father died!"

"I'm sorry, Claude. You know what I mean. Your biological father wants to take you in. I think you should at least meet with him. It'll make things easier for everyone, including you."

"Whatever—"

"I'll call you tomorrow about the arrangements that I'll be able to make for you two to meet."

"Bye."

"All right, goodnight, Claude."

After handing the phone back to Latoya, he said, "Yes, he's my father." Then he put his hands over his face.

Quietly, Latoya drove home with Kelly in the front seat of the car with her. They let Claude stretch out in the back. He was clearly upset.

When she reached her driveway, Latoya told Claude that he should still be happy because he has someone else to be there for him now.

Claude walked into Latoya's house and plopped on the couch, feeling and wanting nothing but peace and quiet because he felt he had something missing in his life that was very important.

Kelly jumped on Claude and asked him if he was all right.

"Yes, but there's a feeling inside of me that I just can't explain," Claude replied.

"I don't understand," Kelly said.

"I'm having a feeling like something or someone else has dropped out of my life."

"Well, I don't know what to say, but I do know that it's not me, right?" Kelly asked.

"No, how could it be you when you just dropped yourself on top of me?"

"Well, I'm here for you, okay, Claude? You can hold me if you're ever wanting to feel love."

"You too, Kelly. I never even asked you how you felt about Thomas dying?"

"It made me sad, of course. But I know he's in a better place, and he's happy for me and you, like he's always been. We're all still best friends, the way I see it."

Even though Kelly said those words, deep down she was feeling so torn apart about Thomas. But she didn't want to burden Claude with her own grief.

"Well, I hope that you know that he hoped for a lot more for us."

"I know. So does my mother and me," Kelly replied.

They then began kissing and holding each other.

"I love you, Kelly, and I hope that whenever that times comes, neither one of us will walk away from the other," Claude said.

"I won't. Are you going to come up to my room with me again tonight?" Kelly asked.

"Kelly, I love you, and even though last night will be unforgettable, I don't want to ever make you feel like I'm using you or only after one thing. I would be okay if you stayed down here and rocked me to sleep tonight. That would be enough for me."

Kelly smiled at Claude sweetly and wrapped her arms around him nice and tight.

Upstairs, Latoya was watching television in her room when more breaking news came on. An unidentified woman had been found under a bridge. Witnesses say she jumped.

CHAPTER 6

"Wake up! Wake up, Claude!"

"What's wrong with you?" Claude asked Latoya. He and Kelly had fallen asleep on the couch.

"Your mother jumped off a bridge."

"What?! Why?! How could she have?"

"I don't know! All I know is that we need to get back to the police station now."

"Please Father God, tell me that this is all not true and is not happening to me," Claude began to cry out. Quietly hoping that it wasn't really her, Claude went out and sat in the car, waiting for Latoya.

She rushed into her car and sped off to the police station. Anthony and the pastor were already there because they had been called first to identify the body. Detective Arnold felt that it would have been too much for Claude to see.

"Where's the detective?" Claude began screaming out as soon as they got there. Claude ran to Detective Arnold's office.

"Detective, where's my mother?" Claude asked.

"From what we know so far, Claude, it looks like a suicide," Detective Arnold said.

"Are you sure it's her, and if it is her, are you sure that she wasn't killed by someone?" Claude asked.

"They got it all on camera. She was on a highway bridge for about two hours, crying and looking as if she didn't know what to do. Then she spoke to someone on her phone. After the call, she got out of her car, stood on the edge of the bridge, and went over it," Detective Arnold said.

"I know my mother. My mother wouldn't have just jumped. She would have gone to her church to talk to her pastor about it all or a friend."

"Well, like I said, we have it all recorded on video. There's no one around her. She doesn't slip. She doesn't stumble. She doesn't fall. Claude, she jumped."

Latoya held her hands over a face, trying to control her sobbing.

Claude pushed everybody out of his way and then ran back in the direction of his neighborhood.

"Get him now so that we can help him keep out of trouble and danger," Detective Arnold screamed out to the other officers.

Five police officers ran after Claude and caught up to him, telling him that if he didn't work with them until it's all solved, they were going to have to hold him at the station.

"I don't care. I gave you a chance already to help me, and you failed. It's my time to go and do what should've been done already," Claude yelled. He began fighting the police officers so that they would let him go, but they slammed him down on the ground and put handcuffs on him. They took him back into the police station and gave him his own private cell.

Anthony didn't know what he could do to help Claude. So he did the only thing he thought he could. He started making arrangements for three funerals.

* * *

"Detective Arnold! We have a call of a shooting inside of a house and we think it has something to do with the man name Stanley that you're looking for."

"All right, let's go!" Detective Arnold said to all of the surrounding officers. "Latoya, I'll call you later. I need to go handle this."

When Detective Arnold reached the scene, a crowd was standing in front of the house. Officers told everyone to step back, and Detective Arnold went through the front door as a few others went through the back. When all of the detectives were inside the house, they began searching for the shooter and anyone else that might be inside. It was too late. Two people were dead, and one of them was Stanley. The other was a young man who looked as if he had taken his own life after shooting Stanley. He had a note addressed to Claude pinned to his shirt.

Detective Arnold put the unopened letter in his pocket before the investigation crew arrived. While driving back to the police station, Detective Arnold wanted to read the letter but felt he owed Claude the opportunity to read it first. When he reached the cell room, Claude was there crying, looking torn apart with scratches all over his arms and face.

"What are you trying to do, kill yourself in here?" Detective Arnold asked Claude.

"My mother did it, so why shouldn't I?" Claude replied.

"Well, I can't stop you, but before you do, here's a letter from someone you knew that just committed suicide after killing the man that you wanted dead," Detective Arnold replied.

Claude opened the envelope.

To: Claude Daniels
From: Your brother, Alan

My father died for your father, and now I've died for you. My father wanted payback for some things that had happened to your father and his friends. Your father wanted payback because he felt he owed my father his life and he ended up getting the opposite.

I was working on it all by myself, I was working for him, but he never knew who I was. I was best friends with his son—can you believe it?—best friends with the man's son that killed my father. I was best friends with his son for five years. That's why I never jumped into that fight you had. I jumped into getting payback another way.

Your father wished and dreamed for you to have a better, more successful life than he had. He wanted you to be a better man than he was. How do I know? He had told me when he called me, asking me if I knew where Stanley was that night after your brother got into a fight with his son during lunch. I never told him where he was, but somehow, he still found him and ended up getting the opposite.

My father never had dreams for me. He never got the chance to. A woman named Susan Daniels once asked me how I felt after my parents died. I told her it was hard to know what I was missing in a father, but my mother, who loved and influenced me a lot, was really missed. She had no one to be there for her the way she wanted someone to be there for her, like how she was for me.

Your mother asked me if I wanted to live with y'all, and I told her no because I'm my own man now. So she told me to learn to encourage myself. How could I have, since I've never had any examples in my life for how to be a better man in life? You can't learn that through books.

You and I have both had bad influences around us. However, one of us had a lot of good to go along with it; and that was you.

I took my life because it was too late for me, and if I would've run away after shooting Stanley, I would have had to live with it all on my heart for the rest of my life. And I just can't do that. It's just too much.

I did this all for your family and my family too, which I always believed was joined the day my father died for yours. In that spirit, you need to do something for all of us who are no longer with you in body but who remain with you in spirit. Make us all proud. All of us, your grandmother, mother, father, brother, my father, my mother, Thomas, and me. Never give up on anything that you set your mind to because you have a lot of angels looking down on you now.

Save the best for last, that's my motto, and that is Kelly. I liked her, but I never tried talking to her because I was always like, that's my brother's future wife. I wish for the best for you two and remember the best ones are always the hardest ones at times, so have patience and love for her no matter what. When the time comes, I hope you'll name one of your children after me, your second brother.

The last thing that I have to say to you, brother, is that your mother called me before she committed suicide, telling me that she was going through the same thing that my mother went through and ended up dying from. She asked me to be there for you and to tell you sorry for her because she couldn't tell you. I hope you understand and forgive your mother for leaving you. I hope you understand and forgive me too, because I was the one your mother wanted to stay at your side. But I couldn't be there for you the way she wanted me to. I chose to take out the enemy that troubled both our minds along with myself because I'd rather die than go to prison. So now, remember that you're doing it for all of us, brother.

- Alan

Claude thought about it all and realized that he had nine people to make happy and proud of him now. However, he still didn't know how he was going to be able to do it.

Detective Arnold released Claude and called Latoya to come and pick him up.

"You're going to have to try to work things out with your father for us because he's really willing to help us all through everything," Latoya said to Claude.

"Yes, I will. I promise," Claude said.

Claude, trying to live up to the person Alan described in his letter, agreed to move in with Anthony. He even agreed to move to Miami, Anthony's hometown. But he would only go on one condition: that Latoya and Kelly move there, too.

That meant Anthony would have to help Latoya find a place to house and a great-paying job like the one she already had in Detroit. But without any questions or hesitation, Anthony agreed.

When Latoya got the news, she was happy. Not for herself, but for Claude. She knew that staying in Detroit wasn't a great idea. Too many memories. If he kept walking the same streets and going to the same school, flashbacks would be all he'd have.

Claude, Latoya and Kelly all moved the week before the funeral. Anthony had been quick about the housing situation. He encouraged them to leave everything behind except for valuable pictures. This would be a fresh start.

Claude and Kelly were going to be homeschooled with Latoya until the next quarter started at the local high school. It would work out well since Latoya didn't have a job yet anyway.

When they went back to Detroit for the funeral to say goodbye to Claude's family and to Thomas, whose funeral was there also, Claude was surprised to see Troy's friends. They had been hiding from the police since the incident. Detective Arnold was there and had seen them, but for some reason left them alone. After the funeral, everyone gave Claude some alone time as they walked out of the funeral home and to their cars. Well, everyone except Kelly she stayed right there by his side holding his hands crying as well.

Claude prayed out loud.

"Father, I don't understand my life. Why must I live my life this way, going through problems day after day? I have forgiven my mother for forsaking me. My brother and the man that I thought was my father killed on a surprising day and time. Having no one here now to accompany me in my dark nights with tears falling from my eyes, having no one here to dry my eyes except Kelly, of whom I believe I'm not worthy yet, because I want the best for her in life, and her mother."

The pastor walked up to Claude, listening to him as he finally opened up and said how he truly felt inside. While Kelly was there with her eyes closed, tears rushed down her face as she listened to Claude.

"Bad mind and attitude? Yes, Father, I know I have. But truly, I know that you know how I'm feeling deeply inside because of the feelings of now living a life that someone else hasn't ever had. Why I ask, Father? Why?"

The pastor put his hand on Claude's shoulder. "Son, the rougher the road is for a person, the better the opportunities and chances available for him. I believe that a person that does right stays strong and learns from his mistakes and from the mistakes of others. It allows him to become a strong motivational leader for many, and someone to whom others can look up to. Claude, never give up and never allow anyone or anything to take you down in life. Stay strong-minded, my son, and never give up hope. Believe in yourself and just know it already. You have one waiting to rebuild a bigger family with you. I'll be here for you whenever you need me to be. Just call me, and if I don't answer, just know you'll always have a father up above that always will be here for you no matter how much wrong you end up doing in your lifetime. Remember, stay strong and believe in the possibilities, no matter how much the odds are against you. Keep going until you've crossed that finish line and into the light.

"Struggles, jealousy, hate, upsets, depression, and bigger challenges may occur along the way, but like I said, never give up and think that you can't make it through because now you have nine angels around you, wishing for the best for you. I know that you've never known that the man you called father wasn't your birth father, but just know he always thought of you as his son and wanted the best for you, and you know that. So don't upset him either, and go for those dreams and goals you've always told him about that he encouraged you in.

"Know he planned to be behind you all the way, Claude. Now you've met your biological father, and I already know that he can never make up for the past. But he can help you succeed right now, and in the future. Believe, my son. Stay strong and believe that your Father God has an unbelievable blessing coming your way, but you must do your part in return. I'm going to go now and leave you. Let out how you feel to your family and father, but just know I'll always be willing to come back whenever you need someone."

Before Claude left to go back to his new home, he decided to go with Kelly and take a last look at the place he had last seen all of his family members smiling and talking with one another like how a true family does. He felt that he wouldn't have another time like that for a long time. That place was back at his old home around their dining room table, where they last ate breakfast together.

Opening up the front door and going in slowly, while looking around to see if there was anything he had forgotten, Claude had just felt like running back out as soon as he saw his mother's picture on the wall, of her smiling oh so brightly, staring at him proudly.

Claude walked inside of the dining room and sat down around the dining room table, with Kelly right behind of him and began to smile as tears began to run down his cheeks, remembering the last time they were all sitting down there, eating, while his mother was praying, thanking the Lord for all the food they had in front of them, and to bless her family abundantly. Kelly decided to stay by the front door to give him sometime to himself however she wasn't planning on being too far away.

Even though it was a funny memory for him, Claude also felt that it was very disrespectful of them to have joked around during the Lord's time. Covering up his eyes with his left hand and slamming his right hand on the table and crying, Claude said, "I'm sorry, Father! I'm sorry! I've done many wrong things in my life and so have my brother and the man that I thought was my father. However, Father, I don't see why it all had to end this way. My mother had a strong mind. She was influential, dependable, intelligent, never unbelieving, caring for all of her family members, tidy, and always kept herself well dressed and appropriate, so that many young girls could've looked up to her, just like how many young and old ladies looked up to my grandmother. I don't understand, Father, why couldn't you just hold her for me while I wasn't around and tell her that everything was going to be all right, for everything happens for a purpose. But, sitting down right here right now, I say to you, Mother, who is at my Father God's side right now, I'm sorry for not being there for you when you really needed family at your side. And I'm sorry for not coming to you to fix the problem that had started between us and my father's old enemy and son. Mother, I feel that Grandmother's death was natural, and I know that she's happy to be at her Father's side also.

"Father, the man that I called my father here on earth, I thank you for him because he was such a real and understanding man, no matter how many wrong things me and my brother would do. He was always there to influence us to do better in a nice and calm, brother-like way. Troy, I hope that heaven has changed you fully into that man you've always told me you'd be in the future, and I love you. Grandmother, yes, Barack Obama, is going to win. I believe it just as much as you did, and I already know that was the last thing that would've made you happy other than seeing your two grandsons live better lives. Thomas, I love you, and I'm sorry that I wasn't there for you. Alan, I wish that you hadn't chosen that path, but you had your reasons, just like my mother. Nevertheless, I wish that you both would've called me before your decision to take your lives."

Claude started thinking obsessively about that night that he was making love to Kelly while his mother was deciding to take her life away. *If only I had known, I would've stopped you*, Claude thought.

Surprisingly, Latoya had come into the house to check up on Claude, knowing that his old home was where he would be after they left him at the burial site to say his last words to his family.

"Claude," Latoya said as she came into the house, seeing Kelly standing by door with her hands over her face crying.

Latoya had then hugged Kelly and told her that everything will be alright because they are all going to stand by one another's side from here on out.

Knowing it was Latoya from the voice, Claude answered and said, "Yes, I'm in here sitting down, awaiting answers."

Walking up to Claude, sitting down right next to him and putting her arms around him, Latoya felt the need to give him a little lesson on life and how one must be happy on such a day, even though it's heartbreaking, because they've gone to a better place.

"Claude, life I feel is nothing else but a test and a time to grow, learning how much we should give our Father God thanks and praise for his love and understanding that he has for his children. We are his children and the same way how a parent wants their child to be someone strong in their life, no matter what, is the same way how our Father wants us to be. Problems come, night and day for many people, and so do blessings. That's why I feel that you should strive to learn from it all and be ready for your blessings from surviving.

"We're all here for you, Claude, and we're not going anywhere, and we won't let you start to doubt your life from all of this. Be and stay strong for me, my only son, for in time it'll all pay off. Allow Anthony to help us throughout all of this and a chance to get to know a little about his son because he's a very nice person, and I'm sure that he's sorry that he wasn't there for you throughout your childhood. You already know that Kelly wants you to do that also. Speaking of

Kelly, just like how Mrs. Anne used to always say to me: 'What makes life worth living is knowing that one day you'll wake up and find that special person that makes you happier than anything in the whole world, right in front of you.' So don't ever lose hope, your expectations, and throw in the towel." So come and let's go and move on from all of this, which is going to very hard. I'm not telling you to forget about them, but to be happy for them and to also make them even happier by accomplishing not only their goals for you, but yours also.

Claude got up with Latoya and began heading toward the front door, having nothing else to say to the house except goodbye.

Smiling as soon as he saw Kelly, waiting for him at the front door, he said, "Let's go," and then put his arms around Kelly and walked out, not even looking back another time.

Claude spent the rest of his time in Detroit with Kelly, laughing and looking back at all the good times that they had there, not only with each other but also with their family and friends.

"I wonder what the future holds for the both of us, Claude," Kelly asked while they began packing their bags to head back home.

"I don't know. Let's just wait and see, and I'm feeling that it's going to be something very surprising," Claude replied with a smile.

Claude and Kelly went back to Miami, Florida ending up living with one another because Anthony was hardly ever home to be there for Claude. They started school being homeschooled by Latoya. Claude began receiving therapy for the loss of his family because there were many nights that he couldn't sleep without Latoya or Kelly close by. Thoughts of his mother's and grandmother's words kept running through his mind about wanting him to be the best man that he could be throughout his life, and how they always strived to inspire him. Thoughts of how Troy always told him that even though he's not the kind of man to give one girl his all or would've ever been. He felt Claude had better not allow a beautiful blessing like Kelly go to waste because not every man is blessed with a soul mate. However, the thoughts about Charles troubled him because he wasn't the man he said he was. But Claude felt though he was everything that a father should be. Unlike Anthony, who had survived so many years without wanting to see or know his son.

Throughout the year while living together there were many times when Latoya wasn't home, Kelly gave sex therapy to Claude to help make him feel better. Also, because deep down inside of her, Kelly was desiring a relationship with her best friend now. However, it was Claude talking to her about never taking it that far. Really though because he didn't want to take the chances of losing the only one now who was able to keep his head up and tears from falling night and day. So Kelly began taking it that they were just friends with benefits. She never liked that, but it was hard for her resist her desire to make love to Claude, who held many other titles in her life now: her adopted brother, the man that took her virginity, her first love, and a whole lot more.

Anthony, who felt that he had money but nothing to do with it except now to see if it could buy his son's forgiveness and love for not being there for him, set up bank accounts for Claude and Kelly, putting a good amount in there for them each month telling them to spend it wisely. After talking to his friend Austin about it, he began thinking about going to family therapy with Claude. However, he knew that wasn't something a young man like Claude would be interested in. So he decided to just wait until the time was right because he wasn't a family guy.

After Claude's graduation, it was time for them to split up for some time because Claude was going off to college in another state while Kelly was entering her last year of high school; however, their love for each other wasn't going anywhere. During the first couple of weeks Claude and Kelly talked every night. But after awhile, Claude stopped answering the calls and only texting back 'I'm with someone right now.' Which, made it seem he was no longer desperate for her love and attention. It made Kelly jealous, and wanting someone else too then.

LIFE

So many challenges, and so many problems,
That we face in it
But yet
So much rewards and happiness
When one stays strong, and does no wrong
But many may not understand
Because, when one's life gets dark
And sees no way out
One, or should I say many,
May do whatever it takes
To see some light
Even when it's wrong
Just to see a change
However, uniting and being as one,
We can make better changes
Back backing, all the dark clouds from around us
And allowing our Father's angels
To shine upon us and come into our lives
To show us
Better ways
That we make our Father
Proud

PART II

TWO YEARS LATER

CHAPTER 7

"Congratulations, Kelly, and it's about time!" Claude said with a bright and shining smile on his face. Claude walked over to Kelly and gave her a hug and kiss on her cheek. "I'm happy for you because now maybe your Mom won't have to be babying you anymore. You're a high school graduate!"

"Thank you, Claude. I'm so surprised that you were able to show for my graduation and not just for the graduation party," Kelly said.

Kelly's friends started laughing.

"Girl, you know Claude wouldn't miss this," her good friend Bianca said.

"Yeah why wouldn't I show up for one of your biggest accomplishments?! C'mon now. You know me better than that."

Kelly looked at him sweetly. "Yeah, you're right. I know you better than that."

Claude grinned to himself but didn't let on anything more.

"Thank you for the love, Claude," Kelly continued. "I'm glad you could be here to support me."

"I wouldn't have it any other way, Kelly."

"So will I be seeing you at the party?" Kelly asked.

"Yes, I'll be busy eating up all the food, but for a sure fact, you will be seeing me doing more though than that."

"Do whatever you want Claude, just as long as my mother doesn't start getting mad."

"Come on, girl, let's go take some pictures, and you know who wants to take some pictures with you too, girl. So let's go," said Bianca.

"I'm about to go and take some pictures with my friends. I'll see you later, right?" Kelly asked.

"Yeah, I'll probably be there before you I'm helping your mother set up."

"All right then, and thank you again."

"All right, see you later, and I don't want you coming to your party late!" Claude yelled after her.

Kelly began walking away with her friends, looking back at Claude, laughing because she already knew that Claude wanted her to be there with him right now.

"I know that wasn't your best friend, Kelly," her friend Catherine said, clutching Kelly's arm. "I just saw him talking to you and kissing you while Donald—you know, your boyfriend, in case you forgot—was standing across the room."

"I'm surprised he came down here just to see me graduate," Kelly replied.

"Girl, he drove all the way from New Jersey to Miami just to see lil' ole' you graduate? I heard from my older sister Victoria that he was supposed to be taking summer classes and working. Kelly, I have a feeling he has a big surprise coming to you soon," said Catherine.

"Well, whatever it is, I hope it'll be one I'll love because I have one for him too that he would never expect but that he's gonna love," Kelly replied.

"Well, I hope so too because you already told me what it is, and I don't think that he would've ever expected that. And the true reason why you're going there, I don't think he'll be happy to hear that," Catherine replied.

"You already know I can't tell him that, Catherine, or else he'll go to my mother about it all. So I'll just wait until I get there. I might make him find out for himself but it's so hard for me to hold things back from him," Kelly said.

* * *

Claude reached Latoya's home, and she was surprised to see him. When she answered the door, her eyes opened wide and she put her hand over her mouth. She gave Claude a big hug and a kiss on the cheek and, then, welcomed him inside. Ever since Anthony had helped Latoya get a job as a mortgage broker, she was always busy and never home because it was a lot of work making sure all of the bills got paid on time. Claude helped out though. Even though he wasn't living in Latoya's house to use all the electricity anymore, he still paid the bill each month. She appreciated his help, and Anthony's too.

"How have you been doing with the man of the house gone for so long?" Claude asked with a giggle.

"I've been doing great, Claude, especially now that Kelly's graduating high school and about to head off for college. I'm three for three. Evette, Shellion and now Kelly. I'm feeling so happy for Kelly right now. And I'm so proud of myself for doing a good job with my girls."

"You have every reason to be. But why didn't I see you at the graduation?"

"Because I don't have no time to be standing up there, watching her and her friends talk and fool around while I got to get all of this food ready and other things for her party. After they called Kelly's name at the ceremony, I came back here to start getting ready. Anyways, I didn't see you either. How did you get in? Didn't you need a ticket to get inside?"

"The same way you know a lot of people is the same way I know a lot of people. So let's keep it like that."

"Boy, tell me how you got the ticket and stop with your 'I got people' talk."

Claude laughed. "One of Kelly's friend's sisters goes to college with me. She couldn't make the trip for her own sister who graduated today too. So she gave me her ticket if I promised to congratulate her sister in person for her."

"You're a sneaky little one, Claude."

"I know," Claude said laughing again.

"You do know that Kelly's following you to school up there, right?"

"Are you serious?!"

"Yep, you two will be at the same college. I'm not surprised, though."

Claude felt like jumping in the air. "No, she hadn't told me yet. I'm so happy right now!"

"Well, I guess she wanted to surprise you with all of that information," Latoya replied. "If she tells you later, act surprised."

Claude had a bigger smile on his face now.

"What are you smiling so bright for?" Latoya asked, already knowing the answer.

"Because Kelly and I have been so far apart for so long. Having her close again will be really nice."

Latoya looked at him with a serious expression. "Claude, you make sure you watch over her and make sure she gets all her work done right and on time. You hear me?"

"Yes, Ms. Brown. Of course."

"I trust you with her. I know you love her."

"Yes, of course I do. I love both of you."

"I know you do. But you *love*, Kelly."

Claude tried not to fidget, but he couldn't help himself.

"No need trying to keep it a secret. You've been bad about keeping it a secret all these years. But it's okay. I don't mind. In fact, I'm happy about it."

"Really?" Claude asked.

"Yes really. I love the kind of person you are, Claude. And I truly feel that you will be the best man Kelly will ever know. If it were up to me, you two would've been together a long time ago. But I know these things take time. And maturity."

Claude smiled broadly and was very happy to hear Latoya's words of encouragement.

"Yes! I am truly in love with your daughter," he said finally. "It's just that if I would have told you, I know a line would have then been put between Kelly and me. Especially because I used to sleep here some nights. I would have loved for her to have come to my homecoming and prom with me, but that year, I had too much going on to complicate things," replied Claude.

"Just say that you were scared to ask Kelly, not of me," Latoya said with a chuckle.

"A real man is never scared to ask a woman out," said with mock macho-ness.

"Yeah, true, and a real man is never scared to express himself to a woman no matter what the answer may be."

"Mom, I'm home!" Kelly said loudly as she walked through the front door.

"Remember what I just said, alright, Claude?" Latoya said.

Looking at Latoya smiling, Claude said, "Alright, I hear you. I won't be afraid."

Latoya nodded her head one good time at Claude and called out to Kelly, "Baby, I'm in here!"

"Did Claude already eat and leave!?" Kelly called back.

"No, he's in the kitchen with me. He's in here talking about what a real man should do in certain situations," Latoya replied.

Claude looked at both of them and screwed up his mouth to fight a grin. "You're making me feel badly now, as if I'm not a real man."

"That's the point. You're not," Latoya replied, laughing.

"Aw, come on, Ms. Brown," Claude said.

"And you're whining too?" Latoya said, laughing harder now. "If you're a real man, prove it to me then." She was looking deeply into Claude's eyes.

Just then, Kelly walked in. She saw Claude and her mother having a moment, and she thought she knew what it was about. She walked up to Claude and held his arm and put her head on his shoulder.

"So instead of just helping to eat up all of the food at the party, you're helping my mother surprise me with a car for my graduation present? Is that what y'all are in here doing?" Kelly asked Claude.

Both Latoya and Claude began to laugh hysterically. Latoya had to use a dish towel to wipe her eyes, and Claude was bent over with his hands on his knees.

"Wooo, this chile' is serious!" Latoya exclaimed when she finally caught her breath.

"It's not about my car?" Kelly asked, sounding disappointed.

"Girl, please. Now reach over there and hand me the paper plates."

The DJ finished preparing all of his equipment and started playing music.

"Sounds like the DJ is ready for the party to begin," Claude said to Kelly. "Can I have the first dance of the night?"

"Yes, I would love that," Kelly replied and looked at her mother, who stood off on the side smiling.

Kelly asked the DJ to play something slow for the two of them.

Lying against his chest as the music played, Kelly began speaking to Claude softly.

"Claude, while we were so far apart, I thought about you all the time, and it feels so wonderful to be able to hold you again."

"You should already know that I missed you too, Kelly," Claude replied.

"I know," Kelly replied and laughed. "Guess what?"

"What?"

"We're going to be going to college in New Jersey together."

"Really?!" Claude said, trying to sound surprised. "That's wonderful news, Kelly!"

"Don't forget about our money also, Claude, because you owe me a lot of it," Kelly laughed.

"Our money, Kelly? I thought it was my money? My father already gives you money."

"Whatever is yours is mine, and whatever is mine is mine, right?"

"I never knew that's how it was."

"Well now you know."

There was a knocking at the door.

"It looks like the party is about to begin. Get ready to party! And don't let me catch you touching up on any of my friends." Kelly said

"I'll *try* not to."

"What?' Kelly replied looking at Claude mock seriousness.

"I'm just playing."

"You better be."

"Well, let all of your friends in to party the night away," Claude said with a laugh.

The party began. Claude was looking at each friend, greeting and congratulating one another. Food was being served, and the dance floor that was set up for a big crowd became overcrowded with girls dancing with one another while most of the males were just watching. Some males tried dancing wild with some of the females, but only few succeeded.

Looking around to see if he could see what Kelly was doing, Claude couldn't spot her anywhere. It seemed she was no longer in the house, so he stood up and looked for the lady in all red with sparkling lips. Claude began to walk outside to see what was going on and to see if he could find her. However, when he got outside, he saw something he thought he never would. Kelly was kissing someone else's lips other than his.

"Damn, who's this fool kissing Kelly!" Claude said with an angry expression.

Coming off Donald's lips slowly and looking back at the front of her house, Kelly saw Claude looking at her. Both Claude and Donald were trying to recognize each other, but because it was dark outside, neither had gotten a clear view of the other and they were not interested in knowing each other either. Kelly turned her head back around to her newly drafted, college-football-player boyfriend to whom she finally said yes to at the prom.

Donald was a typical jock. He was a gifted athlete, but he was also terribly conceited. Girls loved him though, and a lot of Kelly's classmates envied her because of her relationship with Donald.

Kelly was always encouraging Donald to strive towards getting better as a quarterback and in school. That's how he fell in love with her. She was the kind of girl who'd be supportive throughout his football career. He didn't just want a woman in his life that wanted him just for the millions he planned on making. She was everything he wanted, and in Claude's absence, Kelly grew close to Donald. She never told him about Claude, though. And she let Donald believe she was still a virgin who'd never been in love. Those were two things that she knew would break Donald's heart.

What Donald also did not know was that he, Kelly *and* Claude would all be going to the same college. Kelly never mentioned the real reason why she'd picked her school. She let Donald believe that she was following him and his football career.

From the other side of the party, one of Donald's teammates saw how Claude was looking at Kelly. He noticed that it looked more than friendly.

Claude saw the guy looking at him, so he nodded his head in acknowledgement.

But the guy didn't nod back. He mouthed, "That's my homey girl, so go fuck off."

Claude felt rage rising up from deep down inside of him. *Calm down, fool,* he thought to *himself. Don't be stupid. Don't do it.* Then went into a back room to mentally prepare his big surprise for Kelly, sitting inside his pants pocket. He went inside and asked the DJ to turn everything off and told the people by the lights that he had a surprise. He wanted them to turn off all the lights so she would come in and ask what happened.

Hearing that the music had stopped playing, Kelly paused for a moment and laughed.

She turned to Donald. "I'll be right back. I need to know what's going on with the music and lights."

"What's going on in here?" Kelly asked as she moved deeper into the house.

When she took another step, she bumped into someone. Claude was kneeling down on one knee.

"Will you, Kelly?"

The lights were then turned back on. She couldn't believe who and what she was seeing. Tears began falling from her eyes. "What is happening right now?"

"No, Kelly, I'm not asking you to marry me. I'm asking you to hold your word on our everlasting love and friendship because in my hand here is a promise ring toward our friendship and love toward each other. I love you, Kelly, so this is my gift for you as your graduation gift."

"It's beautiful, Claude. Thank you. I love you too." She could barely get the words out.

Claude kissed the ring that he had just put on Kelly's ring finger, stood up and gave Kelly a hug and a kiss on both of her cheeks. "I love you, Kelly. Congratulations!"

"I love you too," Kelly said with a big smile.

"Well, I don't want to hold you up any longer so go on ahead back out there. I think your man's waiting." Claude said.

Outside, Donald stood there wondering what was taking Kelly so long to return. As he looked around, he noticed a woman approaching him.

"Hi, I'm Nancy," she said, standing right up on him.

"I'm Donald," he said back. He took another look to see if Kelly was visible.

"Well Donald, you look really familiar to me."

"Oh yeah," Donald said, loving the attention. "I play football. Maybe that's why I look familiar."

"That's right, that's right. You play quarterback, right?"

"Right," Donald said. He couldn't help but to notice Nancy's lips. They looked wet. Probably because she was licking them slowly.

"Well Donald, I don't know much about football, but I'd sure like to learn."

"Oh yeah."

"Definitely," Nancy said. Then she slipped him her number and walked away. This was just the kind of prospect Nancy had been looking for: a sexy athlete on his way to the pros. She had dreams of becoming a music artist, too. She had no money or connections in the industry, though. So she was willing to do whatever, whenever, however to get the opportunities that she'd always wanted.

"Alright, sweetheart," Donald said, feeling emboldened himself now. "You definitely will be hearing from daddy before he goes off."

"Now that's true love and friendship. That's what I want from my man," some girl on the dance floor said.

Donald had been so wrapped up in Nancy that he hadn't been paying attention. His friend who'd noticed Claude staring at Kelly earlier walked up to him and started whispering in his ear.

"All right, start playing the music DJ so that we could start bumping and grinding again," someone yelled out.

Kelly walked back outside just in time with the music.

"Babe, what was that all about?" Donald asked when she came back over.

"Baby, that's Claude, my best friend, the one I told you about when you had asked me if I only grew up with my mother and my two sisters and no brother to watch over me, from all the boys that liked me. That's him. He was just showing his love for me. He gave me this ring and told me that he'll be always here for me. It was sweet. That's all."

"Well, it sounded like to me that it was a little more than that because of the way how I was hearing about you smiling and blushing in front of him and everybody else."

"You know I wouldn't ever do that to you, my bedtime bear. You're like my good-luck charm." Kelly leaned over for a kiss.

Donald didn't notice. "How come he won't show me his face?" he asked, scanning the room.

"Come on. I'll introduce you to him and my mother."

"No, I'm not ready to meet your mother yet, and I don't think I'd love to meet your best friend."

"Well then, you'll meet him in college because he already goes to the college that we're going to."

"What? You know much about him?"

"Were you even listening to me? Claude is like my family. We moved here from Detroit with him to support him after his whole family died. I've told you this before, Donald."

Donald continued to silently scan around. He wasn't listening at all.

* * *

"So what was that all about, mister? I just see us as friends for now?" Latoya asked Claude in the kitchen while he started to eat his meals for the night.

"All I did was just give her my graduation gift and told her that I love and would always be there for her. That's all."

"That's all, are you sure?"

"Yes, nothing else but congratulations and love."

"Yes, I saw the love, but I'm seeing more than you're saying, Claude, and I must say that when you're going to tell her, make sure you do it with more words and a little poetry because that's what she loves," Latoya smiled.

"No, I don't want to do it like that because my poems are so good that she might end up falling deeply in love and wanting nothing else but me. So I'll wait because I don't want to distract her while her mind is set on school right now."

"Words, words, words, Claude. That's all you got, young man. What about doing it instead of just saying it? I've grown you up better than that, so now I'm waiting for you to show me that I've done great for you and not only for my daughter. Claude, in a way, I don't want you to yet, but don't wait until the last minute."

"Okay, my how-to-get-a-girl instructor, I won't fail you," Claude teased, and then started laughing.

The party ended at four in the morning. Claude was told to stay up to help Latoya and Kelly clean up the house.

* * *

After Latoya left and they heard her room door close, Kelly and Claude started talking.

"Thank you for the gift, and I promise you I will hold on to it as long as I live," Kelly said to Claude.

Claude looked at Kelly and laughed. "You're welcome and I'll probably take you out sometime this week, if you're not busy."

"You don't have to worry about my boyfriend, if that's what you're meaning because he's leaving to go off to college soon. He's going to the same college as us."

"I won't even say anything about that. So you want me to take his place by taking you out while he's not around?"

"Yes, somebody has to take care of the Queen while the King is gone," Kelly replied and laughed.

"Okay, I see how it is."

"Stop thinking like that because you know I'm just playing with you," Kelly said and hugged Claude tightly.

After finishing cleaning up the house, they decided to stop and finish the outside another time. They went to lie down on Kelly's queen-size bed that Anthony had bought for her. They began talking about how many people showed up and how much she loved her party and how surprised she looked when she had seen Claude down on one knee with a ring in his hand, looking as if he was about to ask her to marry him. Kelly said that if that would have happened, she wouldn't have said no or yes because she wouldn't have known what to say.

"So you wouldn't have said no? Tell me why," Claude asked.

"I wouldn't want to break your heart in front of so many people. You'd be embarrassed, and I don't want to embarrass you like that," Kelly replied laughing.

"Answer me seriously this time, Kelly, because I'm going to ask you this question again."

"All right."

"Kelly, what if I did ask you to marry me right then and there. What would you have said to me? Or just tell me what you think you might have said to me."

"I don't know, Claude.

They looked into each other's eyes for a long moment.

They began thinking about how they felt while with each other, and how it used to feel. The feeling became strong, and they both wanted to kiss each other.

"Kelly, yes, I'm still in love with you," Claude said.

Their lips began to get closer, their hearts began drumming, and their eyes closed as they kissed.

Latoya came out of her room and looked around the house for Kelly and Claude, but she didn't see them. *Where could they be now at this time?* Latoya thought to herself. She peeked inside of Kelly's bedroom and saw her baby daughter and Claude kissing. Surprisingly, a smile came on her face because that's who she wanted her daughter's true love to be, but as she walked away, all she hoped was that it wouldn't mess things up between them. If one thing would go wrong while they're still young, it would just mess up everything for them, just like how Claude had told her.

Kelly and Claude began to hold each other closely with Kelly's head on Claude's chest. *Kelly already had a boyfriend, and it was like kissing his lips also,* Claude thought. But he wouldn't want to let every moment like this pass.

Kelly began realizing that the feelings that she had for Claude are still there;. However, her feelings for her man are there also.

That night, Donald called Nancy. He told her that he was in need of a good woman to pleasure him because his girlfriend was stressing him.

"Come on over, sweetie," Nancy said, happy her plan was working. "I'm home alone."

After two sex sessions, Donald was out of condoms, which then made Nancy feel like it was time.

"I don't have any more condoms on me, so I don't want to go through with this right now. So I'll just settle for some head," Donald said.

"I'm on the pill," Nancy said, kissing his neck. "My mother had put me on it years ago because she knows I love sex. I've always used a condom, but the pill is my back up." She moved her kissing down his chest.

Donald was so turned on, his whole body was on fire. "You sure you've been taking 'em?"

"Yeah, baby. Every day at 10 a.m. We're good. I've never had any kind of sexually transmitted diseases either. Don't worry. You're in good hands," Nancy said sexily massaging his dick.

"Okay, let's go again," Donald said. He couldn't resist the temptation.

Getting on top, Nancy told Donald that she was going to ride it hard but still nice and easy for him to love it. She hoped there was still some sperm left over from his first two orgasms.

Nancy rode him just like she said she would. It didn't take long before Donald started to climax.

"Get up, I'm about to cum!" he yelled. Donald loved the feeling, but he didn't want to take any chances.

"Baby, I told you, I'm on the pill," Nancy said, grinding harder. She knew Donald was close to finishing.

"Bitch! Get the fuck off of me," Donald went while climaxing. He tried pushing her off him, but she wrapped her legs underneath him and kept on riding.

"What the fuck?! Bitch, you trying to get pregnant!" Donald then slapped Nancy in the face hard leaving her to land on the floor.

"What the fuck is wrong with you?!" she screamed.

Donald looked at his stomach and saw nothing there. *So that must mean I came inside that bitch.*

"Damn! I can't believe this shit!" Donald said and then looked down at Nancy. "You think I'm dumb motherfucker, huh?"

"What, you don't believe me? Look on my dresser and see the pills that I'm taking," Nancy said holding her face. "Watch, you're going to pay for this shit."

"I don't care. Don't try that shit again with me, bitch. And you better not be lying to me about this because I'll beat the fuck out of your ass. If I hear anything about you being pregnant with my child…" Donald said over her.

"Get the fuck out of my face!"

Donald then picked Nancy up by her arms tightly and looked dead at her. "I mean it, bitch. If you're lying to me, I will beat the shit out of your ass."

"I'm not lying!" Nancy cried.

Donald then let her go, looked on the dresser but didn't see anything on it except makeup and a empty box of tampons. "I don't see shit over there, where is it?"

Nancy looked at the dresser. "I must've misplaced them earlier, but I took one today. I'm sure! Now leave! I want you to leave now before I call the fucking police on your ass!

"You threatening me, bitch?" Donald said with his right hands going across her face again.

She backed up against her bedroom wall and slid to the floor crying. Then she jumped right back up.

Nancy ran towards Donald and began swinging her arms. "You think I'm scared of your ass? You think I'm scared to fight back?" She hit Donald in his face, neck, chest, shoulders, stomach but then he just pushed her down on her bed.

"Keep your hands off me, bitch."

Nancy's cell phone started ringing. Donald immediately walked over towards it to see who it was. "Best friend" is the name that he saw come up. He immediately threw her cell phone down and broke it into little pieces. "Keep your mouth shut about this night, ho', or else before they lock me up, they'll find your ass dead on the beach"

Donald looked back at her again, seeing her getting serious with more and more tears coming down her eyes, right before he was about to say something else, Nancy screamed out again, "Get out now! And if your ass was brave enough to kill me, you would've been done it. Now get the fuck out!"

Donald picked up his clothes smiling and made his way out of her house the same way that he came in. He didn't even look back to see if she was calling the police.

Inside of the house, Nancy ran to the front door and locked it. *I never thought this would happen to me. I'm not going to tell no one about this except Cristal my best friend. But if he does make it to the NFL, and I hope that he does, the whole world is going to find out what he did to me, watch. And I hope that I get pregnant so that his first pay-check will come to me.*

CHAPTER 8

A few days later, Claude called Kelly. He was excited to see her again.

"Hey, you still want to go out tonight?" he asked hopefully. "Remember, we had plans."

"Of course I still wanna go. Why would our plans change?" Kelly knew things had been awkward since her graduation party with Donald there. She wanted everything to go back to normal.

"Oh I don't know. I just wanted to check. Maybe you had made other plans or something. I don't want to intrude or assume anything."

"Nope, no other plans. Just you and me." Kelly let that hang in the air longer than necessary. "So what time are you coming to pick me up?" She asked with a grin.

Claude wasn't sure what to think, but he was willing to roll with it. "Be ready about 7. And wear something really nice."

A few hours later, Claude pulled up to Kelly's house wearing a fine, royal blue tuxedo. He'd made reservations at a fancy restaurant on South Beach and wanted the both of them to look amazing.

Latoya wanted to take a lot of pictures of Claude and Kelly going out. Kelly kept saying it wasn't a date, but Latoya didn't care. It looked like a date to her, and she wanted to capture as much of it as she could.

"Make sure—" Latoya began.

Claude cut her off. "I know, I know. And I will because, remember, I'm the best."

"Okay, I'm just making sure you know how much this night means to Kelly. And boy, don't cut me off again while I'm talking. You know better."

Kelly walked downstairs in a beautiful white and sky-blue dress. She knew those colors were Claude's favorites. She wanted that night to be special.

Claude and Latoya started to clap because she looked so beautiful. Her earrings were sparkly shaped like stars, and her hair was beautifully done, making her look like a princess. Her lips were glossy, and her high heels matched her dress.

"Kelly, you look so bright and beautiful," Claude said.

"Thank you, I guess I'll be your guiding light tonight," Kelly replied.

"Start posing for me, my little babies," said Latoya.

"Well, I guess this will be our first photo shoot together," Kelly said.

"I never knew that you could ever look as beautiful as me, Kelly. I think it's time for a new look for me," said Latoya.

Claude said, "Yes, that's true. But I don't ever think anyone could ever look as beautiful as your daughter is looking right now."

"Come on you two, take some pictures and stop showing off because you're getting me jealous now, and you don't want me to pull out my old photo album on y'all," Latoya said.

"Please don't because I already know we'll be sitting down for hours as you explain how you were feeling in every picture in every pose," Claude said.

"Well then, be quiet and start posing," Latoya replied.

"Hold on, Mom. Let Claude put this necklace on for me."

"Where did you get that necklace with all those stars on it from?" Latoya asked Kelly.

"Claude bought it for me for my prom, but remember, you wanted me to wear the same necklace that you and my sisters wore to your proms?" Kelly replied.

"So you didn't wear it to your prom?" Claude asked Kelly.

"Nope, she wanted me to wear something else," Kelly replied.

"Good thing I did because this is the best time for you to wear it," Latoya replied.

Claude put on the necklace around Kelly's neck as Latoya snapped more pictures. Claude looked down to see if she was wearing the ring he gave her, and she was. He had another necklace for her, but since she never wore the one she had on, he decided to surprise her with it another time. Afterward, Latoya took a lot of pictures of them holding one another.

Claude put out his arm for Kelly to hold onto as they walked out the door and towards the limo he had reserved for the entire night.

"I wish I was able to join you," Latoya said before they walked out the door.

"Maybe next time if you decide to help us clean up the house after a party," Claude said.

"Well, next time maybe you should have cleaner friends come in here and not trash it," Latoya teased back.

Claude walked with Kelly slowly, holding her arm and smiling while telling her that she was strikingly beautiful. The limo driver had opened up the doors for them.

"You first, gorgeous," Claude said to Kelly.

"That's an elegant young lady you got there with you, sir," the limo driver said.

"Yeah, I know. Too bad she's not mine."

In the limo, Kelly sat close to Claude and thanked him for the special night with a kiss that lasted the whole car ride to the restaurant. They were seated right away when they arrived, and Claude was thankful that he had made reservations. He knew he was making a good impression.

At the table, he pulled the chair out for Kelly and waited for her to have a seat. As she sat down, she saw a beautiful letter with flowers around it. It was a poem from Claude titled "Friendship and My Love for You."

"Don't read anything yet, Kelly. Please wait. I hadn't planned it, but after we leave here, I want to go and walk along the shore with you, and then I'd like you to read the letter."

"That sounds nice."

"Good evening, mademoiselle. May I start you off with a beverage?" the waiter asked Kelly.

After ordering her drink and looking at the menu, Kelly asked if there was anything available with more than one hundred calories because all the food looked like diet food.

Claude laughed nervously. "Maybe we should have stopped for fast food before coming to dinner. It might take ten plates from this menu to fill us up."

"I'm sure it'll be okay, Claude." Kelly did not want to seem unappreciative.

They ordered their meals when the waiter came back with their drinks. Making a toast to each other for their friendship and love for each other, Kelly and Claude clinked glasses and a flash went off. They started laughing, and Kelly asked Claude if it was part of another surprise for her.

"No," Claude replied. They looked around and saw it was a cameraman who was around to take pictures of couples.

After they finished eating, they shared a slice of cheesecake with whipped cream on top. Claude cut off a small piece for Kelly and put it in her mouth and the cameraman took another picture as he did so. They started laughing again.

"My turn," Kelly said. Kelly took a fork and cut a big piece for Claude. He thought she might try to play a joke on him, but she didn't. She slowly put the cheesecake to his lips and turned to smile for the camera.

"May I read your poem now?" she asked after the camera flashed.

"Let's go on the beach and sit down. I'll read it to you there," Claude said.

Claude asked for the bill and was asked if he'd like to purchase the three pictures that the cameraman had taken for them also.

"Yes, we'd love them," Kelly replied.

After paying the bill, they walked out the restaurant holding each other's hands happily. Claude and Kelly had walked on the beach and found a nice spot close by the water and lay down. Claude took out his poem and began reading it to Kelly slowly and in a soft voice.

FRIENDSHIP AND MY LOVE FOR YOU

Poetically but passionately, I come to you
With all the love and time
That I have for you

Charming and loving, I've changed myself for you
For you mean the world to me

Delightful and enlightening, you are with me
For when I need you
You forget the world for me

Inspiring and Instigating with your love
That's how you make me feel
Whenever you come and talk to me

You're all, that is all
I wish to ever be, even though
We've been just friends.

I wish to show my love for you
The best I could
Whenever I could
And how I feel I should
I must say
My love for you
Will surely soon to be
More than we've ever
Expected
And wanted it
To ever be

103

Looking at each other, Kelly thought about his words and set her mind to having a night she'd never forget. She held Claude's hand tightly.

"I love you, Claude," Kelly began. "But there is so much that I question about us. Like, what if our relationship doesn't end up how we expected it to? How do you think I would feel if I was to ever lose you? I really, truly love you. But I'm afraid of being with you because I'm afraid of losing you. I don't know if I can handle that."

"Kelly, one thing that I do know is, if anything was to ever happen between us—like, say, if we were to ever stop talking to each other—I know my love for you will never go away. Never. No matter what."

"Tell me how it feels when you hold me."

"How about you tell me?" Claude replied, looking into Kelly eyes as the wind blew through her hair.

Kelly had no words to describe her feelings. So she leaned in and kissed Claude passionately. She thought back to the first time they made love. She hoped she could convey the strength of her feelings through the kiss.

When she slowly pulled her face away, she looked at Claude closely and sweetly. He seemed to get the picture.

Then Claude leapt to his feet and reached out to Kelly to pull her up. He wanted to walk along the beach.

Along the shore, they talked, laughed, held each other, and kicked at the water.

"Are you ready for college?" Claude asked Kelly after a while.

"Who wouldn't be?"

After about two hours of walking, talking, and spending time with each other, Claude took Kelly home and stayed the night in the guestroom, better known as his room. Lying down in her bed alone, Kelly's mind was on Claude, having memories about how good it felt the first time they made love and about how good it made her feel just to hear "I love you" from just him. After a while, Kelly got up to go into the room with Claude because she wanted to hold him. Before she turned the knob, she remembered Donald and turned back around.

"What am I getting myself into?" Kelly asked herself before falling asleep.

CHAPTER 9

"Bye, Mother," Kelly said.

"Bye, Mom," Claude echoed.

"Bye, Momma's little babies. I wish for you the best of luck in college."

Once they were on the road, Claude and Kelly hardly spoke. They listened to music and tried to keep their minds off their feelings for each other.

New Jersey
1:00 p.m.

Ten miles before they reached their destination, Claude felt that if he didn't start talking to Kelly like he normally did, their friendship would start falling apart.

"So, Kelly, what's going to be your major in college?" he said a little too loudly. He was nervous.

"Business management. Is that still your major, too?" Kelly asked.

"Nope," Claude replied.

"What kind of business would you like to run?"

"A luxurious hotel and spa in the United Sates and one in the Caribbean. What about you?"

"I would love to get into hotel management myself. Have my own clothing line for both women and children and my own clothing stores along with it all," Kelly said dreamily. "Wait a minute, Claude. I thought that you once told me that you wanted to be an owner of your own NBA or NFL team."

"I still do, but it takes contacts for me to do all of that. Not just money, right?"

"I don't know. You have to tell me."

"Kelly, I hope what went on between you and me won't affect our friendship."

"No, it won't because I've already been expecting something like that to happen between us."

Claude and Kelly finally pulled up to the college where their final test was about to begin. Amazed by how beautiful and big it was from her view, Kelly said that she would be taking a lot of pictures for her photo album, all over the college, for memories of when she was young, just like how her mother did.

"Haven't you already seen all over this college before when you came here to view it with your high school?" Claude asked.

"Yes, and no, I was to busy hiding from you when we came for the tour," Kelly replied.

"Well, there's your dorm. Make sure you keep it clean and tidy all right because I'll be coming in every week to make sure it stays thoroughly clean."

"I shouldn't have to worry about that. I have you here to clean it for me."

"That's very funny."

* * *

Claude pulled off, hoping that their college life would go well. Kelly ended up getting a room with a girl named Ashley. They introduced themselves to each other and agreed on all the rules of their room. Paul, Claude's roommate, saw Claude coming down the hall and screamed out, "Mr. Clean is back, y'all."

"Very funny," Claude replied.

"Well, you are the one that wants everything cleaned every day and night" Paul said.

"Yes, because I don't like to live dirty, that's why."

"I got my cousin out here now, Claude, about to fulfill my uncle's dream of being a football player. So you know now I'm going to be going to every one of our games."

"So I guess now you're no longer going to be going to our games just for the girls?"

"Of course, I'll just have to do all of what I do at halftime so that I can bring one home, just like how I usually do. Or to a hotel room."

"So what about your cousin? Is he just like you, another girl every week?" Claude asked.

"No, but I heard his girl followed him here."

"Sounds like someone knows how to love a woman in your family, because you don't."

"Claude, I know more about relationships than you. I'm just too young to settle down right now. So I have to keep my gloves on to catch every fly girl that comes my way."

* * *

Kelly was home bored, so she met up with Donald to talk to him about his new teammates.

"Hi, baby," Kelly said, and greeted Donald with a hug and a kiss.

"How is everything?" Donald asked smiling and feeling good because he had just come from having sex with a football groupie.

"Great, and my roommate is so nice. I'm even happier now because my baby is not too far from me anymore."

Kelly was listening, but she was could not avoid picking up the scent in the air. It smelled like a woman's fragrance on his clothing. "Why do you smell like a girl?

Ignoring her question, Donald continued on with their original discussion. "My cousin, Paul, said that he wanted to meet you because of what my dad told him about you and me. Would you like to meet him?"

"Yes, I would love to meet everyone in your family and you haven't answered my question yet. Why do you have some kind of perfume on you?"

"All right, tonight is going to be a beginning-of-the-year party, so I'll call you and tell you what time we're going to come and pick you up."

"All right," Kelly replied without getting her question answered. She pushed any doubts about Donald out of her mind and was just happy to get an invitation to attend the party with him that tonight.

* * *

"Claude, you coming to party with us tonight? Plus you could meet my cousin," Paul said.

"Yes, but I don't know how long I'll be staying there. I'm already tired," Claude replied. He also decided to take the gold necklace for Kelly to drop it off at her dorm on his way back.

Later, when Paul picked up Donald, he wanted to call Kelly to tell her to get ready, but Paul stopped him.

"This is a college party, you don't need her there," Paul said.

* * *

Kelly was waiting for Donald's call when her roommate told her to just call him and tell him that she had a ride and would meet him there. So Kelly said alright and tried to get in contact with Donald, but the music was so loud in Paul's car that neither of them could hear his phone ringing. Kelly ended up calling him back and leaving a message that she'd meet him there.

Reaching the party first, Claude sat down and got a drink, and began looking around to see if he would spot Kelly or Paul around.

Kelly and Ashley ended up reaching the party before Donald and Paul. Looking around, Kelly couldn't see her man anywhere. So Ashley began introducing Kelly to all of her other friends who were there.

"Let's start partying, girls!" Ashley said after they all had met Kelly.

Dancing and having fun, Kelly stayed in the middle of all of her new friends. Claude saw Kelly in the middle of the dance floor and went up behind her and asked for a dance.

While turning around, Kelly said, "Sorry, but no. I already have a man to dance with whom I'm waiting for right now—Claude!"

"Yeah, it's me."

"Why the hell you did that to me for?"

"Come over here," Claude whispered in Kelly's ear. "Would you like something to drink?"

"No, that's all right."

They stood against the wall and talked. Claude was happy to see her smiling face. She began saying that she loved her room and her roommate because they were just alike, clean and neat.

Claude frowned after hearing that. He said that he didn't want to hold up any more of her time with all of her new friends. However, before Kelly walked off, he went in his pocket and handed her the necklace.

"What's this?" Kelly said with a smile on her face.

"I want you looking beautiful all day every day."

Kelly thanked Claude with a big kiss on his cheek and then walked away. Looking back, she blew him another kiss. Claude grabbed that kiss from the air with his hand and then placed it on his chest.

Donald and Paul finally reached the party with a whole crew behind them. Most of them were Paul's friends, and the rest were some football players that Donald had gotten to know. Claude noticed as soon as Paul came into the party because everyone turned to look as they appeared, ready to take over the party.

As Donald walked in, a random girl approached him, and said hi, while smiling and looking at his body.

"What's up sweetie?" he said with a grin.

"Nothing much. But I'd love to put something up for you." Her eyes never left his.

One of Donald's friends yelled out, "That sounds like a invite to me!" Everyone near them laughed.

"Whenever you're ready, baby, I'll be there," Donald replied.

The girl walked up to him and rubbed her thigh against his crotch to feel his bigness. Then he put her hand deep into his pocket to leave her number. She kissed his lips softly and then said, "See you later, sweetie."

Donald and all his friends eyed the woman as she walked away. Then they continued walking through the party, as Donald thought to himself, *Man I'm going to love this college life. Girls on me night and day, sex every day, while my baby is by my side cheering me on.*

"You got lost?" Claude asked Paul.

"I don't go to parties until they start. Here is my star football-playing cousin that I had told you I would introduce to you," Paul said. Donald walked up to Claude.

Claude looked at Donald and began to wonder where he had seen him before. "So you're the future star QB?" Claude asked Donald.

"Yeah," he replied.

"Wish you much luck. Just make sure you don't end up like how I see your cousin about to end up, with a baby mama soon, before he even gets to finish college."

"I won't."

"So you're not like your cousin when it comes down to girls?" Claude asked him again.

"No, why do I have to be? And besides, I got one that is better than all the rest. There will never be another like the one that I have," Donald said.

"That's a lie because with the damn Internet, nowadays, you can find any-body like her," Paul said.

"Yeah, true, but I feel if it was truly meant to be, I shouldn't have to hunt for her."

"While you're looking for her, I'm going to go and find me a girl to dance with," Claude replied.

He went into the crowd and found a beautiful girl dancing by herself. He asked her if he could join her because he didn't like seeing her by herself. She looked at him with a smile.

"Yes, just as long as you don't touch anything that doesn't belong to you."

"Anything that doesn't belong to me yet, right?" Claude replied. She began to laugh and asked him if he thought all his dreams came true. "No, but I hope this one will." He started dancing with the girl.

"So have you been enjoying the party?" Claude asked.

"It's gotten better since I've started dancing with you," she replied.

"What's your name?" "Brittany," she replied.

Brittany was a young lady wanting a good man in her life because she was desperate for love and attention.

"Now, no more questions, just dance and let my dreams come true," Brittany said.

"Ooooh, I think I'm in love with you already, baby."

Brittany looked at Claude and started laughing.

Kelly and Donald had found each other and began dancing. However, when Kelly saw Claude and couldn't believe how he was dancing with some girl, all of her attention went toward them.

Donald saw her looking and asked if she knew someone.

"Yes!" Kelly replied with her head up and a smile on her face, looking into his eyes.

"Who?"

"My brother."

"Well, can I have this dance then with no one on your mind but me?"

"Wouldn't you like to meet my brother?"

"You're joking around with me right because I already know that you don't have a brother."

"I'll show you him."

"Why does he seem to be so bright in your eyes and catching all the damn attention that I should be getting?"

"He's only danced with one girl like that before."

"Let's go, Kelly because I don't even want to know which one of them over there is him. It seems as if you want to be in his arms and not mine," Donald said, looking in her eyes.

* * *

Claude was sitting with Brittany, telling her how he felt about meeting her.

"I felt a strong attraction to you while you were holding me nicely in your arms and looking into my eyes," Brittany replied.

"Well, tell me, can I take you out another time?"

"Yes, I would love that."

"Would you like to leave this party now, and go outside to talk?"

"Sure. But where would you like to go?"

"We could go to the park," Claude said hopefully.

Brittany looked at Claude and smiled. "Guess what? I feel I can trust you. So let's go to your dorm."

Claude and Brittany got up from off of the bench got into their nice cars and drove to Claude's dormitory. He already knew his roommate wasn't coming home that night because he always stayed out after parties. So they were able to talk without any interruptions.

"Welcome to my room," Claude said to Brittany.

"Wow, you're clean, Claude. I wish my brother was the same way that you are because when I was growing up, he used to just make messes and then either I or my mother would have to clean up after him. He would never stay inside of the house long enough so we could scream at him and tell him to either pick it up or clean it up. So tell me a little bit more about yourself if you don't mind me asking, before you start asking me questions?"

"All right, well, I am a nice, young man, not caring what anybody else thinks or says about me because I don't care about popularity. This may be surprising to you, but I want one love for my lifetime because I want to travel all around the world, and I want to do it with that lifetime love."

"Do you think that I'm your kind of girl?" asked Brittany.

"For now, I believe that you're just right."

"Tell me this, why haven't you made a move on me yet? Usually I would have been telling a man to stay a certain number of inches from me, or else I'd leave."

"Sex is not what I'm interested in. I prefer to make love. If I don't have feelings, I don't feel right about sleeping with you. So I'm alright with my hands in my pockets until then."

"You're joking with me, right?" Brittany could not hide her shock.

"No, I'm very serious."

Brittany began laughing at him. "Why is that? You've had too much sex in your lifetime so far, that's why?"

"You're a smart woman. But no. I'm not trying to catch no STD, and I want every time and moment to be unforgettable."

"So in it all, you're a lover not a user?"

"Exactly."

Brittany was quiet for a moment, and Claude wasn't sure if he should change the subject.

"What kind of music do you like to listen to at night?" Brittany asked finally.

Relieved, Claude smiled and put his chin up to think. "I love to listen to slow jams at night. I love romantic music, especially oldies. It makes me feel relaxed and ready."

"Ready for what?"

"I can't tell you, I could only show you."

"Well, show me then."

Claude walked up to his bed where his laptop was laid down, stretched across and turned on a Luther Vandross track that he loved to listen to. Not even expecting it, Brittany walked up behind Claude and began looking at him and asked him to stand back up.

"No, I'd rather you come down here."

"Well, if I come down there, it'll be hard for us to get back up."

"Well, don't you think that I'd love that to happen?"

"Stand up, please," Brittany said.

Claude stood.

Kissing him first on his right cheek, Brittany asked him if he wanted more.

"Yes."

Claude had wanted to prove that he wanted more than pleasure from her, but that was making her feel like he wasn't into her as much as she was into him. However, she decided not to hold anything back and released it. Brittany kissed Claude on his lips and looked into his eyes. He kissed her back after a while and then she stopped. He began staring in her eyes with their lips still touching.

Smiling, Claude started kissing Brittany again. She closed her eyes and rubbed his back, and she loved how he was making her feel. They kissed each other that night, then both fell asleep.

Brittany had a vivid dream while she slept next to Claude.

"I knew you couldn't hold back," Brittany said in the dream, smiling as he began taking off her clothes and then his.

Claude looked at her longing, but said nothing. Then slowly he climbed on top of her.

She grabbed his dick and put it inside of her. He then began grinding, making his way deep inside of her. Brittany thought she was about to explode. Moaning loudly and telling Claude to keep going, don't stop, keep going, deeper and deeper, faster, faster, Brittany could not control herself.

After she was done, she said in a soft tone, "It's your turn." Claude automatically knew what that meant and got up from off of her. Immediately he then lay back down. Brittany climbed on top of him sat on his dick and began riding it fast and hard. She grew sweaty quickly, and Claude liked the beads of it running down her breasts and along her small, firm waist. Then she slowed her riding down and climbing onto her knees. She turned her head back to him seductively and said, "Come on, baby."

Claude began knocking her doggy style as she laid the side of her face flat down on the bed. It felt so good to Claude that he could feel himself about to finish. Knowing this, he pulled his dick out. He didn't want their session to be over.

Brittany, sensing this, turned to face Claude and lowered her head to his crotch. He was going to come right then whether he wanted to or not.

* * *

The loud conversation Ashley and her friends were having on the other side of the dorm room woke Kelly up. Lying there, she let her mind wander, and eventually she began thinking about Claude dancing with a beautiful, sexy girl that wasn't her.

Kelly hopped out of bed and decided to go over to her longtime friend Tiffany's apartment, whom she had promised to visit as soon as she arrived back in New Jersey.

Tiffany was another one of Kelly's close friends whom she felt she could trust no matter what. She had been at the college for two years now; however, she always stayed in contact with Kelly through the e-mail and phone. Since Ashley had so much company over, Kelly asked her nicely to just drop her off at Tiffany's apartment.

Kelly started up a conversation with Tiffany about Claude when she had gotten there while they both were lying down on the bed about to fall asleep. They talked about how strong their friendship had grown. However, seeing him dance with another girl at the party, Kelly said that she felt like Claude was doing something with another girl that she had always thought that she was going to experience exclusively with Claude. She admitted that she was jealous.

"I would've felt the same way too, girl, if I would've ever seen another girl's arms wrapped around a man that I was deeply in love with and hiding it," Tiffany replied before resting her head down on her pillow and drifting off to sleep.

Kelly began to fall asleep too, but Claude was on her mind heavily.

CHAPTER 10

"Girl, you still awake thinking about Claude and that girl he was dancing with?" Tiffany asked Kelly.

"In a way, yes."

"In a way?" Tiffany said with a laugh.

"Yeah, in a way. I'm thinking more about him than I am about the girl. She was pretty, though."

"Don't stress yourself over Claude, Kelly. I don't see why you wanted to introduce Donald to Claude anyway. You know that you have feelings for him."

Kelly made a face.

"It's true. Seriously, tell me what is wrong with being with Claude. I'm all ears. You know I'm here for you."

"I know you are, Tiff. Last night, I just...."

"Go on," Tiffany prodded her.

"I just felt something last night as soon as I saw him dancing with that other girl," Kelly said finally.

"Keep going. What did you feel?"

"Jealousy. And something else that I can't even describe." Kelly looked confused.

"Can I give you some advice, girl? Follow your heart,"Tiffany replied calmly. "It's that easy. Follow your damn heart."

"Part of me knows we are meant to be. He definitely feels that way already."

"Then again, why aren't you with him? And girl, why the hell are you with Donald? He's fine and all. But c'mon, if I knew the guy I was supposed to be with was just across the yard, I'd be all over there!"

They laughed together.

Kelly got serious again. "Claude is going to have a future—a good future. After everything that has happened to him, he doesn't need a distraction. I don't want to hold him back."

"Kelly…"Tiffany began.

"No, Tiff. I'm serious. Everything with me and Claude is almost too intense. It's like, what if we don't work. It would ruin him. It would ruin me."

Tiffany could see that Kelly was really started to get worked up.

"And think about it," Kelly continued. "I already have a great man who is about to become a football player and who wants the best for me. Donald's not a bad choice."

"Yeah, yeah, yeah, you go ahead and let true love pass you by. Donald doesn't deserve you,"Tiffany said, harder than she meant to.

"Am I not ever right, Tiff? Huh, tell me that?" Kelly asked loudly.

"Yes, you are,"Tiffany replied calmly. "But you're paying too much attention to what other people want for you. Outsiders see Donald as a good catch so you're holding onto him. But he's gonna have a good future too. So what makes Claude's future any more precious? I don't get your thinking on this, Kelly. You always talk about Claude as this really strong, capable man, but when it comes to being in a relationship with him, you treat him like he's made of twigs. He can't be both."

Kelly was quiet.

"All I'm saying is, keep everybody else out of it, Kelly. Go with what you feel. Kelly, you got to start caring about your own true happiness and not just what people are going to respond to in a good way. I want you to become the person that I have always known."

"You're right, Tiff. I know you're right. I just can't make that leap yet. I don't know why."

Tiffany shook her head in frustration. "I'm just gonna say it."

"Say what?"

"You're more in love with the fact that Donald plays football and is probably gonna go pro than you are with anything else. You're holding onto the possibility that you might marry a professional athlete. You haven't even slept with him yet. C'mon girl, this relationship with Donald is just for show. It's play-play."

"He thinks that I'm still a virgin, Tiffany," Kelly said harshly. "He's waiting for that special day."

"So you're lying to him also?" Tiffany shook her head. "I wonder how much things his ass has lied to you about."

"I have real love for him."

"You can have love for him, but that doesn't mean you're *in* love with him. Not like you are with Claude. But you know what? This is your choice. I can't stop you from doing anything. I just want you to keep your eyes open."

* * *

When Claude and Brittany woke up, they were glad to be in each other's arms. She looked around and had to remind herself that her dream of them having sex was just that—a dream.

"Thank you for respecting me and not touching me. Honestly, this is the first time I've ever stayed in a man's room all night. Well, actually, all morning for us. Usually, I would leave whenever they would want to start wanting more than my attention."

Brittany pecked Claude sweetly and wrote her phone number down on a small piece of paper.

"Well, what about our date?" Claude asked.

"Yeah…," Brittany said curiously.

"It's lunchtime now and we're kinda funky just waking up," he said with a big smile. "But let me take you out tonight."

She told him she'd meet him back at his room at 7pm and then left. She called later to let him know she made it to her room safely.

While Brittany was showering and thinking about her dream about Claude, she decided to plan a surprise for him. She called him up and asked what kind of food he loved, or if he was in the mood for any particular cuisine.

"Anything and anywhere," he said hungrily.

"Well, make sure that you're ready when I get there. I might be a little late if you don't mind."

"You go ahead and take your sweet little time, as long as I'm still able to have you tonight."

Meanwhile, on the other side of campus, Kelly went to Donald's room to talk to him. She needed to clarify her feelings and explain that she had feelings for her best friend that could complicate things.

"So what about me?" Donald asked after Kelly told him everything.

"I love you, Donald. And I like being with you. That's why this is so confusing. But he's like my family. I love him, too."

"Look, Kelly. I know no relationship is perfect. We've made it through tough times, and now I'm hoping we'll make it through this." He gave Kelly a kiss and told her he loved her and wouldn't give up on her. He started having her best friend on his mind and wanted to know who he was. "What's this dude's name again?"

"Claude," Kelly said softly.

Donald was shocked. "I hope it's not who I think it is."

"You don't know him," Kelly uncertainly.

"I know who you're talking about, though."

"How?"

"He's my cousin's roommate."

* * *

Back at Claude's dorm room, someone began knocking on his door.

"Coming!" Claude replied as he turned off all his lights and the music that he was playing.

Walking up to the door, he blew air into the palm of his hand to make sure that his breath smelled fresh and clean. Satisfied, he then opened up the door. "Hey, you've finally arrived, Brittany. Why you took so long?"

"I told you that I was going to be a little late. I wanted to give you a surprise from me, since you gave me a surprise last night."

"How did I give you a surprise last night?"

"With how you made me feel—as if I could trust you 100 percent—and how you were making me feel while you were only holding me."

"And what's that big special surprise that's over there that I can smell?" Claude asked.

"A homemade meal."

Claude began to laugh. "So you cooked it all?"

"No, I had to go and get this blueberry pie from a restaurant because I know you didn't want me to keep you waiting for too long."

"Well, let me take it in, or would you like to go to the park and eat and talk and then just lie down looking up at the stars. You could wish for one of your dreams to come true, and I could wish for you to become that special one in my life."

"I don't need to because what I want right now is right here in front of me."

"I wonder what that is," Claude said as he walked Brittany inside his dorm room.

Claude placed all the food on his table across from the television. He admired the spread. Brittany had even gotten sweets to go with the meal: Starbursts, Skittles, Snickers, Twix bars, and Reese's Peanut Butter Cups.

"You cooked all of this and brought all of this over here just for me, Brittany, even with candy?" Claude asked.

"No, Claude, it's for us."

"Ah snap, you even brought a movie! Is this one of your favorites?"

"Yep. *How Stella Got Her Groove Back* is one of my favorites. I love Angela Bassett. I also love *Titanic* and *Love and Basketball* too. If you're not really interested, we could watch something else."

"No, no, this is perfect," Claude said. And it was.

* * *

Kelly and Donald were talking things over. They talked about what was disturbing her when she saw Claude. Kelly said that it was because he's like a brother to her, and she was surprised to see him so changed, and in a way that made her love him more.

"Donald," she tried to explain. "I just want you to know that I love him a lot because he's family to me. But my feelings for him are new. I guess they've grown over time, but they're still very new to me. Claude and I have never dated, but we've kissed each other before, just so you know." She was trying to be honest about everything.

Donald looked at her with surprise, but didn't speak for a while.

"I need to leave for a while," he said finally.

"Where are you going, baby?" Kelly pleaded.

"Not far. I just need to get some air. I'll be back, okay." Donald tried to sound reassuring, but he knew it wasn't working.

Before Kelly could respond, he was already closing the door behind him. He needed to talk to Claude himself.

Donald reached into his back pocket for his cell phone.

"Hello?"

"Hey, Paul. What's up, man?"

"Nothing much, cousin. What's going on?"

"Just a question. What's your dorm room number again?"

* * *

Claude and Brittany were eating their meal and talking. After they were finished, he placed the entire dessert on one dish with extra sides of sweets. Coming back with the dessert in one hand and the drinks in the other, Brittany asked Claude where her plate of dessert was because she couldn't eat all of what he had on that plate.

"Right here."

"I can't eat all of that," Brittany replied.

"It's not just for you, it's for us," Claude said, looking in her eyes. He turned off the television and turned on the romantic music that was on his laptop.

Claude took the first piece and placed it on her lips, instead of in her mouth, saying that it was an accident. "Sorry for being so messy, but don't lick your lips because I did it, so I need to clean up my mess."

Brittany laughed with the pie on her lips. Claude began cleaning the mess he left outside her mouth by kissing and sucking on them slowly. Smiling, Brittany wanted to do the same to Claude, but he stopped her.

"No, because you're the baby, so I'm going to feed you, because the baby doesn't feed the babysitter."

"Well, this baby is going to feed the babysitter, or else she'll start crying." She took the fork with some blueberry pie and a red Skittle on top and put it in Claude's mouth. Then she said, "I want my favorite colored Skittle back."

"Well, too late, it has been already given to me, and I don't give back whatever's been given to me to have."

"Well then, I'll just take it back."

Brittany began kissing Claude slowly. She started moving her tongue in between his lips slowly until she had made her way all the way in his mouth. They began a tongue brawl for the red Skittle that he still had in his mouth. After a while, the red Skittle became hers, and into her mouth it went.

Chewing on it and looking in Claude's eyes, she said, "I'm greedy and mean when it comes to whatever it is that I want."

To tease her, Claude put another red Skittle in his mouth to get her to start kissing and playing with him like that again. They started kissing again, and this time, she didn't go for the Skittle.

She moved her hand slowly down and up his neck, his chest, and then onto his back. He began nibbling on her neck as she shook because it gave her a tingling sensation. Claude laid Brittany's body down on his bed and lay on top of her. He began massaging her thighs as he kissed her lips. He went down to her chin, then to her neck to leave his mark.

Claude got up and began giving Brittany a gentle, all-body massage as her eyes closed and her mind was on nothing else but having an all-night romance party with him.

Suddenly, there was a knock at the door. Brittany's eyes opened.

"Expecting a friend?" Brittany asked.

"No! But they better know me to be knocking on my door so hard."

CHAPTER II

Claude's room
10:00p.m.

The knocking continued.

"Coming!" Claude said loudly. Opening up the door, Claude was surprised to see Donald. "Paul's not here, man. I think he went to shoot pool or something."

Donald lifted his head, looking as if his girl had just broken up with him.

"You alright?" Claude asked, totally confused.

"Let me get a couple of words with you about someone."

"Who?"

"Your best friend, Kelly?"

"Kelly," Claude replied with a smile and a surprised look.

"Yeah, Kelly is my girlfriend. I'm starting to have second thoughts about me and her being together. I'm not going to talk to her and make all these promises to her while she is in love with another man."

"Kelly is your girlfriend?" Claude asked.

"Yeah."

Claude started laughing. "I would've never thought that you were that man whom she was telling me about," Claude said.

"At the party last night, she saw you dancing with a girl. She got so jealous. She wanted to be that girl you were dancing with instead of dancing with me."

Claude started laughing. "You're joking, right?"

"No. I love Kelly, and she loves me too. But it seems as if you're in the middle of our relationship and messing it all up."

"Man, I'm not in the middle of anything. And I have company right now," Claude said as he moved to close the door.

Donald put his arm out to hold the door. "Look, I know this isn't your fault. I just need to talk it out for a minute."

Claude stared at him.

"Please."

"All right," Claude said after another long moment. "I'm going to come outside. Give me minute."

"Is everything all right?" Brittany asked as she watched Claude grab his jacket.

"Yeah, my roommate's cousin needs to talk to me for a second."

"Can I ask about what?" Brittany replied.

"My best friend." Brittany's eyes opened with surprise.

"I'll be right back. Don't eat up all the Skittles, okay?" Claude said with a grin.

"Alright," Brittany said with a chuckle. "I'll be right here waiting for you. I didn't plan on leaving tonight anyway."

Claude walked out the door and began walking with Donald. They sat on a bench where no one was around to hear them.

"So what's the problem?" Claude asked.

"Tell me, why does she seem to have such deep, out-of-the-blue feelings for you?"

"I don't know, but she never told me she had feelings for me."

"What is going between you two right now, because it has to be something?"

"Nothing."

"She loves you to death! What do you mean nothing?!"

Claude laughed. "She used to tell me that she loved me, but never in an 'I want you to be my man' kind of way. Only in an 'I love you, brother' kind of way."

"I want to find out for myself about all of this because, in a way, it seems as if a lot of things are not coming out of both of you. And sorry for messing up your night," Donald replied and laughed.

"All right then, see you around," Claude replied.

Walking back to their rooms, they both thought about Kelly and how she made them feel. Claude sat down before he went back to Brittany, and started thinking about what he was going to do—either go after Kelly now, while he was able and had a chance, or just let her go.

* * *

Lying down and thinking about how wonderful it all felt with Claude, Brittany wondered why a guy like Claude didn't already have a love. She felt a soft notebook under his pillow and wondered what it was about because on the cover it was marked Personal. Opening it, she saw a lot of poems as well as a couple of recent airplane tickets to Detroit, Michigan.

"Interesting," Brittany said. So she began reading from page one.

REAL LOVE

Real love
One should never imitate
Because you'll only
Break another's heart
Unforgettable it will always be
For in life
That's an unforgettable memory
That we could never say
It wasn't me
Real love
I feel is just so hard to find
Sometimes, it maybe
Right in my eyes
But still, I'll never know
Just what to do
Real love I have it, but where is it
And will she ever give it to me
For in my eyes, she looks and only says,
Brother, are you alright?

I FEEL

Having you, I feel
Is best for me
Loving me, I feel
Enlightens me
Holding me, I feel
Strengthens me
Seeing you, I feel
Inspires me
And having time for me lets me know
My Lord loves me
Inspiring me lets me know
There's hope for a future for me and you
Strengthening me lets me know
You endure me
Enlightening me lets me know
You care for me
Feeling for the best for us lets me know
You want to spend the rest of your lifetime with me

HOW

Came in the world
Expecting the best
But instead
Ended with less
Having love like no other
That's what I felt
In my mother's mother nest
Tell me, will there ever be another
As best as the best?
For that one love I had for another
Has fallen unexpectedly
How can I be the happiest man in the world
If I fall after every disaster?

FOLLOWERS

Followers are never
Meant to fall
But to rise
From what they have seen and learned
That the right
Become wrong
And the wrong
Become the right
But how does one see it
When their ways
Becomes another one's ways
That has progressed
In their dreams

FRIENDS 2 LOVERS

Friends 2 lovers
How could that ever be?
When that one you love
Is afraid of what may come
Trustworthy or not
A chance is all it takes
Yes, that's what once was said
To me
Without that deep feeling
I'm feeling now deep inside
Afraid of it all, falling apart
Don't be
Because the best ones are
Sometimes the hardest
Yet surprises
That one that you thought would never be
But in the end
The best one
Because our Father works
In mysterious
But loving ways

"He's trying to express himself," Brittany said. "Well, I don't want him saying I'm going through his things, so I'm just going to put this book back where I found it so that he won't think I'm nosey," Brittany said to herself.

Walking back inside of his room, Claude did not know what to say to Brittany because Kelly was so much on his mind. He did not know whether he was going to break up what they were beginning to develop with each other, or just hide it all and try to ignore how he was beginning to feel again when he thought about his best friend. He placed his head on the door and asked himself—*what am I going to say?*—because he wanted to be an honest young man through it all. Luckily, when he entered his room while still not knowing what to say to her, Brittany had already fallen asleep. He knew he had to tell her the next day all about Kelly.

What should I do and say? Claude asked himself as he went inside his room and lay on his bed next to Brittany.

Brittany wasn't asleep. She was lying there, listening to every word Claude spoke to himself until she fell asleep. She got up early the next morning when Paul came home. She woke Claude and told him she was leaving and would call him after classes. Before she left, he told her that he wanted to talk about some things, and Brittany replied, "I already know."

CHAPTER 12

7:30 a.m.

"This man had a girl up in here while I was gone," Paul said as he walked in the room.

"Mind your own damn business," Claude replied and got up to get ready for class.

On the way to class, Donald and Kelly met up and told each other that they loved each other and wished each other a wonderful day. Walking to class, Donald saw Paul and started telling him about all he had found out about Claude and Kelly's friendship. However, he couldn't finish because he only had five more minutes to get to class. So they made plans to talk about it all later.

After class, Kelly went to Donald's football practice so that she could have him feeling good. In high school, he had always wanted her at every practice and every game since he felt that she was his strength and energy whenever he saw her looking at him from the stands.

Paul saw Kelly when she came and sat down, and he got up and started walking over toward her.

"What's up, Kelly? Paul asked.

"You're Donald's cousin, right?" Kelly asked.

"Yeah, but anyways I heard you and my cousin haven't been doing alright," Paul said.

"No, but I feel our love can make it through it all."

"I heard that the one who is causing all the trouble is my roommate Claude."

"Claude's not trouble."

"That's good, because he doesn't feel that way about you."

"How do you know that?"

"Just know that while you got Claude on your mind messing up your relationship with Donald, he's over there enjoying his life every day with some other girl. So just make sure you don't mess up something great for the wrong reasons."

"You're probably just telling me that to get me to forget about Claude."

"If you don't believe me, ask him for yourself next time you talk to him."

Kelly looked at Paul and knew she couldn't trust him. He was too biased.

After practice, Donald and Kelly walked around holding hands and talking, easing their minds from all that was bothering them.

All week, Paul had not gone up to Claude to talk to him about it all because he only had it in him to talk to Donald or Kelly. He only one day watched Claude and Kelly talk and spend a little bit of time together.

At the end of the week was every nearby college's first football game of the season. There were so many people there to cheer their school on as they played. Kelly was there with her friends, and Claude was there with Brittany. At halftime, while their team was winning, Kelly saw Claude and Brittany holding hands as they came from a vending machine.

"Claude!" Kelly called out.

He looked to see who it was and smiled. "That's my best friend," Claude told Brittany.

"Oh, she's in one of my classes," Brittany replied.

"What's up, you having a good time watching the game?" Claude asked Kelly as she walked up to them.

"Great time. And who is this, may I ask?" Kelly said with a smile.

"This is my girl," Claude replied while looking straight into Kelly's eyes.

"Well, it looks like you two are happy with each other," Kelly replied looking at Claude and Brittany. She tried to hide her jealousy.

"Yes, we are," Brittany piped in.

"Well, I guess I'll be seeing you around," Kelly replied.

"Cool. But, uh, let me ask you, is everything good between you and Donald? 'Cause he came to my room a few nights ago asking me about us."

"Yes, we're doing great," Kelly replied quickly.

Claude and Brittany began walking away and back to their seats. *I wonder if that girl told Claude that we have a class together*, Kelly said to herself.

After winning the football game, everybody decided to celebrate and go to the after party. At the party, Claude saw Kelly and Donald together and decided to go and talk to them, even though seeing them made him upset, he tried to understand. As soon as Donald saw him coming, he told Kelly he loved her, which put a bright smile on her face.

"What's up? How are you two?" Claude asked.

"We're doing all right," Donald replied.

"All right, I just came to check up on you because I don't want to be the one getting blamed for any kind of fall in your relationship," Claude said.

"No, you won't get any blame. You won't be getting anything at all," Donald replied. Then he gave Kelly a big kiss and asked her if she was ready to celebrate their football game victory.

"Yes," Kelly replied. Walking away, Kelly looked back at Claude and mouthed she loved him. She wasn't aware that Paul was watching.

Kelly and Donald decided to leave the party with Paul because they had no other ride home. As Kelly went to tell her friends bye, Paul talked to Donald. "Donald, I don't think you can trust her anymore because you won't believe what I saw."

"What?" Donald asked.

"While your girl was holding your hands and walking with you, I saw her blowing a kiss to another man with a smile," Paul said.

"Who?"

"Remember, I'm supposed to be the damn slow one here. Use your fucking head and figure it out. Who were you talking to and walked away from before you went on the fucking dance floor?"

Affected by it, Donald told Kelly, as soon as she had come back, that she had a choice to make between Claude and him. He had nothing else to say and no explanation to give. Kelly looked at Paul and told him that she hated him because she knew he had something to do with it. She had only left them alone for two minutes, so she knew it was something he said.

"You," Kelly told Donald.

"Prove it to him then," Paul said.

"Stay out of our business, Paul. As a matter of fact, I'm tired of you now in our business. Go get a damn life or better yet, go fuck yourself!" Kelly said directly to Paul.

"No bitch, fuck you!" Paul replied.

Donald grabbed Paul by his shirt collar. "Watch what the fuck you say to my girl!"

Kelly could not help but smile. Paul looked genuinely shaken.

Kelly thought about Donald's words and asked herself if her and Donald's relationship was worth her and Claude's friendship. Thinking about it right in front of Donald and Paul, Kelly chose Donald's love over Claude's because she felt Claude would've understood the reasons why she chose Donald. Plus, she remembered all of Claude's promises to her and her promise with the ring that she kept on her finger. *Claude would always be my best friend*, Kelly said to herself. "Yes, baby. I will," Kelly replied to Donald.

Looking at her from the side was Paul with a serious expression, saying that he hoped her words were true to his cousin because he didn't like liars in their family.

"Well, I guess your family hates you," Kelly said to Paul.

When Kelly got dropped off back at her dorm, Donald told her that he wouldn't tell her what to do to make it all clear and final. He'd only wait and see what happens.

Kelly called Claude soon as she had gone back into her room.

"I have something that I need to talk to you about alone and face to face," she said softly.

"Let me know when," Claude replied.

"Tonight. At the small park on the bench, if you don't mind."

"Alright, I'll be there in about twenty minutes. Tell me, what is this all about?"

"Our friendship."

"Come on, Kelly, I don't want to get into it all, especially because my roommate is in the middle of it. I just found out."

"No, Claude, it's about a decision that I have made for myself, and to help us both out." Kelly began crying.

"Are you crying, Kelly?"

"Yes."

"Alright, I'll meet you there now."

Just as Claude was walking through the door, he saw Paul and Donald coming down the hall. Walking toward them, he looked at Donald and told him that he had something that he wanted him to know. But first, he'd be right back. Seeing Claude running down the stairs, they turned around and followed to see what was going on. Claude wasn't looking back to see them behind him. When they got out of the dorm, they saw Claude running toward the park.

"I wonder if he's going to go and talk to Kelly," Donald asked Paul.

"Call Kelly and ask her?" Paul said.

He took out his phone and called Kelly. "Is everything okay, Kelly? Where are you at?"

"I'm going to the park to go and talk to Claude."

"Remember I'm not begging you to do nothing."

"I'm doing it all for myself."

"Call me when you get back to your room."

Donald and Paul began to walk toward the small park still just to see what was really going on for them.

I feel as if I'm about to be in my first soap opera scene, I'm going to make it through it all and get an award for how I've kept it all real with her, Claude thought to himself.

Walking down the sidewalk quietly, Kelly saw Claude smiling and feeling good about something. "Hi, Claude," Kelly said while walking up to him.

Claude stood up and gave Kelly a hug and started saying, "Talk to me about whatever it is on your mind. I'm going to be 100 percent there for you."

"I'm about to lose this one guy I love so much and want to be with. He's a good man for me," Kelly said.

"What the hell are you trying to tell me?" Claude asked suspiciously.

"I'm telling you that I'm willing to do anything for him, because it's like ever since you showed back up in my life, we've been kissing less and not into one another like how we used to be, and I want it back. So that's why I must say, that I want to let you go for his love."

"I don't understand how the hell I've messed you'll up," Claude replied.

"We kissed, Claude, while I knew I had a boyfriend, and you knew also. We were together and feeling each other. But I've felt something from him that I believe is real," said Kelly.

"No, I don't understand how he could make you feel more love than I've ever made you feel, Kelly. I don't have to tell you how I feel about you. I know you know it. I know you feel it. There's no way that you couldn't."

"Claude, I don't want to argue about this. It won't get us anywhere."

"I don't understand that at all, I don't know what's going on in your head right now."

Kelly lowered her head and said nothing.

"Is it because he's probably gonna go pro. Is that what this is about?"

"Claude, how could you say that to me?!" Kelly asked furiously. She did not want anyone pointing this out to her. She did not want to consider that it might be true.

"I'm sorry, Kelly. But I can't imagine what else it could be. But you know what? It's alright. Go ahead and go be with Donald. I'll be with Brittany. But just know I'll always be here for you. Always." Claude leaned over to kiss Kelly's forehead and then stood up.

As Claude turned to walk away, Kelly started crying and asked Claude not to tell her that anymore.

"I love you, Kelly. It's that simple. And it's not going away," Claude said again. He then kept on walking, confident that this little episode would not change anything. He knew that Kelly was not confident about anything she was saying. He would respect her decision because it was what she wanted, but he was not going to take it seriously.

Kelly watched Claude walk about, hoping he would at least turn back around to glance at her. So she was startled when she heard someone clapping.

"It felt good to hear all of that," Paul said with Donald at his side.

Donald walked over toward Kelly and apologized to her about it all. "I hope you're doing what your heart is telling you to do."

"Yes, I am," Kelly answered firmly.

"Come and let me walk you to your dorm," Donald said to Kelly. "I'm sorry for all of this."

"It's alright, I understand."

"I'm surprised he didn't want to fight me or Paul."

"He's mature, that's why."

Donald remembered the promise ring Kelly received from Claude, and said to himself that he wouldn't even ask her about it. He would just wait to see if she would take it off on her own.

Paul and Claude stayed out of each other's way. Paul knew if it ever came down to a fight, Claude would likely kick his ass.

The next day, Claude told Brittany what had been going on. After a moment he asked, "So, what'd you think?"

"About what?"

"About my personal book, because I already know that you read some of it." Claude was smirking.

"Am I busted?" Brittany asked with a giggle.

"Yep, totally busted," Claude said. "Well?"

"Your poetry is good, but some things I don't understand. What inspired you to write?"

"Whenever I watched certain movies and had certain situations in life, I always decided to write about it. But I'm a beginner; so of course, I need to work on it all. But I have written a nice poem before for someone."

"Well, I hope I get one."

"You will."

Claude and Brittany started going out almost every night after they finished studying. Kelly was always going to Donald's practices, games, and then after parties. Their relationship had finally gone back to where it should've been from the start of college. However, Kelly still wasn't as happy as she should've been. Deep down inside of her, she was calling her own self a fool.

* * *

While having sometime to herself, one night Kelly began writing in her diary.

Truthfully, I'm in love with Claude, but somehow, Donald has gotten into me also, and I'm confused—mostly scared of moving out of a relationship with Claude because I want him in my life forever. We've not been talking, but I know I still have him 100 percent. Claude, I'm asking you to please forgive me, and, Donald, I hope you're going to try your best to keep me.

Thanksgiving Day was coming around, and Kelly wanted to bring Donald home to introduce him to her mom. She didn't know if that's what Donald wanted because he had a chance before and never wanted to.

"Are you ready to meet my mother?" Kelly asked while they were at the library studying.

"What am I going to tell my family when they call me and ask if I'm coming home?"

"Just tell them that this year, you're going to spend Thanksgiving Day with your girlfriend's mom. Plus, you won't be too far away."

"Alright but, remember, my family moved to Atlanta for a while after I left."

"Oh yeah, I forgot."

"I'll tell my family, but just make sure you ask your mother first. Where am I going to sleep when we get down there?" Donald asked.

"We have a guest room, so I'm sure she wouldn't mind."

"I won't be sleeping alone every night at your mother's house, will I?"

"Yes, but once she goes to sleep, I'll make sure I come and tuck you in," Kelly said with a smile.

Later that night, Kelly called her mother and asked if Donald could come over for Thanksgiving to finally introduce them to one another.

"What about Claude?" Latoya asked Kelly.

"I don't know if he's coming this Thanksgiving."

"Well, alright."

Kelly called Donald and told him that her mother said yes.

"Can't wait," Donald said.

Immediately after, Latoya called Claude to ask him if he was coming, but he didn't pick up his phone. She left a message telling him to call her as soon as possible because she wanted to know what he wanted on the table this Thanksgiving. Claude called Latoya back after he got the message and told her that he wouldn't be able to make it to this year's family get-together because he's been invited to spend Thanksgiving Day with his girlfriend's family.

This is the first time in so many years that Claude is not coming, Latoya said to herself. She put two and two together and realized that there was something going on between Claude and Kelly. Usually, they would both be listing the things that they would want on the table, and no one could have ever taken away Claude from them on that day.

CHAPTER 13

K elly and Donald decided to drive to Miami, so Donald borrowed Paul's car to save money for a special night out on the beach. They left two days before Thanksgiving Day. Brittany and Claude decided to fly to Bakersfield, California, because Claude didn't want to put all those miles on his Toyota Camry.

When they reached Bakersfield, Brittany's family greeted Claude warmly and treated him as if he was family. They loved the way he carried himself and how happy he made Brittany.

Brittany's parents asked her a lot of questions about Claude to see if she really had gotten to know him and asked questions about their relationship. All Brittany would say was, "I truly love this relationship. All Claude and I have been doing with each other is kissing and holding each other and spending a lot of time together. Nothing else has happened yet, and he's just so happy having me as his girl. I just hope it all works out between us as we both go through college. If it doesn't, the relationship that we have had together will always be a great memory and time for me that I won't ever forget."

"That's wonderful to hear, sweetheart, we're going to end up wanting you back here every holiday, Claude. Because, of course, we'd love to get to know you and have wonderful times with you too. And we would love to get to know your family someday too," Brittany's mother said.

"Yes, I would have loved that too. Unfortunately all of my family members have passed away," Claude replied.

"Well, we're sorry to hear that," Brittany's mother replied.

"It's alright because I know they'll be always by my side. They're the ones that have me motivated to learn and get into a very great career."

"Well, we're happy to hear about your goals and how determined you are. Come and join me in the family room and talk with me about your goals while we get ready for the big games," said Brittany's father.

* * *

When Latoya met Donald, she was surprised to see Kelly with a guy like him. "You're a good-looking young man, Donald. And your muscles are so big. You must work out a lot and play sports."

"Yeah, I play football."

"So are you in love with my daughter?"

Donald was surprised by Latoya's boldness, but he knew he could answer the question easily. "I love her as if she were my wife."

"Hmm, is that right?" Latoya replied suspiciously.

That night, Latoya asked Kelly about Claude and what was going on between the two of them.

Kelly replied, "Claude and I are no longer friends because both of us are in serious relationships right now. Being friends would mess it all up."

Latoya laughed. "He's going along with that just to make you happy, ya know? I've known that boy for years now. I know this isn't what he wants. You know it too."

"I've fallen in love with someone else, Mom," Kelly said with a sigh. "Just let it go."

"Are you in love with Claude?" Latoya asked.

"I don't know," Kelly replied.

"I see you're still wearing his promise ring."

"Goodnight, Mom," Kelly said.

Kelly went to lie down and talk with Donald in the guest room.

When Latoya got up to get something to drink and heard them talking, she headed straight down there. "Not in my house," she said sternly. Kelly knew better than to think she and Donald could share a room.

"I know, Mom," Kelly replied. *I bet, if it was Claude here, she wouldn't have said anything*, Kelly thought to herself.

On Thanksgiving Day, after giving God thanks for such a graceful and wonderful meal, they all sat down, eating and talking about things that they all loved to do with their family members.

After the meal, Donald and Kelly sat down to talk to Latoya about all they had going on and to show their love for one another. They both felt they had something to prove.

Even though Latoya didn't really care, she still smiled and gave them her time and attention.

Donald began by telling Latoya about his life's goals and dreams and had told her that it was all because of his father.

"I have a son that's well-motivated too because of his family," Latoya said before glancing over at Kelly. The she showed Donald pictures of Kelly growing up. All that he was paying attention to, though, was how beautiful she is. She told Donald to look at one of Kelly's happiest moments and pointed out her graduation picture, but Claude's graduation picture was right next to it.

When Donald saw it, he got mad and glared at Kelly.

"It's not my house. Plus, I told you he's like my family," Kelly said.

Latoya only looked at them and didn't say anything. She smiled and asked if everything was alright.

"Where are your sisters?" Donald asked Kelly.

"College," Latoya said before Kelly had a chance to reply.

Feeling nothing but the urge to get up and tear down every photo of Claude in the house, Donald mentioned that maybe Latoya would soon be putting up pictures of him. When Latoya did not reply, and then eventually changed the subject back to college, Donald got even more upset. He tried not to show it. But the longer he sat there, the more he knew Latoya did not think he belonged there.

* * *

Claude and Brittany were having a wonderful time with her family. So wonderful that they all took pictures together and planned to put it all in the family's photo album. Before they left the next day, Brittany's mother walked up to them and told them that if they ever begin to have problems, to talk about it like adults. She also cautioned them not to force anything that did not feel true to them because what is meant to be will be.

* * *

On their way back to school, Donald got the urge to ask more questions about Claude. "Kelly, your mother loves Claude just as much as you do, don't she?"

"Yes. I told you before. Claude's like family," Kelly replied.

What the fuck have I just put myself into? Donald wondered to himself as he drove, shaking his head. "You know what? At some point, you're going to have to make a choice. And I hope you'll choose me. 'Cause I know how to keep and treat someone I love, and not just have them floating around in the air," Donald said.

Kelly looked at Donald and said nothing back, wondering if he meant that Claude should have held on to her and not let her free for others to have, if he treasured her the most.

* * *

Back on campus, Claude decided to move out and get his own apartment because he and Paul were no longer talking or getting along. When he told Brittany the news, she asked to move in with him and agreed to get a job to help pay the rent. However, she wouldn't give up her dorm room because she didn't want her parents to know. Claude told her that he didn't want anything coming in between her and her education, so he told her that she could move in, but she didn't have to find a job because he could get money whenever he needed it.

Brittany was so happy because she would have loved the opportunity to be in Claude's arms every night.

As Claude was moving out of the dorm room, Paul walked in laughing as he saw Claude carrying out his bags. "I hope my cousin didn't scare you out of college," he said with a smirk.

"Shut the fuck up and go eat some pussy 'cause that seems to be only thing that keeps you from talking shit," Claude replied and then walked out the door.

The minute he went back into the dorm for the rest of his stuff, Paul began to talk slick again. "I don't like to talk to bitches more than one time now, so hurry the fuck up and get out."

"What?!" Claude replied. He dropped the bags that were in his hand and rushed over to Paul aggressively with angry expression on his face. Then he immediately grabbed Paul by his shirt and slammed him into the wall. "Watch how the fuck you talk to me 'cause I'll beat the fuck out of you if I have to! Don't let my niceness fool you!"

"Get the fuck off of me!" Paul said through gritted teeth. He struggled to get out of Claude's grasp. "Now it's beginning to look like your parents never brought you up with common sense about who not to fuck with."

Surprised by what Paul had just said because Paul knew his family was dead, Claude got even more aggressive. He drew back his right hand and tightened his grip on Paul with his left. Then he started punching him in the face fast and hard. After the first punch, Paul began to lose consciousness, but Claude got in a few more for good measure. When he finally let Paul go, Paul slipped down to the ground with his back against the wall, lip busted, nose bleeding and eyes slightly closed.

"Now who's the bitch?!" Claude said angrily.

As soon as Claude picked his bag back up and turned around, he saw a crowd of guys from the dorm standing at the door. As he walked out, they all wordlessly moved out his way.

Once Claude had left the room, someone ran over to Paul to see if he needed help.

"No," Paul replied as he regained consciousness. He tried to shake off the pain by moving his back side to side. "I'll get that motherfucker back myself."

When Claude and Brittany moved in together, Claude started to make sure that she spent most of her time in her books like she did before they moved in together. He didn't want to upset her mother and have her saying that if it weren't for their relationship together, her daughter would've been doing better in college. But he was happy to have her with him every day. It made their relationship grow more and more.

Then one night, Brittany finally said what Claude has suspected for weeks. "Claude, I'm in love with you." She was shy about it but her words had conviction.

"So soon?" Claude replied.

"Yes. And I'm certain of it. Claude, I'm in love with you. I love everything about you. I've gotten to know so much about you. My mother just keeps on asking me about you every time she calls me now, and the feelings that I have while I'm with you make me smile."

"I love you too, Brittany. But I have to be honest. I haven't truly fallen in love with you."

"I know. I know that you still love her."

"You know that I still love who?"

"Kelly."

"Well, yes," Claude said slowly. "I do."

They were quiet for a moment.

"How'd you know that?" Claude asked unsurely.

"A woman knows, Claude. But that doesn't change how I feel about you. I've held on to the hope that your feelings for her will fade and your feelings for me will grow. I'm not going to let go of you, no matter what I keep getting told," said Brittany.

"What do you mean, 'no matter what you keep on getting told?' Has someone been telling you things?" Claude asked.

"I've never told you. Well, I've said it once, but it seemed as if when Kelly caught your eyes, your mind just went only to her. Kelly and I have a class together, and she has been telling me things you love and what you love to do. Also, things that you don't like or agree with. I've gotten to know almost everything about you, not only from her, but you too. I don't know if all of this is getting you mad, but I asked her because I wanted to be perfect for you. Just by her telling me all of that, it seems as if she was perfect for you."

Claude looked at Brittany with surprise because he would have never guessed that Kelly and Brittany had ever developed a friendship together because usually, if something like that ever occurred, Kelly would be the one to come up to him and tell him. It all made him feel good, in a way, because that must have meant that Kelly was saying all of what she was saying to help keep him happy and loved. On the other hand, Claude started to feel as if it all wasn't true anymore because all of what Brittany was doing and saying wasn't really her.

"Let's start all over then, Brittany, and give this another chance without you asking Kelly any questions. How about you, Brittany, start asking me all of what you want to know and hear about me because it seems you did all of that because you care for me?" Claude said.

"That sounds good to me," Brittany replied.

* * *

Donald and Kelly had also been going through the same issues, except it was Donald who didn't know what to say and do whenever he was with Kelly and wanted to see a smile on her face. What really was messing it all up, though, was that it seemed as if it wasn't really all about Kelly and their relationship—or their times out with each other. He was worrying mostly about himself and his father's dreams, because he wanted to make it all come true. Kelly was the one putting herself in the picture by encouraging him about doing better on the football field. So it was more about football and his father, even though he loved Kelly and gave Kelly as much time and attention as he could, at least that's what he thought. He felt her sometimes though, but that was mostly when they were together and his hormones began to rise.

One night, when Kelly was feeling a little down and out and needing help and encouragement because she wasn't doing well in one of her classes, Donald knew that Kelly probably expected him to at least try to come and make her feel better, like how she always did for him. But Donald wasn't used to giving encouragement, only getting it. That was what she wanted—his love and encouragement for her future. All Donald did was just tell Kelly that he would take her out somewhere special to make her feel better, and to make up for all the football games that took time away from each other.

Kelly looked at Donald in a weird way. "Why is that taking away our time together? Don't you think that I'm happy when you're on the football field throwing the ball? Don't I love football?"

"Let's go out, sweetheart, so that I can cool you down. Let me take you out so that I can give you all the loving that you've been asking for, especially when we come back," said Donald.

"Where and why do you want to take me out? I need to study and get this done," Kelly said.

"Anywhere that you would like to go, and it's just because it's stressing you, boo."

"All right, surprise me with somewhere special then."

"How about an Italian restaurant?" Donald replied.

"Don't ask me. Just take me," Kelly said.

They started to get ready with Kelly going to take a shower. She was hoping Donald would join her, but he never came in. Donald waited until she was finished and then went to go and take a shower because he started feeling fed up with a lot of things.

Donald and Kelly went out to dinner with no surprise kisses or hugs and no words to bring a smile back on their faces. While waiting for their dinner, Donald was looking at Kelly, wondering what was wrong with her because she wasn't smiling or trying to have a conversation with him. Looking down at her hands as she played with the ring that was on her finger, Donald began wondering what she was thinking about as she looked at it as she played with it. Donald felt the need to speak up about it.

"When are you going to decide to take off that promise ring that he gave to you? Since you say you're no longer friends. It's like you no longer talk, but deep inside, you still do. And with that ring, I feel like you're still holding onto him."

Kelly picked up her head and looked at Donald seriously.

"Baby, my time to clear my mind is right now, right?" Kelly asked.

"Yes, but I think of him and see him every time I see that ring. Don't you?" Donald asked.

It was true that Kelly had seen, felt, and thought of Claude every time she lifted up her hands and saw that ring. However, it wouldn't have been smart to say yes.

"I kept it because it was my graduation gift," Kelly said.

"That ring has got to go. It's holding us back in a way that should be understandable," Donald said.

"Okay, fine," Kelly replied while taking off the ring and putting it into her purse.

"Give it away or something to a friend, or better yet a stranger," Donald suggested.

"No!" Kelly said a little too quickly for Donald's comfort. "I'll give it to my mother."

The waitress came with their food. They ate quietly, looking at each other as if they had nothing left to say. On their way back home, Donald looked at Kelly, wondering what was going on in her head. He wanted to know if she was thinking about Claude.

"You just don't want to tell me the truth, do you?" Donald said.

Kelly picked up her belongings as they pulled up to her dorm room and hopped out of Donald's car as soon as he stopped. She walked away from Donald but then suddenly turned back

"Donald, if you know for a sure fact that I want to be with Claude more than you, tell me, why are you asking me a question that you already know the answer to?"

"I don't know, Kelly. I guess I'm to scared to get my heartbroken."

Kelly shook her head, wanting to tell him goodbye and that she could not take his mind off of not being able to understand another's problems. But all Kelly could do was cry and walk to her dorm room. She wished she had Claude right now at her side. He had always known how to put a smile back on her face, no matter what the problem was. He would've never just let her walk away like Donald had.

When Kelly reached into her dorm room, Ashley saw tears coming down her eyes.

"What's wrong?" Ashley asked. She hoped it was not Donald, but she figured that it was.

"Ashley, tell me, would it be dumb of me to give up on everything that Donald and I have started?"

"I won't decide for you or give you any advice because my advice may be the advice that you don't need to hear, even if it is good. I always tell my friends to just let your heart decide for itself and not your mind."

"Yeah, I understand. That's the same thing Tiffany told me."

Upset by the whole night, Donald went straight to Paul's dorm to talk to Claude. However, when Donald had reached his cousin's dorm and asked Paul where was Claude, Paul replied with his bruised up face and black eye, "I don't know, but he better not let me find him."

"What fuck happened to you?"

"Scalawag whooped my ass and then left. But I got something nice for that motherfucker that'll tear him apart. It'll mean I have to become his friend again. But that shit will be worth it!"

"Well then I'm behind you all the way with this plan because I know exactly what would tear him apart."

"Why are you looking for Claude anyway?" Paul asked.

"He knows some things that I need to find out about someone," Donald replied.

"Ask me."

"What I need to know only Claude has the answers to."

That same night to relieve some of the stress that he was feeling, Donald called a girl over to his room to make him feel better.

After class, the next day, Kelly and Brittany had a talk about all that had been going on, and it seemed as if Claude was doing more to work it all out with Brittany while Donald was doing all he could do to mess up his relationship with Kelly.

That same weekend Claude told Brittany that he had something to handle in Detroit but that he would be back the next day. Brittany never asked what it was, though she was curious. She did not want to be the type of girlfriend who pried too much. When he had arrived back the next night, Brittany woke up to see him looking at the pictures in his wallet as tears fell from his eyes. She then walked over to him and sat down right beside him.

"Who are they?" she asked.

"My grandma, mom, brother and me."

"What's wrong?"

Claude was silent.

She laid her head on his shoulder in solidarity, then asked him to come back to bed.

The next morning, Brittany asked Claude what was wrong with him last night.

"Nothing that concerns you," Claude replied more sternly than he intended.

"Well, excuse me for asking," she shot back.

"I didn't mean it like that," Claude said with a sigh. "I'm sorry."

"Well then I'm sorry for asking. But know that if you don't talk to me, there's no way I can be there for you when you need me. And I want to be there."

"I know, baby. It's just that right now, nothing and no one can help me."

Brittany tried to hide how hurt she was. But it did not matter much. She knew that, in that moment, Claude did not care.

Two days later, after class and before football practice began, Donald finally ran into Claude. He asked if they could talk about some things. Claude answered with attitude because he didn't want to have anything else to do with what they were going through.

"Stay out of my fucking way, Donald. Upsetting me may make you lose your chances of playing this season," Claude said.

"It's important," Donald tried to explain.

"I'll see you again another day."

"Just to help me out with her is all I'm asking. I want to make her happy, and I'm sure you still want that, too."

Claude laughed and walked off. They ended up being around each other again inside of the school's library that weekend while they both were studying for a test and researching. Claude and Donald had not planned to meet up in there however, Kelly and Brittany did.

Kelly saw them and told Brittany as they walked in. After about an hour of talking and watching them, Kelly and Brittany saw when Donald spotted Claude. Donald had decided to go over and try to get some information from him again.

"You studying for a test, too?" asked Donald as he walked up to Claude.

"Studying for my future."

"Same thing I was over there doing just now."

"What do you need from me now?" Claude asked. He did not care that he seemed annoyed.

"I just want to know, what are the best things that I could do to help my relationship with Kelly? Our connection is not where it's supposed to be right now. So I'm asking you to help us with it? Or do you think I should just let her go?"

"It's up to you, not me, Donald."

"But I love her."

Brittany and Kelly crept up behind a bookcase to eavesdrop.

"I know it may make me sound like a pussy right now, but I'd rather beg your ass for help than let her go. That's how much I love her."

"All right, I'm going to tell you a couple of things. Then after it all, don't come back to me again. So take out your pen or pencil and a sheet of paper and begin taking notes, pussy."

Donald fought to hold his tongue. Inside he was seething. But he was playing a much harder game. "Alright, Cupid," he said evenly.

"Kelly loves stars because they shine so bright at night, and that's how she feels about herself. She wants to always be joyous, happy, and thankful no matter the problems, no matter the situation. So buy her something bright. Something that has a big star on it. And tell her you love her. Let her know that even when things are not right in your relationship, she always brightens up your life."

"Okay."

"Also, she loves the colors of the sky, blue and white, like me. So if you're ever going to buy her something like clothing, make it blue or white. And don't just give her money for a gift or to go shopping; take her out shopping to show her that you really care about how she presents herself. She's not into jewelry like how she used to be. But you can still buy her some nice things, and she'll just wear it on special occasions. But really though, she's an all-natural kind of girl. She loves to show her natural beauty especially when she's alone with that one she truly loves."

"Yeah, that's one of the things I love about her too."

Behind the bookcase, Claude had Kelly smiling and feeling good because he knew just what Kelly liked and why. However, Brittany was feeling that it all sounded like they were the best ones for each other because of what Kelly had told her about Claude and, now, what she was hearing Claude tell Donald about Kelly.

"Kelly loves to be taken out to special places where couples go. She likes to be kissed and held all night," Claude said.

"That's exactly why I've allowed her to keep her virginity. I know she wants her first time to be unforgettable. I treat her nicely and I give her what I know she likes. But I wanted to know more," Donald said before pausing. "Don't you want to know why?"

"It means you're a dumbass," Claude said.

"I'm looking at it like I'm a man worried about his lady," Donald replied not really knowing what to say. "And even though you're over here saying I'm not a real man, I'm the one that has her though, right?"

"I wish you and her luck," Claude said. And with that, he grabbed his books and left the library.

Brittany and Kelly, who were still hiding behind a shelf of books, exchanged looks.

"Yep, he's the one for you," Brittany said.

"I don't know," Kelly said as she looked at Donald sitting at the table by himself. He looked as if he didn't know what to do anymore.

* * *

Later that night, Brittany went up to Claude and looked him in his eyes. "Kelly and I heard you in the library today."

"I didn't see you two there."

"Well, we were there. We heard what you said to Donald, and I agree. A real man doesn't need another man's lessons in a real relationship. Even though therapy is good nowadays for most relationships, let nature and whoever do its thing together. He should be able to figure most things out, but not all. The main things about the other, that's what a man and woman, need to know, whenever it comes down to having a true relationship with each other. So am I going to be able to get another night with my baby before he goes?"

"Where am I going?" Claude asked.

"You will see when the train comes."

"Well, until that so-called train comes for me, I'll be here right by your side."

Brittany pulled Claude closer to her and kissed his lips softly at first. Then she pressed her body against his and waited for him to respond. He grabbed her with both hands and kissed her harder. But Claude stopped abruptly a minute later because he knew it wasn't Brittany that he was picturing in his mind while he was making out with Brittany.

"What is it, baby?" Brittany asked.

"I think it's best if I let you go," Claude said.

"What are you talking about?"

"I just think—" Claude tried. "I'm not ready to give to you what you're giving to me. It's not fair. My feelings for Kelly are making things with you more complicated than you deserve for them to be."

Brittany looked crestfallen. She was determined to keep a brave face, though. However, she didn't fail to understand what was going on. It made her upset, jealous, and wanting to cry but there will be another chance is all she told herself.

"I understand, Claude. I'll get my things, and I'll go back to my dorm room as soon as I can. Just do this one thing for me, okay?" Brittany said.

"Okay?" Claude asked.

"Don't you ever let another put their hands on something that's already yours, because you might end up breaking your own heart."

* * *

After class the next day, Kelly and Donald were supposed to be going out on another special dinner. Instead, Donald decided upon a quiet place. He wanted to take Kelly to some place where they could sit down with trees all around them and stars up in the sky.

Seeing each other that night wasn't like any of their other nights because Kelly had remembered every single thing Claude had told Donald that day in the library. Donald changed his mind after thinking about what Claude had told him. So instead of doing all of what Claude said, by letting her look up to the stars to make her happy and smile with him again, his words were changed to goodbye.

"It seems you have already found your match, but I can't get mad because first come, first served," Donald said softly.

Kelly looked at Donald with watery eyes.

"I'm not a perfect man, Kelly. But I want the best for you. And the best that I see for you is your best friend. I'm letting you go because of a comment that was said to me at the end of it all, that I truly keep thinking about because I agree. If our love was truly true, I wouldn't feel so insecure about it. I know I'm not being crazy about what I see between you and Claude," Donald said.

"So you're feeling like you're not a real man?"

"Nope, and I guess he told you."

"No, he hasn't said anything to me about you."

"Well, since I just told you this great news and I've brought you to a nice place with a clear view of the stars, I guess you'll remember me in a good way?" Donald asked.

"Of course," Kelly said with a smile. She gave him a hug and a kiss on the cheek. "And see, I just gave you something to remember me by."

"Thank you," Donald. He tried to smile back, but it was hard. He was the kind of superstar athlete who liked to play the field. But he knew he would have a hard time finding another woman like Kelly. He really did love her.

They got up and walked out of the park together with nothing left to say, with both heads up and not down.

Donald, on the other hand, wasn't happy deep down inside. He remembered his cousin Paul's words about hitting Claude with something that'll likely destroy him, with neither one of them putting their hands on him.

CHAPTER 14

Christmas Day was around the corner and gifts were getting wrapped. Kelly had something special for Claude, and Claude had something special for Kelly. Something that money could never buy.

Kelly had flown back home to visit her mother for the holiday, and the two of them were standing around the Christmas tree, decorating it and putting gifts from friends and other family members underneath it.

"What's in that big box?" Latoya asked Kelly.

"Something special that Claude has always wanted," Kelly replied, and looked at the ring on her ring finger.

"Well then, let me call him and make sure he'll be here to receive this special gift," Latoya replied.

Latoya called Claude to ask him how soon she should expect to see him walking through her front door.

"Soon," Claude replied. He was on his way back down to Florida from Detroit where he wanted to stay and spend Christmas at his family's burial sight.

But he changed his mind at the last minute and decided to do what he knew would make his new family happy.

Latoya had already known that Claude and Kelly had some catching up to do, so this Christmas she expected surprises from the both of them. She was hoping that they would unveil all that they had hidden from each other.

On Christmas morning, as soon as Claude walked through the door with gifts in his hands, he gave Latoya a hug and a kiss along with her Christmas gift and said, "Merry Christmas, Ma!"

Opening up her present with a bright smile, Latoya was amazed because it was an outfit she had wanted from a magazine. Claude had noticed it circled on her dining room table the previous summer. He ripped the page out of the magazine, hoping that Latoya would forget about it. And he made a mental note to buy her the gift later on. Latoya's glee was worth all his effort to keep the gift a surprise.

Claude also had another present for Latoya: a pair of sparkling diamond earrings that he asked Anthony to purchase for him.

"Thank you, my favorite son," Latoya said and then gave Claude another big kiss.

"You're welcome," Claude replied with a smile and then looked at Kelly.

"What did you get for your best friend?" Latoya asked him.

"No, Claude, I want to give you mine first," Kelly said.

"So do I, Kelly, because I've been saving this up for years," Claude replied.

"How about we give each other our gifts at the same time?" Kelly suggested.

"Okay."

They both had a big box for each other and exchanged it at the same time, smiling and looking into each other's eyes.

"On the count of three, let's both open the boxes," Claude said.

"Okay, on the count of three," Latoya said.

Claude and Kelly both stood up and hovered over their gifts.

Claude started talking to his Father, saying, *Please, Father God, let her understand my feelings and how true my love is for her. No matter what she does or how she makes me feel, I will always love her with all my heart. That's why I'm trying to find my way inside of her heart and life before another does.*

Latoya started the countdown. "One."

I hope he knows that what I'm about to give to him is truly from the heart, Kelly thought.

"Two."

I hope hers is special and from the heart, but not better than all of mine, Latoya thought.

"Three!"

Claude and Kelly tore their boxes open.

There was nothing inside of either box.

"What's going on?" Latoya asked. She was totally confused.

Claude looked at Kelly and started explaining his present for her.

"My gift for you, Kelly, is my love and life. Kelly, I love you. I love you so much that I've never thought you could truly be with another man and I said to myself, 'I give up on you and want nothing else to do with you.' I remember when we first met. It was after a fight before the Christmas holiday that I had lost when we were just in elementary school. You asked me if you could help me up, and even though I said no, you still helped me up. Then when those boys had came back to fight me because they had seen me get right back up, you tried your hardest to defend me.

"They laughed at me for it, because I always had my brother or friends helping me up, but that time, I had a girl, you. I asked you why you wanted to help me because you didn't even know me, and you said, 'Because you're kind and have always wanted to get to know me and be my friend,' but I'd never looked your way. Plus you had thought that it would've been a great Christmas present for me, and that was to make a true friend.

"I've always been there for you ever since then, just to make sure no one ever did you any wrong. But whenever you felt as if I was in it too much, I would always take some steps back, like how I did this year, even though it was hurting me. Kelly, I love you so much that even when you take time scream at me I love it because I know if our friendship and relationship was ever perfect, it wasn't true and ever meant to be. Because the best ones I feel are always the ones in which the things you hate the most, come up in your face.

"Breaking true love, families, and happiness apart, that's another thing I've learned that the adversaries do. Your love is just all I've ever felt I needed, ever since my family died and we made love while you were showing me that you cared and wanted everything to be all right for me. I've never complained about no one being there for me since I lost my family, because of the love that you've shown and proven you've had and felt for me.

"Your dreams are all my dreams for you, your compassionate ways, your consideration, and your mature mind that you've grown. I love almost 100 percent of everything about you, and if I could be your best friend, I'm sure I could be your true love, because what's a relationship without a strong friendship? Again, I love you, Kelly. That's why I'm going to ask you to be my wife. And if you say yes, our marriage won't be until after college, because I don't want anything to disturb us while we're working on our future.

"Kelly, I thank you for all of the love you've given and shown me. I thank you for all of the understanding you've given and shown me. I thank you for being my knight in shining armor. I thank you for the life you've helped give back to me, after I lost my mother, father, grandmother, brother, and Thomas. And I would never forget Alan, my second brother, who I feel died because of me.

"I've felt I had to have you, no matter how long I'd have to wait and change. Deep in my heart, I couldn't fight just how much I've been wanting your love for the rest of my life and eternally.

"I've always chosen to be that one that you could always call on, no matter what we were going through. I've tried many times to get thoughts of you out of my mind. Whenever we were together and alone, I'd close my eyes to picture someone else, but then I'd just see you coming to kiss me with a beautiful smile. Your eyes were always on the television while my eyes were on you. That's why now I must say I'm tired of dreaming, and I want to ask you what I've always wanted to ask you. Kelly, your first Christmas gift to me was your friendship, and every Christmas gift that I've given to you ever since then has been materialistic things, things that the world gave to me to give to you. That's why this Christmas my gift for you will be my heart, soul, love, and one question. Kelly Brown, will you marry me?"

"Oh my goodness! I would have never expected this day to be today," Latoya said, putting her hands over her mouth.

Kelly cried with her mouth wide-open and heart beating, knowing that all of Claude's words were truly from the heart because she had felt each tear that had dropped down on her hands every time he told her that he loved her.

"Yes, Claude, I've always wanted to be your all for the rest of your life because I love you, and I would never want to depart from your life in this lifetime or after. You've been my all in one, so I don't know why I didn't trust and have faith in it all. I wanted to wait until the last moment, which could have been too late. And I'm sorry for having you wait so long for what was really already yours," said Kelly.

They then hugged and kissed each other.

Latoya asked the obvious question. "Where's the ring?"

Kelly had put up her ring finger and showed her the ice that Claude had given to her, when he had knelt down on one knee in front of her and many others. The beginning of Latoya's dreams for them had finally begun, and she was going to do her best to help keep that dream alive for them and her.

"I think you two need some time to yourselves so that this day and moment will be even more unforgettable," said Latoya.

"Believe it or not, Mother-in-Law, we've had many unforgettable times in our teenage years. However, that one fear of losing each other had always interfered," Claude replied and smiled.

"Mother, I've been in love with Claude for so many years. But as I was telling him, I feared that—if we had ever broken up—our friendship would have also been affected by it, and that's one thing that I never want to lose. And he was the one that had brought that in my mind. Plus friends had gotten into my mind the problems of us being together, and I wish I had never let them in," said Kelly.

"Well, just have faith and know that if there's ever a problem between you two and your relationship, I will always be right here," Latoya replied.

Kelly and Claude went outside to talk to each other. They never let go of each other's hands.

"Kelly, tell me, would you like it better if I could get a room for a more private time together? Your mother can't keep her eyes off us anymore?" said Claude with a smile.

"Yes, I would love that."

Claude went out and got a nearby hotel room for the night. At that time of the year in Miami, hotel rooms are usually taken. But Claude had gotten lucky. He took it as a good sign of things to come.

Going inside of the room first to check it out, Claude decided to put some white and blue roses inside of it from a flower stand outside the hotel. He put them on the floor and bed with white vanilla-scented candles to light up the room. He got champagne with ice and scented bubble bath.

Claude picked up Kelly and told her to put on a swimsuit so that they could go in the pool and have some fun. Claude had first taken the belongings she had brought along with her and told her to wait outside the room because he didn't want to ruin the surprise that he had inside of their hotel room. Going into the pool, they ended up hugging and kissing and thanking each other for understanding each other's faults, enjoying their private time with together. Claude decided to take her into their hotel room for some tender, loving moments.

"Welcome to paradise, sweetheart, a place where many dreams will come true for the both us," Claude said romantically while looking into Kelly's eyes and smiling.

"This is beautiful, Claude. Thank you for taking the time to do all of this," Kelly said as she entered their hotel room with a big smile on her face.

"Yes, and it's all for you," Claude replied with a kiss on her lips.

They went inside the hotel room.

"Would you like to join me in a bubble bath?" Claude asked.

Without a word, Kelly took off her clothes and lowered herself into the tub. She loved bubble baths, and now she would love it more because she wouldn't be taking one alone.

After an hour of relaxing and talking more about their feelings and love for each other and how special this night was for them, they got out of the tub and showered to wash off all of the bubbles. In the shower, they began laughing and playing passionately, experiencing each other in another happy moment.

Kissing each other's body while showering each other slowly and softly, looking into each other's eyes, feeling that deep sensational feeling, Kelly and Claude grew a strong urge to make love.

With their eyes closed, their tongues touched as the warm water ran from their heads to their toes. Claude began caressing Kelly's lower back with his right hand and then began moving it down slowly to her left butt cheek. He squeezed it and lifted it up to open her legs enough to let his dick in between. She began grinding against him slowly. Kelly's hormones began to rise even higher, making her tremble. She kissed Claude harder and could not stop herself from scratching his back. Then she moved down to his neck. As she sucked on the space between his ear and his collarbone, she could taste the warm water dripping down Claude's body.

Claude pulled his dick from between her legs and began rubbing on her pussy with his index and middle fingers, slowly causing her to moan and bite on his neck. Moving his fingers slowly and steadily, now Kelly's moaning got louder until she began to scream feeling him going in deeper.

Kelly's hands were then on top of Claude's head, pulling him down to her neck, and then unto her breasts. Claude began to suck on them, going from the left one to the right one, and then back again. Kelly began pushing him down more until Claude was on the bathroom floor, pulling her lower half against his face. She spread her legs open and Claude slowly moved his tongue up and down against her vagina. Kelly rubbed on his head with her right hand, while her left hand was high up against the wall as she began to bite her bottom lip. Kelly began to have the urge to feel even more in her. Lifting up Claude's head and then looking down, Kelly saw that titanic had risen and was hard as a rock. Without any hesitation, Kelly sat on it and began pushing and pulling herself on top of it. Claude held onto her butt cheeks and enjoyed the ride. But then just as Claude began to feel it coming, Kelly began to make her way up. Accidently dropping the body wash down which then splashed on the both of them.

After the body wash was showered off of each other, they began heading toward their bed kissing, bodies wet, and made love tenderly nonstop.

All you could've heard from outside the door was moaning and Kelly's words "Yes Claude...Yes!" Sixty-nine ways—that is how Claude planned on giving it to her for the New Year.

* * *

Claude slept and Kelly had her head on his chest with her eyes closed, holding him as if she never wanted to ever let go. In her mind, she thanked him for understanding and forgiving her for being unclear with her feelings for so long. She knew all their difficulties would pay off in the end.

"Thank you. The reason why I wanted your friendship, even more than I had already wanted it when we were young, Claude, was because I felt no one loved me after I had arguments with my mother and sisters. So I went to you, the one that seemed to be needing someone's love and attention too at that moment, when I needed someone to talk to and be there for me," Kelly said with a smile and a teardrop.

CHAPTER 15

Holding each other closely while sitting down on the beach and waiting for midnight to strike and bring in the New Year, Claude and Kelly were spending the last hour of the year talking about their hopes and dreams of having a lifetime together.

Looking into Kelly's eyes and lifting her head up by her chin, Claude said, "You appeared out of nowhere and showed me your courage and love for others, Kelly. I now look back and understand why I couldn't let you go. At first, it was hard for me to understand because my mind was still young. I was so confused while I was falling in love with you because I didn't understand these feelings I got every time I saw you. Every fight and argument that we had, I began to not even fight back after I'd either see you get upset or step aside because I would begin to feel that if I continued, I'd lose you permanently. I need you by my side. I learned so much from you while growing up because of all the help and encouragement you continued to give me whenever I felt like I couldn't accomplish some things, even though you knew nothing about what I was talking about sometimes. Every dream that you would tell me about that I was in, Kelly, I felt that me and you were meant to be because of every smile you had while telling me all about it."

"Claude, it was our destiny to love each other, that's how I feel. We've both had so many friends, but none of the others have spent as much time as we have growing up with each other. You've always tried to be there for me in all of my rough times, and you've helped me to develop a friendship and bond with my mother that I wished we had before me and you ever met."

Claude smiled and felt good because what he had heard meant that he had done unforgettable things in her life too.

"Crying myself to sleep, Claude, is all I used to do every time I thought about your words to my mother for me because I was so scared to speak. Heartbroken, neglected, and I hated how I felt while she went through her trials with my father and their divorce, and you said it all for me. That's why I kept saying that, with you by my side, everything would be all right. I still feel that way. That's why all I'm going to need you to do is love me, trust me with your heart, and be here for me," Kelly said.

As the countdown for the New Year began, Claude's last words for the year 2010 were, "I feel the same way too, Kelly. But you've been more like the light on the dark side of me, and my special someone to love when there was no one to love."

Fireworks shot up into the air to start the New Year, and the relationship between Claude and Kelly has gone from just being friends to lovers.

Claude prayed aloud. "Lucky me, I have someone to love me and I have a real family now. Life has been so unfair to me. Still, I have someone that gives me love at the right time all the time, just as you do, but not as much as you though, Father. She's been my one and only, and I'm not going anywhere because what she does for me makes me feel good and loved inside, because her walk and talk are so sweet. Father, I pray and ask for not another loss in my life, for I feel no one could ever replace this one that I have in my life as my all."

Kelly lay in bed asleep beside Claude, and he kissed her forehead. He was so grateful.

Claude and Kelly's bond blossomed, and their affection and desire for each other led them to a destiny filled with love and trueness for each other. Their friendship had grown from a reliance on each other, from mutual care and cooperation. Their relationship opened doors of happiness for them no matter the obstacles, trials, turbulence, and tribulations that may come their way throughout the rest of their lives.

Meanwhile, earlier that night, Donald had gone to see Nancy. He wanted to see if he had gotten her pregnant. Her father opened the door.

"Good afternoon, sir," Donald said politely. "Is Nancy home?"

"She no longer lives here, since she would rather have sex with men she doesn't know anything about than go to school to get the education that she needs for a good job. We don't know anything about where she's at right now." Then he slapped the door closed.

CHAPTER 16

"Bye, Claude and Kelly. I look forward to you both coming back and visiting me once in a while. Y'all should already know that I'll be thinking of y'all every day of every week because you know that I care and love both of you so much. Also, I trust that y'all will not decide to have any babies while you're still in college because I know that your sex life has already begun. You two have been sleeping alone in a hotel room, with no one there to observe if you're just talking about everything, or if y'all were doing something in there to make up for the hard times that you've been giving each other," Latoya said, trusting that the truth would surface as Claude and Kelly began picking up their bags to carry them outside and to put them into Claude's car trunk.

"Latoya, you should already know that I won't want to turn you into a grand-mother so early in your life. I mean, you're probably only in your late forties or is it early fifties," Claude said with a chuckle as he walked back up to her house door.

"Excuse me, I'm in my late thirties, thank you very much," Latoya said, laughing back. "Kelly, you might be want to get this boy some glasses. Obviously he doesn't see too well."

They all laughed together.

"Mom, Claude is only joking around with you because you seem to be so worried about me getting pregnant before we get out of college," Kelly said with her hands covering Claude's mouth.

Claude moved Kelly's hands and held them down. "Kelly, your mother already knows that I'm just saying all of that to play around with her. We have already had a mature talk about it all, when me and you were younger. Plus, she knows how much your dreams mean to me."

Claude looked into Kelly's eyes and gave her a passionate kiss, right in front of Latoya, while she was just standing up there at the front door smiling and listening to Claude talk to her daughter lovingly. And then Claude said, "I love you and I want your future bright and as happy as I want mine to also be."

"I'm happy to hear that again. I'm guessing that means you two will not be moving in together until you and Kelly graduate college and get your master's degrees," Latoya said, while looking deep into Claude's eyes and hoping for an honest answer.

Holding Claude's hand while feeling excited and with joy in heart, Kelly said, "Mom, I want to move in with Claude. I want to be away from all of the college parties and distractions that come with living on a college campus. Please don't worry, though. You already know that Claude won't allow me to not study for a test or to fail a class. So just know that I'll . . . no . . . let me change that around. We'll be just fine living together because all we do is give confidence to each other daily, and encouragement to do everything that we put our minds to."

"Okay, Kelly, I'm going to be an understanding and trusting mother toward your relationship because I love you both with all of my heart, and I want the best for you in life and not just in prosperity, but also in living a joyous life. I'm happy though that you'll have started off right. Nowadays too many people rush into relationships, not knowing anything about that person. Now both of you come over here and give me a big hug goodbye." Latoya stretched out her arms to hug and hold both Claude and Kelly together.

Walking into Latoya's arms as one, Claude and Kelly thanked Latoya for being so loving and understanding.

Coming out of Latoya's arms slowly, Claude said, "Now that Kelly, your baby, is out of your arms and in mine, I'm sure you're going to start wanting someone to take her place. And no, I'm not talking about another baby. I'm asking you if you're going to start dating again because we don't want you alone in this big house."

Latoya looked at Claude afterward smiled. "I have my house bills to sleep with until I pay them off. And I have you and Kelly to worry about and to keep me happy. So I can't handle anything or need anyone else in my life right now."

"Ignore him, Mom, because you already know how happy and excited he's feeling right now. Now that he gets to take me away from you and have me all for himself night and day, with your permission," Kelly said and smiled.

Claude put his hands on Latoya's shoulder and smiled. "Thank you. I won't let you down."

Latoya looked at Claude and shook her head. "Until you two walk down the aisle with one another after your vows, my little baby will stay my responsibility, alright?"

"Mom, I'm grown now," Kelly replied.

"You won't be called grown until you start paying your own bills. Remember, this is the United States of America, where if a woman or man doesn't have a job, you won't survive or be looked at as a strong person, especially if you're a woman with children to feed and no husband or job I know that will never happen to you, but I'm just saying." Latoya then turned to Claude.

All that went through Kelly's mind after her mother's words were, *Yes that's the people I want to help.*

"No, that will never happen," Claude said, smiling because he was trying to pull Latoya's leg.

"Well, before you'll leave, Claude, go and say hi to your father, Anthony, because he called me asking me about your New Year's Day with me and Kelly. I told him that I didn't know what your plans were, but he seemed to really want to see you. So go and say hi to him and see how he's doing instead of just calling him for money whenever you run out." Latoya tilted her head to the side and grinned. She knew that Anthony sent Claude a little money each month to help him get by, even though he already paid for all of Claude and Kelly's college classes. "Matter of fact, y'all both need to go over there and say thank you."

"Okay, I will," Claude said. "But between us, I just don't feel comfortable, or should I say, close enough to him to talk with him. And I don't know if I'll ever be able to take Charles out of my mind as my real father in my life." Claude looked confused as his past came flooding back. He had not thought about his mother cheating on Charles, or Anthony being his birth father in a while. The memories felt as fresh as ever.

"Don't worry about it all, Claude. Believe it or not, Anthony already knows how much you still think about Charles every time you see him," Latoya said, putting a hand on his shoulder.

"Exactly, baby," Kelly said. "Besides, we're just going to thank him for everything he's doing for us. It won't take long."

"Right," Latoya chimed in. "Y'all go on now before I decide to move up there to New Jersey with you."

Claude and Kelly said goodbye again and walked over to the car, got in, and drove off. On their way to Anthony's house, Claude and Kelly talked about how much of a surprise it was for them both to hear that Charles wasn't Claude's real birth father because Charles and Susan had never shown any signs.

Claude said, "I would've never guessed that my mother was that kind of person or would ever do something like that."

"She wasn't like that for most of her life, Claude. I know she wasn't an untruthful person. She just made a mistake. It was probably because they had some kind of big argument or was confused about something. Then maybe she started to not want to be with Charles anymore. But I guess he had the heart to forgive her, and it seemed as if he loved and wanted the best for you."

"I just can't believe my mother cheated on our family. But I'd rather know the truth than believe a lie."

"I understand why you're happy to hear the truth instead of living a whole life not knowing," Kelly replied as they began driving to Anthony's house.

As soon as Latoya saw that Claude and Kelly were gone, she went straight into her room to call Evette and Shellion about Kelly becoming engaged. Who would have ever known that they would have become so serious so soon?

Latoya picked up her cell phone called Evette.

Evette was home and she picked up her phone when she heard it ringing and asked, "Hello?"

"Evette, hi, how are you doing, my oldest daughter that doesn't bother to come and see me or call me for Thanksgiving Day, Christmas, or New Year's Day. And you did not even bother to come down for your younger sister's graduation. Why, I must ask?"

Evette laughed. "Hi, Mom. You know I'm sorry. Shellion and I have just been busy working and going to school, and I know that we haven't called either to check up on how things were going for you and Kelly, but I'm sure though, Mom, that you'll be very proud of us for the achievements that we have been making in medicine and nursing. I'm sure Kelly is not mad at us because it doesn't even matter if we were there or not because as long as you and Claude were able to make it, everything is all right.

"So how has everything been going for you? How come you're calling me from the same area code that I used to call you on whenever we went down to Miami for spring break?"

"We moved to Miami, sweetheart."

"For real? So I guess that means that Shellion and I will be seeing you and Kelly this summer. Why did y'all decide to move to South Florida, though, Mom?"

"It's a long story, sweetheart, but let me just tell you that it involves a lot of losses."

"Well, Mom, I'm not doing anything right now, so you can tell me about it all now."

"Okay, but first where's Shellion?"

"She just left to go and get us something to eat. I'm sure she'll be back before we get off the phone."

"Okay, well, let me tell you all about what had happened. It all is related to Claude and his family."

"Okay, what's up?"

"Claude's father, Charles and brother, Troy, were shot and killed by an old enemy of Charles's best friend, Kevin. A man named Stanley and his son Robert. Then I had found out that Mrs. Anne, Susan's mother, died also, but naturally of old age."

"That's all so sad, Mom. I loved Mrs. Anne so much because she was such a great speaker. She inspired a lot of people, including us. I can't believe that Charles and Troy got themselves caught in all of that. They had both told me before I left they were going to change and start to become someone that Claude could look up to before he finished high school."

"But let me tell you, it all was affecting Susan so much that she committed suicide, leaving Claude all by himself. He moved in with me and Kelly for a while. Also, Kevin's son, Alan, killed the man who shot Charles and then committed suicide."

"Did Claude want payback? Did he handle it alright? I wouldn't be surprised if he wanted to commit suicide too after all of that."

"At first I saw that he wanted payback, but then he, Kelly, and I started to get really close. That calmed him down in a good, positive way."

"I can see that."

"But after he heard that Susan and Alan both committed suicide, he got angry and wanted payback for it all. The police held him down and put him in a jail cell for a while. He cried throughout the whole funeral. It was so sad."

"Oh my God! Why didn't you tell us? You know me and Shellion would've come home. We want to support him."

"I know, baby. But so much was happening so fast that we were just trying to get through the day. I should've filled you in on all of this sooner. I'm sorry. But if you came home more often, then you'd—"

"Yes, Mom," Evette said, cutting her mother off. She knew where this conversation was heading.

"Well, it's true, Evette."

"I know. And we'll do better. In the meantime, this all is so sad and surprising to me, Mom. So who else was part of all of this stuff with Claude?"

"Oh yeah, I forgot Thomas, Claude and Kelly's second best friend. He was shot and killed on that same day because he was with Troy."

"Thomas was such a funny and exciting guy. He must've been at wrong place at the wrong time."

"Now, Evette, listen to this, out of nowhere a detective that I had met at Claude's house when they had found out about Charles's and Troy's death had told me that Charles wasn't Claude's real birth father in their records."

"Oh my goodness, I never knew that Susan and Charles had ever broken up after they had Troy."

"They didn't. I was told that Susan cheated on him with some rich guy, Anthony Richards. I guess she wanted someone that could help her out and provide for her and Troy, even though she didn't want to break up with Charles."

"So I'm guessing they had called and told him that he had to come and take care of his son, right?"

"Yes, and he came right away and helped out planning the funerals all at once. Kelly and I were the only ones Claude felt comfortable to be with, so he asked us to move to South Florida, where Anthony lived. Anthony's the one who helped with my house and a job so quickly. He's even paying for Claude's and Kelly's tuition right now."

"Mom, how's Claude doing now?"

"It was a shock to him that his mother cheated on Charles, the man that he thought was his birth father. If it wasn't for Kelly and her support toward keeping him calm with her love, I don't think that Claude would be in college right now. I'm not even sure he'd be alive, baby."

"So I guess it was because of all of that that made Claude and Kelly decide to go into their relationship so early in their lives."

"I guess so too, sweetheart. He's doing fine now, and their love and relationship, I would say, is perfect. I wish I would've had something as lovely and real going on with someone when I was their age. Your father and I loved each other, but not like Claude and Kelly."

"I wonder how dad is doing right now, Mom."

"I don't know because we don't talk no more, and he seems as if he doesn't want to have anything to do with his children either. However, next time I'm able to get in contact with him I'll give him your phone numbers and tell him to call you because you want to know how he's doing. Truly, I'm happy that I gave birth to all three of you, but if I would've known that he was going to leave y'all like how he did, I don't know what my decision would've been. However, I thank God for all three of you."

"So, is everything okay now for everybody?"

"Yes, but I'm just afraid of Claude and Kelly's sex life, that I'm sure they've already started, because I want them to finish school first before they have their first child."

"That's true, Mom, because I've known about a lot of girls since I've been in college who have gotten pregnant and had to stop and start taking care of their baby while the father had to slow down in school so that he could start working a full-time job and support his child."

"Well, that's life nowadays, sweetheart, and that's why you have to use your head before you do anything."

"Well, that's what Shellion and I have been doing, Mom."

"So am I going to be really seeing you and Shellion this summer? Because I miss you."

"Yes, I'm going to talk to her about it, plus we'll have to contact our manager at the hospital that we want to take a week or two off for a family get-together."

"Okay, well, I have some phone calls that I have to make before it gets too late, and make sure you tell Shellion to call me when she comes home so that I can hear how she's doing, and call your sister Kelly and check up on her like how an older sister is supposed to do every week."

"Okay, Mom, text me her phone number."

"Okay, sweetheart. It was nice hearing from you, and I can't wait to see you this summer."

"Me too, Mom. Bye."

"Bye."

Latoya and Evette hung up.

* * *

"It's been so long since we've both seen him, Claude," Kelly said as they pulled up to Anthony's driveway.

They got out of the car and walked to the door and rang the doorbell.

Opening up the front door, Anthony was shocked to see Claude because ever since he left for college, he only called and never visited.

"How was Christmas and the New Year for the both of you?" Anthony asked Claude and Kelly.

"Everything we wanted," Claude replied, while holding Kelly's hand.

"Well, that's great to hear. Why don't y'all come in and spend a little bit of time with me before y'all go back off to college?" Anthony asked.

"Okay. I came also to thank you for helping us," Kelly said while walking into Anthony's big, elaborate house.

"So now, tell me how has college been going for you two? Have there been any major issues that you may need my help with? Because I'll always be here for the both of you," Anthony promised.

"No, even though tests are even harder and it takes a lot of studying. But college has been going great for the both of us, right, Claude?" Kelly asked Claude, replying to Anthony's question.

"Yeah, but let me ask you a question, since you've been in the business field for many years," Claude said.

"Okay, go ahead and ask me. It'll be an honor for me to hold a conversation with you."

"When I finish college and become ready to start my business career, are you going to be able to open doors for me within your business until I get enough experience to own my own business?" Claude asked.

"So you want to do what I do? You want to go out there and help businesses come back up whenever they fall by identifying all of their problems and offering solutions and expose them to different marketing ideas that could help them make more money than before they ran into trouble? As well as investing and buying stock?" Anthony said.

"I want to have different business experiences, in every area possible, so that I'll know everything that I need to know," Claude replied.

"Yes, son. Or should I just say Claude?"

"It's okay," Kelly replied for Claude, looking at Claude. Knowing he likely wouldn't have replied back right away after hearing Anthony call him son.

"Kelly, I don't need for you to talk for me" Claude looked at Kelly in a serious manner.

"I was just——" Kelly began to say.

"No, you know you don't need to," Claude cut in. "I could speak out for myself."

"No one said you weren't or couldn't."

"Claude, you don't have to get upset like that. She was just trying to speak out for you," Anthony jumped to say.

Claude looked at Anthony after his words with a surprised expression but no reply.

Seeing the way Claude looked at him, Anthony wondered if his outburst was a good idea after all. Then he said, "Whenever you're ready, just inform me because I'll just be right here waiting for you, so that I can be there for you," Anthony replied, with a smile.

"Thank you," Claude replied. *I definitely still feel it's to late for a father and son relationship to begin for us and at the same time, I don't even think I want it.*

"You have a very wonderful home, Anthony. This is exactly how big I want our house to be," Kelly said.

"It took a lot of time and dedication to get it. When I started off, I had no money, no contacts so I had to work for others, hoping to get referred to other companies by people I had previously worked with. I ended up accomplishing everything every time I was asked to, and then as more people saw what I could do and heard about me, they began referring others to hire me. However, I had no time for my personal life and I didn't even have the time to find a woman to settle myself down with and start a family. I'm living well, yes, but I'm lonely and unhappy at the same time," Anthony said, looking at a picture of him on the wall where he was smiling.

"I'm sorry to hear that, and I hope that special lady out there will show up in your life soon, because you are a very handsome and well-kept-together man," Kelly replied.

Claude wanted to ask Anthony if the reason he slept with an already married woman was because he was desperate for a woman for himself. But he didn't because he already knew that his feelings about it all would only convey too much hatred and bitterness.

"Thank you," Anthony replied to Kelly.

"Well, we have a long drive to go, Anthony, so I guess we'll be hearing from you the next time we come back down to South Florida, or we'll just call you and check up on you from time to time. Thank you again for paying for all of our college classes."

"Did I mention that I'm moving in with Claude?" Kelly asked. "Don't worry, because my mother already knows. Oh yeah, tell me, why don't you and my mother hang out once in a while?"

"I already knew that you and Claude were going to end up moving in together because even your mother expected and said the same thing to me one day when I called her to hear about your first quarter in college. We don't talk much or hang around each other too much because we don't want to get too close. We're both single and looking for a true love, and you and Claude are in love with each other. That'll only just cause big family drama, if we were to ever end up developing feelings for each other, but I must say your mother is very beautiful. However, now since you and Claude are together, I believe that we'll know our limits, so I'll see about it," Anthony replied.

"I understand now. Yes, that is a very smart decision you made. I don't believe that my mother would've allowed it to go that far though because she already knew what the future was going to be for Claude and me. Plus, we would've never broken up for any other because we feel that we were destined to be. Our love for each other is strong," Kelly replied, calmly smiling.

"Thank you for your honest answer," Anthony replied.

Walking outside and saying goodbye to Claude's father, Kelly began wondering if Anthony was a millionaire. His house was so big and he paid for their college education as if his money would never run out. She didn't ask, though. It was too personal a question.

Walking towards the car together, holding hands, Kelly said, "Sorry about what happened in there."

"Just don't let it happen again," Claude said evenly as he opened up the car door for her.

Heading on to I-95 north, Claude asked Kelly if she thought that Anthony was a millionaire but was just not telling them.

"Yeah, I was wondering about that, too," she said. "Like he said, he has everything except a wife, and I've never thought about asking him about his extended family. It doesn't seem right to pry."

They had a long drive back to college. It was good that did not have classes for several more days, though. They did not want to rush.

Making a couple of stops here and there, Kelly began to wonder if this is how they would always be, together while going to school, traveling, and working. However, it struck her that no relationship would ever be perfect like that because everyone wants their own space and time to themselves sometime in their life.

"Ashley knows you're moving out, Kelly?" Claude asked with his eyes on the road, but his mind on her.

"No, but it won't be too much of a surprise."

"Did Brittany get all of her belongings out?"

"Yeah. It's weird that you two were friends."

"I know, but that's just how girls are."

Kelly lay back down on her seat smiling, thinking about Claude. *He's truly my true love, but I'm still afraid of losing him. I'm not sure if he really understands that that's what I'm afraid of the most. I'm going to try to be as understanding, honest, and loving to him as he's always been toward me. Best friends, that's what we are and best friends is what I will always want and need us to be. I'm going to always need that someone to talk to whenever I'm in need of advice and encouragement, or whenever I'm facing a difficult situation in my life.* Kelly looked over at Claude and smiled at him lovingly.

"What are you smiling about?" he asked with a grin. "You must be thinking about something good?"

"Well, I'm feeling like I have everything right now that I want in my life, except a family of my own."

"Don't you think it's a little early for that, baby?"

"Yes, but you asked me what I was thinking," she said with a laugh. "That's what I was thinking."

"Fair enough."

They were quiet in the car for a while.

"Let me ask you something, since you're feeling so good," Claude began.

"Sure, no problem. I have nothing to hide," Kelly replied smiling.

"Was there ever a point in time during our friendship that you've ever wanted to have nothing to do with me?

"Of course not, even though you've made me angry a lot of time, especially when you'd do dumb things with your brother.

"Okay next question: how does it feel for you whenever we kiss and hold each other?"

"That's a question that I can't answer because ever since we were young, I used to always smile whenever I was in your arms. Whenever we kiss, I just feel something I can't describe in words coming over me. And when we make love, oh my God. It's amazing! Remember the first time we made love, baby?"

"That's going to be an unforgettable night not only for me, but also you because you lost your virginity that same night."

"I'm happy it was with you because I feel that someone's first should always be the best and most memorable."

"Have you ever been jealous when you saw me with another girl?"

"Every time I saw your hands on one of them."

"Really?"

"Really. What else you wanna know? I'm an open book."

"Oh okay," Claude said chuckling again. He paused to think.

"I know," he began. "I should probably just wait and see what will happen when that time comes. It's about Tiffany."

"Ask now, ask later. Your choice. Makes no difference to me. We can wait until that time comes if you like."

"Yeah, I'll wait," Claude replied after thinking it over.

Kelly wanted to ask Claude if at any time a decision had come up for him to choose between her love or his family's dreams, including all of the money that they've always encouraged him to earn, what would his decision be. She already knew that all of his accomplishments would be dedicated to his family since they had always wanted the best for him. But what if a decision for his biggest achievement in life included them not having any time with each other anymore to start a family and to have a happy life together?

The question came up into Kelly's mind because of all that Anthony had explained to them about how his career had taken over his life, and how he had no time for himself or for anyone else to come into his life.

Kelly had already figured out that his mind's determination for triumph was going to end up playing a big role in their relationship, even though she wanted the best for him.

I hope that he continues to put us first before any other thing in our relationship, Kelly thought to herself as they finally arrived at their new apartment near their college campus.

CHAPTER 17

5:00 p.m.

After unpacking all of her belongings and putting everything in its proper place, Kelly ordered dinner for herself and for Claude from a nearby restaurant. She felt more at ease with him in their new apartment than any other time since she left her mother's home.

Classes were going to start back up soon, and Claude was happy for it because he was eager to finish school, get his degree, and start working full-time.

The apartment had enough room for the two of them. The bedroom was even large enough to fit Claude's king-sized bed comfortably. He and Kelly both liked to sleep in the dark with no clothing on and the air conditioner set on low. They had gotten used to sleeping in each other's arms with their legs inter-twined and their lips touching, so he knew the sleeping space would be more than enough. His loud snoring might be a little annoying, he thought. Especially on those days when he worked out at the gym and come home dog-tired. Those nights he snored like a lion. He would have to remember not to sleep on his back.

That first night in their new place, they turned off the lights, and they both were in the bed lying down skin on skin, mind on the other, and at the same time giving their Father thanks for making everything turn out the way it was.

"Goodnight, baby," Kelly said with her eyes closed. She was holding Claude closely.

"Goodnight," Claude said with a big yawn.

Claude closed his eyes and fell asleep quickly. He had not slept for two days because he had driven whole way back from Florida. He was even too tired to make love that night.

Five minutes after Claude fell asleep, Kelly's cell phone began ringing.

Kelly had reached over to answer it.

"Hello?"

"Hey, little sis!"

"Who's this?"

"Evette, girl! How are you?"

"Evette! Sister, it's so good to hear from you. I'm focused mainly on school right now, but I'm doing good."

"That's not what I heard."

"What did you hear?"

"I heard you're focused on school and your fiancé."

"I already know mom told you that, but he already knows my head is into school more nowadays."

"That's great to hear. I'm proud of you. Also, Mom told me all about what happened to Claude's family and how you've been his angel throughout it all."

"Yes, I couldn't leave him alone and let all of what happened to him build up in his head and leave him anxious and depressed."

"I always knew that you were going to be together. So tell me, how's the sex?" Evette said with a giggle.

"What!" Kelly was trying to keep her voice down to avoid waking Claude up. But Evette was testing her.

"I'm just playing. Well, I know that you have school tomorrow, so I'm going to let you go. Make sure that you save my phone number, okay? And oh yeah, me and Shellion will be visiting Mom this summer, so I hope that you and Claude will be coming down too. And we're sorry about running away like that but you already know why we did."

"I understand, and we'll be there. Goodnight, sis."

"Bye, little sis."

* * *

The next day Claude and Kelly woke up happy and full of energy and excitement. Claude took a shower, then left to pick up breakfast for the two of them. When he returned, Kelly was just getting out of the shower and had come out of the bathroom with her towel wrapped around her. She took a seat at their kitchen table, ready to eat. Seeing and smelling how tasty she was, Claude was ready to eat her.

After they had finished breakfast, they cleaned up and started getting ready to drive to campus.

When they arrived, they kissed each other and said see you later and walked off to their classes, which were starting at different times. Out of nowhere, Brittany came up to Kelly after Claude turned around the corner. "He's treating you way better than how he use to treat me," Brittany said out of the side of her mouth.

"I'm sorry for getting in the way of what you and Claude had going. This was just bigger than both of us. I hope that there will be no hard feelings."

"No, there won't be any hard feelings. But I'm not going to lie. I'm going to miss him because I really love the kind of guy he is, and I can tell that when he gets older and starts working, he's going to be a get-up-and-go kind of guy every day, without any hesitation, no excuses," Brittany said.

"I'm sorry you're hurting," Kelly said. And she meant it.

"You should be."

Kelly was not sure how to take Brittany's comment. But she did not want to take any chances. "On second thought, Brittany, I'm sorry to say it, but I'm not too sure about us still being friends. I don't need any drama between all of us because of jealousy. My goal is for Claude and me to finish school and get our lives going. I don't want anything messing us up. If having a friendship with you is going to interfere with my goals, then we can't be friends," Kelly said.

"Whatever you wanna do, however you wanna handle it, is fine with me. I'm not trying to be dramatic. I'm telling you how I feel. Deal with it how you need to. But that's not why I came over here anyway. To cut a long story short, Donald wants you back badly, no matter what he has to win you back. He's willing to do it all for you, and that was the message that he asked me to deliver," Brittany said with an attitude.

"Since when you have and Donald become good friends?" Kelly asked. "You seem to know a lot about my relationship with him."

"I just went up to him yesterday and asked him how he was taking all of what had happened. I wanted to see if he was alright," Brittany replied calmly.

"We both went our separate ways. So I don't even want to hear anything else from him. Brittany, we'll talk about this later though because I have class now," Kelly replied and walked into a classroom.

"Okay bye," Brittany replied and started walking back towards her classroom.

Kelly had assumed that Brittany and Donald would be hurt. But she did not think they would be talking to each other about it. She was not sure what to make of the situation. But she was determined to stay focused on her new life with Claude.

On Brittany's way to her class, Donald came up to her out of nowhere. "What did Kelly say? Because I know she hasn't gotten over me that fast."

"Nothing, and she's thinking less of you for sending me to talk to her. It was a punk move. Besides, I'm no one's messenger. So don't ask me to do anything else for you. You're on your own. Like Kelly said, I don't want anything getting in between me and my future. And you holding onto the past, and trying to keep me there with you, isn't good for me. Goodbye," Brittany replied and walked off.

Not caring about her words, Donald still felt that he had a chance of getting back with Kelly. So Donald decided to do what Claude did and just wait patiently for the right time, while dating other girls to keep him occupied.

* * *

Later on that day after, Claude and Kelly got out of their classes and met up back in the parking lot. Kelly had asked Claude to guess who had come up to her as soon as he had gone out of sight.

"I'm guessing Donald," Claude said, getting into the car.

"No. Brittany," Kelly replied.

"That's not too surprising, I guess. Didn't you tell me that you were friends and had a class together?"

"Well, not anymore. And I was just saying that because I don't want to hide anything from you."

"I'll always trust you, no matter what other people might say you did or said. You know that, Kelly."

"I know. I just don't like the way this is all sounding and feeling. I'm getting a feeling that something is going to happen."

"Well then, Kelly, just let it happen. We're honest with each other and good to one another. We'll make it through."

He kissed her again.

"So how was your day?" Claude asked, changing the subject. "I haven't had a chance to see you since this morning."

"My day was wonderful. I was hanging out and talking with Tiffany."

When they finally got home, Kelly remembered that she wanted Claude to take her to buy some food so that he could cook her a wonderful meal just like how he used to do.

"Claude, come on. Let's go grocery shopping because I don't want to keep eating junk food every day when I have a man that can cook for me while I clean," Kelly said and smiled.

"Well, I see that you find that amusing, but I'm going to start giving you some cooking lessons so that we both can cook and clean."

"You know I love your healthy cooking skills, baby."

"Just to let you know every other night from this day forth, we both will be in the kitchen cooking meals," Claude said.

"Okay, but just know that you're putting your life on the line by letting me in the kitchen. Not even my mother would do that."

"Yes, but by the time we get back home and she tastes the first meal that you'll prepare for her by yourself, she'll never want you to ever leave the kitchen again," Claude said while driving to the grocery store.

After they got back from the grocery store, Claude said to Kelly, "I never realized it, but you don't have your driver's license. There are going to be days that we have classes at different times. This weekend we need to go and get your license. Make sure that you study for the test that they're going to give you and the driving test that I already know you'll pass."

"Well, I can't wait for that! For now, Claude, please just help me out with getting all of these grocery bags from the car. It's usually the man that takes them out, right?" she said with a smirk. "But because I'm nice, I'm going to help you."

"Yeah right," Claude laughed back. "Well it's usually the woman that cooks and cleans for the man, and the man enjoys it and gets screamed at about not ever cooking and cleaning for the woman."

Claude jawed back at Kelly as he steadily grabbed the bags out of the trunk. When he turned around, he realized that Kelly had already made it inside of their apartment and had not heard a single word that he had said.

Later on, Claude began cooking dinner while Kelly was studying and loving the smell of her meal being prepared.

"Claude, what do you want to do for your birthday?" she asked.

"I want to spend the whole day with you, and fly all over the world."

"One day we will."

After Claude finished cooking and they both finished eating dinner, the puzzle that Claude left in Kelly's head had come back up. Kelly began asking Claude about it all again. "Just what do you and Tiffany know that I don't know anything about, or are you just playing with my head?"

"Kelly, I don't know how you might take and think about it all."

"Claude, I wouldn't want to hide anything from you and I'm expecting you to come up to me and just let out the past from now on."

"I never planned on telling you either, but since you are still close friends, I thought that I'd just let you know that me and Tiffany made out at one time, but it was only one time, and it only happened because we were alone and had some feeling for each other."

"I already knew about that. You had me over here thinking that it was something else. But I'm surprised you held that back for so long.

"You can't say that you've told me everything because I already know that you've kept secrets about certain things and boys that you didn't want me to know anything about," Claude said.

"I have no big secret, to hide. My mother kept me on lockdown, not allowing anyone in the house except for you."

"True, but everyone has something that no one knows about them."

"Now that I'm thinking about it, I do have a big secret that no one knows about."

"Okay, don't be scared. Just tell me and I won't get mad."

"No one knows about it, Claude," Kelly said and then went over to Claude and hugged him.

"No one knows what?" Claude asked.

"I lost my virginity to you while my mother was in her bedroom," Kelly said with a smile.

"I think that we had better keep that right there between you and me" Claude replied.

"Oh, so now you want me to start keeping everything in again, right?" Kelly asked.

Kelly's cell phone began ringing. It was Latoya.

"Hey, Mom! How are you doing?"

"I'm doing fine, Kelly. How are things going? How's Claude?"

"Everything is going great. We're going to give you a big surprise when we come back home this summer."

"Oh, I can't wait to see y'all!"

"Us too, Mom."

While Kelly talked on the phone, Claude received a text message from Paul that read: "I take back what I said and I hope there's no hard feelings against me still."

After Claude read it, he threw his phone down on the bed. "That's to hard to believe," he said to himself.

"Kelly, one more thing. Make sure that you get Claude something very special for his birthday so that when your birthday comes around, you will get something even better. Men know they should always spend more than the woman."

"Okay, Mom thanks for the advice. Bye."

"All right, bye, my baby."

"What'd your mom want?" Claude asked.

"To make sure I get you something very special for your birthday."

* * *

The next day after Claude and Kelly both got out of school, they were at home, getting ready for day one of how to become a great cook like the magnificent chef Claude.

"Alright, my student. Ready to cook a big meal with the greatest chef today?" Claude asked.

"Yes, I'm ready, baby, but let me tell you a secret. I do know how to prepare wonderful meals too. I just don't *like* to cook," Kelly replied. "There's a difference."

"What! Not even for your Sugar-in-a-Not-So-Tasty way?" Claude asked with a silly face.

"I'll cook for you. But just for you. That's why I'm here right now, right?"

"Yes, but I thought you didn't know how to cook. You faked me out."

"I practiced whenever you or my mother weren't around and always made sure that I cleaned up after myself. I didn't want anybody to find any evidence. And neither of you ever, ever did."

"Alright then. Let me see what you've got. Let's compete. You have half of the stove and I have the other half, and let's see who dishes out a better meal."

"Okay, but I must warn you that you're about to head down a road of embarrassment," Kelly replied and began laughing.

Claude and Kelly began prepping their meals. Claude had no real intention of cooking. He only wanted to know if she would be able to prepare a wonderful dish and show him something that he had never known she could do. If that were true, she would have to make up for all those times he used to cook in the heat for her and Latoya while they watched television laughing and talking.

Forty-five minutes later, their meals were finished, and Kelly's hidden cooking secret was no more. Claude loved her meal and could not believe she had kept her culinary skills a secret. Then he wouldn't have been the only one in the kitchen cooking for her mother after a long day of work.

Later on that night, Claude told Kelly that since she revealed a hidden secret, he was going to reveal another secret about himself. But she would have to wait a little while longer to hear it.

CHAPTER 18

New Jersey
7:00 a.m.

"Happy twentieth birthday, sweetheart!" Kelly said to Claude as she woke him up to soft, romantic kisses on his lips.

Waking up slowly, Claude grinned, and with his eyes wide-open, looked at Kelly. "Good morning, baby. I see you smiling brightly so I know you have not just one, but a couple of surprises for me? And if it's just one, I hope that that one gift for me on this special day is a VIP spot connected to your heart, mind, and soul because there's nothing else I would wish for."

"Awwwww, Claude, you already know that you have a VIP spot connected to my heart, mind, and soul. That's why I had decided to go out and get you something very special and with real meaning behind it," Kelly replied, reaching for that special gift that she hoped he would love. She had put a lot of thought into it.

"Hold on, baby. Don't give it to me yet. I want to go and brush my teeth, freshen my breath, and wash my face so that I can thank you without feeling funky," Claude said while getting out of their bed smiling, filled with joy.

Watching and waiting until Claude came back from the bathroom, Kelly took Claude's birthday present from out of her secret hiding spot, which was in a drawer where she kept all of her tampons and other products for her time of the month. And then she walked over toward their new audio device.

Turning on some old-school slow jams for the moment, Kelly remembered Claude's words to her when he had surprised her with that same special gift.

"I'm not going to say those same words to him that he had said to me. I'm going to give him something new, mysterious, and loving. That'll make him want to work for his big surprise," Kelly said to herself.

Coming out of the bathroom, while making sure his breath was fresh, Claude said with a bright smile on his face, "I'm ready."

"Okay, it's here and waiting for you too, baby. But first, I want you to come on over here and sit back down on the bed here by me and let me talk to you for a minute, sweetie," Kelly replied sweetly.

Claude walked over to their bed and sat down slowly. "What's making you break out the slow jams?

"Close your eyes until I tell you to open them, and then you'll see why I'm revealing your gift to you like this, baby," Kelly replied.

"Okay, but isn't it usually the guy that does this?" Claude asked before closing his eyes, laughing.

"Well, I guess right now I'm the king and you're the queen," Kelly replied, laughing as she said that.

Claude closed his eyes after her reply and could not stop grinning. "You women wish you could become king, but us men have to hold down our main duty no matter what."

Kelly went down on one knee in front of Claude and reached for his left hand and then reached into her pocket and took the gift, a ring, and began putting the ring on his finger saying while Claude began opening his eyes:

Amare, Manutenzione, e Ammirabile
Voi siete per me
Cari, banali, e diligente
Lei mi fa sentire
Onesto, impegnato, e il mio angelo

Desidero per voi di essere sempre
Per questa promessa con anello
Da me a te promettenti
I'll sempre e per sempre di amore e di essere qui per voi
Amore mio

Commesso nei confronti del nostro rapporto di amicizia e di
I'll essere sempre e per sempre
Come onesti, perdono, e la comprensione come lo sono io per te ora
I'll rimangono sempre e per sempre
Il tuo angelo, la tua luce splendente armatura e
I'll rimangono sempre e per sempre
Per Mi sento benedetta, Padre nostro, di noi e ci ha
Restano amici per uno scopo

Qui l'uno per l'altro per sempre e mai come ora amici e amori
Io mi auguro e spero che sarà per sempre e sempre rimanere

"This is your promise ring from me to you, from the heart, even though we're already engaged. I just thought that I'd give you something that you once gave me from the heart, as a token of how equal and true our love is for each other."

"Thank you, Kelly. It fits just right, so this must mean that this gift was meant to be. Let me guess those words that you said to me, I'm going to have to find out what language it is and find someone to translate it for me. I don't know everything you said, but I understand the sentiment. I understand the meaning. And it was sexy as hell!" Claude replied with a smile and a kiss, thanking Kelly for such a thoughtful and unforgettable birthday gift.

"When you find out what language that was—even though you should already know—I want to hear those exact words back from you. Just know that they are from the heart, and for you and only you. You'll be getting some more unforgettable birthday presents from me today, but if you want to understand everything, you'll have to find someone to translate for you. Everything that's happening today took a lot of planning. But baby, it's going to be worth it," Kelly said.

"Well, isn't my birthday going to be an exciting day for me with adventure and finding mystery clues to figure out the puzzle that my love has put in front of me on this day of celebration?" Claude said and laughed.

"I hope you have fun," Kelly said with a smile.

"Is the second one going to be as special as the first one?"

"Why wouldn't it be?"

"Because you've never spent so much of your money on me before."

"Well, you're worth it, and we all change as we grow. Plus, I'll never put money over you."

"I know, I know," Claude said curiously. After a moment, he added, "I'm dying to know what's behind all of this. It's going to take a while for me to figure it all out."

"Yes, it will. But that's part of the fun," Kelly said. "Don't get too ahead of it. Just go with the flow. Enjoy it, okay?"

"Okay, okay. I'll try to sit back and enjoy it."

"For now, just think about my words to you. I've even written it out for you. Good luck putting all the pieces together," Kelly said mysteriously, handing Claude the piece of paper. Then she finished getting ready for her first class of the day.

Thinking about what language she knows so well, Claude thought of Spanish and French. *Or did she learn a little of a new language that she hasn't told me about?* Claude kept asking himself while putting on his clothes and shoes.

"All right, are you ready?" Kelly called out to Claude.

"I've been ready, woman."

Claude and Kelly finally reached their school. Today they both wanted nothing else except good lessons from their teachers and the mystery words in another language revealed by the end of their last classes. But Claude was distracted by the puzzle Kelly had laid out before him. It was the only thing on his mind. "What language did Kelly take?" he asked himself over and over again. He was having a hard time remembering.

Then he remembered that Tiffany would probably know. *I need to get Tiffany's phone number from Kelly's phone, so I'm just going to have to play a nice little game with her called "I lost my phone, so I need yours to help me find it,"* Claude thought to himself.

Getting out of the car as soon as Kelly had parked in the school's student parking lot, Claude quickly began to walk toward the school.

"Where are you going so fast?" Kelly asked Claude before he walked into the school.

"To the bathroom, so wait for me. I'll be fast," Claude said, loudly.

I think that he might be having bladder problems now because he just used the bathroom before we had left the house, or is it because he drank too much orange juice on our way over here, Kelly thought to herself while laughing and looking as Claude was walking inside the school doors.

Kelly got out of the car and opened up the trunk to get her books and folders that she needed for the day. Plus, she wanted to go and research some things on the Internet in the library during her break.

As soon as Claude was inside the building and Kelly couldn't see him, Claude took out his phone, turned it on silent, placed it inside one of his socks, and pulled his long jeans pants over it. He had done that because he had once before played "I lost my phone so I need yours to help me find it" with Kelly because he wanted to know what boy was calling her as soon as they started going back to high school, after their homeschooling. However, Kelly had caught on to it because she was watching him go through her phone.

This time she needs to be a good distance away from me, Claude thought to himself while walking back outside.

When he was back outside, he spotted her talking to some girl he guessed was one of her classmates. Walking up to Kelly as she was talking to her classmate, Claude was prepping himself for a great performance. *This is why I'm thinking also about getting into acting in movies because I'm the best, or should I just do plays.*

"Kelly," Claude said as he walked up to her.

"Hey, baby. I would like to introduce you to Nikki. She also studies different languages just like me. Nikki, this is my fiancé, Claude," Kelly said.

"Hello, nice to meet you," Claude said to Nikki.

"Nice to meet you, Claude, I've heard about you ever since I asked Kelly where she got such a beautiful ring," Nikki replied.

"Good things come to those that wait patiently," Claude said.

"Yeah, you can say that," Nikki replied.

"Kelly, can I use your cell phone for a minute? I just lost mine," Claude said.

"Here, hurry up because I have class in ten minutes, baby," Kelly said.

"Okay," Claude replied.

"Bye, Nikki."

Claude then looked Nikki's way, and she said, "Bye handsome and it was nice to meet you, and oh yeah, happy birthday."

"Thanks," Claude said with a smile and began walking away and looking down on the ground while holding Kelly's phone on his right ear.

"So how is he going to be able to figure out what language you had written your words to him in, Kelly?" Nikki asked because Kelly had just finished telling her all about every surprise that she had in store for Claude.

"Well, if he really put his mind into it all, he'll realize that all he has to do is go on the Internet and type in translate on the search menu and see what comes up and just follow some of the clues," Kelly replied.

"True because the Internet has the answer to every question nowadays, but does he know all of the languages that you've studied in school?" Nikki asked.

"No, and not that language. That's why I gave it to him as a surprise. You should have seen his face while I was reading it to him. He was amazed and shocked, Nikki. And I know for a fact that it's driving him crazy. But he'll be all right," Kelly said.

"Or he can ask one of your close friends that knows all language classes that you have taken," Nikki said.

"Oh yeah, true. That's exactly what I think he's doing right now because he's done that before to me using that same line. Let's go and tell him that we want to help him find his cell phone to hear what his reply would be, I'm starting to think that he's lying to get one of my friend's phone numbers from out of my phone to ask them. And I'm guessing that it's probably Tiffany because she knows," Kelly said.

"Alright," Nikki replied laughing.

Claude walked straight toward the school's front door slowly to play it off nicely, so that Kelly couldn't say that he was trying to walk away to get away from her. Claude began to say to himself "I'm the best" when all of a sudden before he reached for the door to open it, Kelly came up behind of him and said, "Try again, Claude, because remember I have good memory," Kelly said.

"Sorry for jumping in, Claude, but you probably have it somewhere hidden on you, right, Kelly?" Nikki said.

"Probably," Kelly chimed in.

"Y'all would be great private investigators, ya know," Claude said.

"Thank you," Nikki said proudly.

Kelly looked from Nikki to Claude and could not help but to laugh. "Good luck next time, baby."

"Okay, well, I'm off to class now. Is that alright, Investigators Kelly and Nikki?" Claude asked sarcastically. Then he leaned over to Kelly to kiss her. "Have a wonderful day today, baby."

As he walked off to class, Claude looked back one more time and saw Kelly and Nikki still laughing. They both waved their hands and put up the peace sign at him.

Oh boy, it seems like I'm going to have a hard day, but I will not give up on this challenge or any other challenge that may come my way, Claude thought to himself.

At the end of his first class, Claude went up to his instructor, Professor Bell, while taking out the sheet of paper that Kelly gave to him out of his pocket and asked if she knew what language it was.

"No, I can't help you with that, Claude," she said right away.

Just as Claude was about to say "thanks anyway," she piped in again.

"Actually, wait a minute. I probably can help. Well, not me. But my husband. He's a high school English teacher and he's great with languages. He studied several in college. Would you like me to ask him?"

"Thanks for offering, Professor Bell. But I kind of need the answer for this today. It's part of a riddle for my birthday."

"Oh, today is your birthday! I didn't know that. Happy birthday, Claude. So how old are you now?"

"I'm twenty today," Claude said.

"Well congratulations. That's a milestone. No longer a teenager. A young man. I remember my husband at twenty," Professor Bell said with a far off look. "Let me see that paper again. Maybe there's something else I can do to help you."

Claude handed her the paper.

"Okay I'm going to make a copy of this and then I'll get this to my husband at his school and ask him what language it is. Come back to my class in about an hour and a half, okay?"

"Okay," Claude said gratefully. "And thank you."

Professor Bell walked over to her scanner and scanned the sheet of paper and e-mailed it over to her husband, wondering what words Claude's girlfriend had for him and what they meant.

After Mrs. Bell finished, Claude said goodbye and left for his second class for the day, which was starting in fifteen minutes.

He walked around and asked different friends that he had gotten to know, if they knew how to read any other languages.

"No," they all had replied and wished him luck in finding that right person to help him.

Then out of nowhere, Brittany came up to Claude and asked how he was he doing.

"You're not going to tell me happy birthday?"

"Oh, today is your birthday?" Brittany asked. She looked genuinely surprised. "See, I knew there must've been a reason why I ran into you today. Happy Birthday!" Brittany said with a fast hug and kiss on Claude's cheeks.

"Thank you," Claude said.

Walking right past them while Claude's eyes were on Brittany was Donald, and he was wondering what Claude was doing hanging out with Brittany. *Kelly should know all about this,* Donald thought.

Donald decided to hang around for a little while longer with three of his teammates: Miguel, Dontrey, and Renaldo.

"You'll hang around here with me for about five minutes because I want to see what these two right here have going on with each other," Donald asked them.

"Yeah, alright," they all replied.

"Donald, isn't that the lover boy over there that you said stole your girl?" Miguel asked, laughing.

"Yeah, that's him, but I'm gonna wait for her to come back to me," Donald replied while keeping his eyes on Claude and Brittany as they spoke to each other. *But about what?* Donald wondered to himself.

Claude told Brittany that he had to go to his next class. As he walked away, he saw Donald and his friends standing nearby looking at him suspiciously.

"Hmm, I wonder what that was all about," Donald said loud enough for Claude to hear.

"None of your fucking business," Claude replied, shaking his head and smiling. He knew what Donald was trying to do, and he did not want to fall for it.

"Yo! Watch your fucking mouth when talking to me!" Donald said.

Claude never looked back. He just kept walking.

Brittany turned around and saw Donald staring Claude down as he walked away.

"Come over here, Brittany, and let me ask you something," Donald said to Brittany after Claude was out of their sight. "What was that all about?"

"It's really none of your business, Donald. Damn. But for your information, if you want to know so badly, it's his birthday, so I was just wishing him a happy birthday that's all. I have to go now," Brittany replied.

"Goodbye, sweetheart. I hope that you and I could hook up with each other for a special night out. I promise that you won't ever regret it," Renaldo said to Brittany.

"Whatever," Brittany replied.

"After your night with Shorty, I would love to take you out and have a special night with you too, and then you tell us just who is the better man for a beautiful queen like yourself," Dontrey added.

Brittany looked back and smiled, saying to herself: *What am I going to do with myself? I can't feel for any man right now but Claude, and he doesn't want me.*

"Look at that, Renaldo. I made that bitch smile, unlike you who just made her wish she had never seen your fucking face before," Dontrey said, laughing and looking at Brittany walk away.

"Don't talk until you get a girl, pussy," Renaldo replied after pushing Dontrey back.

But then Dontrey began walking back up in Renaldo's face, with a serious face. "I ought to bitch-slap your ass, like a bitch, since I'm a pussy," Dontrey replied after slapping his hand before Renaldo pushed him back again.

"Both of y'all just shut the fuck up and go and find another bitch to talk to," Miguel said.

"Yeah, because she's in love still with that fool Claude," Donald said to all three of his friends.

"Alright let's go, y'all. I got to get to class," Renaldo said and then got off the wall and began walking.

The rest of them had gotten off the wall and followed behind him.

After Claude's second class had finished he remembered to go and check and see if Mrs. Bell had gotten all of the information for him and had translated Kelly's poem into English.

Claude got up and started walking straight toward Professor Bell's classroom. On the way, he saw Kelly's friend Nikki again talking to someone. But he had just walked by her and didn't say anything.

However, when Nikki saw Claude pass right by without saying hello, she decided to go talk to him. "Sorry about messing up your plans for getting to know what language it is all written in. To make up for it, I'll tell you what language it is in, but I won't tell you what it says."

"Sounds good to me!" Claude said excitedly.

Nikki moved closer to Claude and said, "This will be my birthday present to you from me."

"Thanks," Claude said, unsure how to take what Nikki was saying.

Nikki moved in to hug Claude. But when she did, she grabbed his ass with her right hand, and with her left leg, she pried his left slightly apart and moved her thigh up on his dick. Then she whispered in his ear that Kelly's words were in Italian, and finished it off by giving Claude a soft kiss on his right cheek. "Have a wonderful night," she said before walking away.

Claude stood there without moving. He was not sure what to do. But as soon as he turned around, he saw Donald and his friends right behind of him, looking at him.

"You a player!" Renaldo yelled.

"No, a P-I-M-P!" Miguel said.

"You knew a lot about Kelly, but it seems like you know a lot about girls, period—even your girlfriend's close friends. You're the best, Claude, the motherfucking best," Donald said and began walking off.

"You're the best! 'Cause shit, I wish she would've came and grabbed my ass." Dontrey turned around and then screamed it out one last time, while Renaldo just laughed and shook his head.

"I'm tired of this shit from you," Claude said and began running toward them, calling out Donald's name.

"What do you want, P-I-M-P?" Donald said as he turned around.

Claude stepped into his face. "Look, I've tried to be cool with you, and I respected you while you were dating Kelly. But it seems like you can't do the same, fool. So the coolness that I had once for you has now been heated up, and the temperature is going to keep on rising until you start minding your own fucking business because I know you want her still. And don't think that because your fucking friends are right here beside you, I won't knock your ass out. Again."

"Alright, alright cool down, P-I-M-P. And again watch your fucking mouth whenever you're talking to me! I'm not trying to start any problems with you because I don't want any charges filed on me for attempted murder. Plus I'm here on a scholarship, so my days of fighting are over for now. But look at this now; I thought that you were more mature than me. I guess I was wrong," Donald said and turned around and began walking off while his friends laughed the whole time, shaking their heads and wondering if Donald was about to fight another man for his girl.

Watching as they walked away, Claude said, "Remember, once you cross that line with me, there won't be another way of ever crossing back over." He made sure he spoke loudly, while others around them looked on.

Donald put his thumbs up in the air as he walked away, laughing with his friends.

Claude thought to himself, *I can't believe that I was about to fight him about something that I already have. I have to do better. Plus it's my birthday, so I have to do better.*

Claude started walking toward Professor Bell's room, and as soon as he arrived, she turned around and saw him. "I was just thinking about you," she said. "I have just read and printed out the e-mail that you gave to me for translation. Here, allow me to read it to you."

"Okay," Claude replied. He was a little nervous.

"Alright, here goes," Mrs. Bell replied and then began reading it to Claude.

Loving, Caring, and Admirable
You are to me
Cherished, Remarkable, and Diligent
You make me feel
Honest, committed, and my angel
I wish for you to always remain
For with this promise ring
From me to you promising
I'll always and forever love and be here for you
My love

Committed to our friendship and relationship
I'll always and forever be
As honest, forgiving, and understanding as I am for you now
I'll always and forever remain
Your angel, your light and shining armor
I'll always and forever remain
For I feel our Father blessed us and had us
Remain friends for a purpose

Here for one another forever and ever as friends and now lovers
I hope and pray it'll forever and ever remain

"Oh, this is so astonishing and surprising. I didn't know that young people had it in them nowadays to fall in love at such a young age. I thought that the new generation that y'all are in nowadays only look for sex and pleasure for about a month or two and then y'all move on. Unless the female gets pregnant, because the male always ends up not wanting to leave the female because of all the child support payments that he'll be having to make for eighteen years straight."

Claude had begun laughing and began to tell Professor Bell that yes, it's true for some men nowadays. But guys like him that start a friendship before a relationship always end up keeping that wonderful friend and love in their life forever.

"So how did it all begin for you two?" Professor Bell asked.

"I have to go to my last class now, but let me just say that she was there for me before we were friends when we were just in elementary school, and since then I've felt like I owed her a lot back, and a strong friendship between us began to form that we never would've expected."

"So y'all have gone from just being just friends to being a couple?" Mrs. Bell asked.

"Exactly," Claude said shyly.

"That's lovely."

"Thank you, Professor. And thank you for your help and time today. I hope one that I'll be able to make it up back to you."

"No, that's alright. I just want you to keep being faithful and true to her because that's what it all seems like you are to her, and that's how a true man should remain for the love of his life," Professor Bell said with a smile.

"Okay, and I promise you that I will for the rest of my life," Claude replied and thanked her again with a hug this time.

Before Claude had walked outside the door, he had remembered to ask Professor Bell what language it was in.

"Italian," she said.

"Okay thank you. That's the same language that her friend had just told me too. Alright, bye," Claude said and walked out happily, while Mrs. Bell was smiling and happy for him because she'd wished for that special someone to come into her life when she was that young. But that special someone did not come into her life until she was in her late thirties. Feeling joyous and so happy, Claude went straight to his last class.

When Claude finished class and was walking outside toward the student parking lot, he couldn't believe who he was seeing talking to each other face-to-face and right by his car, as done on purpose: Kelly and Donald were talking to each other.

When Donald saw Claude walking toward them, he told Kelly that he would talk to her later because it seemed as if he was about to come up to him again and try to start up another fight with him.

"All right, bye, and I'll make sure to tell him, okay," Kelly said.

"Okay," Donald replied.

As Claude began to see Donald walking away with Kelly smiling and saying goodbye, he began to walk slowly, thinking to himself, *don't flip, stay calm.*

"What was that all about, Kelly?" Claude walked up to her and asked.

"Please don't get mad. Donald just told me to tell you happy birthday for him because he was scared to. He thinks that you would've probably wanted to knock him out."

"How does he know it's my birthday?" Claude asked.

"He said that he saw you with two different girls, and they both had hugged, and kissed you, saying happy birthday and I heard one even grabbed your ass," Kelly replied with a smile.

"Tell me just who were these girls that he told you were hugging and kissing me?" Claude asked.

"Nikki and Brittany, but I told him that I will trust you no matter what he or another might tell me you did, baby," Kelly said and gave Claude a kiss. "Let's go home."

Getting into the car, Claude said to himself that it seemed like Donald wanted to start trouble with him and to make him and Kelly start arguing. But Claude was not going to allow that to happen, even if it meant transferring to another college.

"So did you get the message translated, baby?" Kelly asked, breaking Claude's train of thought.

"Yes, I did."

"Did you find out what language it is by yourself, or did someone help you?"

"Italian, and one of my professors helped me."

"Thank you and I'm sorry but it's just that he mentioned something about your birthday, and it caught my attention right away," Kelly said, while driving off campus.

"I love you, Kelly."

"I love you too, and tonight we're going to have some fun listening to one of your favorite singers of all time. But first when we get home, you'll have to answer my question and then read it to me."

"I'll read it out right now, if you want me to."

"No, I want to wait until we reach back home."

CHAPTER 19

Claude and Kelly reached their apartment and lay on the bed talking about how if Claude were to ask more questions about Kelly's interests in school other than business management, he would've known all of the different kinds of languages that she has studied and learned a little bit about them. However, Claude's reply was only that he didn't want to play 20/20 with her because then Kelly would want to play 20/20 with him every week, and he doesn't like to be questioned that much. He loved Kelly, but he also wanted their relationship to have a little mystery to keep things interesting. Every person needs at least a little privacy.

"I'm ready now, Claude. Go ahead now, baby. Read it to me and tell me what you think of my words," said Kelly.

"Alright," Claude replied and began reading the words Kelly dedicated to him and their relationship and love for each other. Kelly lay in his arms smiling, as if she was proud to see Claude reading on his own.

Loving, Caring, and Admirable
You are to me
Cherished, Remarkable, and Diligent
You make me feel
Honest, committed, and my angel
I wish for you to always remain
For with this promise ring
From me to you promising
I'll always and forever love and be here for you
My love

Committed to our friendship and relationship
I'll always and forever be
As honest, forgiving, and understanding as I am for you now
I'll always and forever remain
Your angel, your light and shining armor
I'll always and forever remain
For I feel our Father blessed us and had us
Remain friends for a purpose

Here for one another forever and ever as friends and now lovers
I hope and pray it'll forever and ever remain

"From your words in this, Kelly, I understand how I make you feel all that you wish to feel from that special one, and that you're planning to be with me forever and ever. You wish to remain my all, for we were blessed from our Father who's in heaven with a friendship and then blessed even more to have gone from friends to something more. However, Kelly, you don't really need to give me a ring to have me feel that because as long as I have your love and your with me always, I'll be alright, and remember even without it I know and feel you with me. Remember, we're one," Claude said.

"Exactly, baby. I already knew that, but I was just trying to give back to you everything that you've given to me as a sign that there's nothing that I wouldn't do for you," Kelly said. Then she gave Claude a sweet kiss.

"Thank you. Now all I want is my fiancé to tell me how many more things she has in store for me. I've been wondering all day what else you have planned," Claude said.

Kelly got up and sat down on Claude's lap facing toward him, saying before she began to kiss him, "Just wait on it patiently, baby, just like how you waited on me patiently, baby, because you knew that I was coming." Then she began grinding on him.

Claude and Kelly kissed each other passionately, holding each other closely with their eyes closed and mind set on making love.

Kelly slowly rubbed Claude's back with her head tilted up so that Claude could kiss her neck. After about a minute of enjoying it, Kelly turned to face Claude head on. "It's your birthday, baby, so I'm going to give it all to you." Then she lay Claude gently down on his back.

Slowly, Kelly began to climb on top of Claude as if she was a lion prowling over his body in search of food. She unbuttoned his shirt first. Then she rubbed his chest and sexy abs. "Damn, my baby is sexy," she purred.

Claude caressed her thighs.

Feeling as if she had on too much clothes herself, Kelly peeled off her shirt and unbuckled her belt. She never took her eyes off of Claude.

She lowered herself back over Claude and started kissing and sucking on her baby's lips. Kelly's hormones began to rise as she felt Claude softly touching her skin. Feeling her nipples harden as they touched Claude's chest, she grew more and more aroused. She grinded on his dick, licking and kissing from his lips, neck, chest and abs. Then she reached for his pants.

She unbuckled his belt and took off his pants and boxers in one seamless motion. Seeing it standing straight, tall, and thick, Claude's dick seemed like a magnet and Kelly's hands metal, because that's how quickly she went for it. Massaging it gently as if it was a little baby being put to sleep, she wrapped her lips around him and lowered her head down as far as it would go. Claude moaned in pleasure.

Looking down and seeing how Kelly was handling his dick, Claude realized he was having the best birthday of his life. But he wanted to see her face. He reached for her to come closer to him.

Kelly looked over from his crotch and brought her head up to speak. "I wanted to do it, baby."

Somehow her wanting to do it was enough for him. He wanted to be inside of her. So he positioned her on top of him and Kelly got the picture. She straddled him gingerly as he began putting his dick inside her.

The minute Kelly felt Claude's dick going inside her, she began to grasp unto Claude's head as it went in nice and slow. Kelly then began to move up and down on it until it made its way all the way in and then began grinding on it. There was no one else around and the walls weren't hollow so Kelly no longer felt she had to be silent when they were having sex.

Kelly's moaning excited Claude like never before. He began moving in her faster and faster, and Kelly began grinding on his dick harder until Kelly was practically screaming. She began moaning louder with the words "yes, yes!" Feeling her orgasm coming, Kelly began making louder noises. She felt Claude trying to roll her over to get on top, but Kelly then pushed him back down saying, "Stay!" It kind of cut off the orgasm a little but Kelly caught back up quickly when she felt Claude's hands back on her ass and breast as she sat on his dick moving round and round, up and down on it. Feeling herself coming, Kelly laid down on Claude holding him tightly as the sensational feeling went through her.

After Kelly came, she began grinding on Claude's dick like she wanted to come again. She kissed him slowly at first and then began sucking on his tongue and moving her head up and down like she was saying she wanted something else in her mouth now. She decided to try a new position while she was still on top. But she turned around this time and rode Claude even harder than the first time.

Claude could feel that he was about to come, but he did not want to do it yet. So he lifted Kelly up in the air and positioned himself right behind her. He wanted to have sex doggy-style. He pumped slowly whenever he felt himself about to come and then faster when it went away. He did this until Kelly had her second orgasm. After that, he took his dick out and came on her butt.

After a nice shower, they laid down on the bed together holding one another naked. Kelly was there lying down on his chest looking down on his dick as she began to play with it. "I love you," Kelly then said.

"I love you too," Claude replied.

"I'm not talking to you," Kelly then said and then went down and kissed Claude's dick. Which made it stand right back up. Kelly facial expression went from just a smile to being stunned. Afterwards she went looked up at Claude with a big smile. "Don't worry, I love you too." And she began kissing Claude while getting back on top of him for another session.

It ended up being an evening of romance instead of studying.

6:00 p.m.

Kelly's cell phone rang, and it was Nikki.

"Hello?" Kelly answered.

Nikki said, "The limo driver said that he'll be at the address that you gave me at 7:30 p.m., and the two sets of clothing that your mother sent up—one for you and one for Claude. I left school early and put it in your closet in the back. I'll give you back your door key tomorrow when I see you at school.

"Alright, thank you, Nikki."

"I hope that you'll have a wonderful time tonight, Kelly."

"We will."

"Okay, bye, Kelly."

"Bye"

Kelly decided to wake up Claude to let him know that they had to start getting ready because she already knew how much Claude loved to take his time to look the best that he can whenever they go out to special places, just like she did.

"Wake up, Claude! We have to start getting ready now to go out to that special event that I told you that I wanted to take you to," Kelly said.

"Alright," Claude said as he stretched and yawned. He was working up the energy to climb out of bed.

After her shower, Kelly dried off and wrapped her towel around her, walking toward their closet to get the clothing that she had asked her mother to get Anthony to buy for them.

Kelly took them out and placed Claude's on the bed along with a couple of pieces of jewelry: a ring, watch, and chain that his father had asked Kelly to give to him for his birthday. She put out a pair of dress shoes that Latoya had bought for him for his birthday to match the set that Kelly wanted to get.

Claude exited the shower, and when he took his towel up from off the bathroom sink and wiped his face dry with it, he looked to see what Kelly was doing in the room, and he saw a nice white-and-blue tuxedo.

"This has to be personally handmade," Claude came out of the bathroom and said to Kelly.

"Yes, it is. Your dad knows a professional fashion designer, and they had showed me some of his work, so I picked out this set for you and told him what colors I wanted it in. Do you love it?" Kelly asked.

"Yes, I do. You already know that white and blue are my two favorite colors," Claude replied.

"Now guess which two other people also put things into it all as their birthday present for you?" Kelly asked.

"Please just tell me. I can't take any more guessing games, Kelly," Claude replied with a nice smile.

"A nice pair of dress-up shoes to match your set, and some white and gold jewelry with diamonds to make you glisten whenever the light shines on you tonight, and your mother-in-law and father bought all of those for you for your birthday. And of course, I told them that I had to get some too," Kelly said, smiling.

"So how were you able to find out the right size for me in this whole suit?" Claude asked.

"Claude, your father is a businessman. Don't you think he knows a lot about the right sizes for a man, especially because when you two are practically the same height? I told him that you like to wear everything at least two sizes bigger because you don't like tight clothing," Kelly said, while moving toward her set of clothes she'd hung on the closet door.

"Okay, now let me see what you're wearing because I can tell that's what's in that black, long bag right there that you're trying not to let me see."

"No, I don't want you to see because I want to surprise you when I come out of the bathroom with it on," Kelly said and walked inside of the bathroom and closed the door.

Claude and Kelly both got dressed and put on their jewelry with the diamonds to make them shine all night long. When Kelly opened up the bathroom door because she was finished getting dressed, Claude had immediately turned around to see how beautiful and spectacular she looked. She looked beautiful in her white-and-blue handmade dress and her beautiful sparkling necklace and earrings and her white high heels. Claude told himself that he was going to definitely have to stay at her side all night to keep other suitors away. Not that he was the jealous type. But he did not want any problems.

"I think I might have to watch you all night tonight because I wouldn't be surprised if all eyes are going to be on you, wherever we're going to," Claude said, smiling.

"Thank you, baby, and you're looking just as good. But of course the lady has to look more beautiful," Kelly replied.

"About that saying right there, we'll have to talk," Claude said.

"Well, it's seven thirty-five, baby, so that means our ride is waiting for us outside," Kelly said, picking up her handbag and her camera.

Claude smiled and thought to himself, *Don't tell me this girl got a limo for us tonight too.*

Claude walked out the door and saw the nice white limo there to pick them up. *This is going to be a spectacular night for us!*

"Claude and Kelly Daniels?" the driver asked while opening up the limo door.

"Yes it's us, thank you. But before we go inside, can you please take a couple of pictures of us together by the limo?" Kelly asked.

"Yes, of course I will, ma'am," the limo driver replied.

"Come on, Claude. Let's take a couple of pictures together," Kelly said.

"Of course," Claude replied, walking toward Kelly, who was already standing by the side of the limo.

"Say cheese!" the limo driver said and laughed as he took a couple of pictures of them standing beside each other and hugging each other, decked out in their white and blue.

After they were finished, the limo driver returned Kelly's camera and walked back over to the limo door and opened it. "I hope you enjoy your ride. And Happy Birthday, Mr. Daniels."

"Thank you," Claude replied and followed Kelly into the limo.

The limo driver started off to their destination, where a variety of events always took place at the center, and Kelly knew that tonight's special guests would be a perfect evening for Claude's birthday.

On the way, Claude and Kelly sat next to each other talking and looking at how beautiful the pictures of them had turned out, as they smiled and held each other lovingly.

Exiting the car holding hands, the limo driver said to them, "Have a wonderful night, and I'll be here waiting."

"Thank you," Claude and Kelly replied.

Entering the dinner and entertainment center together, still holding hands, they were seated at their dinner table by the stage by a host. Claude began saying to Kelly, "I didn't know New Jersey had nice places like this."

"Claude, every state has entertainment for their visitors and residents," Kelly replied.

"Hello, Mr. and Mrs. Daniels. Here are your menus, and would you like to order any kind of beverage to drink before your waiter comes to take your orders? Also, let me just say that I was told that you are under twenty-one, so I can't serve any kind of alcoholic beverages at this table," the host asked.

"Raspberry ice tea will be just fine for me," Kelly replied.

"I would like that too," Claude replied.

"Alright, well, I will go and get the beverages, and your waiter will be with you shortly to take your order," the host replied.

"Thank you," Claude said.

"There's going to be a wonderful performance here tonight that you'll love. And don't ask me by who," Kelly said.

Claude smiled and then just said, "What a great night this is going to be!"

"Well, I hope that I'll be able to say the same thing on my birthday this year," Kelly then said, looking back into Claude eyes.

"So this is what all of this is all about?"

Kelly grinned. "Here comes the host with our drinks."

"Here are your drinks and a couple of napkins. Your server will be with you shortly," the host said.

"Thank you," Kelly replied as she picked up her drink and took a sip of it.

"So what are you going to order, sweetheart?" Kelly asked.

"Fish, my favorite. How about you, Ms. I-know-everything-about-my-fiancé?" Claude said.

"Good choice you just made. I'll have the same, but I'd like mixed vegetables with mine please," Kelly replied.

"I figured that you'd always want to be like me," Claude said, laughing.

"Whatever," Kelly replied, just looking at Claude while he laughed.

"Let's get back to this special treatment conversation, Kelly. Tell me, if I give you a nice massage tonight, what will I be getting back in return for it?" Claude asked.

"A smile on my face and a thank you," Kelly said.

The server then came to their table and introduced herself.

"Hello, my name is Anne, your server for the night. How are you two love-birds doing?"

"We're doing wonderful, it's his birthday," Kelly said, looking up at Anne and smiling happily.

"Happy birthday. It's wonderful to see you two enjoying yourselves before all of the fun and excitement even gets started tonight. Well, are you two ready to make a special order for yourselves?" Anne asked, smiling at the both of them.

"Yes, we are," Kelly replied.

After writing down their orders, Anne said, "Okay, well, your orders will be ready in about fifteen to twenty minutes. Until then, we'll be having the reggae band Morgan Heritage performing 'She's Still Loving Me,' and then after that we have an R&B artist, Mary J. Blige performing 'Real Love.'"

"You're lying. For real? Those songs are oldies but goodies," Claude said. He was not even trying to hide his excitement.

"Yes, they're both here tonight. Remember this is a couples' dinner and entertainment center," Anne replied.

Claude looked over at Kelly and said, "Thank you, baby. You're the best, and I shouldn't be surprised that you know my favorite kinds of music."

"Well, like I said before, Claude, I know everything about you," Kelly replied.

Anne laughed. "All right, Mr. and Mrs. Daniels, enjoy yourselves while I go put your orders in."

As soon as Anne walked away from their table, the lights over the tables dimmed and the stage lights over the stage began to shine brightly.

Errol took the stage again and asked if everyone was enjoying themselves, and if they hadn't, they were about to. They had two special artists in the house to sing two great love songs with some of the most powerful lyrics written.

Everybody turned their heads toward the stage to see who the first performer would be—Morgan Heritage came onto the stage to fire the place up with "She's Still Loving Me."

Claude and Kelly began feeling excited and wanted to dance as Morgan Heritage performed, but there was no dance floor.

"I dedicate this song to you, Kelly, because you're my one and only, and I'm not ever going anywhere," Claude said and turned his head back to the stage to listen as Kelly smiled and said to herself. *Yes, I already know that you're not going anywhere, baby, because you already know that I'll be willing to go out and find you, even if I might get lost.*

Kelly moved her seat closer toward Claude's and held his hand as they listened to the song.

After Morgan Heritage's performance, Claude and Kelly's connection with each other felt even stronger, and they really wanted to act on it. They were both trying to control themselves because they were in a public place. They could tell it was going to be on when they finally got back home.

"That was a great performance, wasn't it?" Errol asked everyone.

"Yes, it was, and I loved it!" a lady sitting around a table replied loudly.

"Well, everyone, I hope that we're not interrupting your meals, but we're about to bring on the stage now Mary J. Blige," Errol said, and the crowd gave her a big round of applause.

Mary J. Blige sang while everyone grooved along with the beat. During the performance, Claude turned his head toward Kelly. "I've already found my real love," he said. Then he gave Kelly a soft kiss.

After Mary J. Blige's performance, everyone's orders arrived. Claude and Kelly's meal was wonderful, and when they were finished and Anne asked if they wanted any type of dessert, they decided to get something sweet to go.

"And what may it be?" Anne asked.

"Cheesecake for the both of us," Kelly replied, never taking her eyes off of Claude.

When Anne brought back their desert and the bill, Kelly pulled out her credit card and paid for everything. Claude was happily surprised. Usually he paid.

Claude and Kelly were just about to leave when Errol introduced a poet named Jonathan Anthony Burkett to the stage.

"Hold on, baby," Claude said. "Let's hear what this brother's gonna say."

"Okay, but you know I can't wait to get you home," Kelly said, licking her lips. She then turned her attention to Jonathan.

"Hello, everyone," Jonathan began. "I dedicate this poem to every true and happy relationship that is in this house today, and for those that are just starting to let that special someone see what's really inside of you. I hope you enjoy it."

BONA FIDE AND PHILOSOPHICAL

An overwhelming ebb and flow of emotions
We feel as we hold one another and think back
On how magnificent our love has always been

A deeply rooted and well-bonded friendship
Was all we had at first
To flourish, grow, and succeed
Into what we have now
In what is known as true and abundant love

Accepting one another despite and in spite
Of our differences
We have shown how exhilarating and amazing
The ride can sometimes be
Even with challenges and obstacles
Along the way

We've had many, evoke a gamut of sentiments and thoughts
Towards our loving relationship
However, our thoughts for and about one another
Have never changed

For emotive and touching, our story have been for many
Having us then saying unto others
Comfort towards the other
Creates a profound bond between loves
Allowing it to gradually blossom
Into something deeply rooted and then
Cultivate into something beautiful

Heartrending yet heartwarming
Our relationship may be
For unceasingly and as one
We pushed our relationship to be
What it is now
Bona fide and philosophical

"That was beautiful. I love his words, Claude. Especially the title. 'Bona Fide and Philosophical' is how we are," Kelly said as they got up from the table to head out the door.

"Yes, especially his words saying that comfort towards the person you love creates a profound bond between you. That means that to create a real bond with me, you must comfort me day and night," Claude replied seductively.

"Yeah, but that only comes after *you* comfort *me* day and night. Remember 'ladies first,'" Kelly replied with a smile.

"You always have a comeback about ladies first," Claude laughed with a shake of his head. "Baby, when are you just going to accept your duty to be my sex slave and just let it be?"

Kelly moved to within a centimeter of Claude's lips. "Whenever you learn to do the same," she whispered.

Claude cleared his throat and put his hand on the small of Kelly's back. He wanted to hurry to the limo so that they could get home.

Their limo driver was outside right where he said he would be. When he spotted them, he jumped out of the front seat to open the door for them.

"How did the night go for the both of you?" the limo driver asked.

"It was wonderful, with big surprises and inspirational words about a wonderful relationship that I know we already have," Claude replied.

"That's great to hear," the limo driver said, and closed the door after they entered the limo.

As soon as the driver closed the door, Claude and Kelly began to kiss and make out. Kelly kept trying to unbuckle Claude's pants, but he wanted to wait until they got home to get to the really good stuff. He wanted to get comfortable and put it down like he knew he should. The back of the limo was sexy in theory, but not the same as their king-sized bed. The idea of waiting for home made Kelly want him even more right then.

Once they finally arrived home, Claude handed the limo driver a $100 tip in addition to his payment for the night.

"Thank you," the limo driver with a slight bow.

"Goodbye!" Claude and Kelly replied together. Then they hurried to get inside their apartment.

Walking through their front door, Claude and Kelly were already taking each other's clothes off. Kelly dropped the cheesecake on the kitchen counter, and then followed Claude into the shower.

By the time they had finished cleaning each other, kissing underneath the shower as the water washed off all of the body wash from their skin, Claude and Kelly had the urge for a romantic night of love and pleasure.

Clean, fresh, and aching for each other, Claude and Kelly came out of the shower and were drying each other slowly. They began to make their way to the bed remembering to grab their tasty dessert. Claude lay down on the bed first on his back, and Kelly took half of the cheesecake spreading it on his lips, neck, and chest. Slowly licking and sucking on Claude's lips, neck, and chest until it was all gone.

"Hmmm, this was the best meal I've had all day," Kelly moaned.

Claude got up and lay Kelly down slowly and softly, and then began slowly rubbing the rest of the cheesecake all over Kelly's body and eating up every spot the cheesecake touched. Claude and Kelly began to make love slowly and meaningfully without a worry on their minds.

Later on that night, Claude and Kelly talked to each other about how deeply rooted their relationship had gotten and if it could ever be pulled up or die because they were not connected enough, or willing to understand and believe.

"I feel that yes, some things will happen between us that we won't handle maturely or maybe even together. But I feel that because of our friendship, nothing could easily kill our relationship. I'm talking about the whole thing between Donald, Brittany, and us. That's why I was thinking that we should try to both move to another college together next year," Kelly said.

"Where should we go?" Claude asked.

"Anywhere, really, but I was thinking about mostly somewhere down in Florida. It'd be nice to be closer to my mother."

"Alright, let's go to the library and look it up tomorrow," Claude replied, holding Kelly gently in his arms.

"Okay."

"One more thing, Kelly. If down the line, you do end up ever wanting a little space for yourself, promise me that it won't ever be too far."

"I promise. Now let me ask you a question."

"Alright."

"Can I get my full body massage now?"

Claude just lay back down, closed his eyes, and said, "Good night, baby."

Kelly chuckled. "Okay, I see how it is, and I'm going to remember this," she said, and then went to sleep.

CHAPTER 20

Waking up bright and early the next morning, Claude and Kelly were feeling alive and ready for another day of school because their bodies seemed to draw so much strength from the previous night's lovemaking.

"That was a wonderful night we had, baby. It was like a dream come true for me, boo. I only remember dreaming about having a wonderful night like how that one felt. However, it's not going to be as memorable as the first time we made love in my bedroom because that time it felt like I was giving you all of me, even my life and soul," Kelly said, envisioning the first time they were together.

Claude closed his eyes and began remembering why that night for them was so powerful.

"It was all so sensational and real, and yes, I now look back and feel that it all was meant to be, but I remembered why I left myself so open for your love to come in so deeply. It was because I felt like everything in my life, including my soul had just been destroyed and shattered to smithereens. I didn't think I could ever get put back together because all of the pieces of me had perished. Only one person could've made me up again, and that was my mother, who had killed herself. It was you, though, Kelly, and all of the love that you had for me that helped to make me into who I am today. And those promises that I made to Charles Daniels about all of the accomplishments that I was going to succeed in—I'm keeping them, and I'm keeping the last name." Claude was trying not to get choked up, but he could not help himself.

"I know, Claude, and I want you to just look at it as a lesson and message for you," Kelly replied.

"Just what lesson and message that may be?" Claude asked.

"To never take life, family, friends, and someone that loves you for granted. To spend and enjoy every year, month, week, day, hour, minute, and second of your life as if it was your last, because you never know when that time may come for you to go. And I must say also, Claude, that if you were to look back at it and think about how we both ended up coming to the same college, even though I was following another guy, it seems as if faith was keeping us together," Kelly answered.

"Yes, I agree with you on that one. I feel that it's up to us now because faith has already done its job in helping us to realize that we were meant for each other," Claude said, reaching over to kiss Kelly's hand. "Let's start getting ready for school."

With their minds still set on their first night of lovemaking, Claude and Kelly took a shower and started getting dressed.

On their way to school, for the first time since they arrived back, they were simply just sitting inside their car driving quietly and listening to music. It wasn't because they were mad at each other; they did not need to talk.

They got to school and took their belongings out of the car and made plans to meet in the library after both of their last classes. Then they kissed goodbye and headed in opposite directions.

Kelly checked her cell phone to see where Nikki wanted to meet before their first class. On the way, she passed Donald, Miguel, Dontrey, and Renaldo. They were just standing and talking to one another about how they'd love their next year's football season to go, who they'd like to have the opportunity to play against and on which teams they'd like to break records.

Donald spotted Kelly and walked over toward her as she kept her head straight ahead. She was not in the mood for Donald.

But when he shouted out, "Good morning, Kelly!" she instinctively turned around.

He waved to her flirtatiously and she regretted having paid him any attention. She did not want him messing up a wonderful day by having Claude catch her talking to Donald again. So she sped up her pace.

Donald had to jog to catch up her. "You can't say good morning now?"

"Good morning, Donald," Kelly said dryly as she kept up her pace.

"That's better," he said looking at her. "Damn girl, are you gonna slow down so I can talk to you?"

"Why in the world would I do that, Donald? You know I'm with Claude. You're just trying to start trouble."

"That's only partially true. I'm not trying to make trouble for you, but you need to know something."

"What's that, Donald?"

"I'm still love with you, Kelly. And I'm going to wait for you. I don't care how long it takes."

"Well, if you were smart enough, you'd see that the best thing for you to do now is to just move on to one of the hundreds of women that you have in line."

"Kelly, you're the only one who matters to me. I swear."

"Donald, I don't have time for this. You're going to make me late for class."

"Fine," he said, stopping Kelly by holding her shoulder. "But just know that your man, he doesn't just have one person wanting him anymore, sweetheart. I've been seeing him get real close with one of your friends lately. I just thought I'd let you know, boo."

"Don't call me that. And stop spreading lies."

"Believe me. Don't believe me. Your choice," Donald said with a shrug. But you know I never lie to you." And with that, Donald walked back to his friends.

Kelly was trying not to listen, but she could not help but to hear what Donald was saying. *If there was anyone wanting Claude and he knew about it himself, he would've already told me, even if she is one of my friends. Unless he has a good explanation of why he doesn't want to tell me, but I'm not going to put this on my mind because I would rather see it and hear it for myself than believe anything these guys are telling me,* Kelly said to herself.

As Kelly walked toward where she was to meet Nikki, Claude sat down on a bench thinking about how much he missed his family and how proud his mother and stepfather would be of him if any of them were still alive. All of a sudden, Paul walked up to him.

"I'm sorry for how everything went down, Claude. But you got what you wanted, and now my cousin is more focused again on his dreams."

Claude looked at Paul uncertainly.

Paul was determined to get a conversation going. "So how has everything been going for you and your queen?"

Claude just looked Paul straight in the eyes. "Perfectly. And you can go back and tell your cousin that I said that too."

"Man, I don't know what the hell is still going on between y'all still. Frankly, I don't care any more. I just wanted to say what's up, that's all. I'm saying to myself now that I can change and that I can depend on myself to make that money and not just my cousin no more."

"That's great to hear if it's true." Then Claude got up from the bench and walked away.

Kelly met up with Nikki at a picnic table and told her about Claude's wonderful birthday night.

Later on, after Claude and Kelly finished their classes for the day, they met up in the same library where Kelly had decided to break up with Donald because of her feelings for Claude.

They had a couple of things that they had wanted to look up on the Internet, including researching new colleges that they might transfer to.

"Claude, I remember that day when you and Donald were up in here talking about me, or should I say when you were telling Donald about the kind of things that I love. I was just behind the bookcase smiling and feeling surprised about it all, with Brittany at my side."

"Yeah, you could say that I was the teacher and he was the student throughout it all," Claude replied as he looked up Florida universities. They read about a college in Jacksonville and then one in Tallahassee. They all looked pretty good.

"Let's just print out some information and then read about them when we get back home because I have some work I need to get done for class tomorrow. Yesterday my mind was just set on you and you alone. So I'm about a day behind with my studies," Kelly said and began taking out all of her notes that she had taken down in class to look up and study.

"I guess I'll use this time also to research and study because I was just planning on looking up information and then bringing it back home," Claude said.

"Well, a library is better for me because at home I'm just going to feel lazy as soon as I see the bed," Kelly said.

"No, because that's where you get your workout on," Claude said.

"Whatever," Kelly replied and laughed.

"I'm going to stop distracting you, so go ahead and do what you need to do. I'll be right over there looking for a book to help me out with my math skills if you need me," Claude said.

"Okay," Kelly replied and gave her schoolwork all of her attention while Claude walked over toward another area in the library that held books on business, investing, and mathematics.

During study time for Kelly, Victoria, the older sister of Kelly's high school friend Catherine, came up behind her and recognized her from spring break, when her sister had introduced them.

"Hey, Kelly! How have you been doing, girl? My sister told me that you were here with Donald, but I hadn't seen you anywhere yet. I've seen Donald at after parties after his football games. Where you been, girl?" Victoria said.

"Hey Victoria! It's good to see you. You haven't seen me because Donald and I are no longer together."

"Oh, I'm sorry to hear that. You seem really good though. Landed on your feet?"

"Yep, I'm with someone else now. I'm engaged!"

"Oh wow! That's great to hear. Give me your phone number so that I can give it to my sister and y'all can catch up with each other," Victoria said.

Kelly wrote down her phone number and then gave it to Victoria.

"So how is Catherine doing?" Kelly had then asked.

"She's doing fine. It seems like college isn't for her, so she's planning on becoming an actor," Victoria replied.

"It sounds like you're going to have a millionaire in your family soon," Kelly said.

"Yes, hopefully, but you know with the competition out there, there are no guarantees."

"Well, tell her I said good luck."

"I'll make sure I do that."

"Alright, I'll see you later, Victoria."

"Bye Kelly."

After Claude and Kelly finished studying and they were on their way home, they decided to stop by a restaurant for another dinner out. Afterwards, they went out to a nice park and sat down.

Claude's phone rang. It was Latoya.

"Hello?" Claude answered.

"How have been doing, Claude?"

"Everything has been all right. How about you, have you started dating yet?" he teased.

"Boy, don't go there! How was your birthday?"

"We had a wonderful time, and the gifts that you bought me—I was very thankful for them, especially that blue-and-white suit. I meant to call you this morning to tell you how much I loved it."

"Well, I'm happy to hear that. How about the entertainment? Was it great?"

"Yes, it was. Morgan Heritage and Mary put on a great performance and then ended it all with a nice poet."

"So how has school been going? Have you been studying and passing all of your classes?"

"Yes, of course. I told you that I'm putting my all into it, and Kelly and I haven't been distracting each other."

"I would have to hear that from her to believe that, Claude."

"Oh, so you don't believe your son-in-law any more?" Claude laughed.

"Of course, but I can't have you talking for my daughter. I need for her to be talking for herself. She is a grown woman, right?"

"Yes."

"Plus, if I didn't think so, I wouldn't have been letting you sleep naked and under the sheets together at night, right?"

Claude took the phone from off his ear and from around his mouth and began laughing. "How do you know that we sleep naked under the sheets?"

"I know, okay? And, Claude, Anthony said that he's going to call you after we get off the phone. I'll call him and tell him when we're done, so don't worry."

"Alright."

"So when will I be seeing you again?"

"When school finishes. And after this school year wraps up, you might start seeing us every other weekend. We're thinking about transferring to a college near you."

"Oh, that would be so perfect! I don't want to get too excited. Y'all have to do what's best for y'all. But you now I'd be thrilled to have you both closer."

"We know, we know. Here I'm going to put Kelly on the phone to tell you."

"Okay."

Claude handed Kelly his cell phone.

"Hello?" Kelly said as she placed the phone on her ear.

"Hello, sweetheart. Are you okay?"

"Yes, I'm doing fine, Mom."

"So tell me why are you and Claude coming down here for school all of a sudden?"

"Donald won't leave me alone, and Claude still has his ex coming up to him even though we're kind of still friends, and that seems like it's going to start a conflict between us and pull us away from the time that we need to study."

"Alright, I understand, but until you come down, I want y'all to stay away from both of them."

"Alright, Mom."

"And did your sisters tell you that they're finally coming down to see me this summer? I'm hoping that you'll be able to make it down in time too after you and Claude move to whatever college y'all decide to go to."

"Mom, you already know that I will be there, no matter what. I miss them too."

"Alright then, Kelly. Bye, and tell Claude to keep the phone on him because I'm going to tell his father to go ahead and call him now. Oh and, Kelly, one more thing: don't you ever forget to call me if you ever need anyone to talk too about something whenever Claude isn't around to talk and help you out in a situation."

"Thank you, Mom. Bye."

"Bye."

Kelly gave Claude back his cell phone as another phone call came in, and she asked him what Anthony wanted to talk to him about.

"I don't know. I guess to wish me a happy belated birthday?" Claude replied as his cell phone rang.

After he finished talking to Anthony, Claude asked Kelly if she thought he should go for his master's degree in business

"Yes, of course, that's what I'm going for too, boo."

"Well, I don't know about it because I truly feel a bachelor's degree would do the job for me, only because I want to start my career as soon as I can. I'll think about it. Anyway, let's go home," Claude replied.

Claude and Kelly got up and headed home feeling so good. It was about ten o'clock and Kelly was already sleepy, so when they got in, she just jumped on the bed and went to sleep. Claude sat down on the other side of their bed studying some things that he needed to really understand for his classes.

Back on campus in their dorm rooms, Donald and Paul were talking about how at first Donald was just going to leave Kelly alone and then move on to brighter and better things in his life.

"I just can't keep her out of my mind anymore, plus she's the only girl that I feel I can trust, who does not want to be with me only because of the career

I'm seeking. Paul, you just don't know what I mean when I say, 'I love that girl,'" Donald said.

"Yes, I do. But think and look back at this, Donald. You were in love with a girl that was in love with her best friend but was keeping it all hidden inside of her. You never know, she probably could've been thinking about Claude while she was kissing you. So let her go and let's go and find some new girls. Plus, you'll be alright because I'm going to break them up in the future one way or another," Paul said.

"That's easy for you to say, but it's not so easy for me. You know what? Check this out."

"What?"

"I'm going to ask Brittany to give me a try, just to get Claude and Kelly's attention. I'm sure that if both of them see each other paying attention to me and Brittany, a conflict between them will be started."

"Sounds stupid to me," Paul said.

"Shut up and pay attention as the master unfolds his plan to get his sweetheart back. You might learn something."

Donald remembered that he had Brittany's phone number from when Kelly used it one time to reach her when they were classmates. He called her and asked if she could just come outside and talk to him about something that had been running through his mind constantly.

Donald and Brittany met up outside in a parking lot.

"I hope I didn't interrupt anything that you were doing that was important," Donald said.

"No, you didn't. So what do you want to talk to me about?"

"Us," Donald said, looking in her eyes.

"What about you and me?" Brittany asked.

"At first I just wanted to be your partner in crime because I was still thinking about Kelly. However, from the first time we talked to the last time, I have wondered why you never had any kind of interest in the kind of person that I am."

"You were into Kelly, and I was into Claude so much that I guess neither of us came up in each other's mind as more than just friends."

"Well, I'm sorry about that, but I'm sure that you know how it feels to want someone back."

"Yes, I do," Brittany said before pausing. She looked at Donald curiously. "Why are you playing Mr. Nice Guy with me now?"

"Because I like you."

Brittany laughed. "You expect me to believe that?"

"I was hoping you would give me a chance," Donald said, lowering his head.

Brittany looked up and saw that Donald looked sincere. "Look, I'm sorry. I didn't actually think that you were being real with me."

"I didn't believe it at first either, but I felt it and to prove it, here."

"What?"

Donald stepped closer to Brittany's face and gave her a soft kiss with his eyes closed that brought a little wiggle to Brittany's hips.

After the kiss, Donald said, "I'm sorry, and I hope that you can forgive me and will give me a chance to be your man."

Brittany was surprised at her own change of heart. Donald's proclamation was so unexpected. But it did not feel as weird as she would have expected it to. Before she could stop herself, she found herself speaking. "Yes," she said with a big breath.

"So now, can I get another kiss? That first one was nice as hell," Donald said with a laugh.

Brittany tilted her head up to him and they kissed again.

After a while of talking and forgetting about Claude and Kelly, Donald and Brittany began to connect with each other, and the craziest thing about it all was that it was all not meant to go that far because Donald had only had plans of using her. But as they talked more and more, he realized his words to her were more sincere than even he knew.

CHAPTER 21

When Claude and Kelly reached school, Nikki was in the student parking lot waiting on them.

Kelly got out of the car.

"Hi Kelly, where's Claude?" Nikki asked.

"In the car, sleeping," Kelly replied.

"Why, what happened? Was it all too much for him last night?" Nikki asked, and began laughing.

Kelly was laughing also and said, "No, he was up studying last night, and I guess he fell asleep early this morning."

After awhile Claude finally woke up and got out of the car.

"Guess who called me last night after I gave him my number in the beginning of the school year and asked me to be his girl?" Nikki said to the two of them.

"Who?" Kelly asked.

"Paul," Nikki replied.

"What did you say?" Kelly asked.

"At first I was like 'hell, no,' but after he apologized to me he told me that he was ready for a special girl to come into his life and he couldn't think of no one else but me. So I said 'Yes, I'll give you a chance, but one mistake and we're done.' He said he understood and that he would say the same thing too if I was him and he was me," Nikki said.

"Well, I say that you still can't trust him," Claude said.

"In a way I say the same thing, but I still want to give him a try because I would love to have a man as fine and as nice as he is," Nikki said.

"Well, that's your decision. Make sure you put your foot down in the relationship early. You don't want him playing games and trying to rule you," Kelly said.

"Girl, there's no man could ever rule me. Cheat on me without me catching on right away, maybe. But rule me? Girl, hell no!" Nikki replied, seriously.

"Well, I hope everything works out well for y'all," Claude chimed in. "Baby, I've gotta get to class. But remember that we have to let the school know about our transfer, so go ahead and do it today and then later on today we'll decide which school."

"Alright, boo. Bye," Kelly replied.

Claude walked off to his first class

"Y'all are transferring to another school?" Nikki asked.

"Yeah, we want to get away from everything that's distracting us a little," Kelly replied.

When Claude walked into the school, Brittany walked in right behind him. Looking back, Claude expected Brittany to say hi to him, but she only walked past without even looking right at him like the way she used to do.

Looks like she's finally gotten over me.

However, as Claude watched Brittany walk by, he saw that she was about to pass Donald, but she didn't. Brittany stopped, hugged Donald, and gave him a kiss and waved at his friends standing nearby. Then she walked toward where she'd been headed.

Shocked and amazed by what he had just seen, Claude told himself that they were just trying to play games with his head because she had seen him when she had passed right by him. *This is just a mind game and a joke.*

That day, Claude and Kelly let the school know that they were going to transfer to another college because of problems that they felt were going to distract them from schoolwork. The school administrators said that they understood and they hoped that they found another school before they stopped accepting students.

After school, Claude and Kelly went to the library and picked the Florida school they felt was the best place for them to go together.

That night Claude and Kelly was up watching "The Monique Show" laughing at her jokes while holding one another and talking about one day getting seats for her show for a nice, fun night out together.

Valentine's Day
6:45 a.m.

"Good Morning, baby. It's Valentine's Day!" Kelly woke up and said to Claude.

"So did you get me anything, sweetheart?" Claude asked as he opened his eyes.

"Yes, of course, and here it is," Kelly said, giving Claude a kiss on his lips.

"That's all?" Claude asked.

"Yes, so where's mine?" Kelly asked smiling.

"Look on the side of your bed and you'll see it."

Kelly jumped up and looked beside the bed to see what it was, and there was nothing there. "Where is it?" Kelly said. "I don't see anything, baby."

"Well, I guess someone must've taken it then," Claude said as he got up and headed for the shower.

Kelly looked at Claude. *Claude thinks that I don't know him by now because I already know that he has something here for me, but he just wants to surprise me with it. So you know what? I'll just play along with it all.*

When Claude got out of the shower, Kelly got in right after him. Smiling, she said, "I know you got me something special, baby. You can stop pretending you forgot."

"Don't get too excited. I got you something this year that I've never gotten you before: nothing. So be happy and accept my gift," Claude said, grinning mischievously.

Kelly did not look amused.

"What? You said you wanted something different."

Kelly rolled her eyes and got in the shower. *I know he got me something. That brother ain't stupid.*

When Kelly got out of the shower and began to dry off, Claude came up behind her with a red rose. "This rose, baby, is right from the heart and all that I feel that I need to give you on such a special day as Valentine's Day, because I feel that my love alone for you is better than any material thing here on the planet Earth. And if you say that my love for you is not enough, well then, I'm not the right man for you."

"Yes, of course your love alone is enough for me, and thank you for this special red rose and your love," Kelly replied, giving Claude a hug and another kiss on his lips.

"That's all I get, Kelly, a simple kiss on the lips?" Claude said, looking shocked.

"I didn't brush my teeth yet, baby, so I didn't want to kiss you without fresh breath."

"Smart decision, a very smart decision," Claude replied as he made a funny face.

After brushing her teeth, Kelly walked out of the bathroom with a towel wrapped around her body and a smile on her face, and looked to see where Claude was. Claude saw her smiling and began wondering what she was so happy about. Kelly walked up in Claude's face and began to kiss him romantically and lovingly, making Claude feel for her much more, so he began taking off the towel that was wrapped around her and placed her on the bed and made love to her.

On their way to school, Claude told Kelly that he wanted to take her out to a Valentine's Day event that would start at 6:00 p.m. and go until the next morning.

"Of course," Kelly replied, "because anywhere would be better than just sitting down at home with nothing to do."

When Claude and Kelly got to school, a lot of couples were hugging, saying, "Happy Valentine's Day" to one another and giving each other teddy bears, roses, and chocolate-shaped hearts.

Claude and Kelly decided to just remain with each other until it was time for their classes to begin.

Sitting down talking and holding each other closely, Claude and Kelly had two unexpected visitors come up to them—Paul and Nikki.

"Hi Kelly. Hi Claude. Happy Valentine's Day!" Nikki said happily with a teddy bear and big red lollipop in her hands.

"Happy Valentine's Day to the both of you too," Kelly replied.

"Paul, I see that cupid has shot two big arrows straight into your heart and head that made you finally fall in love with someone," Claude said, smiling curiously and shaking his head.

"Yeah, he has, but we're not in love," Paul said.

"Going anywhere tonight, Kelly?" Nikki asked.

"Yes, we are," Kelly replied.

"If it's the same event we're going to, I guess we'll be seeing you there later tonight then," Nikki said with a smile.

"Yes, and we'll be looking for you too," Kelly replied.

"Alright then, you two, we're going to go now. Bye," Nikki said.

"Alright. Bye," Kelly replied.

"Well, isn't that amazing to see a pimp and a private investigator together?" Claude said to Kelly.

"Not as amazing as we would've been to everyone back when we were in high school," Kelly replied with a smile.

"Why?" Claude replied, knowing that Kelly was about to make a joke because of the way she was smiling.

"Because back then, everyone referred to me as beauty and referred to you as the beast, that's why," Kelly said and began laughing.

"That's funny?" Claude said while only smiling.

"Yes, very funny," Kelly replied.

"Well, what if I was to tell you that you looked just as much of a beast as me, or should I say even worse, with your hairy butt cheeks and your hairy neck, back, legs, and toes?" Claude said and smiled.

Kelly stopped laughing and moved from underneath Claude's arms and said, "That's not even funny, what you just said. But what is funny is that you be the one kissing all of those body parts morning, noon, and night. So that must means that you've swallowed a couple of those hairs. You're not even supposed to be making fun of me like that," Kelly said screwing up her face.

"Alright, let's go to class now," Claude said, and began walking with Kelly. Their classes were in opposite directions, so they kissed each other goodbye when they had to turn in the opposite direction.

After school, Claude and Kelly were walking to their car and saw Donald helping Brittany into a car and closing her car door for her. Both of their eyes stayed on Donald as he walked slowly to his side of the car, looking happy and then driving off.

Claude and Kelly didn't say anything about it to each other. But they were thinking the same thing.

When they got home, Claude was able to clear both of their minds by taking out his Valentine's Day present for Kelly. It was a beautiful white gold necklace that he had gotten for her before they were a couple, and it had a heart as the charm. In the heart, it had the initials C and K and underneath it: "Through life and eternity."The necklace shone brightly.

"Thank you, Claude! I love it!" Kelly said with a smile looking at herself in the mirror after Claude fastened it around her neck.

"Well, I'm happy to know that you love it. Now you have two necklaces that I have given you."

Kelly jumped in Claude's arms and said, "I knew that you had something for me, even though you were acting like you had nothing but your love for me.That was fine with me of course, but I know you so well that I couldn't expect only that from my baby," Kelly said and began kissing Claude.

Kissing for about an hour straight and telling each other "I love you," Claude and Kelly began making love once more.

6:30 p.m.

When they reached the event, Claude and Kelly walked around to find just the right spot for the both of them to be when the performances began. Other couples were hanging out, relaxing with one another, drinking and talking as the music played.

The music played continuously for an hour as Claude and Kelly sat down smiling and talking. Donald and Brittany came and sat down right next to them, but no words were exchanged between the couples.

When Paul and Nikki arrived, they looked for Claude and Kelly and Donald, and they were stunned when they saw them seated next to one another.

"Paul, let's just stay out of all of this because I want nothing to do with what's probably going to happen here today," Nikki said seriously.

Paul laughed. "Yes, but not too far away though."

Sitting next to one another quietly, Claude saw that Kelly was not feeling comfortable at all in the position that they were in, so Claude turned to Brittany and Donald. "Out of all of the seats that you could've gone and sat down at, why did y'all have to choose to come and sit down next to us? Go and find another spot."

Brittany said, "Sorry, but we didn't see any other seats. Yes, we knew that you weren't going to want us by you, but we had no choice. If you want us to get up now, fine we'll do that for you, Claude."

"We don't have to fucking go nowhere," Donald said, loudly and angrily.

"Please, you two, just calm down right now," Kelly said to both Claude and Donald.

"What the fuck do you mean you don't have to go nowhere? Everyone here is supposed to be enjoying themselves, not trying to make one another jealous," Claude said, trying to reason with him to get them to get up and leave nicely.

"Yes, I understand what you're saying, Claude," Brittany replied. She wanted to keep things calm so she turned to Donald and said, "Let's just get up and go somewhere else, baby."

"No one is trying to make anyone jealous here. But if you are, I can't blame you," Donald replied with a smile.

"Get your ass up and sit down somewhere else!" Claude yelled.

"And if we don't choose to do that, bitch?!" Donald said in Claude's face.

Kelly and Brittany both got up and asked for them not to fight and asked for all of them to get up and go separate ways right now.

"No, we were here first," Claude screamed. Now his mind was set on fighting.

"I'm going to ask you again, Claude. If we don't move, what are you going to fucking do about it?" Donald asked looking Claude straight in his eyes.

Claude started laughing and shaking his head, saying, "You've done crossed the line with me now."

At that, only Kelly knew what Claude meant and what he wanted to do. However, she did not jump in front of Donald to protect him because she knew that it would make Claude even more upset.

Claude raised his hands and balled them into fists. He then punched Donald with a fast and hard punch to the head and then rushed at him fast again, with a couple more hits to the face as Donald fell back a couple of steps. Claude kept on hitting Donald hard, with nothing but blows to the head until Donald dropped down to the concrete floor hard on his back.

Kelly felt sorry for Donald and got up and began to try to pull Claude off of Donald, grabbing one arm as hard as she could. Then Brittany thought to herself, *Let me try to help too because Claude would never hit me either.* So Brittany began to pull on Claude's other arm as hard as she could also, telling him to please stop hitting Donald because he's hurting him. The crowd around them backed up and watched.

Hearing and seeing the crowd go on as if a fight was going down by where they had just seen Claude, Kelly, Donald, and Brittany, Paul and Nikki ran back to see if it was them. Kelly and Brittany were still trying to pull Claude off Donald.

One security guard came and helped Kelly and Brittany pull Claude away and held him back. Then Kelly and Brittany left Claude with the security guard to see if Donald was all right, but when Claude saw them go to try and help Donald, he got even madder and pushed down the security guard and rushed after Donald again. Kelly, Brittany, and a man in the audience tried to help get Donald to stand up. His face was covered with blood. Claude tackled Donald again hard, throwing him to the ground, then got back up and started stomping on him. Kelly was so shocked and angry that she ran up to Claude and slapped him in his face, telling him, "Stop right now because you're getting yourself into trouble."

Claude stopped and said to Kelly in her face, "What, you're defending him now?"

"No, I'm not, but please just stop!" Kelly said with tears pouring down her face as Brittany had Donald in her arms while he lay on the ground and she looked up to see what Claude's reply was going to be.

Paul and Nikki came and said, "What's going on here?"

"Stay out of it," Kelly replied to them, because she didn't want Claude to start fighting Paul.

"Let's go!" Claude said.

"No, I can't just leave Donald and Brittany like that," Kelly said as the tears continued to fall down her face.

Paul looked at Donald. "I'm going to have to call for help."

"Help is already here," Nikki said as she turned around and looked at the police.

"Let's not be a part of this, Nikki. I'm trying to stay in school, and, Brittany, look after Donald for me and call me later," Paul said and walked with Nikki in the direction opposite of where the police were coming from.

"Alright then fine, take the car keys and I'll find my way back home by myself," Claude said and gave Kelly the car keys and turned around and began walking out by himself.

However, the police arrived and the security guard that Claude had pushed down pointed him out.

"Get down on the ground now!" the police officers said and went over to Claude and handcuffed him. The police picked him up and put him in the back of the police car.

An ambulance was also called for Donald, and he was taken to the nearest hospital.

Kelly and Brittany were asked to sit down and tell the police officers what had happened and what caused the whole fight in the first place. Right before

Kelly was about to explain to the officers that it was a misunderstanding situation, Brittany began to say to the police, "It was mine and Kelly's fault. There is jealousy between me and Kelly, so they didn't want to see us fight, so they began to fight each other, saying that the other should go and move to another spot somewhere else. So, it was our entire fault—they were just trying to defend their dates."

"Is that true, Kelly?" the police asked.

Kelly looked at Brittany and said, "Yes."

"Alright, then we'll just have to see if Donald would like to press charges against Claude because he's been really beaten up," one of the officers said.

"Alright, we understand," Brittany replied.

"So if Donald doesn't want to press any charges, then Claude will be free to go because there was nothing broken here and no one else was hurt during it all."

Claude was in the backseat of the car, not mad at Donald anymore. He was mad at Kelly for defending Donald when she should've been only on his side.

She still has feelings for him, Claude thought to himself.

However, as soon as the police took Claude to jail, Kelly and Brittany went to bail him out, but he didn't want to get in the car with them. He decided to take a taxi home and told Kelly that he'd meet her there.

Kelly and Brittany decided to go and check up on Donald before they went home.

At the hospital, after Donald had gotten cleaned up, the police asked Donald to tell them his side of the story.

Because Donald was used to fights growing up in Miami, he never believed in calling the police for revenge. Doing so would only cause more problems. Donald told the police officer that it was all his fault and that no, he didn't want to press charges against anyone.

"Alright," the police officer said and walked out as Kelly and Brittany walked in.

"How are you feeling?" Brittany asked Donald as he lay down on the hospital bed.

"I'm doing fine. How are you doing?" Donald asked and smiled.

"I'm doing alright too, baby. I'm just happy to see you," Brittany replied.

"How about you, Kelly?" Donald asked.

"I'm sorry for all of this, and I'm about to go now because I don't want Claude to get angry again about me wanting to be there for you and not him, but it's good to see that you're all right," Kelly said.

"Thank you, and do me a favor? Drop Brittany back at the Valentine's Day event so that she can get the car I rented. Tell Claude for me that he's smart because he got me before I got him, and that I don't want any trouble in school. But when we do get back to Miami, tell him that he owes me a fight," Donald said with a smile.

"Alright, I'll tell him everything you said, except for the last part, Donald. Now let's go, Brittany," Kelly said.

Kelly dropped Brittany off to get Donald's rented car and went home where Claude was just sitting down outside and looking mad, wondering what took her so long to get home.

"I'm sorry, and, Claude, Donald said he's sorry too and that he doesn't want any problems in school, so he wants to let it go," Kelly said and walked up to the doorstep.

But there was no reply from Claude, so Kelly went straight inside. When she was inside, she looked on the bed and saw a rose on there and a letter saying, "Baby, I know that you thought that was all, but here I had one more thing for us: two tickets to Italy for spring break since you love their culture so much. I love you. Happy Valentine's Day. Now come on over to me and give me a kiss."

Kelly started crying and saying, as if Claude was right in front of her. "I'm sorry, but you were wrong too."

"I know I was, but it all got me to see that you still have feelings for him," Claude said as he came in and closed the front door.

"I only felt sorry for him during the fight, just like I would feel sorry for anyone else that you beat up like that," Kelly replied, crying.

"Kelly, you not only defended him, but when I asked you to come on and leave with me, you looked at me crying as if I just tried to kill the man that you love," Claude said.

"I have a heart for people, Claude. I don't want to be with him, but I do still look at him as a person."

Claude didn't believe her. "How about this then? Until you don't have a heart for your ex no more, let's just be friends!" Claude said.

"No!" Kelly cried.

"No, what?" Claude asked.

"I won't let this problem break us up. I won't ever make anything break us up," Kelly said firmly.

"So how are you going to fix it?" Claude asked.

"By asking you to understand the kind of heart that I have inside of me. Because, Claude, you already know that I'm not an aggressive person. I'm soft, Claude. I'm so soft, kind, and understanding that even if someone that has tried to kill me is getting beaten up, I will have the heart to try to help them," Kelly said with meaning.

Claude held his head down and said, "Well, I'm not."

"I know you're not, but I know that you can understand. That's why I'm asking you to understand what was going through my mind as I saw you beating him up. I slapped you, yes, to give you something else to focus on because I knew that you wouldn't hit me back. I knew that you loved me so much that, you wouldn't put your hands on me, and did you? No, you didn't," Kelly said.

"You're right. I couldn't," Claude replied.

"Claude, I'm not going to beg you not to break up with me. I'm going to tell you that I'm not going to let this mess us up. Everything that I've said to you, Claude, was all real and from the heart. I'm going to read it to you again," Kelly said meaningfully. Then she walked to her drawer and got out the letter that she had given to Claude to translate.

"Alright," Claude said. "I understand and I'm sorry."

"No, let me read this to you again."

Loving, Caring, and Admirable
You are to me
Cherished, Remarkable, and Diligent
You make me feel
Honest, committed, and my angel
I wish for you to always remain
For with this promise ring
From me to you promising
I'll always and forever love and be here for you
My love

Committed to our friendship and relationship
I'll always and forever be
As honest, forgiving, and understanding as I am for you now
I'll always and forever remain
Your angel, your light and shining armor
I'll always and forever remain

For I feel our Father blessed us and had us
Remain friends for a purpose

Here for one another forever and ever as friends and now lovers
I hope and pray it'll forever and ever remain

"Claude, you've also given me your words and promises. Now let's see if you keep them because I've made mine now and committed toward our friendship and relationship as I said I would be, and that's what I'm doing right now."

"I'm sorry," Claude said and gave Kelly a hug.

"Now, there's one more thing that I would like for you to do," Kelly said.

"And that is?" Claude said.

"Be a man and apologize to Donald. I'm going to tell him to do the same thing the next time I see him. As a matter of fact, I'm going to call Brittany and ask her if she talked to him about it yet," Kelly said.

"You'll have to wait until when I'm more over this, Kelly. That's asking too much of me right now," Claude said.

"Okay then, I will, and don't ever think that I'm going to ever let you go so easily. I've been there for you through worse things, and this is easy compared to the rest of the problems that have gone on in our lives," Kelly said.

"I know. And I wish that all of what you've been through for me had never happened."

"I understand. Now come over here and hold me and rock me to sleep because I'm proud of you for becoming so understanding," Kelly said and lay down on the bed.

Claude lay down next to her. "I've really changed a lot for you."

Kelly didn't reply; she only had said in her mind. *These challenges that are about to come toward us, I'm ready for them, and I'm happy that we've made it through the first because even though the words did come through Claude's mouth, the love and understanding that I have for him and the love and heart that he has for me changed his mind.*

* * *

Back at home, Latoya and Anthony were staying in contact all the time, mainly talking about how they both wanted someone special again in their lives. Anthony was spending most of his time working, but thinking about slowing down all that he was doing in the business field to find something steady where he would be able to start a regular life again. Latoya, on the other hand, was working hard and after work always going to the gym and working out as much as she could because she wanted to be looking good and feeling nice.

CHAPTER 22

On their way to school, Kelly asked Claude some questions about their trip to Italy for spring break. "Are we still going to go to Italy? Because I would really love to go."

"I don't see why not. I know you'll love it. And I'll love you loving it," Claude replied, smiling.

"Thank you, and I'm happy to hear you say yes because I was holding on closely to those tickets last night, knowing that a trip to Italy is going to be an unforgettable memory for the both of us. I can't wait to see if the way I've been taught to speak their language blends in with them," Kelly said, smiling and feeling excited.

As soon as Claude and Kelly arrived at school, they began looking for Donald's car, to try to get everything resolved with him. Believing he was still at the hospital when they couldn't find his car, they decided to walk into the main campus building to wait for more information about him. However, when they went inside, they saw Paul and Nikki walking up.

"What were you trying to do to my cousin last night, beat the life out of him?" Paul asked.

"I'll talk to him about that the next time that I see him," Claude replied evenly.

"What, you want to fight him again?" Paul asked as he stepped forward aggressively.

Kelly looked at Claude, hoping he would keep his composure.

"No, I'm going to apologize to Donald about all that went down last night," Claude said, looking Paul in the eyes to show that he was serious about it.

Nikki looked at Kelly. "Kelly, your words really do have a big effect on Claude."

"Yes, it's the connection between us that allows us to listen and respect each other's thoughts and words when one doesn't agree with what the other does," Kelly replied looking at Claude.

"The doctors released Donald from the hospital, but he had a headache, so he said he was going stay home and sleep all day," Paul said.

"He'll be alright. And we all have classes to get to," Nikki said.

"Yeah, we'll see y'all later," Kelly said and gave Claude a kiss and walked away while Nikki looked on.

After school, Claude met up with Brittany. She was not happy to talk to him or see him because of what he had done to her man.

"Brittany, you alright?" Claude asked.

"I always thought that you were a better man than that, Claude. I don't even want to breathe the same air as you right now, so just get away from me," Brittany said angrily.

"Don't worry, I didn't walk up to you to take up your time or try to become your friend again. All I wanted to do was apologize—to say that I'm sorry for last night," Claude said.

"I'm not the one that you should be apologizing to," Brittany said and began walking away without looking back to see Claude's reaction to her reply.

Watching Brittany storm off, Claude called out loudly, "I'm sorry!"

Brittany heard what Claude said but kept walking. *You have no idea what I want to hear out of you.*

Later on that day, after Claude and Kelly's last class, they met up inside of the school's library for some research and study time.

After Claude finished studying, he got restless. "Baby, are you about done studying? I'm ready to go."

"I need more time, baby," Kelly replied. "These mathematical problems are tough, and I don't understand them yet."

"Do you need my help?" Claude asked.

"No, I'm going to try to figure this all out by myself," Kelly replied.

"All right, call me whenever you're ready to go because I'm going to get something to eat," Claude said.

"I'm hungry too, baby, so can you just wait for me for a little while longer?" Kelly asked.

"Alright, I'll be waiting outside for you then. If I can't leave here right away, I at least want to get some air," Claude replied, picking up his belongings and heading out of the library.

As Claude walked toward his car, Donald's teammates were talking about what had happened to Donald. They spotted Claude and walked up to him.

"Do you need any help?" Renaldo asked. He noticed Claude putting all his school stuff in the trunk.

"What the fuck do you want?" Claude shot back.

"How has everything been going for you, Claude?" Miguel asked calmly.

Claude closed the car trunk, "Y'all surrounding me like you about to do something!"

"No one here wants to start a fight, so don't piss your pants. I just asked Miguel and Renaldo to walk with me over here so that we can talk to you about Donald," Dontrey said.

Claude could not tell what his angle was. "Say what you have to say then," he said suspiciously.

"If one of us gets in any kind of trouble for this, we'll all have to face the consequences. We don't want that," Dontrey said.

"I've already made up my mind about what I'm going to do next," Claude replied.

"Alright, but before we go, can you at least tell us what you're going to do?" Miguel said.

"Why, so you can see if you need to get to me before I get to you?" Claude said. He was not going to give these guys an inch.

"Man, we're just trying to stay out of trouble. Daaaaaamn!" Renaldo said. He sounded exasperated.

"Look, I don't want to be dealing with this either. I have serious goals I'm working towards, and I'm not trying to get sidetracked on some bullshit." Claude finally relaxed his shoulders.

"So we're agreed," Dontrey said, though it was more of a question.

"Yep, don't start nothing, won't be nothing," Claude said nonchalantly.

Miguel let out a big sigh. "The whole situation seems to be under control. So let's go and get something to eat because I'm hungry. This whole conversation is just making me feel like I'm in a fucking soap opera, and I'm not even the type of guy to sit down and watch it. So why the fuck would I want to be in one? I'm ready to go." Then Miguel began to walk off.

"Yeah, it is all sounding like a damn soap opera," Dontrey replied with a chuckle. Then he stepped a little closer to Claude. "You're an honest man. I like that about you. Just make sure that you stay that way."

Claude looked Dontrey over. *How is he not wanting me and Donald to have problems with each other, but he's sounding like he's warning me about something that's going to happen? What a dumbass fool.*

Claude turned from Dontrey and climbed into the driver's seat of his car. He laid the seat back so that he could sleep while he waited on Kelly.

About an hour later, Kelly opened up the car door. "Let's go and get something to eat, baby," Kelly said as she began putting on her seat belt.

While he and Kelly were driving around and looking for a place to eat that interested them, Claude's phone rang. It was Paul.

"What?" Claude answered.

"Donald said that he wants to talk to you and Kelly, if you don't mind."

"Where?"

"By my dorm room. As a matter of fact, just call us when you get there and wait for us in the parking lot."

"Bet. We probably won't get there for an hour or two. We're about to go somewhere."

"Alright, just call me whenever y'all arrive."

"Cool."

"Who was that?" Kelly asked Claude.

"Paul. He said that Donald wants to talk to us. I don't know what about. But I figure it's the least I can do to keep the peace after our big fight."

After Claude and Kelly found a place to eat, they headed toward Paul's dorm room.

On their way, Kelly's cell phone rang, and surprisingly, it was Tiffany.

"Hi, I've missed talking to you, Tiffany," Kelly said as she answered the phone.

"I've missed you too, girl. Has life been good?" Tiffany asked.

"I've been having my bad and good times. But life for me is still wonderful, especially when I have Claude by my side. How about you, girl? What's been going on?"

"My life has been all about school lately because I'm tired of being here now. I'm ready to start living a normal life, but I'm doing well in my classes, so I can't complain. Anyways, I heard from one of the football players that Donald's ex-love's boyfriend had put him in the hospital."

"Oh my goodness. Word has spread that fast? I thought we were out of high school!"

"Donald is part of the football team. If anything happens to one of them, the whole team knows it. Fans too."

"Whatever. Everything has been going alright because they're planning on leaving the whole problem alone and moving on. It's not like anyone will get paid for letting everyone know about Donald's life and relationship problems."

"You may believe that, but be careful. People are talking about it now, especially the athletes. Everyone is saying you were right there behind him as they fought over you. So they're saying that you're probably thinking you're the shit."

"Tiffany, I'm not worried about what they have to say about it all."

"I wouldn't be either. I just want you to know what folks are saying."

"Well I appreciate it, girl. Hey, can I talk to you later? Claude and I are out running errands."

"Of course, girl," Tiffany said.

"Alright, I'll catch up with you later. Bye."

"Bye, Kelly."

Claude called Paul and told him that they were waiting for them downstairs.

"So what was Tiffany talking about?" Claude asked Kelly.

"The same thing that everyone else is talking about—the fight between you and Donald," Kelly said as she opened the car door. *I can't wait until all of this is finished with. My schoolwork is the only thing that I expect to be stressing me like this.*

Five minutes later, Donald and Paul finally came down to talk to Claude and Kelly. Then out of nowhere, Brittany showed up in front of Donald as soon as he had arrived in the parking lot. "Who told you that I would be over here tonight?" Donald asked Brittany.

"Paul, he said that it would be very smart of me to show up for this conversation between you, Claude and Kelly," Brittany said as she reached for Donald's hand. She wanted him and everyone else to know that they were sticking together in this.

Walking right behind Donald and Brittany was Paul. As they approached Claude and Kelly, Donald started to speak. "Claude and Kelly, we want to start off by saying we're sorry. We knew that it was only going to start controversy between us at that moment and time."

"I want to apologize also, Donald, because I was wrong," Claude said sincerely.

"How about to make up for it we go on a double date with one another, along with Paul and Nikki."

"Oh no!" Kelly and Brittany both replied out loud simultaneously.

"It'll just be too weird and uncomfortable for us, but it was nice talking and working things out with you. I'm also tired and we have classes tomorrow, so we'll talk to you later," Kelly said. Then she turned to Claude. "Baby, let's go home."

"Alright, goodnight," Brittany replied.

Claude and Kelly headed back home to get into their bed to rest for another day of school and study.

Donald and Brittany decided to stay and talk to each other about how they were going to work on things for themselves so that there would be no more conflicts between them with Claude and Kelly; however, deep down inside they each wanted their first love back.

Paul and Nikki no longer wanted to be a part of all that was going on between the others because they realized it wasn't doing any good for their own relationship. It was only taking time away from talking and getting to know each other better. However, it was all a valuable lesson for them about not being around a couple where one is your ex's partner, and the other is your partner's ex.

* * *

Meanwhile in Miami, Anthony called Latoya earlier and asked if she would mind joining him and a couple of his friends for dinner. Expecting her reply to be an unsure one, he was surprised when she said, "Yes, I would love to go out and enjoy myself tonight."

When Anthony picked up Latoya, he was astonished by her appearance, seeing the result of her working out and eating a healthy diet. She looked even more eye-catching than he remembered.

When they had reached a nice restaurant to meet Anthony's friends, Latoya loved the night already because they had live musicians playing, and the ocean and the moon made a wonderful view.

Anthony saw his friends and told Latoya to come on over there with him so he could introduce her to their dinner companions.

"Hello, everyone. Were you waiting long?" Anthony asked.

"No, we're still waiting on my wife," Stephan replied.

"Who's this beautiful lady that you have brought here with you tonight, Anthony?" Mike asked, smiling and looking at Latoya.

"Oh, I'm sorry. Let me introduce you to one another. Everyone, this is my son's fiancé's mother, Latoya Brown. She's highly respected, caring, and professional in all her ways. Latoya, this is Austin, Stephan, Mike, and Chris. They're all really good friends of mine," Anthony said, pointing out who each one was.

"Hello, everyone, it's very nice to meet you," Latoya said to the group.

"It's very nice to meet you too, and I must say that you're a very nice-looking young lady, Ms. Latoya Brown," Mike replied, reaching out to her right hand and kissing it.

Latoya smiled. "Thank you for your compliments, Mike."

"It's nice to meet you too," Austin said and reached out to shake her hand.

Stephan and Chris also reached out to shake Latoya's hand.

"Here comes my wife Michelle right now, everyone. She's always late if I'm not around to take her to wherever she's going," Stephan said, shaking his head.

"Hello, everyone," Michelle said and then gave Stephan a hug and a kiss.

"Michelle, you already know Austin, Mike, Chris, and Anthony. This is Anthony's son's fiancé's mother—did I get that right?" Stephan asked.

"Yeah, you're good!" Latoya said with a laugh.

"I was just introduced to her for the first time myself, just a while ago," Stephan said.

"Hello, Latoya. It's very nice to meet you. I haven't heard much about you, but I'd love to get to know you. You're a very beautiful lady, I must say. If I was in your kind of shape, I'm sure my husband wouldn't mind taking me out every night, like how he used to do," Michelle said to Latoya, laughing.

"Thank you and it's very nice to meet you also," Latoya replied, smiling. This group was making her feel really good about finally getting out of the house.

"Well, everyone, let's head on in," Anthony said. "The food's supposed to be excellent. I made us a reservation."

As they started walking in, Mike came up slowly behind Latoya and asked her if he could walk her in, the way a nice gentleman like himself should always do for a beautiful lady like herself.

"Yes, I would love that," Latoya replied, smiling.

They were then seated at a table for eight, even though there were only seven of them.

"Alright, everyone, this is not a night that we're supposed to be talking about business and plans for making more money. It's supposed to be just a night of relaxation and enjoyment of each other's company," Anthony said while everyone was settling around the table.

"Don't worry about me talking about money. I plan on spending the night getting to know Latoya. I'm very interested in getting to know her," Mike replied as he moved himself closer to her.

Anthony smiled and asked the others about their Valentine's Day.

"Our Valentine's Day was wonderful," Michelle said proudly. "We went out to a nice restaurant and rented out a luxurious boat for the rest of the night. It was wonderful because along the ride, we heard no noise, and it just felt like we were in a world all by ourselves giving each other love."

"Yes, that sounds very romantic. What about you, Austin? Where did you take your fiancée, Anna? Because I remember you had told me that you were going to propose to her," Anthony said.

"Ahh, that was very sweet and nice of you to do it on Valentine's Day," Michelle said, smiling.

"Yes, I surprised her with a ring, but she surprised me with something else also that same night. It broke my heart and made me feel like I had wasted all of the money that I had ever spent on her," Austin said, shaking his head.

"What did Anna say?" Stephan asked.

"She liked the ring, but she turned me down," Austin said.

"Oh no!" everyone replied.

"Yeah," Austin went on. "She knows that I want to start a family right away. And she's not ready to slow down her modeling career to settle down. She's really ambitious, and I love that about her. But I want more balance for both of us. And she doesn't want that right now. She's all about working. I tried talking it out with her, but she just walked right out. She didn't want to discuss it at all."

"Wow," Michelle said incredulously.

Austin was quiet for a moment. "Exactly. I couldn't believe it. After all those years, she walked right out and never looked back."

"Well, now you see why I said that it was going to be very hard to keep a girl like her," Chris piped up. "All models do mostly is concentrate on keeping themselves looking beautiful and sexy. Plus, from what I heard, most of them don't even want babies. And if they do, their first one won't even come until they're in their forties because they don't want to take the chance of getting a stretch mark on their body. I'm sorry it happened to you, man. You two made a wonderful couple."

Michelle tried to be reassuring. "Well, at least he gave it his best and didn't back down from it all. Don't worry, Austin. The next time that she calls me about going shopping or just hanging out, I'll find out what's going on in her head."

"Thank you and when you do, tell her that I'm still waiting for her. I know that she doesn't mean what she's saying. She's going to come around eventually," Austin replied.

"How do you know that?" Chris asked.

"I saw it in her eyes, that's how," Austin replied. "I probably spooked her by wanting to get super-serious. But I don't believe she's willing to throw everything we have away. I just don't believe that."

"Well, I must say, don't give up on her like how I gave up on Myra," Anthony replied.

"Oh yeah!" Chris said excitedly. "Whatever happened to you and Myra, Anthony? Y'all were like a match made in heaven. You can't tell me that you don't sometimes talk. You must."

"When we finish talking about everyone else's Valentine's Day, I'll tell you'll all about it. It's a long story," Anthony replied.

"What did you do for Valentine's Day, Chris?" Michelle asked.

"I gave myself a rose and told myself "I love you" and then began playing video games," Chris replied because he knew that Michelle knew that his girlfriend broke up with him because he cheated on her with one of her coworkers.

Everyone laughed except for Latoya, who did not get the joke. "Why, what happened?" Latoya asked.

"It's all my fault. I cheated on my girl with her coworker," Chris replied.

"Oh," Latoya said cryptically.

"Latoya, don't even think of trying to make him feel badly about it," Michelle said. "It makes no sense to even try to influence him to be a better man because a man like him will listen to you when you tell him something, but will never take it seriously. This is not even the first time something like that has happened. He's a bad man, searching for a girl that'll allow him to bring another woman into the bedroom with them at night time."

"How about you, Latoya? What did you do?" Mike asked, smiling at her.

"All I did was go to work, go home, and made myself some salad for lunch. Then I put on some workout clothes and worked up a sweat. I sat down for the rest of the night watching movies and thinking about how my daughter and her fiancé were spending their night together," Latoya replied.

"Well, it sounds like you were lonely. I wish that Anthony had introduced me to you earlier because I would've taken you out somewhere nice," Mike replied, smiling.

"So, Mike, you're telling me that you would've actually left your office— where you spend every night and every day—to take Latoya out, even though you're in the middle of a big deal with a major company?" Austin asked.

"I finished my deal before 4:00 p.m., thank you very much. And even if I wasn't, I don't believe I would've chosen another boring deal over a once-in-a-lifetime date with this smart, beautiful woman."

"I think that Mike is falling hard, y'all," Anthony said, laughing. "Latoya, what'd you do to that man?!"

Latoya blushed.

"Well, if he'll stop making only compliments and ask Latoya out on a date, he might just have a chance with her," Michelle replied.

"I want her to feel that she can trust me and be comfortable around me first before I decide to ask her out, Michelle," Mike replied with his eyes still on Latoya.

"So was that all that you did for real on Valentine's Day?" Latoya asked Mike.

"Yes, I'm single. And yeah, Austin, Anthony, Chris, Stephan, Mike, and Michelle will tell you that I've lost many women because of my career. I was once homeless and wasn't able to keep a woman then either. So not much has changed in that department," Mike said.

"Well, it sounds like you have a very interesting story," said Latoya.

"Yes, but I must say that I would rather hold off on all my good stories until you let me take you to lunch sometime."

"You've got yourself a deal," Latoya replied.

"Oh Lord, Mike finally has a date. I'm guessing that means that you'll be calling my husband less now to take you out for dinner because you're oh so lonely," Michelle said to everyone, smiling.

Everyone laughed.

"So, Anthony, it's time. Tell us what happened with Myra?" Chris asked.

"All she was wanted to do whenever she was off was take away my time from work, and whenever it was time for her to start scheduling models for runway shows, she never wanted me to bother her. Whenever we both had the same day off, it was wonderful, but there wasn't much understanding going on when I needed her understanding. Plus, she wasn't into business the way I am. That bothered me. I was like Mike, except I didn't ignore over a thousand women. Myra and I still talk and hang out from time to time."

"Well, you need to take your own advice," Chris said. "You and Myra obviously have something special, even if the road is a little bumpy. You probably need to try again. And you better hurry up. She might be married with five children already."

Everyone laughed.

"Married? Maybe. Five children in less than five years? I don't think so," Anthony said, taking a sip of his water. "If I ever feel the time is right for Myra and I to try again, I won't be afraid to ask her out. But until then, I'm happy to be her friend," Anthony replied.

"I plan on helping you out with your decision, Anthony, if you don't mind me doing so," Latoya said, looking at Anthony to hear his reply.

Anthony had only smiled while nodding his head yes and said, "Okay, I'd love that."

Everyone ordered dinners and ate, talking to one another about how they thought each other had handled a relationship whenever they got into one. Latoya and Mike started to have their own private conversation, and they did not realize it, but the others at the table were kind of listening in. Everyone was excited to see Mike hitting it off with someone they liked.

After everyone finished eating and talking, they all walked out of the restaurant and said goodbye. Latoya and Michelle exchanged phone numbers. "I'll call you soon," Mike said.

As Austin, Stephan, Michelle, and Chris walked away, they looked back seeing Latoya and Mike saying goodbye to Anthony.

"Where are they going at this time of the night?" Michelle asked everyone.

"Mike is probably trying to find a way to ask Latoya if he can drive her home. I bet he wants to see where she lives!" Stephan said with a laugh.

"Yeah, I think that's exactly what's going on," Austin chimed in. "He's gonna stalk that poor woman."

"No, I think it's because he wants tonight to be their first night all alone with each other talking and romancing in the moonlight. I noticed that they were feeling into each other," Chris replied.

"I think the same thing," Michelle replied and turned around. *Remember, girl, never on the first night.*

Mike was in luck. Latoya did let him drive her home. Once they pulled into her driveway, she invited Mike in for coffee. She popped in a movie and they fell asleep on the couch cuddled up.

* * *

8:00 a.m.

Claude and Kelly woke up and had a wonderful breakfast that Claude had bought earlier. Eating breakfast calmly and quietly, Kelly asked Claude to turn around and tell her what the date was because she had a report she had to do by the eighteenth. Turning around and looking at the calendar, Claude turned back around in silence with tears beginning to run down from his eyes.

"What's wrong? Why are you crying, baby?" Kelly asked Claude as soon as she saw the first tear run down his cheek.

Kelly went over to Claude and wrapped her arms around him and held him closely to her heart, asking him what was wrong. Kelly picked her head up and turned around and looked at the calendar and then asked herself, "I remember this date, but whose birthday is it today?"

Thinking and asking herself time and time again in her mind whose birthday it was today, while holding Claude close to her heart, Kelly remembered and whispered, "Happy Birthday, Susan."

CHAPTER 23

8:45 a.m.

Holding Claude in her arms at their dining room table, Kelly said to him, "I'm here for you, baby, I'm here for you. Your mother is here for you as well, and I'm sure that she's smiling happily and proudly to see where you're at right now in your life. Plus, baby, understand all of the love that your family has for you. It's all inside of me because I have an unlimited amount of love that's all for you. And I not only show it and say it, I also express it by giving it to you, right baby? Whenever you want and need it—morning, evening, and nighttime before we go to our bed, and then even sometimes in the middle of the night, to help to put you back to sleep feeling good and to get a good night rest."

Claude's face all of a sudden brightened with a smile, though his tears still fell. He lifted his head slowly and looked deeply into Kelly's eyes. "Thanks."

Kelly smiled brightly as she began to wipe Claude's tears from his face. "I love you too, sweetie."

"I miss them all though. My mother, my grandmother and grandfather, Charles, my brother Troy, Thomas, and Alan. I've realized how precious and irreplaceable a family's love is. I get a lot of love from you, Kelly, but I feel a mother's love, like the amount of love and understanding that my mother had for me, is irreplaceable." Claude looked into Kelly's eyes and placed his hands on the side of her face, rubbing it gently.

"I've realized that myself, sweetheart, and I sort of know just how you feel. I also had taken your mother in as my second mother. However, a mother won't be happy unless her children are happy and thankful in their lives, baby. So for all time, keep a smile on your face with joy and happiness inside of you, so that she'll always be looking down from heaven happy and smiling by our Father's side," Kelly said softly rubbing Claude's back.

"Let's go to school now. I don't want you to be late for your class because of me," Claude said.

They left for school moments later with their school things. They had their information they needed for research, and after their last class, they planned some serious study time at the campus library. When they reached campus, they were greeted by Donald and Brittany and then saw Paul and Nikki. Surprised by all of the polite, peaceful greetings, they stood by one another watching Miguel, Dontrey, Blane, and Renaldo agreeing that being true in life really does bring peace and harmony in one's heart.

"Psych!" They all said and began laughing, agreeing that they'd never see themselves doing what they were all seeing, which was two couples that hated one another becoming best friends.

Moments later, everyone went to his or her class.

* * *

Back in Miami, Latoya had woken up in Mike's arms, and it felt good and snuggly. Before they parted from each other that morning, they made plans to go out that same night again. They wanted to go somewhere fun and exciting, as if they were both still kids.

While at work, Latoya was feeling happy and energetic. She believed that she had found that true man that she had always prayed and hoped for, ever since she and her children's father had separated. They'd felt that they weren't meant to be, however, had second thoughts about what they had said because their children were meant to be in their lives. In the end he neglected them and left without ever trying to get back in contact with any of them.

Latoya felt that Mike was about to bring excitement back into her life in a different way than all of the love, excitement, and journeys that Claude and Kelly, her two babies, used to give her.

Mike was happy for all of what and who had been put in front of him, and for a wonderful opportunity to make a change in his life. He wanted what Al Green sang about: love and happiness. Mike began to say to himself that Latoya is the one he had been seeking for so long because of how loving she is. If she'd seen him homeless on the street, she would have been likely try to help him. He wished that he'd have had the chance to meet her earlier in his life. However, at the right time, because he'd been the kind of man that wouldn't have opened his heart to another, for fear of breaking it.

However, for introducing Latoya and Mike to each other, they both began wanting to bring Myra back into Anthony's life, one hundred percent.

After seeing Latoya and Mike leaving together after just a couple of hours of seeing and getting to know each other for the first time in their lives, Anthony felt his first stings of jealousy because he was alone when all his friends were coupled up. He decided right then to go after Myra again—the woman he felt was his true love. He decided he had made a mistake by letting go of what they had so easily.

* * *

Back at school, Kelly ran into Ashley, her old roommate.

"How has everything been going for you, girl?" Ashley asked Kelly, hugging her happily.

"Everything has been wonderful. I'm doing good in school, and my baby has been keeping me happy," Kelly replied, finally letting go of the hug.

"That's great to hear, so I'm guessing that you haven't been going out to any more college parties because I haven't seen you anywhere ever since you moved out of our room," Ashley said.

"I've been still going out, but not to any parties. I'm not trying to get into anything with anyone," Kelly replied.

"That's understandable," Ashley said.

"Have you been dating anyone lately?," Kelly asked.

"I'm not seeing anyone because I'm never ever going to get into a relationship with any of these boys in this college. A relationship for me right now would not work out well at all. I want to be able to go out, shake my ass and dance, as well as spend time with whomever I want to, and not just one man that I feel would want me to be around him and only him all the time. Life has too much to offer for me to be put on lockdown to just one man," Ashley replied.

"Well, I hope that your decisions are what really make you happy," Kelly said.

"Yes, I'm sure, girl. So what are you doing for spring break? My girls and I are going to South America to party," Ashley said.

"Claude and I are going to Italy," Kelly replied.

"That sounds amazing!" Ashley exclaimed.

"Very interesting, because we're both going to see new things that we've never seen before in our lives. And I can't wait to taste the food. I hear it's unbelievable," Kelly said.

"Well, just make sure that you ask what it is first before ordering it and putting it inside your mouth," Ashley said with a chuckle.

"You're right girl," Kelly said and laughed. "You're so right!"

"Well, I'm going to get out of here now, Kelly. I'm getting tired of all of this studying and schoolwork I have to do. The only reason I'm still here is because I love the parties, and I need a degree to make money. Shoot, you know that without money, you can't do anything in America. Not even sleep."

"Well, alright then, Ashley. It was nice running into you. Have a good spring break. Bye," Kelly said.

"Oh, believe me, girl, we will and I'm so sure of that," Ashley replied.

* * *

After work, Latoya called Michelle and asked if she would like to work out with her at the gym because she wanted to talk to her about Anthony and Myra's relationship.

"Sure, why not. I'm sure that my husband wants me looking just as good as you were looking last night when we were at dinner together."

Latoya laughed and gave Michelle the gym's address and said she'd meet her there in about half an hour.

Later on, when they both reached the gym, Latoya greeted Michelle with a hug and said, "Let's go and burn all of those calories that we gained from last night's dinner."

They started by stretching out their bodies and then went on a workout machine to help strengthen their calves, thighs, and hips.

"So what did you want to talk to me about? Because it sounded like you wanted to get in contact with Myra," Michelle said.

"Yes. It sounds like Anthony really wants to be with her. Seems like he needs some advice or some help convincing Myra that his feelings are true."

"Well, yes, what you're saying is true, Latoya. But, if he really wants us to talk to Myra about how he feels about her, I believe that he would've already asked one of us. If he's no longer afraid or ashamed to confess his mistakes during their relationship, he would've told her that already."

"Yes, but I still think he could use a little reinforcement."

"Okay, I'll call her and schedule a get-together for just the three of us. We can have a woman's night out to talk about everything."

"Thank you."

"No, Latoya, Anthony should be the one saying thank you to the both of us right now. So tell me how was your night with Mike?"

"Just know that I woke up in his arms this morning."

"Whew girl!" Michelle said laughing.

"You know you need to stop."

"Oh please. You can't tell me he stayed the night, then expect me not to have a reaction. Well at least I know that you must've woken up happy."

"I did, I did, Michelle. I don't know about Mike, but I've been feeling good all day and we have plans to go somewhere fun tonight."

"So things are going well early. That's good. But be careful. Mike's a good guy, but you don't have to rush anything."

"I'm not. We fell asleep on the couch together last night. He didn't even try to kiss me. He was a perfect gentleman. Right now we're going to get to know each other more and see if anything more develops." Latoya sounded Zen about it, but she was just trying to hide her excitement and hopefulness.

After about three hours of working out and then resting and stretching out, Latoya told Michelle that it was time for her to go so she would be on time for her date with Mike.

They said goodbye and both left the gym.

* * *

6:00 p.m.

Claude and Kelly left the library and stopped by a fast food restaurant to get something to eat and went straight home because they still needed to study and had work that they had to complete.

When they arrived, Claude went to lie down before a long, hard night of studying.

After a while, Kelly's cell phone rang, so she picked it up and then looked at the phone number that was displayed on the screen. She didn't recognize the phone number, but she answered it anyway.

"How have you been, girl? This is Catherine, your old high school friend that you seem to have forgotten all about."

"Catherine! Hey girl! Everything has been great. Victoria must've told you we ran into each other."

"Of course she did. Victoria's a trip."

"I know," Kelly said. "So how've you been doing? I haven't forgotten anything about you, girl."

"So I'm sure Victoria told you that I dropped out of school to become an actress."

"Yeah, she mentioned it. But do you, girl! I bet you're really talented."

"Thanks, Kelly. I'm taking acting classes and stuff. I like it a lot," Catherine said. "Don't tell Victoria, but I would love to become an R&B artist. I didn't want to spring all my news on my family at one time."

"That's great to hear! I'm so happy for you."

"I heard that you've taken your best friend in as you're present and future man."

"Yes, girl. We're engaged."

"Did Donald cry when you told him?"

"No, he didn't. He just took it, and then we went our separate ways. He's got a new girl now, but he's still sniffing around me. I already know that he's going to try to get at me again. It doesn't matter that he says that he's in love with Claude's ex-girlfriend."

"What?! Girl, that's too much drama for me."

"I know, right?" Kelly laughed.

"Well, girl, that's life. I am happy to hear that you're with the man that makes you happy and not the man that'll only make you happy with the amount of money that he has coming to him."

"I wish him much luck in his football career. But he's just not the one for me."

"So when am I going to get to see you again, girl?"

"Most likely in the summertime because we're going to Italy for Spring Break."

"Wow, girl I'm envious! You got you a good one! Taking you to Italy. That's a big trip."

"Yeah, we're really excited."

"How about Memorial Day? What are you two doing then?"

"I'll ask Claude if he wants to go back down to Miami because I already know there'll be a lot going on there around then."

"Alright, I hope that he says yes because it's been such a long time since I've seen you."

"I miss you too, Catherine. But, girl, I have a lot to study right now, so I'm going to save your phone number and call you whenever I know I'm coming down."

"Okay, girl. Go study and make me proud!"

Kelly laughed and told Catherine goodbye and put her mind back into what she was studying before she had received Catherine's phone call.

* * *

9:00 p.m.

Back in South Florida, Latoya was getting ready for a fun and exciting night with Mike. She did her hair stylish and neat and wore a sexy outfit. Staring at herself in the mirror, Latoya said to herself, "Girl, it looks like all of the time and work that you have put into getting yourself in shape has paid off, and just in time too."

When Mike reached Latoya's house and saw what she had on and how beautiful she looked, his mind went blank, and he thought to himself, *You've got to hold on to this one because you'll never find another as perfect.*

Latoya locked her front door, then turned back. "Hello, handsome."

"You're a beautiful woman. In fact, you're the most gorgeous woman, and I know I'm that right man for you," Mike said to Latoya the minute she had turned back around.

"What makes you so sure of that," Latoya asked, smiling and looking at Mike as if she wanted him to give her something.

Mike had not been with a woman in so long that he forgot what it looked like when a woman wanted to be kissed.

"You'll see," Mike replied walking Latoya to her side of the car. "How was your day, beautiful?"

"Today was just as wonderful as every other day for me. However, I felt so hyped and energetic, had a smile on my face and I couldn't take you off my mind because of a strange feeling that I feel inside of me. It started from the time that the both of us woke up this morning together. It was as if all day I felt you holding me closely in your arms," Latoya replied, smiling.

"Well, I hope that you feel just as energetic as you've been all day because I have made plans to have some fun with you," Mike said as he closed the car door and ran to his side of the car.

When Mike was inside the car he put on his seatbelt before turning on the motor. He had been in an accident before and took all the precautions possible to be safe.

"Seatbelt on," Mike said to Latoya.

Latoya buckled her seatbelt saying, "Can't wait to see where we're going."

Mike started his car and headed for a skating rink.

When they arrived at the rink and saw how crowded it was, they both got very excited because the more people that were there, the more the fun and entertaining it would be.

However, Mike was not as happy as he seemed to be because he was worried he was about to be the laughing stock for the night. He hadn't roller-skated since elementary school.

As if on cue, Latoya asked, "So Mike, are you good at this?"

"No," Mike replied nervously. "But I thought it'd be fun and different."

"How about I teach you? Now let's go and skate because this music they're playing has me feeling ready to go," Latoya said and then got up.

Mike got up, but he immediately fell to the ground as he tried to take his first step in the roller skates.

Latoya laughed and helped Mike back up. "Hold onto me," she said sweetly.

Mike laughed too as Latoya helped him up.

Stepping slowly into the rink, Latoya held Mike very close to her. When they started to skate, Mike fell down a couple more times, and every time he fell, Latoya laughed and so did everyone else that was passing by, even the school kids that were there practicing with one another.

After a few more falls and laughs, Mike got his balance together and began skating all by himself. What a wonderful, exciting, and funny night it already was for Latoya.

After they left the rink, they went to get ice cream nearby and decided to get only one serving of some butter pecan ice cream.

Eating their ice cream and taking lick after lick, smiling and looking into each other's eyes, Mike and Latoya began to kiss passionately.

"It feels like I'm eighteen again," Latoya said.

"There's only one way to tell," Mike replied, smiling.

"How?" Latoya replied, smiling.

"Let's go," Mike replied.

Mike took Latoya to a nice dancing club where they mixed hip-hop, Spanish music, disco, and R&B all together for everyone to enjoy.

Dancing the night away, Mike and Latoya didn't leave the club until two in the morning.

Mike slept at Latoya's house again that morning after Latoya asked him to stay and rock her to sleep. They slept together that morning with their clothing still on, even though they both wanted everything off.

That same morning, Latoya and Mike woke up holding each other. They kissed each other with their mouths closed since they hadn't brushed their teeth yet. Before Mike left, he said to Latoya, "I would love another exciting night with you, tonight?"

"You have permission to take me out any night that you'd like to," Latoya replied happily.

Later that day, after Latoya and Mike had left for work, Latoya received a phone call from Michelle saying she had been in contact with Myra and that she only had time to meet with them tonight because she had already made some plans for this weekend with some of her girlfriends.

"Okay, tonight it is then," Latoya said.

After Latoya and Myra got off the phone, Latoya called Mike and canceled their date, saying that something important had come up and that she'd make up for it the next time they were together.

Surprised about the change of plans, Mike had nothing to say except, "Okay, have a wonderful day." Mike was sad that Latoya canceled, but he knew she must have had a good reason.

* * *

Later on that day, Claude and Kelly were at home together watching television. Bored, Kelly suggested they go shopping for some new clothes because she wanted the both of them to travel to Italy in style.

"You're buying everything for me today because I spent a lot of money already for your birthday."

"I'm not going to even reply to that because you're forgetting that your mother and Anthony were the ones that helped you out."

"I'm ready now, so let's go, Claude, my sweetheart and honey bun," Kelly said as she picked up the car keys.

"Oh, so when the man is about to spend his money is when the woman treats him the nicest? I understand now. I'm not even sweating it," Claude replied with a laugh. Then he walked out of the front door with Kelly.

As Claude and Kelly drove to the nearest clothing store where Kelly loved to shop, they discussed how they'd love to see the other dressed when they reached Italy, even though they already were pleased with the other's usual style.

When Claude and Kelly finally reached a casual clothing store for men and women of all sizes, Kelly went inside and saw all the new stylish clothing on display and smiled. She looked back and said to Claude, "Sweetheart, while I shop, do the math and keep up with the total amount of everything that I want, okay, baby? And I love you. Remember that as you add up everything together for us."

Not surprised at all about what Kelly said, Claude looked for a comfortable seat, a pen, a sheet of paper. He wished he could find a bell to ring for when she passed her spending limit for the night of two thousand dollars.

Just as he got comfortable, he heard his phone beep. He had a new text message. "We could be friends with benefits," the message read.

"Who's this?" Claude texted back.

"You don't need to know that, just know I know how big it is," the person texted back.

Claude did not reply to that message. He was too concerned with figuring out who it could be. Then he received another message with a picture of a naked female with the head cut off. Attached was a note that read, "Whenever you're ready, I'm here."

Claude immediately erased the photo and turned his phone off before putting it back inside his pocket.

* * *

8:00 p.m.

Latoya and Michelle met up and went to the gym again together as planned. After they worked out, Michelle followed Latoya to her house to take a shower and then they got ready to go and meet Myra.

Latoya and Michelle reached the restaurant on the beach that Myra had requested. Myra saw Michelle getting out of her car and handing her car key to a parking valet as another lady was escorted out of the car. Walking up to Michelle slowly, Myra began saying loudly with a bright smile on her face, "Girl, I haven't seen you in such a long time! How have you been doing? You look so brand-new, as if you've been working on the shape of your body with a strict diet for your man."

Michelle ran over to Myra as she was also beginning to speed up, and they hugged each other and kissed each other's cheeks.

With one of her arms still around Myra, Michelle said to her, "I've been doing wonderful! My body is getting into the shape that women my age hardly have nowadays even though I'm only going on my second day. I would like to introduce you to Latoya. She is Anthony's son's fiancé's mother. She's great!"

Latoya walked over to Myra and gave her a hug, saying, "It's nice to finally meet you after hearing so many wonderful things about you from Anthony."

"Thank you. It's nice to meet you too," Myra replied.

"Alright, girls, let's go inside and sit down, talk, and have a wonderful dinner with one another," Michelle said to Latoya and Myra.

"This is such a wonderful restaurant, Michelle. I don't think I've seen this one since I've been down here in South Florida. I remember the first one where I met with you and Anthony's friends," Latoya said to Michelle as they walked in with one another looking at all of the fancy items and pictures that the restaurant had on display.

"Latoya, remember there's still a lot of things and places that you still don't know about here," Michelle replied as the hostess approached them.

"Table for three," Michelle said to the hostess, Gladys, as she began looking at the board for available tables.

"Make sure you watch how you eat tonight, Michelle. I don't want all that hard work that you have been putting into getting yourself back into shape be put to waste," Latoya said as Gladys showed them their table.

"Latoya, believe me. I won't let all that hard work and time that I've been putting into getting my fat stomach and body back into shape again be put to waste because I'm not doing it just for myself. I'm trying to keep it tight for my man," Michelle replied as they followed Gladys.

"I think that I need to start joining you at the gym. I want men chasing me too!" Myra laughed.

"Here's your table for the night, ladies. And thank you for your time and patience. I must say that yes, a sexy and in-shape body leads to endless nights of touching and unforgettable moments. However, not enough sleep for work the next day, if you know what I mean," Gladys said to all of them and winked.

"Yes, however, there are men that can't ever go longer than three minutes in bed and then can't get it back up for the rest of the night. So three minutes out of our sleep time isn't nothing," Michelle replied to Gladys, laughing.

"Well, whatever man that you meet that can't go no longer than three minutes, y'all tell me please so that I can stay one hundred feet away from him because I want my man to be like Superman," Myra said, while everyone laughed. Even the ladies at the table right next to them were laughing and saying, "True that, girl!"

"Yes, true that. I've dreamed about having that kind of man all my life. I found one when I was in Jamaica, but the words 'serious relationship' were nowhere in his dictionary," Gladys said.

"Well then, maybe I need to go and visit down there for a couple of months and see if I can bring me back home one of them," Myra replied, smiling.

"Alright, everyone, someone will be coming to the table to take your order for the night, but I will be bringing back drinks for you. So what would y'all like to drink?" Gladys asked.

"Water," Latoya replied and then looked at Myra.

"Water for me too," Myra replied.

"I would love to start off the night with some water with you, but I'm trying to enjoy my night, so let me get some vodka, Gladys. And Latoya, you're driving when we leave. I thought I'd just let you know that right now," Michelle said with a grin. "Here are the car keys."

"Vodka!" Latoya said out loud, making everyone around look at their table to see what was going on.

"Relax, relax, I'm just playing, Latoya. Gladys, let me get some water and then later on I'll make an order for one of my favorite champagne drinks," Michelle said, laughing.

"Girl, you already know that you shouldn't be drinking, especially when you're in your forties," Myra said.

"True, however it's better to do it when you can, before health problems start. Well, then I'll be back with y'all drinks soon," Gladys said and turned around and walked off.

"Michelle, if I would ever see you drinking crazy right here in front of me, I would call Stephan to come and get you to bring you home and then put you on restriction for such a decision," Myra said and laughed.

"I drink from time to time still, but not to the extent of making myself drunk," Michelle replied.

"Well, I better not see you drink anything, especially while trying to get into shape," Latoya said.

"Relax, I'm not going to kill myself. It sounds like y'all two have much in common," Michelle replied.

"No, we just have mature and responsible minds, that's all," Myra said while looking at Latoya.

"You talk and act the same way Anthony described you," Latoya said to Myra.

"Anthony was talking about me?" Myra asked curiously.

"Anthony described you as a very unique and motivated kind of lady that always speaks the truth and knows how to speak her mind in positive and extraordinary ways at all times. He said you were loving and understanding to both young and old. In addition, you're a great mother even though you don't have any children in your life, except your nieces and nephews, and you always want to be there for them since they look up to you for being such a strong independent woman, who works hard for any and everything she wants," Latoya replied as Michelle listened in surprise, as if all that she had heard was out of the blue.

"Well, it sounds like you have had a whole discussion about me at one time. I'm not surprised that he has mentioned me. Well, not only to you, but to everyone that he knows. I know he loves me. But he seems to love his success way more. By the way, I also talk about him day and night with my friends about how much I wish that we both had that right mind to develop a true and never-ending relationship between us," Myra said.

"Well, that's another thing I wanted to talk to you about, and that's making both of your dreams of being with each other in a true and real relationship come true. But it has to start from the both of you putting aside money and prosperity first," Latoya said.

"May I say that it seems like you are scared to open up and give your hearts to each other, stop fearing that you'll make less money, and you don't need anyone telling you all of this because you are grown up now. Myra, Anthony is ready to give his career up for you. Plus, I told him that with the amount of money that I heard he has saved up, as if he's never spent a dime that he has made all throughout his career, he doesn't need to work and stress himself out for something that's replaceable. He needs to start enjoying life as much as he can, while he still has the chance to. However, I must ask, are you ready to put aside some things for a man to come into your life?" Michelle asked.

"Yes, I am, but I didn't want to be the only one because that would've only brought heartbreak in my life," Myra replied.

"Well, girl, thank you, and I'm happy that we've gotten all of this out of the way because now I just want to enjoy myself with a wonderful meal and talk with my friends about us," Michelle said, feeling relieved.

"Wait, one more question," Myra said to Latoya.

"Was it something that you said to him to motivate him to go after something other than money in his lifetime?" Myra asked.

"No, but then again yes. But it wasn't just me. It was his son's and my daughter's relationship with each other that has had all of us so surprised and jealous. It has made us more aware of how sensitive we need to be," Latoya replied.

"Well, I can't wait to meet the both of them because it's all sounding like they'll be magnificent motivation for me and Anthony," Myra said.

"They'll be back down here this summer, so don't worry, y'all will get to meet them, and I'll make sure of it," Latoya said.

Gladys brought them their drinks. "Someone will be with you'll shortly, and I hope that y'all have a wonderful night, ladies."

"Thank you," they all replied and watched as Gladys walked off, smiling back at their table.

"I already know that she wishes she was able to come and sit down and talk with us about all the things she heard us talking about," Michelle said.

"Money comes first though, Michelle. Money comes first," Myra said.

"See that's your problem. Money, money, money, that's all that is in your head. Myra, do this for me and let the money stay inside of the bank and not in your head anymore, girl. You need to go and start spending some of that money on Anthony, and I'm going to say the same thing to him too. So, Latoya, how has everything been going for you and Mike, okay?" Michelle asked.

"Wonderful, just wonderful," Latoya replied, smiling.

"You've been going on dates with Mike?" Myra said loudly.

"Yes, nosey. Why?" Latoya laughed.

"Don't worry about Mike being all about money either anymore, Myra, because it seems as if he's in love and doesn't only want pleasure and love from a woman anymore. Well, at least from Latoya," Michelle said.

"Well, it sounds like I've been missing out on a lot of things that have been going on between everyone. I'm not going to get into anyone's business until I get what I really want from Anthony again," Myra replied.

"Well, I don't blame you," Latoya replied, smiling, feeling happy that Anthony was about to get back what he had been struggling to find.

Their waiter for the night came to their table and asked them if they were ready to order their meals.

"Yes, we are ready, thank you," they all replied.

They ordered healthy dishes with champagne for the end of the night to give a toast to a wonderful friendship that had begun among them so brightly and a toast toward their relationships with their men.

* * *

11:00 p.m.

After hours of shopping, Claude and Kelly headed home with one of them surprised by how much money was spent, and the other happy because a whole new closet of clothing and shoes was bought for the both of them.

Before they lay down and went to sleep, Kelly asked Claude a question that he couldn't answer without thinking about it for the rest of the night or probably even longer.

"Has my love for you taken over your mind?"

CHAPTER 24

11:00 p.m.

Claude and Kelly woke up late because of a special midnight routine that had gone on longer than usual. Those always took place whenever both of them caught each other's eyes in the middle of the night at the same time. Then, with their legs in between each other, the start of their cravings for sensational pleasure would take over.

"Kelly, I fell asleep last night with that same question on my mind, and it took a lot of thinking because every time I said no, I asked myself why I bought so many things for you without asking why you want it or the price of it. I told myself that I was going to keep track of everything that you wanted last night, and as soon as I saw a smile on your face, whenever you said that you liked and wanted something, I felt good and cared for nothing else but that you were happy with it. Baby, my love for you is all-consuming," Claude said as he rubbed her back slowly and softly and began massaging it gently.

"Me, too baby," Kelly said as she looked up at him. "I know I show it differently. I appreciate that you've been the one supporting us. I know it's not easy. What can I do to ease that burden for you?" Kelly asked honestly as she rolled over to rub Claude's shoulder slowly and gently while her leg was moving slowly up and down in between his legs.

"We've done everything that a couple can do inside of a bedroom, dining room, bathroom, kitchen, and car. I have some stuff in mind for Italy," he said seductively. "But let's wait until we get there."

"Well, I was hoping that you would've said something that I've been wanting, but I just remembered that I wanted all of that on our honeymoon," Kelly said.

"And what will that be?" Asked Claude.

"I want to surprise you with it now, or should I say I want you to surprise me with it, just like how you've always been surprising me," Kelly said, laughing and lifted her head from off Claude's chest and bit his chest, laughing.

"Why'd you bite me?" Claude asked.

"To help get you up. Today I want us to go and take some pictures of us. One of my classmates told me about this photo studio nearby, and the photographers take excellent pictures there, baby, so how about it, boo? Do you want to go and take pictures with your baby, or have your sweetheart keep on sinking her teeth into you again and again until you say yes?" Kelly asked.

"Well, from the way it's sounding, I don't have a choice to say no, right? So of course then it's a yes," Claude replied.

"Thank you, baby, I love you," Kelly said and gave Claude a kiss before she got off the bed to put away all the clothes they'd bought the night before.

"Well, this here is what I wish to see, 24/7," Claude said, smiling as he sat up on the bed staring directly at Kelly's body.

"What is that may I ask?" Kelly said.

"Kelly Brown or should I say Kelly Brown-Daniels walking around with no clothes on, smiling and stretching herself out. Now if she was dancing now to some slow music, that right there would make my day," Claude replied, laughing.

Kelly laughed too. "Well, one day you might get it again if you continue to be a good boy. But until then, baby, go back to sleep. As a matter of fact, let's go and take a shower and get clean so we can get dirty. Afterward, we'll choose a photographer to take our pictures," Kelly said and began throwing all of the clothes on the bed.

"You know, I would love to take some real photos when we get back down to Miami because down there they have some hot spots for photo shoots," Claude said.

"Alright, then we'll do more when we get back home, baby. Plus, some with my mom and sisters because we're all going to be spending the summer together," Kelly said as she began walking into the shower.

During their shower together, Kelly heard her phone ringing, so she jumped out to answer it without looking to see who it was.

"Hello?"

"How are you doing, girl?" Nikki asked.

"Fine, how have you been doing?"

"Girl, everything has been going great for all of us, especially for me because my man treats me like I'm the best girl in the world."

"That's great. So what's up?"

"Oh, I called you to ask if you and Claude would like to go bowling with Paul, Donald, Brittany, and myself tonight."

"Oh, I don't know about that."

"Come on girl, please? I haven't seen you anywhere other than school. C'mon please, Kelly. Plus, there is going to be a lot of other couples out there walking around, and you never know if you might run into an old friend from out of nowhere."

"Let me check with Claude. If he says no then it's no. But I'll ask, okay?"

"Okay, just make sure he knows that it's going to be all about competition, meaning couple against couple, and you already know what that means, girl."

"What, Nikki? Because I don't know."

"The winning couple gets a grand prize."

"And that is?"

"Oh yeah, I forgot to tell you that two hundred and fifty dollars has to get put down from every couple before the game begins, so that the winning couple will get seven hundred and fifty dollars."

"Okay, I'll let him know all about it."

"Call me later okay, and let me know what his answer is? Because Paul and Donald were the ones that really asked me to ask if you and Claude wanted to come. I only wanted *you* to come though."

"Okay, Nikki, bye. We're about to go somewhere right now."

"Bye, Kelly."

Kelly hung up the phone and went back inside the shower with Claude, not planning on asking him about it all until after their photo shoot.

As soon as Claude and Kelly had dried off, they dressed in the clothes they had picked out for each other to wear.

"What do you want to do after we take our pictures?" Claude asked.

"I don't know yet. I haven't made up my mind about something," Kelly replied, smiling.

"Hmm, it sounds like you already have something planned out already," Claude replied.

"Maybe," Kelly said thinking hard. "Just maybe."

* * *

2:00 p.m.

Back at home in Miami, Latoya left work early because all the assignments that she had for the week she completed the night before. Latoya called Anthony to tell him how well the conversation between Myra and her had gone.

Feeling happy and excited about the chance of a new start with Myra again, Anthony called her immediately and asked her out on a date.

"Yes," Myra instantly replied, and they agreed to go out on Saturday. Anthony told her that he would come and pick her up from the house at 8:00 p.m.

Now Latoya was at home wondering how Claude and Kelly were doing, as she sat down waiting for Michelle to come and pick her up to go to the gym and workout together, as they planned to do for the remainder of the month.

I wonder how my two little angels are doing, Latoya wondered to herself again and then picked up her phone and called Kelly's phone.

When Latoya called Kelly's phone, there was no answer, so she had left a voicemail for the both of them. Latoya decided to call Claude's phone, but there was also no answer, so she left another voicemail for the both of them again saying to give her a call back because she wanted make sure that everything is going fine for the both of them.

Then Latoya called Mike and asked how his day had gone for him so far.

"I've been thinking of you," Mike replied, hoping that she would want to go out with him tonight again.

"Ohhh, I miss you too," Latoya replied.

"Will I be seeing you again?" Mike asked sweetly.

"I'll call you tonight and tell you when and where." Latoya replied. Mike began smiling brightly on his side of the phone call.

"We'll see each other later then," Mike said.

"Yes, and Michelle is here for me so that we could go and workout and stay looking sexy for our men, so I'll call you later, bye," Latoya said, smiling because she knew that she had just told Mike what he wanted to hear out from her.

While Michelle was driving to the gym, she saw that same bright smile on Latoya's face from the time that she had picked her up to the time that she pulled up to the parking lot at the gym.

"Who has brightened up your day so much, Latoya?" Michelle asked.

"Me, myself, and I, Michelle. Now let's go and workout our bodies and make them sexy for our men," Latoya replied.

Surprised by her reply, Michelle said to herself, *She either got some sex last night or she's about to get some tonight.*

* * *

4:00 p.m.

After their photo shoot, Claude and Kelly went to get some lunch at a Spanish fast food restaurant.

Sitting around the table talking about how exquisite they looked together in the shots that the photographer had shown them, Kelly said they looked so good together that if they were to ever enter into a couple's photo contest, they would win.

"Nikki asked me earlier today if we wanted to go to a bowling alley with her and a bunch of other people. I said that I'd think about it, and that it depended on you," Kelly said, hoping for Claude not to get upset about it.

"Who asked you?" Claude asked.

"Nikki," Kelly replied.

"So that means Paul, Donald, and Brittany are gonna be there too?" Claude asked.

"Yes. So would you like to go and enjoy ourselves there with them tonight? I mean it's not like we're not going to be by one another's side all throughout the night," Kelly replied.

"You know what? Why not? I mean everything from the past is the past, right?"

"Right," Kelly looked up at Claude smiling.

Reaching for her phone to call Nikki, Kelly looked on her phone and noticed that her mother had called. So she pressed the talk button on her mother's name and tried calling her back, but Latoya never answered her cell phone.

Kelly said to Claude, "My mom was calling me, Claude, but she's not picking up now. Will you try calling her from your phone for me, baby?"

"I dropped my phone in your purse. It should still be somewhere in there."

"Oh, here it is," Kelly said, fishing the phone out. "It looks like she called your phone too. I hope nothing's happened," Kelly said. She tried calling her mother again, but she still didn't pick up.

Claude could tell that Kelly was getting worried. "She's probably busy, so let's just try calling her back in a few hours."

"Claude, she must've been calling the both of us for something very important."

"Didn't she leave a voicemail, baby?"

"Yes."

"Well then, listen to the voicemail. Isn't that what voicemail is for, Kelly? Don't worry until you have to," Claude said, laughing.

"Okay, but there's nothing to be laughing about here, Claude. This could be serious." Kelly was really starting to get worked up.

After listening to both of the voicemail messages on her and Claude's phones, Kelly realized everything was fine.

"See, I told you," Claude said.

"I'm glad you were right. She had me scared for a minute. Let me call her back and tell her we're okay. I don't want her worried about us like I was just worried about her."

After she left her mother a voicemail, Kelly called Nikki and told her they'd be there later on for a whole night of fun and competition with them.

"Don't forget the money," Nikki had replied before she hung up the phone with Kelly.

"We won't," Kelly replied. "Bye." She turned to Claude. "Oh yeah, I forgot to tell you that she had asked us to bring two hundred and fifty dollars to help hype up the competition even more," Kelly said.

"How much?! Kelly, that's a lot of money for bowling," Claude said.

"I know, but the grand prize winner takes home seven hundred fifty dollars. Aren't you a really good bowler?"

"Yeah, I am," Claude said, thinking it over. "Alright, let's do it. I like our chances of bringing back home more money than we're leaving the house with."

Later on
8:00 p.m.

Claude and Kelly left home and headed toward the bowling alley. Along the way, Latoya finally decided to call them back after hearing their voicemail.

"Hi, Kelly, how has everything been going for you and Claude?" Latoya asked.

"Wonderfully, Mother, everything has been going wonderfully. We're doing great in school, and our relationship has been blossoming into something spectacular for the both of us," Kelly replied happily.

"Well, that's great to hear, honey. So what are y'all going to be doing together during a wonderful night like tonight?"

"We're going bowling with some of our new friends right now, Mom, to get a couple's competition under way for the grand prize of about seven hundred and fifty dollars."

"Well, I hope that y'all have a wonderful time tonight and that y'all drive carefully and don't let me hear about y'all ever drinking and driving either because I want my two little babies making me a grandma in the future."

"Mother, you already know that we don't drink alcoholic beverages, no matter what."

"Yeah, lots of parents think that about their little ones that are all grown-up now, and in the end they find out a little too late, so I'm just telling y'all from now, not to okay, Kelly?"

"Okay, Mom, I understand. Thank you for your love and concern toward us. What are you doing tonight, Mom?"

"Nothing much at all, baby, I'm going to be home tonight watching television and eating the night away."

"Well, don't eat too much food so late in the night, Mom, and then get back out of shape again because I already know you've been losing weight because of all the work and walking up and down in your new job, and eating less."

"Baby, it's not just from the job. I've been losing weight and getting into shape, because I've been going to the gym and working out a lot lately."

"Oh, that's good to hear, Mom. I'm proud of you, and I can't wait to see you when we come down this summer."

"Tell Claude that I said hello and that I can't wait for my two little angels to come back home and show me all of the good grades that you have been getting."

"Alright, Mom, I'll make sure that I tell him everything."

"Oh yeah, Kelly, I hope that y'all have been using condoms, and don't tell me that y'all haven't been having sex because I wasn't born yesterday. I already know that there is no way two young college adults can sleep in the same room on the same bed and are fiancés and not having sex every night while you'll still can——"

"Mom!"

"Kelly, don't *Mom* me! I'm serious, okay? I want the both of y'all to finish college first."

"Okay, thank you again for the advice. I love you. Bye."

"I love you, too. Bye."

Kelly got off the phone, and turned to Claude. "Mom said hi, and to tell you that she misses you and that she can't wait to see her two little angels come back home again."

"That's what made you scream out Mom so loud just a while ago, Kelly?" Claude asked.

"No, she began saying that she hopes that we're not drinking and driving, and then she started having this whole sex talk with me saying that she knows that we've been having sex every night, since we sleep together every night and that she hopes that we've been using condoms because she wants us to finish school before we have our first child together," Kelly explained, shaking her head.

Claude started laughing too. "Well then, if she wanted to know so badly, Kelly, you should've told her how good I've been giving it to you every night then, because remember we never hide anything from your mother."

"Shut up!" Kelly replied, watching Claude as he laughed.

"Don't worry, baby. I won't try to get you pregnant until we're both ready and have finished school," Claude said.

They reached the bowling alley, so Kelly called Nikki to ask where everyone was at.

Nikki replied, "We're all inside of the bowling alley waiting in line for a spot to start the tournament."

"Alright, we're coming in now," Kelly replied.

A couple seconds later Claude received a text message saying, "I can't wait to see you."

"Stop playing games. Who's this?" Claude texted back right away.

"Your friend with benefits," the next message read.

Claude did not text back.

When Claude and Kelly entered the bowling alley and found Nikki and her boyfriend whom she was hugging upon like always, Claude shook his head and began saying to himself that it's about to be a three on one.

Claude said that because he saw Donald, Paul, and Blane stand up all together laughing with one another after Nikki kissed Paul bye and walked over in their direction, with Brittany, and another girl whom he had never seen before.

"Kelly, I would like to introduce you to Gina, Dontrey's future wife," Brittany said after hugging and saying hello to her.

"Who's Dontrey again, Brittany?" Kelly asked.

Brittany pointed over toward all of them, saying, "Him over there standing up next to Donald in the white shirt."

"Oh, okay I remember him now," Kelly replied.

Claude then walked over to where the guys were.

"Nikki, are y'all ready to begin?" Paul said loudly.

"No, not yet. We're talking about some things," Nikki replied.

"I already knew that was going to happen as soon as I saw all of them walking up to Kelly and asking me to join y'all so that they can be alone," Claude said.

"Alright then, forget them, where's your money at? Let's get this going between us alone then," Paul said.

"Right here, where's yours at?" they all asked Paul.

"Of course I have my two hundred and fifty dollars. Here let's put all of the money into this empty cup," Paul said as he picked up a cup from off a table next to theirs.

"Hi Claude," someone said to Claude while he went to get his bowling shoes.

Turning, he saw that it was Victoria, Catherine's older sister.

"Oh hi, I'm doing all right. Let me guess, you're looking for Kelly?" Claude asked.

"Yes, and I'm sure that she's here, if you're here, right?" Victoria asked.

"Yes, she's right over there with those three girls talking and laughing while she's supposed to be getting ready to bowl," Claude replied.

"I would like to introduce you to my man, Tyrone."

"What's up?" Tyrone said to Claude.

"We men are about to bowl for some money. Are you going to jump in? You might as well because they're all going to be talking over there for a while," Claude said.

"Yeah, I know, so why not?" Tyrone replied.

"Alright then, bye, sweetie," Victoria said and gave Tyrone a kiss and walked over to Kelly and all the rest of her friends.

"So how much money do I have to put in to get in the game with you?" Tyrone asked.

"Two hundred and fifty dollars," Claude replied.

"Cool, I'm in," Tyrone said.

When Claude and Tyrone put on their bowling shoes, Claude walked him to their table and introduced him to Paul, Donald, and Dontrey. After that, he told him where to put the two hundred and fifty dollars.

"So now the winner gets one thousand two hundred and fifty dollars, so are you ready?" Paul said to all of them.

"Claude, Tiffany's boyfriend, Brian wants to bowl with you'll!" Kelly yelled to him.

"Alright, tell him to come!" Claude replied loudly and began walking to meet him halfway.

"What am I going to do with all that fucking money when I win it?" Paul asked himself with one of his fingers on his cheek.

"Paul, stop dreaming because you're not winning a damn thing," Donald told him.

"Stop using your mouth, Donald, because until you'll beat me, I expect mouths to remain shut at all times," Paul replied.

When Brian arrived at the table, Claude introduced him to everyone and said, "Look at all the girls talking over there. I thought that tonight was supposed to be a couples' tournament."

"Man, you should already know that whenever a group of girls like them get together, they take us men out of the picture," Brian said.

The tournament finally began as the girls talked to one another on the other side. Later on, Miguel and Renaldo came, but they only watched the others bowl and made jokes about everyone else because it was too late for them to get in the tournament, and they didn't have the money to join.

* * *

10:00 p.m.

Back in Miami, Latoya had Mike come over to her house after she cooked dinner for both of them. After their meal, Latoya ordered a movie from On Demand for them to watch in her bedroom.

Lying down on the bed together, watching the movie, Latoya and Mike couldn't hold it all in anymore, and they began kissing each other into the night and then headed under the sheets, holding on to each other and never ever wanting to let go.

* * *

1:00 a.m.

The bowling tournament was over, and the winner of the fifteen hundred dollars was Brian, so the men were ready to go. However on the other side, the girls' conversation with one another still wasn't over, and they weren't tired yet. However, when they saw their men about to walk outside of the bowling alley together, all of them ran over to ask them just where they thought they were going, without letting them know.

"We're all going to a club to go and hang out, just like how you girls are doing," Miguel replied, smiling.

All of the girls exchanged looks. "Hell no, you're not!" they said simultaneously.

"Girls, I think that it's time to take our men home. Well at least mine. Goodbye, everyone," Victoria said and reached over for Tyrone's hand and walked out with him, smiling.

Everybody else did the same and grabbed their men's hands and walked out with them to take them home.

"So how was your night, Kelly?" Claude asked as they began driving home.

"It went all right, how about yours?" Kelly replied.

"I enjoyed myself. So what were you girls talking about over there that you couldn't make it back over to us?" Claude asked.

"Nothing much at all, baby, but I had a wonderful time tonight, and that's all that matters, right?" Kelly replied.

"You girls are so weird, how the hell were you'll able to hold such a long conversation with one another for so long and hardly know one another?" Claude said.

"Baby, if you were a woman you would understand. But since you're not, it'll be too hard to get you to understand. So did you win us any money, baby?" Kelly asked.

"No, Tiffany's man won all of the money," Claude replied.

"What?! Now I see why you had wished I was there with you because you needed my help," Kelly said.

"Kelly! You wouldn't have been any kind of help for me, baby. As a matter of fact, I don't even know if you would've even been able to lift up the bowling ball," Claude said, laughing.

"I'm better than you, so you need to stop talking like that to an advanced player, alright, beginner?" Kelly replied smiling.

"What?! Kelly, please don't tell me that you're challenging me. Please don't, because I wouldn't want to embarrass you," Claude said, looking at Kelly feeling good.

"Stop talking, please, Claude. You do not want me to grab the wheel and turn this car back around, right now. As a matter of fact, we'll do it another time because it's too late now," Kelly said.

Claude laughed and shook his head. "All talk and then excuses, that's all you women have for us men."

Kelly looked at Claude proudly. "Thank you for growing up into a better man. Thank you and I love you."

That same night multiple naked pictures like the one sent before appeared on Claude's phone with a text message saying, "These were for my man but I'm sharing them with you now."

Claude did not even bother to reply this time. He simply deleted the pictures and held onto Kelly tighter.

* * *

8:00 p.m.

Anthony drove up to Myra's house in a white stretch limo and got out of it carrying beautiful white and blue flowers in his hands.

Knock, knock, knock.

Myra opened up her front door for Anthony, and he reached out his hands to give her the flowers.

However, Myra only looked at him and then the white limo that was behind him and then, surprisingly, pulled Anthony inside of the house with her, jumped in his arms and began kissing him. Holding her up by her butt Anthony began heading straight towards her dining room table and placed her down on top of it softly, while pushing everything from off of it. Myra then ripped his shirt open and began kissing his chest as she began unbuckling his belt and then pulled down his pants.

After seeing Anthony, Myra began saying, "I'm ready for you, big daddy" to spice up the moment and make him feel good.

Anthony reached down to lift up Myra's dress and then he pulled down her panties with his teeth. He moved his mouth to her crotch to pleasure her like no man had ever done before. After feeling that sensational feeling for ten minutes straight, Myra got up and made love to him as the limo driver stood at the limo's door waiting for them to come out.

* * *

"Spring Break"

Spring break arrived for Claude and Kelly, and they could barely contain their excitement about Italy. During their visit, they toured throughout Italy's legendary beaches where Julius Caesar, Mark Antony, and Octavius Caesar set out on their sea voyages. They then visited Rome and saw amazing statues in the

Piazza Campidoglio. They took a lot of pictures to keep their memories fresh. Then Claude and Kelly took a trip to Verona, the setting of Romeo and Juliet.

"Our love and life together will never be broken up," they both agreed as they stood imagining just how Romeo and Juliet's true love had begun.

"That night"

"Claude, our love reminds me of the sun and moon. It shines so brightly every moment someone looks up at it, and it's because of that that I feel our love will grow and grow through every passing year. I want you to know that I'll be with you in all you say and do because I love you and I want the best for you. I thank you for being my friend, lover, and soulmate, and I feel that our Father God will always be beside us to help us bear every troubled time that may come for us. Spring, summer, winter, and fall, Claude, my love for you will be there for you throughout it all," Kelly said as she lay down in Claude's arms, listening to the waves come in and feeling his heart beat on her chest.

"Thank you for being a true blessing from above. For you have been the star that shines on my path and the fire that warms my heart. I plan to never let you stray too far because you have brought my life and mind peace. Somehow, ever since I lost my family, your love immediately surrounded me, quieting the pain in my heart. I've been holding you so close to my heart because it ensures we'll never be apart. I feel the bond we share will never fade and we will feel it whether near or far, for it's your tenderness and beauty that make my heart take flight. Kelly, I have endless love inside of me just for you. That's why I feel so satisfied in my life from every kiss and gentle touch that you give to me, and that's why as I hold you in my arms, I feel a lilting soft romance," Claude whispered softly, and began kissing Kelly as they lay down on the Adriatic coast of Italy in the moonlight.

Couple of days later.
2:00pm

While hanging out with his teammates, along with a couple of girls talking about doing a sex tape with the girls. Donald received a text message from an unknown phone number that read, "Stephan Duncan was born today wondering. Where's Daddy?"

Donald immediately deleted the message.

Two weeks later, Cory, Stanley's oldest son had been released from serving two years in California jail. Police had locked him up for assaulting a police officer after the officer kept boasting about knowing something about who followed his partner home and killed him in front of his wife and daughter after work. Cory kept his mouth shut. He knew his cousin Romeo was involved, but he refused to snitch.

Cory immediately made his way back to Detroit to see how his family was doing. He had not heard from anyone or about anyone since his prison sentence began. Before he went to see his family, he tried to stop by his father's house first. He arrived only to find out from one of his father's friends that Stanley and Robert were killed by one of his father's old enemies who had been killed too. Only the youngest son, a college kid named Claude who had somehow gotten away, remained alive.

Feeling for vengeance at all costs for his family's death, Cory immediately asked, "Where the fuck is he?"

His father's friend looked at him seriously. "That's the problem. No one knows."

Jonathan Anthony Burkett was born in 1987. He is a bright writer inspired by many as he continues to struggle in life. Devoted for achievement in his lifetime, he is willing to take any test. He told himself that he would never give up, no matter the trials and tribulations. He decided to write to help him move toward a bright future for himself and because he knows that's what his grandparents want for him.

To learn more about Jonathan visit him at

www.jonathanburkett.com

www.facebook.com/Friends2Lovers

DESTINED TO BE

In every journey there is meaning
Following growth and understanding
Though every now and then, an individual
Feels as if that predicament has no significance

Along my voyage in life
I have come across dilemma and uncertainty
Feeling skeptical of whether or not
I was destined to

Desiring now a change in my existence
A new course in life
I have chosen to take
For I wish to no longer live my life unfaithfully

Repenting for my sins
Taking the time to replenish
To confirm to myself
I was destined to be

Self-reliant in my goals and dreams
I've chosen to be, for in life
There is only one which I can trust and depend on
To be there for me

Respectful unto others
I've chosen to become
No matter the companionship
Others show unto me

On a new course in life, I must now go
Finding prosperity, and not destruction
Finding fellowship, and not revulsion
Finding brightness, and not darkness
Thinking right, and not wrong
And giving love instead of dreadfulness

A change in my life
We will now all see
To show through all
I was destined to be